ANNE HILLERMAN

ROCK WITH WINGS

A LEAPHORN, CHEE & MANUELITO NOVEL

HARPER

An Imprint of HarperCollinsPublishers

HARPER

An Imprint of HarperCollins*Publishers*
195 Broadway
New York, New York 10007

Copyright © 2015 by Anne Hillerman
ISBN 978-0-06-227052-8

First Harper premium printing: December 2015
First Harper hardcover printing: May 2015

10 9 8

By Anne Hillerman

Rock with Wings

Spider Woman's Daughter

Tony Hillerman's Landscape:
On the Road with Chee and Leaphorn

Gardens of Santa Fe

Santa Fe Flavors:
Best Restaurants and Recipes

Ride the Wind: USA to Africa

In memory of my mother, Marie.
She gave me the title for this book . . .
And in memory of Cindy Bellinger.
She gave me simple, sage advice on how to finish
ROCK WITH WINGS: Keep writing!

ROCK WITH WINGS

1

Officer Bernadette Manuelito had been sitting in her unit by the side of the road for an hour, watching the last of the twilight fade and the pinpoints of stars appear in the blue-gray sky. In that time she had seen two vehicles, both with the classic yellow-and-red New Mexico plates with the Zia symbol in the center. The gray Subaru advanced at close to the speed limit, with no signs of driver impairment. The old green Buick cruised along more leisurely, with the windows rolled down and country music flowing into the night air. She knew the car and the driver and knew he was headed home after a long shift at the Four Corners Power Plant. If he'd had a beer or two, his driving didn't show it.

After that burst of activity, things slowed down.

Bernie climbed out of her unit to stretch her legs, enjoying the scents of summer in the cooling air. This sort of assignment, if she was lucky, involved hours of monotony punctuated by a bit of routine traffic work. If she wasn't lucky, violence or the threat of it shattered the boredom. The challenge, and the secret to survival, was to stay alert without getting paranoid.

Over the police radio she learned that sheriff's deputies, New Mexico State Police, and BIA officers also assigned to help with this drug intercept operation were snacking, gazing at the moon, and shooting the breeze. Those fortunate enough to be waiting where their cell phones worked might be chatting with friends or sending texts.

The drug bust was a bust so far, but the night was still young.

Bernie climbed back into her Ford SUV and was listening to an audiobook with her purple earbuds when she saw headlights approaching. The big silver car with a white Arizona plate flashed toward her, speeding past her through the junction. Pulling onto the pavement behind it, she clocked the car at fifteen miles over the speed limit—a lot for this twisting, narrow road. She radioed dispatch with her location and the plate number, then switched on her light bar. After about two minutes, she saw the flash of brake lights in front of her.

Good.

Traffic stops made her nervous, especially at night. After a certain hour, she knew the odds that the driver was drunk or on drugs increased. This driver didn't seem intoxicated, though. At least, nothing she'd seen so far made her suspect it.

The car ahead—a Chevy Malibu, she could see now—slowed and pulled over at a wide spot on the shoulder. Bernie slipped in behind it, leaving her light bar and headlights on to warn oncoming motorists. She radioed in again with her location. Before she got out to talk to the driver, she turned on the dash cam switch. The feds stressed that every possible arrest had to be recorded.

The machine stayed dormant. Bernie turned it off, and then clicked it again. This time, thankfully, the green record light blinked. She clipped on the microphone and reached for her flashlight.

As she walked toward the Chevy, she could see one shape in the front seat, illuminated by her headlights. There was no one in the back. The driver lowered the window, and she felt a wave of chilled air flow past her from inside the car. Bernie shone the flashlight onto his face. His eyes looked normal. His hands were on the steering wheel. Not a Navajo, he was in his thirties, clean-shaven, wearing dark-rimmed glasses and a black baseball cap with a wolf logo. She moved the light past him for a quick scan of the front seat. No visible weapons, only work gloves, sunglasses, and a dark leather case that looked like it might hold a camera or binoculars. Nothing suspicious.

"Sir, please turn off the engine. No reason to waste the gas. May I have your license, registration, and proof of insurance?"

He killed the engine, squirmed a bit to reach into his back pocket, and pulled out a brown leather wallet. He handed her an Arizona driver's license with a photo that matched his appearance. His hand stayed steady. So far, so good.

She waited for him to reach for the glove box, the place most people kept the other documents she needed, but he sat staring straight ahead. She read the name on the license.

"Mr. Miller, would you show me the car's registration and proof of insurance?"

Miller didn't respond. Beads of sweat had appeared on his forehead. He gripped the steering wheel so tightly that the veins on the back of his hands stood out. Both her training and her intuition told Bernie to proceed with care.

She spoke louder. "Mr. Miller, my camera here is recording our conversation. We do that for our mutual protection. Have you consumed any alcohol or drugs today?"

"No. No, ma'am."

"Sir, I need to see the car's registration and proof of insurance."

"The papers are, um, in the glove box. But so you'll know, I have a gun in there too."

His breath didn't carry the smell of beer or liquor. He shifted away from her, leaning toward the glove box and reaching with his right hand.

"Don't." Bernie raised her voice. Telling, not asking. "Sir, roll down the window on the passenger side."

He pushed a button, and the window lowered.

"Do you have any weapons on you? Another gun, a knife, anything like that?"

"No."

"Please get out of the car and walk around with me so we can get the gun and the papers I asked for."

She heard the click of his seat belt releasing. The interior light came on when he opened the car door. He was about five foot six, with a slight build, though a bit heavier than the 150 pounds stated on his license. He wore a tan long-sleeved shirt, khaki shorts, and hiking boots.

The man walked ahead of her around the front of the car to the passenger side, the light from her headlights helping them negotiate the rough dirt on the shoulder. He moved without any swaying or wobbling. No obvious signs of impairment.

"Is the glove box locked?"

"No."

"I'm going to open it and remove the gun." She looked at him. "Is it loaded?"

"Of course. Why else—" He didn't finish the sentence.

She reached in and felt the catch, clicked the box open. A light flickered on, and she saw a dark green plastic case, the kind that might have an owner's manual packed inside. The gun lay next to it. She removed it and left the compartment door open.

"Mr. Miller, it is illegal to have a loaded gun in a vehicle on the Navajo reservation."

He shrugged and said nothing.

"Now I need you to get the papers I asked for."

He reached for the case, opened it, and handed her the insurance card and registration.

"Please sit back in the car for a moment."

She could see well enough in the headlights to tell that Miller's name was on the documents, and his insurance was valid. She went to her unit and called in the updated information. Because of the drug bust party, the system was operating at maximum efficiency. She waited only briefly to discover Miller had no outstanding warrants. The Chevy was registered to him, too. Good, she thought. Just a guy speeding on a usually empty road on a night when a cop happened to spot him.

But his silence and his nervousness bothered her.

Bernie walked back to the sedan. If things went as she expected, she would return the gun with a stern warning about speeding. Or, maybe, a speeding ticket. Depended on his attitude.

She handed him the car papers and his license.

"What business are you in, Mr. Miller?"

"Construction." He was chewing his lower lip, and perspiration glistened on his pale skin. The night was warm, but not hot. Unless he had a medical problem, something other than the ambient temperature was making him sweat.

"What do you build?"

"Oh, whatever."

"You have a job out here?" Bernie wanted to hear him talk a bit more, make sure he wasn't impaired.

"Yeah." The fingers of his right hand tapped on the steering wheel.

When he didn't elaborate, she tried something different. "Where is it that you live?"

"Oh, outside of Flagstaff."

"Flag, huh? Do you like it?" Flagstaff was high, almost seven thousand feet, a railroad town on the edge of the Colorado Plateau, cold in the winter. The best thing about the town was its views of the San Francisco Peaks, Dook'o'oslííd, home of some of the Holy People: Talking God, White Corn Boy, and Yellow Corn Girl. The Hopi held the peaks sacred too, as the dwelling place of their kachinas from July until the winter solstice.

"It's quiet, you know? They have NAU there—that's Northern Arizona University—lots of bike trails, and Lowell Observatory. The Grand Canyon is practically next door. Some nice bars. A good brew pub. My dog and I walk about anywhere without getting hassled."

He kept talking now, telling her about his dog, referring to it with the fondness of someone discussing his child. He spoke too fast, even for a white man. Was his nervousness a normal reaction to being stopped at night? Or was he high on something?

When he finally fell silent, she asked, "Why are you in such a hurry tonight?"

"Ah, no reason in particular, I guess. No, ma'am. I wasn't paying attention. You know how that is? You look down at the speedometer, and you surprise yourself."

"Where are you headed?"

"Oh, to Gallup to spend the night. Then home tomorrow."

Gallup was at the south end of 491 in New Mexico. Shiprock anchored it on the north. "You have friends out that way?"

"Um, no. I like the Comfort Suites, you know, on the east side of town. They take dogs when my pooch is with me." He started tapping the steering wheel again.

"And where did you come from this morning?"

"I had a, um, a meeting in Albuquerque."

"Since you're in a hurry, why are you here on 491 instead of the Interstate?" Avoiding the state police, FBI, and a drug arrest was the obvious reason, even though he wasn't the stereotype to be arrested for drugs. He didn't have enough bling. Not enough bluster in his attitude.

She waited. Miller didn't let the silence hang for long.

"Oh, I love the desert. It's not against the law to drive around at night. It was a free country, last I heard." He wiped the sweat off his face with his palm, took off his cap, ran his fingers through his hair. Put it on again.

"You seem nervous." She kept her voice neutral. "Why is that? Drugs, sir? Maybe a prescription you're taking or something?"

Miller removed his glasses, looked at them, rubbed the bridge of his nose. Pursed his lips and exhaled. "Too much coffee, maybe. Maybe that and I'm just, well, excited about being out here, I guess. And getting stopped by the police? That's enough to make anyone sweat a little."

"Mr. Miller, do you have something in this car that you shouldn't have? Something like amphetamines, cocaine. Counterfeit money. Fake IDs, stolen credit cards, illegal weapons, explosives. Liquor? You know that's illegal on the Navajo Nation." She smiled at him. "If you do, you should tell me about it now, before I find something that will get you in a huge amount of trouble."

He was thinking about it, she could tell.

"I mentioned the gun." Miller's voice was barely a whisper.

"Right, you did. That was smart."

"I didn't realize it was illegal out here." He took his hands off the steering wheel and wiped them on ...orts, then put them back.

"Yes, that's what you said. I am asking you if you have anything else in the car that is making you nervous. Something you want to tell me about now before I find it."

He wrinkled his brow. "Don't you need a search warrant to look in the car?"

"I'm only asking, sir. Based on your behavior, I have reasonable cause to search the car for contraband. I can get a warrant. If I do that, we will have to wait here for the judge to be woken up and to fax it to my office in Shiprock, and then they will radio me. That process takes time, and you said you were in a hurry. If you don't have any contraband, it would be easier on both of us if you opened the trunk for me to take a look. Does it have a release down there under the dashboard?"

"Can't we work this out between the two of us? You seem to be a reasonable gal—uh, person. Like you said, arresting me would be a big hassle for both of us."

She hadn't said that, but she let his comment linger on the summer air. The increasing light from the rising moon made it easier to observe him. His left eye was twitching.

"OK," he said. "I'll give you a hundred dollars if you let me drive out of here. Give me a speeding ticket if you need to. You'll never see me again, and this can stay between us."

"A hundred?" Now she had him for speeding, and for attempting to bribe a police officer.

"Five, five hundred. That's all I have on me. I don't want any more trouble."

"Too late." Bernie put steel into her voice. "Open the trunk now, sir."

Miller looked like he might throw up. He pushed a button. She heard the catch unlock and saw a line of light appear between the trunk lid and the car's body as the lid sprang upward a quarter inch. She walked to the back of the sedan and pushed the lid up. The gleam of the trunk light caught the shaft of a rifle he'd lied about, a shovel, and two shallow cardboard boxes filled with dirt. She aimed her flashlight inside the trunk and then on the boxes. She played the beam around but discovered nothing more, at least on the surface. No obvious contraband. But smugglers were getting smarter. Maybe the car had a hidden compartment. Something in the trunk, in or under those boxes, or hidden in the sedan must be worth a lot more than $500.

Miller turned his head out of the window toward her. "How did you know about this?"

She was tempted to say, *Know about what?* But instead she waited to see what Miller would do next.

"You can have the rifle, too. It's a good weapon. I've got the five bills in my wallet. I can be off the rez, out of New Mexico. Gone, and you'll never see me again. No paperwork for you. We keep this between us."

"Sir, please step out of the car."

"You're kidding."

"Do it now."

She waited for him to comply, aware of the gun at her side.

"I am arresting you for attempting to bribe a police officer. I am going to handcuff you now for safety." She sucked in a deep breath of relief e didn't resist.

Miller stood hunched and silent as she read him his rights. He looked frighteningly pale now, even for a white guy in the dark. A word she seldom used popped into her head: *flabbergasted*. He could be the poster boy for the definition.

Bernie stowed him in the back of her SUV, called in to dispatch, updated the situation, and made arrangements for the car to be towed in. She was lucky. It was a slow night, and the tow truck driver would be there soon. Miller's car would first be secured in Shiprock until the federal drug agents could come for it and find the contraband.

Grabbing her cell phone, she took pictures of the interior of the trunk from several angles, since the dash cam couldn't capture that. She focused on each box and the rifle. "You seem like a decent guy," she said to Miller as she climbed into the front seat. "Why don't you give me the whole story now, while we're waiting here?"

"I've said too much already."

"I'm a good listener. What's in those boxes?"

"I need you to call someone for me. His card is in my wallet."

"The phone service is spotty out here. You can make your call when we get to Shiprock."

"You'd save us both some trouble if you'd make the call now. It's complicated."

Bernie looked in the rearview mirror, noticing that Miller kept his eyes on his car. "Everything is complicated these days. We're going to wait here until the tow truck comes. You might as well tell me what's in the car. Why it's complicated."

Miller said nothing.

The tow truck arrived, and she drove Miller to the Shiprock station to be held until he was transported to the big new jail in Tuba City. The officer on duty at Shiprock, Wilson Sam, was a rookie, of course. All the more experienced officers were working on the drug net.

"Tell me what you learn about those boxes of dirt," she asked Sam. "I'm curious. I've never seen drugs smuggled that way."

"I'll let you know if I hear anything." Sam chuckled. "I'm not exactly at the heart center of information."

"What's happening with the rest of the drug operation?"

"Nothing much yet. State police picked up a few small-timers who happened to be in the wrong place with a burned-out headlight or who forgot to use a turn signal. The San Juan County deputies found a stolen car and a couple of folks with outstanding warrants. But no big shots with a backseat full of cocaine or a suitcase of meth. Either the feds had it wrong, or word leaked out."

"Did any of our team get anyone?" she asked.

"Only you so far. Congratulations."

At home, Bernie was happy to see Chee's truck in the driveway. He'd avoided the drug stakeout because he'd put in his request for vacation a day before she got around to submitting hers. He teased her about his knack for planning. Because he had the day off, he got to pack and get everything set for their little trip. And then, when he went back to work a day ahead of d handle the harder job, the cleanup.

She decided not to take a shower; she didn't want to wake him. Looking in the refrigerator, she found half a sandwich and some lemonade Chee had saved for her and ate at the kitchen table. She could hear the rhythmic chuckling of the San Juan River and a symphony of crickets through the open windows. The air felt good, finally cool after the hot summer day.

Vacation. Bernie had never actually taken a vacation, except for her honeymoon in Hawaii two years ago. And this trip would be different. No surf, no beach, but plenty of sand.

2

Jim Chee said his morning prayer, then grabbed a cup of the good coffee Bernie had made. He cooked Spam and potatoes for the burritos and wrapped them in flour tortillas. They smelled so good, they tempted him, but he reminded himself that they were road food. He and Bernie could eat them in the truck without too much of a mess.

He was loading the sleeping bags when Bernie came back from her run.

"Sleeping bags? I thought we were staying at Paul's house."

"We are, but I know Paul. I never can tell exactly what the situation will be."

Chee's cousin and clan brother Paul had telephoned two weeks ago on a Saturday morning—too early, of course—and invited them to check out his new Monument Valley guest hogan.

"I need somebody to take my tour," he'd said,

"and tell me how I can make everything better. I figured you two would be perfect."

"What tour?"

"Oh. I'm starting a photo tour business. 'Sunrise, sunset, and everything in between,' that's my slogan. I'm calling it Hozhoni Tours. Or maybe Picture Perfect Tours."

Hozhoni, the word that described a beautiful, peaceful place and that same state of mind. Chee approved. But the other name? "So you've become a photographer now?"

"Even better—a photography coach. I told you I got some work as a substitute driver with some of the tours? I watched those guys with the big cameras take pictures of arches, buttes, spires, rocks, and other guys with big cameras. I listened to people complain about not being somewhere at the right time for the right light. After a while, I started to realize what camera people want. They don't care much about geology, the history, or what made the ruins. They want photo opportunities." Paul chuckled. "I got my tribal license, and my first group is booked. This would be a great time for you to visit."

"What's the difference between a photo tour and a regular tour where people take pictures?"

Paul laughed, a deep, cheerful sound that reminded Chee of the fun they'd had together as boys. "My tours are special, brother. Personal tours with personal attention. Small groups only. I'll show them the right angle, the perfect perspective, unique sites. I'll let them use my horses as models, too."

"Hold on a minute. Let me talk to Bernie about it."

Bernie, his beautiful Bernie, had been sitting on the deck with a book, waiting for him to get off the phone so they could drive out to her mama's place before it got too hot. He remembered the title: *Helping People with Head Injuries*. She could use a break, he thought, and they both had time off coming. A few days away would be nice. He had been thinking about taking her on a little vacation. This trip would be easy, interesting, and practically free.

Bernie had never been to Tsé Bii' Ndzisgaii, the Valley of Rocks, known on maps as Monument Valley. Chee had visited many times, helping Paul's family with their livestock, working side by side with his cousin and his uncle, fixing the generator and refilling the water tank at the well at Goulding's. And then shooting baskets on the packed-dirt basketball court until it grew too dark to see the rim. He remembered the pleasure of getting up each morning amid the breathtaking buttes and spires. Chee never tired of the place.

He had explained the invitation. "Paul lives in Mystery Valley. It's part of Monument Valley, right next to it, but not included in the park. *Bilagaanas* have to be with a Navajo guide to see it because it's not open to general tourists. It's full of arches and windows, holes in the rock that are like eyes to the sky. Beautiful. Remote, too. He hauls water, doesn't have electricity except for the gasoline generator. No cell phone service out there either."

Bernie looked up from her book. "It sounds wonderful. Quiet. Relaxing. I'd love to see it." Then her expression darkened. "But what about Mama? What if she gets sick or something?"

"Think positive. Mama's fine, and Darleen lives with her. And it's not like we are going to California or somewhere. It's only a two-hour drive from Shiprock to Paul's place."

"OK. If we can get time off and Darleen agrees, let's do it."

Chee got back on the phone.

"Great," Paul said. "The hogan should be all done by then."

They stopped at the trading post at Teec Nos Pos. While Bernie pumped the gas, Chee went inside to get her a Coke, a treat to officially launch their vacation.

The place was busy as usual, a mixture of Navajos shopping for meat, vegetables, and maybe a sack of Blue Bird flour, and tourists checking out the weavings in the rug room or looking for jewelry or a little wooden horse or some other souvenir made by one of the locals to hang on a Christmas tree. A woman Chee knew was working the cash register.

"You should have been here yesterday for the flea market." She rang up the Coke and gave him his change. "Everybody and his brother had something to sell. Where are you off to?"

"Monument Valley."

The woman nodded. "I hear that hotel the tribe built is fancy. You staying there?"

"Not this time."

"I think Rhonda is staying there. She's making a movie."

"Rhonda?"

"Rhonda! Can you believe it? Yeah. Here on the rez."

He would have asked, "Who is Rhonda?" but there was a line of customers waiting patiently behind him. And, he thought, it didn't matter anyway.

His phone vibrated just as he left the store. He pulled it out of his pocket, saw that it was Captain Largo, and took the call.

Chee knew the drive through the north-central section of the Navajo Nation always took Bernie's breath away. She marveled at the purple hue of the Carrizo Mountains and the softer colors in the rounded hill beyond them. She asked him to stop at Baby Rocks and took photos of the formation, which resembled an artist's clay rendition of a flock of totem poles. He pulled over again when they reached a pullout with a view of Comb Ridge, frozen waves of rock. They climbed out and Bernie took more pictures while he savored the beauty.

"You're really quiet today," he said. "Everything OK?"

"I keep thinking about that dirt, you know, the boxes in that car I stopped yesterday? I'm dying to know how he used that to hide drugs. Or to hide something else. I keep replaying the scene and wondering what I missed."

"If that guy hadn't offered you five hundred bucks, would you have been suspicious?"

"Sure, wouldn't you have been? Why would somebody have boxes of dirt in the trunk? Why was he so nervous and sweaty?"

"That's the thing about being a cop. You run into all kinds."

"I know. I almost wish we could have put off our trip just so I could find out what that guy was up to. You know, see for myself how he hid the drugs."

Chee took a breath. Now, he decided, was as good a time as any to tell her. "Speaking of work, Largo got a call from the guy in charge of the office in Kayenta. They opened a little substation at Monument Valley because of all the visitors this summer and a movie that's being made there. The filming is taking longer than expected, and some of the officers on duty had a training scheduled. Largo asked me, as long as we were out this way, if I could fill in for them for a few days."

Bernie looked at him, waiting for the rest. He shrugged. "How tough can it be, babysitting some Hollywood types?"

"But what about our vacation?"

"We still have four days. I don't have to go to work until the end of the week. By then, you'll probably be sick of me anyway."

"Why didn't you tell me sooner?"

Chee heard the irritation in her voice.

"He just called when we stopped for gas. You know, we can use the money."

"I know."

She turned from him and looked out the window. "I guess that goes with the territory when you're married to a cop. We'll just make the most of the time we've got."

"Good plan," he said. "We'll call this vacation lite." They passed the junction for Bluff, Utah, and headed on to Kayenta, Arizona, the last town before Monument Valley.

"You hungry?" Chee asked. "There's a hamburger place here that has a Code Talker museum. It's pretty cool."

"I'm OK. I can't wait to see the monuments. Let's stop there on our way home."

Paul greeted them with enthusiasm and a snack of sweet watermelon. Then he offered them a tour that started with a vehicle parked under a ramada.

"This is my joy, my baby." Paul gave Chee a playful punch in the arm. "I want to take you guys for a ride."

The baby had six wheels and looked like the hybrid offspring of a bus and a heavy-duty pickup. The front was a truck chassis, the back a platform with seats on both sides of a central aisle and metal siding that came halfway up. A striped awning deflected the sun. The cover and the vehicle itself were yellow, the color of fertility, a sign, Chee thought, that Paul intended not only for his vehicle to stand out but also for his business to grow. Someone had carefully painted "Hozhoni Photo Tours" on the hood.

Bernie climbed up inside. "Nice Jeep. You can haul a lot of people with this."

"It looks like a Jeep, but it's an old military vehicle. It has a speaker system so the driver can talk to visitors. I call it a People Mover. The folks who ran the tours at Canyon de Chelly used it and I bought it from the old Thunderbird Lodge. Chee and I had some fun back in the canyon. You remember that, bro?"

Chee nodded.

"We'll make a trial run in it later. Let me show you the rest of this place."

They admired the solar shower he'd constructed, walked past an aged corral with a pair of horses, saw his single-wide and the hard-packed dirt basketball court next to it. Then came the new hogan. As Chee had suspected, but not mentioned to Bernie, it was far from finished.

Paul didn't ask for help, but they offered to work inside it, sweeping the dirt floor, smoothing down the rugs Paul had brought, adding dowels where visitors could hang their clothes. Although traditional Navajo families slept on the floor on cozy sheepskins, Paul had wisely decided non-natives would be more comfortable with the option of a cot, and Chee and Bernie put them up and added the new bedding.

Paul had followed the traditional plan for building, so the octagonal structure had no windows. The single door faced east, as the Holy People advised. Ventilation was through the door and the smoke hole in the roof. Hogans provided a cozy living space for families in the winter. In the summer, traditional Diné herders went with their sheep to the fields, camping and using ramadas for shade and cooking. Tourists could sleep inside on a summer night if they wanted, Chee thought, but he preferred the open air, his sleeping bag, and moonlight.

After they worked in the hogan, Bernie made the mistake—at least that was how it looked to Chee—of asking if there was anything else they could do to help. There was, and when they finished, tourists from New Zealand, Japan, Michigan, and elsewhere wouldn't worry about tripping over anything on their way to the outhouse. The wind came up, contributing fine red dust to the process of building the path.

Chee had failed to mention to Bernie that Paul liked to talk. Really liked to talk. That quality could make him a perfect tour guide, but the constant chatter combined with working in the heat usually gave Bernie what she called "the start of a headache." She looked hot and sweaty, but his Laughing Girl didn't complain about cleaning up someone else's debris. "It's beautiful here," she said. She was right, Chee thought, as always.

When Chee found her alone, he suggested that they go see a movie. He liked the idea of sitting in a cool dark room after a dusty warm day working outside.

"A movie? There's a theater in little Kayenta?"

"Not in Kayenta. At Goulding's."

"Goulding's? Is that a town near here? I haven't heard of it."

Chee shook his head. "You haven't lived, girl." He explained that Goulding's was an historic lodge named for the couple who put Monument Valley on the map, thanks to their appreciation of both the massive red buttes rising from the valley floor and the potential Navajo workforce. They enticed Hollywood director John Ford into using the scenery in classic films such as *Stagecoach*, *She Wore a Yellow Ribbon*, and *The Searchers*. Monument Valley's sandstone buttes became the landscape synonymous with the word *western*.

"Some of my kinfolks made movies out here in

their spare time. You ever heard of a guy named John Wayne? Well, my relatives helped him get famous."

Bernie laughed. "Gosh, I can't believe you never told me all this before. So, does this mean they have a movie theater at the lodge?"

"Well, it's not a theater like in Farmington. It's a room with chairs, where they show those old films starring the Duke. You can't buy popcorn, but it's cool in there."

"Indians always end up the losers in those old Westerns. Do you really like those movies?"

"Sure. You know, when Paul and I played cowboys and Indians with our friends, I always wanted to be a cowboy. I was in junior high when I realized a guy could be a cowboy and an Indian at the same time."

"And a comedian, too."

He grinned. "It's five o'clock. Quitting time. I'll buy you dinner at the lodge to go with the movie. A real date."

"What about Paul? I don't want to hurt his feelings."

"Don't worry. I'll talk to him."

She headed off to take a shower with the sun-warmed water and put on clean jeans and a T-shirt.

"You two lovebirds go on," Paul said. "When you get back we can hit the highlights of the sunset tour. I'm going to take you up to Enchanted Mesa first, and then—"

Chee let him explain the route for another five minutes. "Cousin, why don't you tell us all about that when we are on the tour, so we can critique you as a guide?"

Paul nodded. "You get going. They get busy at this time of year."

Before dinner, they headed into the cluster of buildings that formed Goulding's Lodge, first to the quaint old museum with upstairs rooms where the Goulding family lived, and then to the exhibits about the geology and the world of movies downstairs.

Bernie stopped in front of a photograph, a still from one of the films. "Hey, look at this." She drew Chee's attention to a group of Anglo cowboys and others who looked like Navajos but wore costumes designed to resemble Indians of the Great Plains. She indicated a man who sat with a single cowboy on a bench. "That guy reminds me of somebody."

"You know what they say. All Indians look alike."

"He looks like your friend Robert. The one who made that bracelet for me."

Chee studied the picture more closely. "You're right. He does."

The movie of the day, *Stagecoach*, was about to start in the little theater. Chee had seen it in high school when a substitute came for history class and brought the movie with her. He still remembered the date it was released, 1939, and the fact that scholars credited the film with reviving the Western movie genre. Class ended before *Stagecoach* was over, so they were allowed to watch the finale the next day. Chee had felt a fondness for it ever since.

After that, they walked to the restaurant. A young Navajo hostess showed them to a seat by the window, perfectly situated for a view of the Mitten Buttes across the highway to the east. Bernie asked Chee to order her usual, a hamburger and a Coke, and took pictures while her husband made up his mind.

He looked up from studying the menu. "Did you like the movie?"

"Yes, especially the scenery, those shots of the monument with the stagecoach in the foreground. And Navajos pretending to be Apaches." Bernie laughed. "Some of those riders chasing the travelers did look like your relatives."

"I told you we were a handsome bunch."

A large blue tour bus was heading up the drive toward the lodge. It stopped in front of the motel office, and a man in a khaki hat that tied beneath his chin climbed down the steps. He returned to the bus a few minutes later with a large brown envelope in his hand. The bus chugged up the steep incline and stopped near the dining hall front steps. The door opened again and Hat Man climbed out. Then the other passengers started unloading, walking toward the restaurant.

The waitress returned. "If you're ready, you better order. Looks like we're gonna be slammed in a few minutes."

"Is this place big enough for all those people?" Bernie heard a mumble of conversation from the newcomers as they filled the entranceway.

"That's a small group compared to some. It's always like this in the summer. Bus after bus. But the customers aren't too bad, except when they're grumpy. Food always cheers them up."

Chee grinned. "Yeah, my wife says the same thing about me. So, should I have the pork chops or the Navajo taco?"

"I like the pork chops."

"OK, then. And a burger and Coke for my bride."

The waitress left, and Bernie took another photo through the window.

"I'm going to send these to Darleen to show Mama." She glanced at the phone, and frowned.

"There's probably a stronger signal outside, back by the museum," he said. "You can get a different shot out there, too."

"Thanks. While I'm out, I'll call Largo before he goes home and see what happened with that drug bust."

Neither Mama nor the captain liked chitchat. Chee knew she'd be back before her burger arrived. But before Bernie could leave, the waitress returned. "The salad bar comes with the pork chops. There's soup up there, too."

"Thanks."

"Are you from around here? You look kinda familiar."

"My clan brother Paul lives in the valley."

"He's the one starting the new tour business?"

"Right. He's specializing in taking people to places for the best photographs."

"Good idea. I hope he makes it." She smiled at Bernie. "You go ahead and have some salad if you want. Keep him company."

The server left to bring water and menus to the bus people, who now filled all available tables and booths. The room echoed with the buzz of conversation.

"I didn't realize this place was so popular. Are they speaking French?" Bernie asked.

"It could be Russian for all I know." He looked around. "We're surrounded and outnumbered."

Bernie's phone chimed, and she reached for it, studying the display. "It's Mrs. Darkwater." She pushed the answer button and covered her left ear. "Wait. I can't hear you. I'm going where it's not so noisy and the signal's better."

"If that doesn't work, tell her to call my phone. Sometimes it gets better reception."

Bernie walked quickly into the front hallway. She didn't know why her mother's neighbor was calling, but it gave her a deep sense of dread.

"Hello." Mrs. Darkwater's response was muted by the background blare of the television.

"I can barely hear you. Is everything OK out there?"

"Hold on." A pause, and the TV went silent. "Your mother told me you were going up to Monument Valley for a little break. Hot there, I bet."

"It's about like Shiprock. A little warmer. Beautiful."

"That's good." Bernie heard Mrs. Darkwater sigh. "My husband, he's up in Dulce, and you know how you always ask me and him to keep an eye on your mother."

What had happened? Bernie's heart sank, but she knew better than to interrupt.

"I have to go to Chinle to help my son Marshall with Junior. Junior is the one who made those pictures of the rodeo that I have on the refrigerator. Marshall took him to the one up in Cortez."

Would Mrs. Darkwater stay on track and save the

stories of Junior's artistic talent and her son's success as a good dad for another day? "I remember that. How's Mama doing?"

"Well, I hated to call you." Bernie heard a change in Mrs. Darkwater's tone and felt her chest tighten. "When I went over there a little while ago to tell your mother good-bye, she was still in her clothes from yesterday. She was just sitting on the sofa, not even watching the TV. Not reading. Nothing. Staring."

A stroke, Bernie thought. Mama had a stroke. But why hadn't her sister called? Darleen lived with Mama, and her job was helping take care of her.

Mrs. Darkwater kept talking. "I thought something had happened to her, but she said no. She felt OK. Then I asked about you, because I know she worries about you, especially because of your friend who got shot. She told me you were fine, off on a trip. That's good, honey."

Bernie listened, waiting, though she wanted to scream, *Get to the point!*

"Um. I don't know how to say this, so I'll just blurt it out. Your sister didn't come home last night. I am sorry to call you. Your mother told me not to call, not to bother you on your vacation, but I have to leave, and I worry about her all alone." Mrs. Darkwater's voice had an end-of-story sound to it.

"What happened to Sister? Why isn't she there?" Bernie pushed the vision of her little sister dead in a car crash out of her mind.

"I asked your mama that. She just shook her head." Mrs. Darkwater sighed. "My son needs for us all to drive to Chinle pretty soon now. I promised him I would help with the boy, since Marshall has to work. I thought you might know someone else who could stay with your mother."

Bernie tried to think of available friends and relatives, and came up short. "May I speak to Mama?"

"Sure thing. But I'm not at her house, so I'll go over there real quick and call you back." Mrs. Darkwater hung up.

While Bernie was outside on the phone, the waitress brought dinner. Chee tasted the gravy—a creamy little brown lake surrounded by a mashed-potato dike. Very good! He cut some bites of the pork chop to go with the potatoes, tried the corn, and decided he was a happy man.

Bernie returned, frowning. After two years of marriage, Chee had become fairly adept at reading her moods, but this was something he seldom saw—sadness, confusion, anger, and worry mixed together. Searching his own conscience, he couldn't think of anything he'd done lately to upset his bride. It must have been the phone call. Bernie loved burgers, but she wasn't eating and didn't seem to want to talk.

"Do you want to tell me what Mrs. Darkwater said?" Chee asked finally.

"Sister didn't come home last night. I don't know what happened. Mama's been alone since yesterday, and Mrs. Darkwater can't stay with her, and her husband is out of town."

Chee chewed his pork chop, listening for more. The dining room had quieted as the tourists ate. The waitress returned with a box for the burger and a Coke refill. Bernie sat in silence.

"Eat a little, sweetheart, before the fries get cold. I'll make some phone calls about Darleen."

Bernie cut the burger in half, picked up a piece, and then put it down. She took a sip of the Coke. "Let me talk to Mama first to find out what she knows. Mrs. Darkwater was going over there to call me and get Mama to the phone."

"You know, I have Largo and Bigman on speed dial. They'll help us figure out what's up."

"I know. It's just that—"

Her phone chimed. Bernie answered, "Hello?"

She put the cell on speaker, and Chee moved closer. "Yes, I'd love to talk to Mama."

Chee pictured Mama seated in her favorite chair at the table and Mrs. Darkwater standing in her kitchen with the old-fashioned yellow phone receiver pressed to her ear, and then covering the mouthpiece with her left hand, telling Bernie's mother that her elder daughter was on the line, before finally handing over the phone.

"Daughter, are you having a nice trip?"

"Yes, Mama. But Mrs. Darkwater said something's happening with Sister."

Silence. Then, "She has not come home. I tried to call her on that phone she has, but she did not answer me. I waited for her all night."

The phone went silent. Chee heard Bernie's mother sigh.

"Mama, was Sister arguing with you, something like that?" Darleen had never run away before, but maybe she'd needed some space to cool off.

"No. Some friends came by, and she drove off

with them. She was happy. That's all." Bernie's mother paused. "You find out what went wrong and bring her back here."

"I'll find out."

An accident, perhaps? Chee wondered. Or maybe Darleen's drinking had led to an arrest.

Bernie shifted gears. "What did you eat today, Mama?"

"I didn't get around to that yet."

"Is there something in the refrigerator for you to make a sandwich?"

"I'm not so hungry."

Chee watched Bernie drum her index finger on the table next to her plate. Mama could be as stubborn as her daughter.

"At least have some peanut butter and crackers. Maybe there's some juice. You don't want to get weak, Mama, especially with the heat."

The phone faded to silence, and then Mama said, "The sun can be hot in that valley. You be sure to have plenty of water. Make sure the Cheeseburger has water, too."

Mama and Darleen had given Chee that nickname before he married Bernie. Funny, he thought, since Bernie preferred her burgers cheese-less.

Bernie exhaled, and Chee saw the worry on her face. "Could you hand the phone back to Mrs. Darkwater, please?"

"She's not here."

"But she just called."

"I told her to leave with her son and the little one. Darleen will be home soon."

"Mama, listen. We don't know when Darleen will be home. I will find out what happened to her. Do you know the names of the friends she left with?"

"One was that Stoop Man. And his sister, too." Mama's voice had an edge now. "Daughter, I need to say an important thing."

Bernie and Chee stared at the cell phone, waiting.

"If you come here now instead of staying there with the one you married, I will be angry with you. T'ahi'go." The word translated to something between "livid" and "furious."

"You hear me, daughter? Understand this."

Bernie's eyes glistened. "Use your walker, Mama. Be really careful. Drink something."

Bernie's mother was probably not sipping water like she was supposed to, Chee realized, because without Darleen as a safety net, using the bathroom was difficult for her. She had given herself a black eye that spring when she slipped and fell against the tub.

"You be careful, too," she said to Bernie, and hung up.

Bernie looked at the phone and then shifted her gaze to the picture-perfect view of the expansive valley. Chee thought how much they'd been looking forward to this vacation. He thought about the private tour in the People Mover, and Bernie's face when he told her how the red stone buttes and spires began to glow at the first hint of dawn. He thought of who they knew who might be willing to stay with Bernie's mother, and discarded every idea as quickly as it popped up.

"I need to check on Mama and figure out what's

happening with Darleen." She looked like she was fighting back tears. "Oh, honey, I'm so—"

Chee touched her lips with his fingertip. He had already left cash for the bill and a tip on the table. He reached for his truck keys. "Don't forget to take your burger. I might want it later if you don't."

3

They made good time, Chee driving as fast as he could safely. Before they reached Agathla Peak, Bernie had called the hospitals in Shiprock and Farmington. If her baby sister had been in an accident fairly close to home, the ambulances would have taken her there first. Through friends who worked in the emergency rooms and gave her the information confidentially, she learned that Darleen had not come in for treatment, been admitted, or been transferred elsewhere. Good, but it left the mystery unsolved. Of course, there were other hospitals in the area—Gallup, Cortez, Durango—but those were farther away, and Bernie didn't have contacts there. She'd put that off until she ran into a dead end.

Darleen could have been arrested. If she were, it probably had to do with too many beers.

Bernie thought about calling Bigman and decided not to, at least for now. If the Navajo Police had picked up Darleen, she knew someone would be in touch. Even if they had stopped Darleen and let her go, Bernie and Chee would find out about it soon enough. Theirs was a small and close-knit community. She'd have to live with the embarrassment.

She phoned a girlfriend who worked for the San Juan County sheriff's office and could have discreetly found out if Sister had been arrested by one of the deputies. But the woman was out of the office, and Bernie didn't have her cell number.

So she sat and fidgeted, edgy and uncomfortable in this unknown territory. She could have asked Chee his opinion, but she wasn't ready for it yet.

They rode in silence to Kayenta, where Chee turned on to US 160. They cruised east on a paved two-lane highway with no traffic signals, stop signs, cell service, or patrol cars, and plenty of scenery. Bernie studied the landscape as it rolled by, watching the first tinge of pink sunset brighten to brilliance and then fade again to soft gray. She turned on the radio and channel-surfed, finding only static. Turned it off again. Looked out the window until she could see the first pinpoints of starlight in the summer sky.

Chee broke the silence. "When Paul told me he could use some help, I didn't realize how much.

"Paul's a nice guy, hard to say no to. It felt good to do something physical instead of sitting in my unit all day.

"He told me how much he liked you. I mentioned that your sister was single and cute. I told him she was a strong girl, too. A good worker."

"You didn't!"

Chee laughed. "I didn't. You think I should be a matchmaker?"

"Don't you dare." She moved closer to him, slipped off her shoes, and put her stockinged feet up on the seat beneath her. Chee wrapped his arm around her.

His phone rang from the center console, where he'd placed it along with his sunglasses. Bernie looked at the screen. "It's Paul." She answered and put it on speaker.

"So where are you guys? Guess I should have told you to get back before sunset."

"Oh, man, I should have called you," Chee said. "Bernie's mother had an emergency and we had to drive back to Toadlena. I forgot to let you know."

"It's OK, bro. I would have canceled your tour anyway. The People Mover won't start."

"What's wrong with it?"

"I don't know. Maybe you can take a look."

Chee asked more questions and they listened as Paul tried to define the problem.

"That sounds easy to fix."

"I hope so," Paul said. "Easy for you, anyway. I'm not great with this stuff."

"You can do it. Take the phone outside, and I'll walk you through it. First, open the hood and find the battery."

They waited, and then Paul's voice was back over the speaker. "Is there a latch or something? It doesn't want to go up, man. Oh, wait, I got it now."

Chee started to explain, but it soon became obvious that Paul needed more than a verbal map to discover the mysterious world beneath the hood of an aged vehicle. "Do you know somebody who's good with cars?" There had to be a shade-tree mechanic in the Monument Valley community who could help him; living in out-of-the-way places bred self-sufficiency and cooperation.

"Yeah, sure, bro, but you are my go-to guy tonight. I'll try doing what you say."

"Good."

"Speaking of good, here's some good news. Outback Expeditions—that's Ron Goodspring's company—he called me after you and Bernie left for the movie. Ronnie's got four people from Norway wanting a sunrise photo tour, and he can't handle them. I just landed my first referral." Paul talked in enticing detail about where he would take them— Skull Arch, Honeymoon Arch, House of Many Hands ruin. "We'll probably stop so they can take pictures of horses on the sand dunes, too. When will you and Bernie get back?"

"I don't know. Everything's up in the air at this point. We're not sure what's happening with Bernie's mom."

"It depends on Mama and—and some other stuff," Bernie chimed in. "Nice to have met you if I don't make it back this time."

"I hope everything works out OK. You all stay in touch."

"Thank you," Bernie said. "Come see us in Shiprock."

Paul hung up, and Bernie snuggled closer. "I appreciate you not mentioning Sister."

"I didn't want to spoil our double date."

Chee focused on passing the occasional RV or delivery truck and watching for animals on the road as he considered the problem with Paul's vehicle. How could he explain in the simplest terms how to fix it in time for the morning tour? Maybe, just maybe, things would work out with Darleen and Mama, and he and Bernie could salvage some of their vacation before he had to go back to work.

Bernie hadn't talked to any of her law enforcement contacts, he noticed. "Are you OK?" he asked.

"I guess," she said. "I'm trying not to worry. I just want to sit here and think about this, figure out what comes next. Sister probably did something dumb, but I hope she's OK. She said she'd give Mama more help while we were gone, and I trusted her. I shouldn't have."

Chee started to add that they didn't know Darleen's side of the story, but thought better of it.

They reached the turnoff for Many Farms and Mexican Water, Arizona. Just beyond that was the road that could have taken them north to Utah. A few minutes later, Chee read the big Welcome to New Mexico sign. It was interesting, he thought, that the state considered this obscure border important enough to mark. When they reached 491, with its big trucks roaring toward Gallup or the Colorado border, he turned south.

"I think I've come up with the start of a plan," Bernie said. "Tell me what you think."

"Go ahead."

"My job is to make sure that Mama is safe. I should have been on top of this sooner. So I'm making a list of relatives I can call to give us some help or who might know somebody to stay with Mama. I'll work on that, then deal with whatever trouble Darleen is in."

She squeezed his hand. "And I thought some more about that guy with the boxes of dirt. Maybe instead of hiding something in the dirt, he was interested in the dirt itself—hunting for pot shards or charcoal from an old fire pit, or something like that. You can barely take a hike out here without running into an archaeological site."

"Hmmmm."

"That's lame?"

"I didn't say that."

"You didn't have to." He felt her shift, straightening her legs. "Thank you for coming home with me."

"Every pretty girl needs a chauffeur." But he heard her use the word *home* for her mother's house. When would his house, their house, be home? Maybe with a kid or two playing outside?

Bernie pushed her hair behind her ears. "Did I tell you about those beer cans stacked up in Sister's bedroom? I've seen her drunk when I've gone to Mama's. One day she could barely get out of the car. I didn't want to think about it, but now I have to. I should have been tougher on her. Maybe this will be a wakeup call. What do you think?"

He hesitated. "We don't know what happened, except that your mother is home by herself, and that's not a safe situation. You're right to make Mama your top priority."

"Sister should have called me, not just left Mama alone."

"I agree. I could check on her, see what I can find out." After his years in law enforcement, Chee knew most of the major players in the Four Corners.

"When we get to Mama's."

Finally Chee turned the truck onto Bernie's mother's road and stopped in front of her little house. Mama usually went to bed early, but tonight the living room lights shone into the evening.

Bernie opened the passenger door. "Are you coming in with me?"

Chee shook his head. "I'll hide out here until you see how things are. If she asks, tell her I had to make those phone calls about Darleen."

Bernie nodded. "I can't blame you."

Chee watched her walk to the porch, open the front door, and disappear inside.

Mama must be unhappy with her baby daughter. When she saw Bernie, that would make two people on her bad side. And when she found out he was there too? He knew from long experience some situations were best left to the women.

Chee felt comfortable in the truck, away from the emotion-packed world of mothers, daughters, sisters, and family drama. He was happy to help; happier to stay out of the way. He liked Bernie's idea of focusing on more help for Mama. If it worked, maybe they could plan another vacation—or even continue this one.

After a while he climbed out onto the road to stretch his legs and his back, feeling the residual warmth radiating from the tan earth. Another day with no rain, and no rain expected anywhere on the Navajo Nation or in the Four Corners for another week. Some years the summer rains had started by now, but this late June only brought baking heat.

Chee heard his phone ring back in the truck and trotted to catch the call. Cell service was spotty on the reservation, but, amazingly, their phones worked near Bernie's mother's house.

It was Paul. "So how's Bernie's mother?"

"I'm not sure yet. Bernie's in there talking to her. I'm waiting, looking at the stars. How are you doing as a mechanic?"

"Not good. I searched for the battery. It looks like a box, right?"

"Right."

"I guess this thing doesn't have one. If Bernie's mom is OK, could you come back tonight? Help me fix the People Mover? I hate to lose that job."

"Let me see what's up in the house of women. I'll call you."

Chee climbed back out of the truck again and looked at the sparkling sky. The stars always made him feel small, a little speck of life in the giant scheme of things—many of them unknown and complicated.

He walked toward Mama's house. He could see Bernie sitting on the couch, Mama next to her. His mother-in-law looked like she'd lost weight, precious pounds she couldn't afford to lose.

He knocked, and Mama and Bernie turned. Mama put her hand on Bernie's leg and said something he couldn't catch, and he realized he was in trouble. Bernie rose and opened the door.

In the years he had known her, Mama had been unfailingly polite, but tonight she dispensed with the pleasantries. "You came, too?" She didn't wait for Chee to respond, or invite him to sit down. "You talk to this one. Talk some sense into her."

Chee stepped inside. He had seen Bernie handle difficult situations and wondered what she had said so far. Whatever it was, it hadn't worked.

Mama spoke to him again. "You two should not have come. I don't know why she makes such a fuss about me."

Bernie said, "I could use some coffee. I'm going to make some for all of us." When she walked past him to the kitchen, Chee could tell she had been crying.

Chee turned to Mama. "The night sky is beautiful. Would you like to go out to the porch with me and see the moon?"

Mama considered the offer, then nodded. She struggled to rise from the couch, and he moved toward her, offering his arm. Her grip was surprisingly strong, but she was trembling. He gently leveraged her to standing. She felt as light as bones baked in the sun. She pointed to the corner with her lips, the same way Chee's aunt had always done. "Get that walking machine."

Chee knew she meant the walker. He waited for her to stand more steadily and then helped her take a few steps. When she reached the back of the couch, he pushed the walker where she could grab for it.

Moving slowly, she headed to the front door. Chee opened it, and they made their way outside. They stood for a while, and then Bernie's mother sat in the wooden chair, and Chee lowered himself onto the cement at her side.

Mama had grown up in a society where sons-in-law kept their distance, but the traditional Navajo world was changing. Chee thought some of the changes, like the end of the taboo against a woman's mother and her husband ever catching sight of each other, were for the best. Death had taken Chee's mother years ago. He considered Mama's presence in his life a blessing.

"Did my daughter see Tsé Bii' Ndzisgaii?" Mama used the Navajo name for Monument Valley.

"Yes. She smiled and smiled. My wife will tell you how beautiful it was. She took some pictures."

Mama nodded. "I remember my uncle's stories about how the Holy People left us those big rocks out there so the Diné could find our way through that place."

Somewhere a coyote yipped, and another answered.

Mama spoke again. "Your wife thinks I am too weak to be alone."

Chee watched a cloud flirt with the moon, and waited.

"She is stubborn, that one. She doesn't listen to me so well anymore. You tell her to save her energy to take care of her sister."

Chee said, "My wife looks like she's been crying."

Mama stared ahead, and the silence sat so long that he wondered if she had fallen asleep.

"She is angry with her sister, and she worries too much. And I think she is still sad about the old one who got hurt."

Chee realized she was referring to the attack on Lieutenant Leaphorn that Bernie had witnessed.

"I told her not to come here," Mama said. "When I look at her, I know her heart is still heavy, uneasy, restless, ever since that bad thing happened."

They watched the cloud float in front of the moon, covering it like frost on a cold morning. Chee said, "May I share an idea with you?"

Mama nodded once.

"My wife would like to figure out how to best help her sister. She would enjoy your company. Seeing how strong you are would lighten her heart, help her return to *hozho*." *Hozho*, harmony, contentment with the inevitable—a central tenet of the Navajo way. "I believe if you asked her to spend some time here at your house, she would say yes."

He studied Mama's face for a reaction. Discerned none. Continued.

"Some people say that it is a good thing for daughters to be with their mothers so they can learn from them. They say it doesn't matter if the daughter thinks she is already a grown woman, she can still benefit from her mother's wisdom."

The wisp of a cloud drifted away, and the moonlight brightened. The fragrance of coffee wafted out onto the porch.

Chee stood. "May I bring you some coffee?"

Mama reached to the walker for support and rose gingerly from the chair. "My daughter knows how to make good coffee. I want to go in to sit with her. And you come in, too."

Chee held the door as Mama moved inside and pushed into the kitchen with measured steps. She eased herself into her regular chair. Bernie poured coffee for her and brought it to the table, along with the sugar bowl and a spoon. She poured a second cup and handed it to Chee.

He took the mug by the handle. "I'm going back out to the porch to make some calls about my sister-in-law. I'll tell you what I find out."

After he left, Bernie took her regular seat and waited. Mama looked at the coffee in her cup, tried a sip, and added more sugar. She put the cup down and pulled herself a little taller in the chair. "Elder daughter, I have been thinking things over. I would like you to stay so we can decide how to help your sister. It would make my heart happy to be with you."

Bernie was glad that her mother considered it rude to look someone in the eye. She quickly brushed away her tears. "I will be happy to do that, Mama. We will figure things out together."

Suddenly, the night seemed sweeter.

4

Chee had good connections and a bit of luck. After a few calls he discovered that Darleen was in the San Juan County Detention Center, arrested for disorderly conduct and placed under protective custody because she was drunk. He was glad he'd found her, glad that she wasn't in the hospital or dead, glad that she hadn't been arrested for DWI. After decades of highway tragedies, New Mexico's legislature had made the state one of the nation's toughest places for drunken driving. He told Bernie privately, stressing the good news—Darleen was safe. His wife would decide when and what to tell Mama.

After that, he called Paul and told him Bernie had to help Mama, but he would be back tonight to do whatever needed doing. Chee appreciated the fact that his clan brother didn't ask why Chee hadn't been invited to stay, or when Bernie would return.

"If we can't make the People Mover start," Paul said, "we could use your truck and my truck. You could follow me. Maybe a couple of them won't mind sitting in the back, you know? You and I used to do it when you came to visit."

"Don't worry. I'll get your baby going." Chee figured that even if they didn't know it was illegal, tourist passengers would balk at riding in an open truck bed.

"I've been nervous about this, brother. It means a lot to me." Chee heard the relief in his cousin's voice. "I've been making some notes for tomorrow for the *bilagaanas*. I can brew a thermos of coffee, and I've got a can of milk, some sugar cubes. Would you stop and get some of those little doughnuts? I'll pay you for them. You know, the white ones with the powdered sugar outside?" Paul made a soft clicking sound with his tongue. "I wish we had some of those breakfast burritos like the ones you used to make. That would be perfect."

Chee stopped at the grocery in Shiprock, amazed to find it still open. The mini doughnuts looked shopworn, so he bought what he needed for burritos along with a case of bottled water. The customers would probably want it. It would be warm, but it was the best he could do. Then he went by the trailer along the San Juan that he and Bernie called home and picked up his police uniform and weapon. He'd need them for his vacation-interrupting assignment.

Chee's drive back to Monument Valley was long and solitary. He told himself to stop feeling grumpy, to remember how lucky he was to have a wife who cared for her relatives and who expanded the circle to include his relatives, like Paul. He already missed Bernie.

When he got there, he fixed the People Mover by

flashlight. The repair didn't take long—it was just a matter of reconnecting loose battery cables. He was thankful that old engines didn't require computer analysis.

Chee wasn't usually an early riser, but before sunrise he and Paul went to work making burritos. Chee cooked the filling, and Paul wrapped the tortillas, sealed the burritos in foil, rolled them in towels, and put them in an insulated bag. Chee set up the coffeepot and placed it over the fire in the fire pit. Paul had found six cups, the old-fashioned kind their grandmother had used. Because this was Paul's first time guiding a tour, Chee agreed to come along as an observer. He could suggest improvements for the next time.

The guests—two couples from Norway—were ready at the visitor center at 6:00 a.m., bright-eyed and excited. They seemed amazed and a bit intimidated to find themselves in the big, open, nearly waterless landscape with a real Indian as a guide. Paul further wowed them when he told them that Chee, his assistant for the day, was a genuine Navajo Nation policeman.

The visitors nodded and introduced themselves: Filip, Emma, Emil, and Nora. They spoke rusty high school English.

"You came here on holiday like us?" Emma, a woman in a long-sleeved hiking shirt, asked.

"Yes, but I'm going to be working here, too, helping with a movie."

The woman looked at him with more interest. "You are in this movie?"

"No, ma'am." He tried to explain the situation, which led to more questions about the Navajo Nation police and how they operated. He wished he'd kept his mouth shut; he knew from experience that talking more than necessary only led to trouble.

He helped the visitors into the People Mover and they bounced along to Paul's place, where they toured the hogan, admired the ramada, and praised the coffee. They gobbled up the burritos once Paul showed them how to scrape off most of the green chile and explained that they could do so without hurting his feelings.

After breakfast, Paul pulled the People Mover keys out of his pocket and tossed them to Chee. "You drive so I can concentrate on giving out the information. I'll tell you where to turn for the photo vistas."

The tour went remarkably well. To Chee's amazement, Paul knew quite a bit about photography and had a jovial way of sharing advice without being pushy. He told Chee to stop at all the right places for pictures. Paul also explained the geology of the park and talked about its plants and animals without going overboard. The customers knew enough English to understand the essence of the narration and ask questions. They took dozens of photos of horses on the sand dunes.

Chee enjoyed driving the big vehicle and revisiting places he'd loved years before. When Paul discussed the area's human history—ancient Pueblo people, Spanish and Anglo miners, and the Navajo families who lived in the park today—he thought about Bernie's theory, that the dirt from her traffic stop might be tied to archaeology. He reached no conclusion.

Chee steered them out of Mystery Valley and onto the main Monument Valley road, a rough dirt track that looped back to the Visitor Center. The sun warmed the midmorning air, which blew in through his open window and buffeted the guests on the People Mover's bench seats. Ahead a sight-seeing van, fully packed with customers, churned up a red cloud of dirt. The suffocating dust left him two alternatives. The first was to slow down to a crawl for the long miles back to the visitor center to stay well behind the van, while the passengers in the back baked, got sunburned, and grew bored.

The second, more manly option? Ignore the painful speed limit, pass the van, and let them de-celerate or eat his dust.

He sailed by the vehicle smoothly, but a giant pothole lay just beyond it. He avoided the crater only to encounter a barricade the road crew had created to keep the trail from flooding. The People Mover plowed directly onto a hill of rocks and sand that took up half the roadway. Chee winced at the scraping noise and then felt a *thunk* as something big and hard made contact with the underside of the vehicle. The People Mover continued forward just fine, but the realist in Chee didn't trust it. He had no choice, of course, but to drive on.

As Paul helped the guests unload at the hotel, Chee noticed oil dripping onto the asphalt of the parking lot. After the customers left, he showed his cousin the dark puddle. "I think that's from what-ever I clobbered back there."

Paul shrugged. "It had a leak already. They have oil at the store behind Goulding's. We'll add some when we need it, take some with us. No problem."

Chee's phone rang. "Just a second." He hoped it was Bernie.

Instead, he heard a different woman's voice. "Sergeant Chee? It's Monica, the administrative assistant at the Monument Valley substation. The captain asked me to call you. He's hoping you can start work early. Something's come up."

"What do you mean by early?"

She hesitated. "The captain can give you the details, but we're really short around here. He asked me to see if you could meet with him this afternoon, so he can brief you on your assignment."

"Let me make a couple calls, and I'll get back to you, Monica." If the situation with Bernie's mother was going to take time to resolve, he might as well make himself useful. And whatever trouble he'd created for the People Mover would have a price tag. Why not meet with the captain and get the lay of the land?

"Where's the office?" he asked, and she gave him directions.

There was no answer on Bernie's cell number. He didn't leave a message, instead calling her mother's house and their home number in Shiprock. No Bernie anywhere. He called Monica back, and told her he'd be there.

Paul gave him a questioning look, and Chee explained.

"I thought you were on vacation for a few more days."

"If Bernie can't get back, I might as well go in early."

"Stay with me as long as you want, bro. I was thinking we could fix up that old corral while you're here. I might start some horseback tours."

Chee had noticed the corral. Fixing it was not an option; Paul needed to rebuild the whole thing, to make it safe for tourists who'd probably never been within smelling distance of a horse.

Paul kept talking. "We can work on that when you're done with the police stuff. We could do it the old way with junipers. Remember how Uncle would bring in a bunch of trees, and we would trim off the branches to make the posts?"

Chee nodded. The work had been hot and dirty, but they enjoyed it because Uncle told them stories of his army days in Vietnam.

They added oil to replace what had leaked out and bought more to take with them in case of an emergency. Back at Paul's house, Chee scooted under the vehicle. He spotted the problem easily: a steady drip that led his eye to a hole in the oil pan. Fixing it would require draining the oil—or letting it simply drip out—welding the hole closed, adding more oil, and making sure the weld held.

Chee maneuvered himself back out, dusted off his clothes, and explained the situation. "Since I did the damage, I'll take care of it for you."

Paul said, "I told you, it had a leak before. I'll pay for half with some of that money I get from the tourists. I'm glad you can fix it."

"I hope I can fix it. Do you know where we can find a welding torch, a rod, and a socket wrench that will fit these old bolts?"

"I'll find somebody who can loan us that stuff."

In the late afternoon Chee took a shower, put on his uniform, and tried unsuccessfully to reach Bernie again. Then he drove his truck to the Monument Valley Visitor Center.

The temporary police substation occupied two offices on the expansive Visitor Center's lower level. Chee introduced himself to Monica, dispatcher/receptionist/answerer of questions, a fortysomething Navajo woman. Monica reciprocated with her clans. They weren't related, but of course she knew Paul.

The captain was expecting him.

Leroy Bahe rose from his cluttered desk. "Jim Chee. I haven't seen you since we worked together in Tuba City. How long has it been? Back when you were a bachelor." If large-and-in-charge was a requirement for police work, Bahe qualified, hands down.

After they'd talked about their mutual friend, Hopi officer Cowboy Dashee, Bahe's sister's graduation from truck-driving school, and his son's success in the marines, Bahe asked about Lieutenant Leaphorn. "I heard about him getting shot. I hope he's doing OK."

"The Lieutenant's getting better. My wife and I spend time with him when we can. He can't talk much yet, but the doctors think he might regain that. His friend Louisa is helping him."

Bahe nodded. "Glad to hear it. I understand you almost got barbecued in a storage locker."

Chee chuckled. "Yeah. Gave me a whole new respect for gasoline."

"So you're willing to work here an extra day or two?"

"Largo mentioned something about babysitting some movie folks."

"You bet. You get the Hollywood assignment." The movie, Bahe explained, was a horror film with permission from the Tribal Council to shoot in the park. "Mostly what you'll do is make sure their equipment doesn't block the roads. You might have to handle a trespassing call every once in a while that their paid security can't or won't deal with."

"Monica said something about starting sooner than I'd planned."

Bahe nodded. "I'd really appreciate it if you could start today. I just got a call that somebody out in movieland went for a drive and didn't come back. I could use you now."

Chee waited for what Bahe would say next. In the Navajo tradition, if something was important, you mentioned it four times.

Bahe scanned his computer screen. "Melissa Goldfarb, thirty-five. Blond, five foot five, one-twenty pounds. Her boss says she drove off in a red Chevy Cruze. You could do some nosing around about her first before you actually have to go searching. Maybe she decided to head back to California because she got bored or overworked or angry about something."

"How long has she been gone?"

"Only twelve hours. These movies folks already sent their own security man, but he couldn't find her. Evidently she's not the type to go psycho, so her boss is worried she's lost or hurt or something out there."

Usually the police waited forty-eight hours

before looking for a missing adult. Bahe read Chee's expression. "The Tribal Council delegate from around here worked hard to get the movie. Nobody wants any bad publicity out of this. And the guy who called, a producer named Delahart, vaguely threatened to go to those entertainment news shows and tell America what a dangerous place the valley is unless we help them with the search."

Chee said, "Wouldn't it be better to send someone else if she's really lost out there? I mean, someone who knows the area?"

"Darn right. But I don't have anybody else, so you're my guy." Bahe grinned. "What do you say?"

"Sure thing." He'd figure out how to tell Bernie. "If I start today, you think I could leave a few days early?"

"You never know." He stood and handed Chee a set of keys. "I'm thinking this is a publicity stunt they'll spin to have something to do with zombies. But Delahart was a good enough actor to convince me to check it out. The unit's out back. Be careful. I remember your driving from Tuba and the problem with that lawyer's car. What was that gal's name?"

"Janet Peet. That accident could have happened to anybody. Her little dream ride had a lot of problems."

"And a few more when you finished with it."

"How do I find this Delahart guy?"

"Easy. Take the loop road into the park, and right before Ford Point you'll see some yellow and black signs that read 'TUR.' "

"TUR?"

"It stands for *The Undead Return*. The name of the movie."

Chee liked the SUV Bahe had loaned him, a newer unit than the one he used at Shiprock. Nice ride. The air-conditioning blew hot air on his feet and at his face, but it turned cool by the time he'd adjusted the seat, positioned the mirrors, and clicked on his seat belt.

Now that he was looking for them, Chee noticed the small yellow signs. Why, he wondered, hadn't the lost woman, Melissa, just followed the signs back to base camp? He doubted that she was lost. More likely she'd had an argument with a boyfriend or somebody in the company and taken off. Or maybe she wanted a change of scene and drove into Kayenta or over to Mexican Hat.

Chee cruised down a sandy wash, up a hill, and around a few curves, picking his way through the ruts, holes, and rocks on the exhausted dirt road. The route had been designed to offer fairly close views of the magnificent sandstone formations and, not coincidentally, several wide, safe parking areas where visitors could pause for photos and buy jewelry, pottery, cold drinks, and souvenirs from local families who set up tables to sell their wares.

A little sign indicated the turnoff, and a few minutes beyond that he saw the movie base camp. A pale-green late-model sedan of some sort was parked just outside of the camp entrance. As he drew closer, a man with a ball cap climbed out and hailed him.

"*Yá'át'ééh*, Officer. What can I do for you?" The parking attendant had a name badge that read "Gerald."

"*Yá'át'ééh*. I'm looking for the man in charge, a gentleman named Delahart."

Gerald took off his cap, rubbed his head, put the hat back on. "You don't want to talk to that guy, and he's not here anyway. Mr. Robinson is the supervisor. He can help you. Drive straight in and park by the trailer that says 'Production Office.' Just ignore the No Parking signs."

"You might be able to help with something else." Chee paused, making sure he had Gerald's attention. "A woman could be missing. Somebody named Melissa Goldfarb. Did you see her leave?"

Gerald shook his head. "I just got here for the night shift. Missy is missing? No kidding? So are you working with Officer Tsinnie?"

"I'm just filling in for a few days. I haven't met him, or anybody at the station yet, except Captain Bahe and Monica." Tsinnie was a fairly common name; Chee knew several Officer Tsinnies.

"Him's a her." Gerald chuckled. "But I'm sure she's been called worse."

Chee pulled up close to a group of structures and parked near an unlit trailer with a sign that read "Production Office." Beyond he saw a larger trailer, lights on inside and a standing figure profiled in the doorway. The person trotted down the steps and up to the car, not even waiting for Chee to turn off the engine.

"Officer, I'm glad you're here." The man was tall, something over six feet. He stooped over to speak into the window. "Greg Robinson, assistant producer."

Robinson moved with the grace of a person who stayed in shape. Chee placed his age as early fifties. "So, the missing woman isn't back yet?"

"No. I wish."

Chee opened the door of the SUV, forcing Robinson to step back, and climbed out.

"She said she was taking the day off," Robinson said. "She got in her car. That was it."

"Did she tell anyone what her plans were?"

"Well, not exactly. She said she wanted photographs and some time to collect her thoughts." He paused. "It can get crazy around here."

"Tell me about her."

Robinson repeated the description Chee knew: blond hair, blue eyes, slim, early thirties, wearing shorts and a white T-shirt. "She's full of life. A great gal. A hard worker."

"Was she alone when she left?"

"I guess so. Nobody else is missing." Robinson shrugged. "And, before you ask, no drug or booze issues, no teed-off lovers, no arguments with co-workers I know of. We've been on a tight schedule, lots of pressure. I can see why she wanted time to herself, a break. But Melissa didn't show up for the evening meeting. That's totally not like her."

"Is she an actress?"

"No, she keeps track of the money. That's one of the hardest jobs around."

Robinson looked past Chee, out toward the vast empty landscape. "Are you going to call in a crew with some of those search dogs?"

"First I'll drive around, take a look for her myself. Try to remember if Melissa mentioned where she was going to take her pictures. Was there some landmark she wanted in a photograph?"

"None of us have been out here long enough to

really know our way around. It's easy to get lost in this desert. I feel like I've been dropped onto another planet. Perfect for the movie, but it's starting to get on my nerves."

Chee gave Robinson a card with his cell phone number. "Let me know if she comes back, or if you think of anything else that would help." That is, he thought, if his phone worked out where he was headed. "If you can't get me and it's important, call the office."

He turned off the air conditioner and lowered the windows as he drove out of the movie compound, listening for another vehicle or perhaps a woman calling out for help in the quiet desert. He savored the warm evening air that filled the SUV, dry as dust. No worry about mosquitoes here except after those rare, blessed days when the valley got some of its five inches of annual rainfall.

The view matched the dictionary description of *spectacular*—a brilliant sky packed from edge to edge with Technicolor pinks, magentas, and oranges that made the monuments look even more rugged, imposing, and otherworldly. Diné stories confirmed Chee's observation that this place was special and blessed. The valley had been the interior of a giant hogan, with stone pinnacles tourists called Gray Whiskers and Sentinel as its doorposts. His people also considered the two soaring buttes known as the Mittens to be the hands of a Holy Person, left behind in stone to remind the Navajos that they weren't alone.

The vivid colors gradually faded to soft pastel. Wispy clouds added ambience, like see-through scarves that make bare skin beneath more alluring. If he were a photographer, he'd be taking pictures.

Chee knew from past visits that the best sunset shots were on the Utah side of the valley, the vista points he wished he'd had the chance to show Bernie. He stopped at the Monument Valley Park security gate, explaining to the attendant who he was and describing the woman he was looking for. The guard seemed interested. "I started work at eight tonight," she said. "I didn't see any car like that leave, but she could have come through before my shift."

"What about the person who had the earlier shift?"

The guard shrugged. "You can ask, but he has so many cars to keep track of. I doubt he would remember."

Chee gave her a card with his cell number. "If you see Melissa come through before I get back, could you ask her to call me?"

"Sure thing."

Chee turned north, crossing from the Arizona section of the park into Utah on US 89. From here Monument Valley, foreboding and beautiful, spread to his right. Deep shadows accentuated the contours carved into the sandstone by wind, time, and water. The monuments looked muscular, supernaturally splendid, and eerie in the dying light. The movie people had the right idea, Chee thought. Why go to the trouble of building sets, or creating them with computers, when nature herself provided such a grand backdrop?

Looking for the red Chevy, he checked turn-outs and cruised down side roads that promised the grandest views. Back on the pavement, he discovered an RV with a portable barbecue grill outside, the occupants settled in for the night at their improvised and illegal campsite. He ignored them, focused on finding Melissa Goldfarb.

Heading back toward the Arizona border and the park entrance, he drove faster now, rechecking turnouts and parking spots to make sure he hadn't missed the little car.

Back at the park entrance, the guard waved him through. "Nobody's come in since you left."

Chee tried to think like a white woman from Los Angeles. What if she'd gone to one of the two hotels that served valley visitors? Maybe someone staying there invited her to a party. If that was the case, she probably wasn't in as much danger as she would be if she'd wandered out into the dry, empty valley.

He considered what Robinson had said about the woman needing to get away. He should have asked if she was depressed, but nothing in Robinson's description hinted at that. Just stress, modern life's most common malady. Seeking quiet and solitude, she might have driven down one of the local, private roads, thinking that she could get an unusual photograph. Perhaps her car had gotten stuck in the sand. What if she had decided to leave it and walk out? What if instead of following the road, she'd taken a shortcut? Lots of what-ifs.

Chee cruised the seventeen-mile loop road again. All the vendors had packed their wares and headed home, leaving the park to the night creatures and movie stars. He drove more slowly, hoping his headlights would find the worst of the road's ruts and obstacles. At all the obvious places a person would stop for a photo, he looked for a glint of chrome or window glass, finding nothing. The park encompassed more than 91,000 acres, according to Paul's spiel for visitors. A good place to disappear.

In his years as a policeman, Chee had spent more nights on patrol than he could count. His grandmother had been correct when she had warned of *chindis*, restless, troublemaking spirits that emerged after twilight. Most of the crimes Chee responded to went down in the black hours beyond midnight. The darkness outside seemed to summon the darkness inside people.

Heading north past a shuttered crafts stand on a side road that looked as if it could lead to more views, Chee noticed a faint glow from the arroyo. Headlights? The illumination grew brighter as he approached. His unit's lights flashed against the open tailgate of a truck parked off the road. Beyond it, he saw a tent lit from the inside. Past that, nothing but sand, a few shrubs, rocks. No red car.

He parked but kept his headlights on, positioning them to shine on the tent. He had left the other campers alone, but they were outside the Navajo Nation's jurisdiction, beyond the park proper. He walked toward this tent with his flashlight shining.

"Navajo Police. Hello. Anyone in there?"

He saw shadows in the tent, shapes rising from the floor. Chee's experience made him wary when facing the unknown. "Come out," he called. "I need to talk to you."

"What do you want?" The man spoke with an accent.

"I need to ask you some questions. Don't you folks know it's illegal to camp here?" Chee waited for the response.

"Sorry. Can we pay you the fee?" A female voice.

"Is that you, Melissa?" Chee said.

"No."

"Come on out here and talk to me. Both of you."

The tent rustled, and a gray-haired woman in shorts and a T-shirt emerged. "Heinrich is coming. He's pulling on his shoes." The woman took a few steps toward Chee. "My husband couldn't find anywhere else to camp. We are doing no harm. We shall be gone by morning."

An elderly man with a potbelly emerged from the opening and stood next to the woman.

"Heinrich Schwartz," said the man after Chee introduced himself. "And this is Gisela."

"I'm looking for a lost person. A blond woman driving a red car, or maybe walking around taking photographs. Have you seen her?"

"We haven't seen anybody," Heinrich said. "Nobody but you."

The woman nodded. Chee thought she looked a bit like Louisa, Joe Leaphorn's companion. He should call Louisa and find out how the Lieutenant was progressing.

"Have you seen any vehicles tonight?"

The man rubbed his scalp. "A truck with a trailer that stirred up dust. A motorcycle. One of those touring shuttle buses, empty. It made a lot of noise, too."

"And that little car with loud music," Gisela added. "It was red."

"Which way was the car headed?" Chee asked.

The woman gestured with a pale arm. "It went by about an hour ago."

"Did you see it again after that? Or hear it?"

"We did not," the man said. His *w*'s sounded like *v*'s.

"Where are you visiting from?"

"We live in Germany."

"Bavaria," the woman said.

"Germany? Ma'am, from your English, I would have assumed you were American."

She nodded. "You're right about that. I was born in the States, but I grew up in Germany and moved back there when I met this wonderful man. Finally I persuaded him to see the West, and now we're in trouble."

"We went to the camp across the highway," the man said, "but it was full. We went to the campground in the park, but it was closed too. Where else can we go?"

The couple looked tired. They stood in silence, backlit by the glow from inside their little tent. Chee looked at their neat campsite.

"The next closest camp ground is Navajo National Monument, on the way to Tuba City. But they might be full too, and that's a long drive. Tell you what. You can stay here tonight if you promise you will pack up and move out first thing in the morning. And no more illegal camping. You understand?"

Heinrich spoke quickly. "Yes, sir. We promise. You are kind. We will pay you the camping fee?"

Chee shook his head. "You can buy something for your wife from the next vendor you see. Help the families who live out here. Welcome to Navajoland."

He could see Gisela relax. "My grandfather worked here back in the 1930s. He loved this place and the people." She held out her arm. "I have this Indian bracelet he bought many years ago. He said it was made by a Navajo man."

Chee looked at the sand-cast silver. "That is beautiful."

"I'd like to get something like this for my daughter."

"If you don't find what you like out here, I have a relative who's a jeweler, lives in Gallup. He might be able to come up with a copy for you."

The woman pulled a wallet from her pocket and gave him a business card. "That would be wonderful. He can use this e-mail."

Out of habit, Chee made a note of the husband's name and the license number of their truck on the back of her card.

"I hope you find the woman," Gisela said. "I wouldn't want to be lost out here."

Chee headed in the direction the woman had indicated. Unless Melissa had already returned to the movie camp, he felt confident that he'd find her, help her if she were hurt, give her a lecture if she wasn't.

He heard faint music long before he saw the red car. When he got closer, he recognized the sound as jazz, a saxophone playing something vaguely familiar. He followed the beat to a Chevy parked on the road at the top of the ridge and stopped in front of it. The music was full bore, loud enough to scare the coyotes. Getting out of his unit, he reached through the open window, pulled the key from the ignition, and put it in his pocket. The music died.

"Melissa?" he called. "Melissa Goldfarb? I'm

Navajo Police. Your friends are worried about you."
If she could hear the music, he figured she could
hear him.

Silence.

He shone his light on the road, noticing other
tire tracks and something white. He walked over to
it. A poker chip, standing on end like a wheel. He
picked it up and put it in his pocket.

He went back to the red car and found footprints
leading away from the driver's side up a steep, sandy
hill, and similar prints coming back to it and heading away again. The footprints were smaller than
the ones he made and had a concentric circle design
on the soles. He followed the tracks, calling out,
"Melissa!" He listened, but there was no response.

The moon was rising, and after about fifteen minutes of slogging through the sand, he saw a figure
silhouetted in its light at the top of the rise. A person
and a tripod.

"Melissa!"

The figure turned toward him, tensed. "Who's
there?"

"Sergeant Jim Chee, Navajo Police."

"I have a gun," the voice called back. "You have
ID?"

He knew from the voice he'd found a woman. "I'll
shine the flashlight on it, but you won't be able to
see it from way up there. Are you Melissa?"

"Yes."

"Your boss called the police station, and they sent
me to look for you. Are you OK?"

She laughed. "So that's what this is about. You
scared me half to death. I'm better than OK. I'm

fabulous. Come up here, Sergeant Jim Chee. Look at this view. Unbelievable."

He climbed up the sand slope, his smooth-soled boots slipping a little. He was breathing harder by the time he reached the ridge and had worked off some of his irritation at being ordered to do something by a civilian he'd come to help.

"What do you think?"

The vista across the valley, lit by the rising moon, was stunning. The moonglow subdued the colors, tamed them. The monuments looked ethereal, like enormous petrified creatures frozen in time on a landscape huge enough to accommodate them.

"I'm safer here than in LA, don't you agree?" She didn't wait for his answer. "I've got great shots of the sunset, and now the moonrise with these formations."

"I think you're lucky to have people concerned about you. You need to get back to them." He sounded stricter and more official than he meant to.

"Whatever. I'm done anyway. I can't believe they actually called the police." She removed the camera from the tripod, stowed it in the pack on the sand next to her, and took out a water bottle.

"Want a sip?"

"No, thanks."

"Hey, what happened to my music?"

"I turned it off."

He would have guessed that she was a few years under thirty. She looked more like a long-distance runner than an accountant. Maybe lugging around camera equipment kept her in shape.

Melissa picked up a backpack and hoisted it onto

her shoulders. She grabbed the water bottle and a walking stick, and then reached for the tripod.

"I'll take that," Chee said.

"Thanks."

He led the way back, a different, more direct, and steeper route. They were about halfway to their vehicles when he heard a grunt behind him and then some swearing. He turned. Melissa lay sprawled in the sand, facedown.

He went to help. "Are you hurt?"

"I don't think so." She pushed herself onto her side and then sat up. "Something tripped me. I dropped my water bottle and my walking stick back there somewhere. Just give me a minute to catch my breath."

He turned on his flashlight to look for the equipment and found why she had tripped. Out here in the empty middle of Monument Valley, somebody had carefully outlined a rectangular shape with a line of rocks, perfect for stumbling over in the dark.

It looked remarkably like a gravesite.

After Chee left, Bernie realized that she hadn't eaten dinner, and that her burger was headed back to Monument Valley. She coaxed Mama into sharing some canned soup. As usual under Darleen's command, it looked as if a dust devil had roared through the kitchen.

Finally she helped Mama to bed. Her mother seemed weaker than the last time she had visited. Bernie tried, with partial success, to convince herself that it was due to recent stress and Darleen's irresponsibility.

She thought about sleeping in Darleen's bed, but its tangled sheets, the bedroom's clutter, and the fragrance of unwashed clothes that assaulted her when she opened the door inspired a new plan. She found a clean sheet in the closet and appropriated the soft blue Pendleton blanket that lived on the back of Mama's chair. She'd need it in the early morning, when the house would be cool.

Bernie's Navajo name meant Laughing Girl, but she didn't see much to laugh about tonight. Chee had worked a minor miracle in persuading Mama to invite Bernie to stay, but Sister had spoiled what was left of their vacation.

Mama was too thin . . . but she'd always been thin. And she was weak, really too unsteady to be here alone, and too stubborn to acknowledge that she could use a bit of help.

Bernie had told Mama that Darleen had stayed in Farmington, that she was OK. It was true, but it wasn't the whole truth, and Mama knew it. Bernie had never been a good liar.

"Did that girl get arrested?" Mama asked.

Bernie simply said yes, and Mama didn't pursue the subject. They hadn't mentioned Darleen again.

Bernie made a nest for herself on the couch. She took off her shoes and socks, noticing the gritty floor against her bare feet. How tough could it be for her sister to sweep once in a while? She added house cleaning to her mental list of tasks for tomorrow. She'd go to the grocery to restock the pantry and cook something Mama liked, with enough to freeze for later.

Then it dawned on her that her Toyota was back in Shiprock.

She'd seen Darleen's car outside. If she were lucky, her sister had placed an extra key in the drawer in the kitchen, as Bernie had requested. She put her socks back on, got up, and rummaged in the drawer with no success.

Bernie went back to the couch and took her socks off again and curled up in her snug little bed. She remembered that she hadn't called Largo to inquire about the drug car, but her phone was in her backpack in the kitchen, and it was too late to reach him now anyway.

Usually Bernie slept through the night without interruption, dozing on despite the racket of summer thunderstorms, nagging problems at work, or complications with her mother, her sister, or Chee. But tonight she lay awake, restless. She tried to focus on her breathing and the stress-reduction techniques she'd learned in police training. Instead of getting sleepy, however, her brain drifted to recent events, replaying them like unwanted stimulants.

The Lieutenant, her mentor, healing from the bullet to his brain. She'd tell him about the oddly nervous man with the boxes of dirt when she saw him next. He liked interesting cases. She pictured the way he'd smiled at her, for the first time after his injury, when she'd seen him last week. That thought brought her peace.

She must have fallen asleep, because when she opened her eyes again, dim predawn light filled the room. She checked on Mama, who seemed not to have moved an inch. She considered a run, but didn't want to leave her mother alone. Instead she went outside and stood quietly, welcoming the new day. Surely it would be easier than the one that had passed.

When she pulled her phone from her backpack to check the time, she noticed two things. A text from her boss: *Call re scheduling.* And nothing from Chee.

She called Largo at the office, figuring she'd leave a message. But he was in.

"Manuelito, don't you have anything better to do on your vacation? Ever hear of sleeping in?"

"I saw your text. We had a situation with Mama, and I had to come back." Before he could ask, she added, "I think she's OK. She had a restful night."

"Glad to hear it."

"What's new with Miller? Do you know where he hid the drugs?"

"Before I get to that, would you like an update on your sister?"

Bad news travels fast, she thought. "I guess. Sure."

"She'll be released sometime today."

"Do you know what she did?"

"Not exactly. She got drunk and got rowdy." Largo gave her the name of the arresting San Juan County sheriff's deputy. "He can tell you."

"And what about Miller?"

"No news so far."

"Really?"

"Really."

"I wasn't wrong about him. Why would an innocent guy offer me five hundred to give him a speeding ticket?"

"The dogs didn't find any drugs. The feds are going over the car tomorrow. Chill out, Manuelito. I need to talk to you about something else."

Bernie fought back her disappointment and listened as Largo went on about the challenges of scheduling. He stopped without making the ask.

"If Sister gets home tonight, I could take a shift tomorrow."

"I'll plan on that, unless you say otherwise."

She put the unwashed dishes Sister had left in the

sink, added soapy water, and told herself to cheer up. As she started breakfast, she heard Mama calling for her.

Her mother was sitting on the edge of the bed. "Bring me the walking machine."

Bernie pushed the walker to her. "May I help you up?"

"That's what this thing is for." Mama hoisted herself to standing, took a moment to find her balance, and then moved slowly toward the bathroom. Bernie walked beside her.

"There are things we need to speak of. But first, we have our coffee."

Bernie knew the code. Her mother had advice for her, probably another lecture on her role in keeping Darleen out of trouble. But if Mama was still angry with her, she couldn't read the signs. Perhaps her irritation had switched to Darleen.

Bernie wiped off the table so they would have a clean place to eat. She poured Mama her coffee and found some raisins to add to the oatmeal, along with sugar and cinnamon. No milk, so they did without. Somehow, the oatmeal with the raisins made her think of the boxes of dirt sprinkled with rocks. At least she had Miller on tape. The recording proved that something was up with him and justified her traffic stop.

Mama complimented Bernie on her cooking, but only ate a few bites. "Save the rest for me for lunch."

"No, ma'am. If I can find the key to Darleen's car, we'll get some groceries and I'll treat you to lunch in Shiprock."

Mama nodded, and then reached across the table and put her hand on top of Bernie's.

"My daughter, I have been thinking about your friend, the one who got shot."

Bernie knew she meant Leaphorn. The statement caught her off guard.

Mama put her hand on her chest, over her heart. "When a bad thing happens, it leaves a bruise here."

Bernie set her spoon down. The incident had emblazoned itself in her mind. She had pulled her weapon for the first time since she'd been an officer. She would have killed the perpetrator if she could have. And if she had acted more quickly, she might have intervened before the shooter hurt her mentor. "I don't want to talk about that."

"I understand. I am happy you are here, my daughter. We will laugh together. We will cook today."

Bernie felt relief roll along her spine like a warm breeze. Mama didn't have a lecture for her this morning. "What shall we make?"

"*Atoo*'. The meat came already from Mrs. Darkwater's nephew. Potatoes, onions in the drawer there."

Mutton stew, and no one made it like Mama. It took time, but it was worth it. And, Bernie thought, cooking would keep her from dark thoughts and obsessing about Miller.

"We need corn, maybe some squash," Mama said. "In the old days, I had it from the garden. Now we have to go to the store."

"We might have to make do with what we have here. I looked where I asked Darleen to put the extra car key, and I couldn't find it. She might have one of those magnetic key cases on her car, I don't know."

A cloth pouch hung like a saddlebag from Mama's

walker. She reached into it and pulled out a pink, sparkling heart—Sister's key ring.

"She gives me these in case she's drinking. She's a good girl."

Bernie hadn't driven Darleen's car for so long that she'd forgotten its idiosyncrasies. First, she figured out how to unhook the wire that kept the trunk closed so she could lift Mama's walker inside and then refasten it to keep the lid from bouncing open as she drove. She helped Mama with her seat belt, then realized she couldn't open the driver's door.

"Put your arm through the window. You have to do it from the inside." That explained why the car was so dusty. If Darleen rolled up the window, she had to climb in the passenger door and scoot over to drive.

Then the car wouldn't start.

"Push on the floor." Mama demonstrated.

Yes, Bernie remembered, pump the accelerator a few times to get the gas moving so the ignition could catch.

She looked at the fuel gauge. Full? Then she remembered that it didn't work.

She drove holding her breath, hoping there was enough gasoline to make it the ten miles to the gas station and convenience store at the intersection of the Toadlena road and the four-lane highway, NM 491.

"What's that up there?" Mama said.

A tan creature was moving from the road into the empty field beside it. "I think it's a dog." Stray dogs were a long-standing problem on the reservation.

"Glad it's not a coyote." Coyotes in your path meant bad luck. If a person couldn't turn around or go a different route, a special prayer helped keep evil away.

The dog loped along the road's shoulder, then back onto the asphalt, then off again. Not exactly trotting—more like staggering. The canine version of a drunk.

Bernie slowed down, watching it. One summer when she was a girl, she'd encountered a pack of dogs, and one of them had bitten her before her uncle scared them off. Ever since, most dogs, especially big ones, made her nervous. The animal trotted away from the highway lopsidedly and lay down in the weeds. Maybe distemper, she thought. Or maybe a car had hit it, and that was why it walked funny.

Parking beneath the overhang at the gas pumps, she pulled out her cell phone to call about the dog, but the battery was dead. "I'll be right back. Would you like something?"

"Too expensive."

Inside the store, Cathleen stood at the cash register. Bernie gave her $20 for gas and asked if she could use the phone.

"What's the matter? Don't the radio in your car work?"

"I'm off today. I need to tell animal control about that dog."

"There's more than a few of 'em around here."

"The tan one. He's walking funny. I think he's sick."

Cathleen turned serious. "We found two dead

ones out there." She pointed to the back of the store. "Not shot or nothin'. Must be a dog flu."

Sandra, the Shiprock station's dispatcher, receptionist, and go-to girl, answered the phone. "I heard you were spending the day with your mom. What's up?"

Bernie explained about the dog.

"I'll let the guys know." Animal control had an overwhelming job. Lack of money and access to clinics for spaying and neutering, combined with the practice of leaving unwanted animals along the highway to fend for themselves, had created a bad and long-standing problem for people with livestock.

After filling the tank and making a note of the odometer reading for Darleen, Bernie put air in the tires. Darleen didn't have a tire gauge in the car—if she had one at all—so Bernie estimated the pressure, hoping she got it right. Heat and overinflated old tires led to blowouts.

It was a typical June morning on the Colorado Plateau: clear, warm, with a few clouds beginning to form in the brilliant sky. This time of year—Ya'iishjaatsoh, according to the Navajo way of calculating the seasons—brought the hottest weather, broken only by the longed-for arrival of summer rains.

The trip to the grocery took longer than expected. Mama insisted on pushing her walker down every row at the store, examining the merchandise and declaring most of it too pricey.

"Does Sister bring you to the market with her?"

"No. She goes after her class."

"What class?"

"I'm not so sure about that."

Bernie had encouraged Darleen to get her GED. Maybe Sister had listened to something she said after all. If, in fact, Darleen actually *had* enrolled in something. Bernie pushed the critical thought away and focused on filling the cart.

After shopping, they drove to Bernie's trailer for her stew pan, and for her mother's bathroom break. Mama paused outside to study the loom Chee had built. "Cheeseburger did a good job."

"He did."

"Something like this needs to stay busy."

"I'm going to use it one of these days."

Mama ran her hand along the smooth frame and stayed quiet, but Bernie sensed the unspoken *When?* and *Are you sure?*

Then they stopped for a burger and an ice cream cone at the Chat and Chew. But Bernie couldn't get Miller out of her mind, and the police station was only a few minutes away.

"Mama, I need to check on something at the office," she said.

"Park in the shade. I will wait in the car. Don't be too long."

Sandra looked up from her magazine when Bernie came in. "You took the world's shortest vacation."

"I guess so. Is the boss here?"

Sandra motioned toward his office with a slight twist of her chin.

Bernie knocked, and Largo waved her in. He politely inquired about Mama and learned she was waiting in the car, and no, she didn't want to come in. Mama didn't like being in the police station.

"Since I had to come into town, I thought I'd see if they'd found any drugs yet in Miller's car."

"I haven't heard anything new."

Largo didn't seem happy. She waited.

"No stolen credit cards or bootleg booze, explosives, or anything illegal so far."

Largo stood, rolled his neck, stretched his long arms behind his back. "I don't know what to think about that dirt, Manuelito. Maybe Miller was stealing Indian land a little at a time. Next thing you know, one of these Arizona tourists will try to run off with Tsé Bit' a' í Ship Rock itself."

Bernie cringed at the joke.

"I wasn't going to arrest him at first, sir. But even before he tried to bribe me, Miller acted guilty as could be. I figured he had a lot at stake to offer me that much money and the rifle to let him go. It's in my report, and it's all on the tape, too. You can see him fidgeting."

Largo exhaled. "The camera wasn't working."

"You're kidding? I checked it. The light was on."

"You didn't record anything."

"Not again." She tried to keep her tone neutral, her frustration at bay. Failing equipment was an ongoing problem. "I've got some pictures of the boxes and the rifle in the trunk of the car. I'll add them to my write-up. That might help."

"It might." But Bernie heard the doubt in his voice.

"So, sir, the bribery will be a 'he said, she said'?"

"Afraid so. Take another look at your report.

Make sure you've put everything in, whatever you remember."

"Yes, sir."

"Can I count on you tomorrow?"

She shook her head. "I don't know yet, sir. It depends on my sister. If she's not available, I'll need somebody to stay with Mama."

Bernie watched Largo sit down again. The men in the department didn't have the complication of dealing with their mothers. Their sisters and aunts and maybe even their wives handled that.

"I trust you on this bribery deal, Manuelito, but you know, without the tape it will be hard to prove. There's one good thing about this."

She waited, wondering what came next.

"The FBI is interested."

"Why? And that's a good thing?"

He chuckled. "Your encounter with Miller might be what saves this whole operation from being a complete fiasco. They are sending a team to search the car again with some high-tech gizmos. Maybe Sweating Man invented a new explosive. Or maybe they'll come up with something else suspicious. You've heard of fertilizer being used to blow things up, right?"

"Yes, sir. Timothy McVeigh."

"Maybe those guys will discover an aged cow pie, sheep droppings, some horse dung in one of those boxes."

Bernie could feel warmth in her face.

"Manuelito?"

"Yes, Captain."

"Don't beat yourself up over this. Miller probably

won't sue us. The Navajo Public Safety Department doesn't have enough money to be worth it."

Bernie drove Mama through town with the windows down, imagining that the breeze made her cooler. She tried to shake off the embarrassment and failure that had followed her from the station, but it clung like a burr to a sock. When she reached the big highway and sped up, Mama rolled up her window. Bernie realized that winding the crank on the driver's side caused no change in the level of the glass, another reason Darleen left the window open.

"Is there some trick to this window?"

"Your sister pulls it up halfway first." Mama pantomimed the action with both hands. "You can roll it from there."

Bernie expected her mother to fall asleep on the ride. Instead she said, "Oldest daughter, we need to talk now about your sister."

When Mama said, "We need to talk," she meant that Bernie needed to listen.

"We need to help so she doesn't become an *adlaanii*."

Bernie kept her eyes on the highway. *Adlaanii* were relatives and friends who had damaged or severed their connection to their family, their clan, and their friends, because of alcohol. She wondered if it was too late, if her sister already was an alcoholic. Besides the beer cans, she'd spotted an empty vodka bottle in the trunk when she loaded the walker.

"That one wants to go to the art school for Indians in Santa Fe. You know, the Eye something?

It could be a good thing. I want you to help her do that."

The Institute of American Indian Arts—IAIA for short—drew students from around the country, and even foreigners. Some of the Navajo Nation's best-known artists had studied there. Darleen liked to draw, but as far as Bernie knew, her little sister hadn't even completed her GED. Bernie was skeptical, but she kept silent.

"Getting away from the ones who encourage her to have beer," Mama continued, "that would be good. She will come home to see us on the weekends. That's what I have to say."

"I'm glad you wanted to talk about this, Mama. In my job, many of the people I encounter get in trouble because of drinking. Sometimes going to jail helps them realize they should give up alcohol." And, Bernie knew, sometimes an arrest meant losing a job, falling behind on car payments, and putting additional stress on relationships. "Sister has to decide to stop drinking. No matter where she is, Santa Fe or home with you, or what she does, she will have a chance to drink. The choice is up to her. Being somewhere else won't solve the problem. And you and I can't solve it for her."

"Coyote lives with us," said Mama. Coyote, prince of chaos, a troublemaker, trickster, transformer, and more. "But you help your sister."

A sudden blast of wind shook the car, and Bernie gripped the wheel and tapped the brakes. The gust had pushed the horse trailer in front of her into the left lane, and a car that was passing her put on the brakes, narrowly avoiding an accident.

"Mama, promise me you will never get in the car with Sister if she has been drinking. You could both die. I've seen it."

"Daughter, why do you worry so much?"

Bernie watched a flock of small white clouds assembling on the horizon, looking like cotton balls on a child's painting of a perfect day. They scudded against the deep turquoise backdrop, casting black shadows that moved over the dusty country below. The clouds were too small and too independent to build to thunderheads. At best, they'd screen the sun later to provide a bit of cool; at worst, they would make dry lightning, starting fires in the mountains.

By the time they got back to Mama's house, midday heat had settled in with full force. Too warm for anything except a big glass of water—or maybe her first Coke of the day—and a good book.

"It's so hot, Mama. Let's wait until later to start cooking."

"Summer." Mama said it as though that was all the explanation needed. "You remember this when you get cold at Késhmish."

Christmas, and most of December, brought the area below-freezing nights, but the worst of winter came in January and February. Bernie remembered the deep snow a few years past that had created an emergency for livestock, and the welcome sound of New Mexico National Guard helicopters flying in hay to keep animals from starving. The Navajo Nation had worked with the state to help families isolated by the blizzard and the mud that followed it.

Bernie carried the groceries into the kitchen and checked Mama's phone for messages, but only the hum of the dial tone greeted her. Nothing from Darleen or from Chee.

Mama supervised as Bernie laid out the ingredients for the stew and a knife for each of them. As they had done so many times before, she and Mama sat at the kitchen table together. As usual, Mama didn't do anything halfway. When she made stew, she made enough to share with friends and relatives.

First they cut the mutton into serving-size pieces and divided it between the big pots. They added water to cover it and salt and pepper, put on the lids, and set the pots on the stove, one in the front and one on the opposite burner in the back. Bernie waited for the water to boil and for the phone to ring, Sister asking for a ride home.

They chopped potatoes, carrots, onions, squash, and celery. Mama noticed Bernie looking at a scar on one of her fingers, a white crescent.

"When I was a little girl, I wanted to help with the *atoo'*." Every time Mama told this story, it was slightly different. "My grandmother told me no, but when she wasn't looking, I grabbed the knife and tried to cut some meat. I nearly chopped off this finger." Mama wiggled the finger, examined the scar. "My grandmother stopped the bleeding. My finger hurt a lot, but then she made me learn how to do the job right."

Some say perspiring is good for you. Bernie had read articles about women paying to do yoga in a hundred-degree room. It wasn't that hot at Mama's house, she didn't have to pay to chop, and they would have stew as a reward. What a deal!

The pungent smell of bubbling mutton interrupted her thoughts. Mama reached for her walker.

"I'll check on it." Bernie turned down the stove to simmer and skimmed off the foam from the boiling meat. Bringing them both a glass of water, she went back to work.

Mama looked at the pile of chopped vegetables. "We will put this in later. Now we should have a little rest."

Bernie helped Mama take off her shoes and watched her stretch out on the bed. These afternoon naps still caught Bernie by surprise. Mama had always had more energy than she and her sister rolled together. It always seemed like Mama was supplied with extra batteries. But not anymore.

"You sleep, too, daughter."

Bernie didn't tell Mama she wasn't sleepy. Instead, she sat on the porch with a book from Mama's bookcase, a mystery she feared she had already read. The shade made an oasis of relative coolness. Her eyes scanned the words, but her brain couldn't focus. The questions about Miller replayed themselves. She wished Chee were there, or at least someplace she could reach him, so they could brainstorm.

She forced herself to stop obsessing about Miller, and thought about her sister. Mama was right. She could have done more to help, but she hadn't wanted to. Darleen knew how to aggravate her, knew exactly what to say, what to do, how to be, to push her frustration buttons. Maybe, just maybe, the Darleen who came home from jail would be different from the one who had left.

After a few minutes, she put the book down and, despite the heat, went for a run.

It didn't take long to work up a sweat in the day's

heat. She kept going until she wasn't thinking about anything anymore. Then she turned around and ran back.

When she came in from her run, she picked up Mama's phone. Finally, there was the rapid beep. She called up the message, listened, and saved it.

When Mama woke up, Bernie put the phone on speaker and replayed it.

Darleen's voice filled the room. "Mama, I'm OK. I'm leaving Farmington soon. I love you."

Mama stared at the phone then turned away. Bernie saw her raise a hand to her cheek to wipe away a tear. She couldn't remember ever seeing her mother cry before.

The Diné Bahane', the mythic origin story of the Navajo people, concerns balance, give-and-take, facing challenges, and making one's way in the world, negotiating the constant presence of dark and light, life and death, *hozho* and its counterpart, *hochxo*. This certainly seemed to be her journey at the moment and her sister's, too.

Bernie wondered if her sister was hitchhiking home. She hoped Darleen was safe.

Mama seemed to read her mind. "Don't worry about that one." She patted Bernie's arm. "She will be here tonight. She is ashamed. You don't have to think like a policeman all the time."

Afternoon turned into evening. Bernie and Mama made tortillas to go with the stew—it was too hot for fry bread—and ate together. After she helped Mama to bed, Bernie went outside. She breathed in the crisp air of the high desert evening and listened for a car on the road or the beat of Darleen's footsteps as she walked in from the highway, but she heard only the nonhuman sounds of the night.

If Darleen didn't make it home tonight, or was too out of it to be trustworthy, Bernie would take Mama with her to Shiprock tomorrow and go to work. Mama could spend the day at her trailer while she was at the station. She had to be there when the feds did their special check of the car so she could see what Miller had hidden and where.

She didn't want to live with another mistake.

She knew what had happened to the Lieutenant wasn't her fault. But if she had been a little faster, a little smarter, a better officer, she might have snapped to what was about to unfold in that parking lot in time.

Back inside, Mama was asleep. Bernie curled up on the couch, opened her book, and started to read.

The noise of a vehicle in the driveway startled her. She glanced at her watch. A few minutes until eleven. Through the living room's open windows she caught snippets of a muted conversation, the closing of a car door, the sound of tires on the road.

Moments later, Darleen came inside.

Bernie had been thinking about this moment, preparing for it. But the sight of her little sister, her exhaustion and sadness, swept away all Bernie's plans, replacing them with joyful gratitude. She hugged Darleen until they both stopped crying.

Darleen pulled a wad of tissues from the pocket of her jeans and offered one to Bernie. "I was hoping you wouldn't have to come, but I am so glad you're here."

"Me, too," Bernie said. And she meant it.

"I'm starting over. I don't want to be an *adlaanii*. I saw enough drunks to— to— I don't know. Is Mama OK?"

Bernie nodded. The Navajo language was interesting, she thought. It had a word that meant "drunk," but there was no simple way to say "Sorry." Perhaps the ancestors realized that each offense left different damages, and each required a complicated making of amends. A trite phase didn't cut it.

"Mama and I made some *atoo'*. Want some?"

"I'm starving. But I have to take a shower first."

By the time Darleen returned, the stew was hot. Bernie ate again with her, noticing the dark circles under her sister's eyes.

Darleen got up for more stew. "Did Mama ask you to come?"

"No. Mrs. Darkwater called."

"What did she say happened to me?"

"She said you hadn't come home and that Mama stayed up all night waiting for you."

"So I guess Cheeseburger is here, too."

"No, but he drove back with me."

"Back from where?"

"We were on vacation, remember? Chee found out that you got arrested."

"I so totally screwed up. I was drinking and I said some stuff to a cop—" Darleen stood and put her bowl and Bernie's in the sink. "What if I tell you and Mama about it in the morning? I don't want to relive it twice, and I can barely keep my eyes open now."

After Darleen went to bed, Bernie returned to the couch, snuggled into her nest, and turned off the lamp. Now that Sister was back, she ought to feel better, but worry still tugged at her. Maybe Darleen really would start over. Maybe Chee would call tomorrow. Maybe she'd figure out what Miller was up to.

The new day was just a few hours away.

6

Chee quickly played the flashlight beam over the rectangle of rocks. From the way the earth rose, he assumed the mound inside the border was recent. He didn't see a cross, nameplate, or memorial marker, but he knew a burial site when he stumbled over one. The hair on the back of his neck stood up, and his stomach felt unsettled.

He looked back toward Melissa. "Are you all right?"

"Nothing damaged except my pride. Is this a grave?"

"Sure looks like one."

No Navajo he knew would bury a family member like this. In the old days, no one built graves. Now things were different. Some veterans requested interment in military cemeteries. Christian Diné wanted to rest in sanctified ground. A few of the most traditional still disposed of the deceased the way the family of Joe Leaphorn's beloved wife Emma had done. Designated males escorted the corpse to a cave far away from the family's living quarters. They walled up the remains to prevent predation and to let natural mummification take place. Then the men underwent a cleansing ceremony to free them from the *chindi*.

Melissa stood next to him, looking at the mound. "An odd place to bury someone. Makes it hard to come for a visit."

"Let's get out of here."

They trudged through the sand to their cars, moving a bit more carefully now. The night seemed less inviting. Chee tried to shake off his unease. He'd seen family graveyards established by the *bilgaana* and Hispanic ranching families in Arizona, Utah, and New Mexico. Perhaps that was what had happened here. Before the US government gave the valley to the Navajos, they shared it with miners, ranchers, and western explorers. But he rejected that theory. The grave was new.

"Do you live out here?" Melissa asked.

"No, I'm from New Mexico."

"That's a long commute."

Chee explained, briefly, about Paul, the new substation, and his interrupted vacation.

"This is my first time here," Melissa said. "It's amazing. The scenery is the best thing about my job."

"The man who called about you, Mr. Robinson, he said you were the one who keeps track of the budget. That sounds like a lot of work."

"I used to like it, but lately it's crazy making, especially now that the production is behind schedule. Robinson worries about everything that could impact the budget, and I guess that includes me going off to get some photos. I think Chief Worrier is in his job description."

Chee radioed Captain Bahe while Melissa loaded in her equipment.

"I've got good news."

Bahe sounded tired. "You found her?"

"She's fine."

"Great."

"And some bad news. We stumbled over what looks like a fresh grave out here."

"Where?"

Chee gave him the location as best he could.

"Check with Robinson and find out if that's part of a movie backdrop, or whatever they call it. Ask if they've got a permit for it."

Chee bristled at the instructions. Did Bahe think he was a rookie? "Will do, sir."

Melissa was standing by her car, waiting for him. Chee felt for her keys in his pocket and found the poker chip. He showed it to her. "Did you drop this?"

"Not me."

"We'll drive back to the movie camp together. You follow me."

"I'm sorry you had to go to all this trouble."

He handed her the keys to the red car. "It's nice to find a missing person who's not really missing. I like having a case where everything comes out OK."

She smiled. "I'll tell the guys back there not to worry so much."

The air had cooled into comfortable shirtsleeve

weather. Except for the sound of his engine and Melissa's car behind him, the evening was calm and silent. Chee saw a shooting star and blew at it out of long-instilled habit. Some said the falling stars brought bad luck otherwise. The lights were off at the German campers' hideaway.

He imagined the folks at the Monument Valley hotels, in their rooms watching television, the same shows they could see back in Indiana or wherever home was. Meanwhile, nature served up a celestial light show against a backdrop of million-year-old geology.

When Chee reached the entrance to the movie site parking area, Gerald waved him on through. He parked next to the dark administration trailer, and Melissa pulled up next to him. She climbed out of the car and extended her hand. "Come back when you're not working and watch some of the filming. You might get a kick out of it."

Hearing footsteps behind him, Chee turned to see Robinson. "Hey, Missy. Everything OK?"

"Couldn't be better. I'm sorry you guys worried about me. I wasn't lost, you know, but it was a pleasure to meet Sergeant Chee here."

"They're ready to head out to the film site. The van leaves as soon as you get there. On the way out, Turner can fill you in on the meeting you missed." Robinson turned to Chee. "I appreciate you finding her."

"I've got a question for you about something we ran into out there."

"Sure. You have time for a sandwich? I was on my way to get something."

The word *sandwich* reminded Chee of how small and long ago lunch had been.

He was surprised to see so many in the food tent. People dressed in tatters, decorated with makeup that made them look pale and ugly, sat chatting with others wearing shorts and T-shirts, eating together as if dinner with zombie guests was perfectly normal.

"We do a lot of filming at night." Robinson looked around at the crowd. "We love this moonlight."

Chee selected a thickly handsome roast beef on rye, served with a pickle. The apple pie in the dessert case made him think of Lieutenant Leaphorn and how the man loved almost anything sweet. He examined the machine that made coffee—a fancy glass-and-stainless-steel contraption. The device offered half a dozen choices and could have even given him a double *café macchiato*—whatever that was. He pushed a button that read "Dark Roast Hawaiian."

He sat across from Robinson, watching as the man carved off a forkful of tomato with a green leaf—some herb—on top and a soft white platform beneath it. "What's that you're eating?"

Robinson put his fork down. "It's called a Caprese salad—sliced tomato, fresh basil, and fresh mozzarella cheese. It's good. Movie companies eat well. We buy some stuff out here, but we have food suppliers who cater to our whims and charge accordingly. It costs an arm and a leg to bring union food trucks out here, but it's a requirement for any big production." He picked up the fork and cut a bite of cheese and tomato. "Are you a movie fan?"

"I work a lot at night, but my wife and I go when we can. Or watch them on video."

"Maybe you know some of the ones I've been involved in." Robinson mentioned names that sounded vaguely familiar to Chee. "This is the biggest job we've done. Delahart, he's the producer, finds investors, and Missy and I try to make the money last as long as possible."

Chee finished the sandwich and mentioned the grave.

"No kidding? Here we are making a movie about zombies, and you find a grave? How strange is that? Maybe one of those missing miners, those guys who got the buttes named for them, maybe he's buried there. You and Missy might go down in history."

"No. It's new, still mounded up. Did the company get special permission for it?"

"Not that I know of. This is the first I've heard of it." Robinson took another bite of his salad. "So, are there Navajo zombies? Do you guys worry about that?"

Chee considered the fact that Robinson didn't want to talk about the grave, and what that meant. "No, not zombies. Some people believe in skinwalkers, shape-shifters who come out, usually at night, to cause trouble. And there are evil spirits that linger after a person dies, making problems. Our ghosts are more complicated." The old ones believed that talking about *chindis* called them forth. Chee was ready to change the subject.

Robinson nodded. "When things go haywire it's nice to have something to blame that's beyond our control. I think that's one reason people like horror movies. That, and they like to be scared."

"Do you enjoy watching them?"

"Well, horror movies tend to do well at the box office. At least, that's what we're hoping."

Chee tried bringing the conversation back to the reason for his visit once again. "What can you tell me about the grave?"

"Nothing. Sorry." Robinson looked at the clock over the food line. "I've got to run. Have some dessert if you'd like. They do a good job with the pie. Thanks for finding Missy."

As he savored the last of his coffee, Chee noticed three Navajo men in the food line. When they settled in at a table, he selected a piece of apple pie—a juicy one, in the Lieutenant's honor—and introduced himself to the men, mentioning his cousin Paul.

The one who called himself Randy wore a black Stetson with a band of small silver conchos. He motioned to Chee to join them. "I know that guy. Good man. I remember him from high school. I heard that he got one of those big old Jeeps they used at Canyon de Chelly."

Chee told them the story about the People Mover and Paul's tour business, and then they sat in silence for a while.

"So did they hire you to be an actor?" Randy asked.

"No. I'm a real cop. I got called to find a missing lady who wasn't really missing. Then I got invited to have a sandwich."

All the men nodded. "You are having a good evening," Randy said.

When Chee finally asked, none of them had any-thing to say about the grave. But they didn't seem surprised at the question.

Chee had just opened the door of his unit, ready to drive back, when Robinson jogged up.

"Glad I caught you. We've got some trespassers. Our security guy was going to give them a warning, but they turned belligerent. Can you help us?"

"Where are they?"

Robinson pointed to a trailer. "Over there in the production office. The guard is waiting for you with them."

"OK, I'll be there in a minute."

He radioed the station with the news about the trespassers and Robinson's professed ignorance of the grave. Bahe had gone home, but Monica filled him in. "We handle those trespass calls every once in a while. Usually bored local kids."

But instead of Navajos, Chee found two young white women and a well-muscled rent-a-cop. His name badge read "Samuel." Chee wondered if that was his first name or his last.

"*Yá'át'ééh.*" Chee introduced himself to the guard.

Samuel didn't return the greeting. "What hap-pened to Tsinnie?" Leaning against the back wall, arms crossed, he turned his gaze from the girls to Chee.

"I don't know. I'm the new guy. Temporary help."

Samuel uncrossed his arms, moving his hands to his hips. "Well, you need to arrest these two for trespassing and having an illegal firearm. And for being smart-asses."

The suspects, squeezed together knee-to-knee on a love seat against the office wall, looked to Chee to be in their late teens. They stared at the floor.

"So, trespassing and a firearm. What happened?"

Samuel studied one girl, then the other—focusing long enough to make them uneasy, Chee noticed. "I was driving patrol when I heard something up by one of the cast trailers. I drove over to check it out, and I saw these idiots outside Rhonda's place, trying to break in."

The girl in the black T-shirt with a silver ring in her eyebrow looked up. "We weren't—"

"Just a minute. Let him talk. You'll get your turn." Chee spoke to the security guard. "Who's Rhonda?"

Samuel looked at Chee as though he thought the officer was an idiot.

"Rhonda Delay. Even you people out in the sticks here must have heard of her. She's our star, man. She's queen of the zombies. She's the one who causes the headaches when numbskulls like these two try to sneak in for an autograph or a picture of her." Samuel made a sound, a humorless laugh. "Nobody should be back there where she's at. Strictly off limits. I rolled down the window, told them to move away from the trailer. Instead, they took off."

"We didn't—"

Chee gave Eyebrow a hard stare. The other girl, her brown hair pulled back with a headband, never looked up.

"I had to chase them. That's when I saw this on the ground." Samuel reached into his pocket and pulled out a pistol. "It wasn't there when I cruised by earlier, so I knew one of these two dummies dropped it." He put the gun on the desk next to Chee and went back to leaning against the wall.

Eyebrow made a snorting noise.

Samuel was grinning now. "Hear that? They have what I call attitude. Bad attitude that needs an adjustment. Laugh at me all you want, baby doll. The last laugh will be on your own skinny behind." A vein pulsed blue through the thin skin at his temple.

The girl jumped to her feet. "You think you can bully—" She took a step toward the guard, and he toward her.

Chee moved between them. "Young lady, sit down." He gave Samuel a look. *Chill, man. You're the grown-up in this situation.*

The guard stepped back to the wall.

"Anything else to add?" Chee said to him.

"Stupid little twerps. They're all yours." A wave of warm air rushed in as Samuel opened the door and went outside.

Chee sat in the desk chair and rolled it closer to the girls. "How old are you?"

"Eighteen." Eyebrow spoke first.

"How about you, miss?"

Headband mumbled, "Sixteen."

"Do you live around here?"

"No. We're on vacation. Our dad brought us here. It was boring until we found out that Rhonda's movie was here, too."

"Your dad drove you out here?"

Eyebrow said, "Not here, to the hotel, you know, the one across the highway? He's asleep. I drove to this place."

Chee said, "Can I see your license?"

Eyebrow rustled through a purse as big as a duffel bag, extracting a lime-green wallet. She pulled out a laminated card and handed it to Chee. Her fingernails were green, too, with something glittery on the ends.

He took the card, one of those graduated driver's licenses issued to teenagers in Arizona. Courtney Isenberg from Sedona. She'd turn eighteen next month. The license came with restrictions designed to ease the young person into the world of freeways and road rage. Among other limitations, the person who held it could not legally drive between midnight and five a.m. unless a parent or guardian was in the car with the young driver.

"Thank you, Courtney."

He looked at the other girl. "What about you?"

"I left my wallet back at the hotel."

"What's your name?"

"Alisha. Alisha Isenberg."

"Are you sisters?"

Alisha nodded. She looked up for the first time, and Chee saw that her eyes were swollen and her lips trembled.

"Tell me why you're here."

"Because of that jerk," Courtney said. "We weren't doing anything."

Chee frowned at her. "You know what I mean."

"We heard about the movie, and that Rhonda starred in it. We wanted to see her. That's all."

"Did you plan to shoot her?"

Courtney stifled a giggle. "Shoot her? Are you kidding me? She's amazing. Everyone is crazy for her. I wanted to take a picture of her, or at least her trailer. We weren't doing anything. She wasn't even there. That mean guy said she went to Las Vegas."

He turned to the younger girl. "How about you?"

Alisha looked surprised. "What?"

"Why are you here?"

"The same."

Courtney said, "She's the one who knows how to use a gun. Dad's been giving her lessons at the shooting range. He's all proud of her. He keeps it in the glove box, so she took it in case we saw a wolf or something."

Chee felt his phone vibrate and ignored it. He looked at Alisha. "I've never seen a wolf out here. You have anything to add?"

Her eyes had filled with tears. "I want to go back to my dad and the hotel."

"Does Dad know you two are out here?"

"I don't know."

Courtney said, "I don't get why us being out here is such a freaking big deal."

Chee wondered the same thing, but he had to do his job. He used his best policeman voice. "I'll explain it. Besides the trouble you're in for trespassing on a closed movie set, you are also trespassing inside the boundaries of a Navajo Nation park that's closed to visitors at dusk. It's dangerous to be roaming around here, especially at night. I'm here because a crew member got lost out there. I found her, but the next person might not be so lucky."

"OK. Whatever."

Chee had to wrap this up. He gave Courtney a hard look. "Based on your license, you're not allowed to drive after midnight unless it is an emergency. You could lose your driving privileges over this incident."

Her smirk disappeared.

He didn't know exactly when she'd driven out, but his tactic worked.

Chee looked at the handgun, a well-cared-for Glock. Loaded.

He put their gun in his pocket. "I'm going outside to make a call and think about what to do with you two. If you come up with some suggestions for me—appropriate consequences—let me know when I get back."

He opened the trailer door and trotted down the steps into the still night air. Looking at his phone, he saw a text from Bernie: *Everything OK here. Call when you can.* He texted back *Working now. Will call soon*, and added *Love you.* Why hadn't she typed that?

Samuel was standing outside the food tent, smoking a cigarette. He walked in Chee's direction. "You gonna be working out here long?"

"Just a few days."

"Where are you from?"

"Shiprock."

"Where's that?"

"New Mexico, up near the Arizona and Colorado border."

"Is it a town?"

"Yes."

"Sounds like the middle of nowhere."

Chee said nothing.

Samuel dropped his cigarette to the dirt and stepped on it. "What about those girls?"

"What about them?"

"They're hot. Especially the one with the headband. The one with the eyebrow ring has a mouth on her. But the little one . . ." Samuel smacked his lips. "She's dynamite. I'm gonna be dreamin' about her."

Chee let the remark slide over him like oil on water, like slime on the surface of a lake. Time to head back to the trailer, get this settled.

The girls grew quiet when he opened the door. Chee sat down next to them. "What have you come up with?"

Courtney spoke. "We'll sign a promise that we'll never do this again. We'll pick up trash along the road tomorrow like prisoners do. We could write an essay about trespassing and not having guns. I really need my license."

The younger girl rubbed her arm and stared at the floor.

"What about you, Alisha?"

"Whatever," she said. "I just wanna go home." She looked pale, tired, scared.

Chee nodded. "I'll think this over as we drive out of here."

He escorted the girls to his unit and put them both in the backseat together. They were quiet as he radioed in an update. He followed Courtney's directions to their car, a dust-covered dark blue Audi.

He climbed out and opened the back door. "Here's what's going to happen now. Alisha, you will stay with me. Because this is a special circumstance, Courtney, I'm going to allow you to take that car back to the hotel where you are staying. If I see any driving violations, I will make sure you don't drive again for at least a year. When we get there, you are going to introduce me to your father, explain what happened, and apologize to him for the trouble. That goes for both of you. Understand?"

"Got it," Courtney said.

"Alisha?"

"I understand."

He waited while Courtney started the Audi and followed as it bounced along in the moonlight toward the park exit, traveling below the speed limit. She wasn't a bad driver.

He spoke to Alisha. "I noticed you rubbing your arm back there. Did you hurt it?"

"It's OK."

"What happened?"

"He—he—" And then her voice grew small and tearful. "Nothing. I don't wanna talk about it."

Dad, Jeff Isenberg, was a fortysomething man with a military haircut who seemed suitably shocked by the turn of events. After the girls apologized, Chee said, "I need to talk to your dad about this in private."

"Go to your room," Isenberg said. "I'll deal with you after the officer leaves."

Chee reminded him about the restrictions on Courtney's license, gave him a mini lecture on responsible gun ownership. He sensed that Isenberg wanted to argue with him, but the man simply said, "Got it."

"One more thing. I noticed Alisha rubbing her arm. She might have gotten hurt out there. I asked her about it, but she didn't want to tell me. She seems a lot more upset than her sister."

"She's the sensitive one. I'll make sure she's OK. Nothing means more to me than my little girls."

Back at the substation to type up the report, Chee found a message: "Go home. Meet with me and the detective assigned to the grave case at 7 a.m."

He would have liked to go home, but instead he drove to Paul's place. Paul was waiting up for him.

"How's it going? How's my couch-surfin' crime fighter?"

"OK. Ready for sleep."

"Well, here's some good news for you. We've got a sunset tour tomorrow."

"Great. But what about the People Mover?"

"All good, bro. Somebody knew somebody who found everything we need."

"That's great." Chee knew what was coming next.

"Could you fix it?"

He hesitated long enough that Paul added, "Not now. Maybe in the morning? You know I stink at this stuff."

"I've gotta be at work at seven."

"No problem then. We can do it after you get off. That should be around five, right?"

One thing Chee liked about Paul was his optimism.

7

Bernie awoke as the sky changed from gray to a color closer to pale pink. For a split second, she wondered where she was. The house was quiet, Mama and Darleen still slept. She rose and dressed and went outside to watch the sunrise. She felt energized this morning, grateful that her mother was still with her, that she had married a good man, that she had work she enjoyed, and that Sister was safely home. She sang her morning prayers. It would be a good day.

By the time Mama shuffled toward the kitchen, Bernie had made the oatmeal, and the familiar aroma of fresh coffee was filling the room. Mama wrapped her gnarled hands around the mug Bernie had poured for her. "When I was a girl, we had that Arbuckles coffee. It was good, too. Do they still make that coffee?"

"Gosh, I don't know. I never heard of it."

"It came with a yellow-and-red label that had a woman with wings on it. I loved to look at that woman." Mama spooned some sugar into her cup. "Did Youngest Daughter get home?"

"She came in late."

Mama looked up, waiting for more details.

"She ate and went to bed. She said she would tell us what happened this morning."

"I will be happy to have both my daughters here today."

"I can't stay. I talked to Captain Largo. He needs me at the station."

Mama shrugged. Bernie felt disappointment circle the room and settle into the pit of her stomach. It was an old conflict, balancing her enjoyment of work with her duty of—and pleasure in—spending time with Mama. And Chee made life even more fun and more complicated.

When she'd finished her coffee, Bernie stood. "I'm going to wake Sister. I have to go soon."

She rapped on Darleen's bedroom door. "Time to get up. We have to leave in half an hour."

"You go on without me." Darleen's voice sounded muffled, as though she were lying on her stomach or talking through a pillow.

"I don't have a car, remember? You're driving me to Shiprock."

"Oh, right. Save me some coffee."

Bernie had gently helped Mama into the front passenger seat, folded the walker into the trunk, and was fiddling with the wire clasp when Darleen walked out with a mug in one hand.

"I need my keys, Sister," she said. "I'm your chauffeur today, you lucky girl."

Bernie unzipped the front pocket of her back-pack, felt the smooth metal of the keys and the heart-shaped ornament, and put them in her sister's hand.

"There's some junk in the backseat," Darleen said. "Just move it so you can fit."

The backseat looked like a cross between a flea market and a trash bin. Bernie shoved everything—Darleen's sweat shirt, a plastic bag filled with who-knows-what, some books, and even what could have been old class assignments from high school—to the other side of the car and sat behind Mama. She made room for her feet among the empty water bottles, beer bottles, crumpled napkins, and discarded cigarette packs that cluttered the backseat floor.

On the seat next to her was a notebook, the page open to a pencil drawing. She picked it up. It showed two people in masks and a big creature, a jaguar or something, on a leash.

"This drawing is good. I like the animal."

"It's supposed to be a panther. It stinks, and you just proved it. It needs to look like it could bite somebody's head off. Not, you know, like something dumb."

"I said animal, but I thought it was a jaguar."

"It's terrible. I forgot it was back there. I should have burned it."

Rather than argue, Bernie let the comment hang. Darleen had a knack for drawing, but she was always critical of her work. Bernie readjusted her feet and thought about the empty cigarette packages and the beer bottles. She hadn't smelled smoke on Darleen or in the car, so it must be some of her friends who were smoking. Good. She'd talk to Sister about the beer again, about drinking in the car, and drinking in general. Sister wasn't old enough to drink legally, and Bernie had lectured her about it until she couldn't think of what else to say.

The breeze through the open front windows blew Bernie's hair into her face. She found a band in her pack to use for a ponytail.

"I am ready to hear your story," Mama said to Darleen.

"It was stupid. I was stupid. I went to a party with Stoop Man and his sister. Some of their friends live in a cool place in Farmington, along the river, and they had a barbeque. It was fun, and she and I drank beer and did some shooters."

Darleen adjusted the rearview mirror. "Then he was driving us home, and this dog wandered into the road, just came out of nowhere. He turned and missed it, but then the car swerved. We went into a ditch. Nobody got hurt or anything, but it was scary. We tried to push it free, but we couldn't get it unstuck because of the sand. So Stoop Boy started hitching, trying to get a ride so we could get towed. His sister and I just waited. Our phones didn't work there, of course.

"He was gone forever, so she and I decided to finish the six-pack in the backseat because there was nothing to do out there and we were, like, bored to death. Anyway, this sheriff's deputy came by and asked what was up. We thought that sounded dumb, so we started laughing. The cop asked if we'd been drinking, and she said not enough, and we both kept laughing. Well, then he asked how old I was, and

I said eighteen. Then that guy wanted me to pour my beer out and I argued with him about that, you know, that it was wasteful and he should mellow out. But he wouldn't listen. The cop acted like he knew everything."

"Beer. Whiskey," Mama said. "They get people in trouble."

"It was all a big, dumb mistake. I just didn't think I'd go to jail."

Bernie said, "You were way out of line."

"I wasn't driving. Nobody got hurt."

So much, Bernie thought, for her sister learning a lesson. "But you shouldn't be drinking. You're too young, and it gets you in trouble. You know that."

"I didn't mean for you and Mama to worry about me."

As Darleen approached the convenience store at the 491 intersection, Mama said, "We saw a crazy dog here yesterday. You be careful."

"I know all about those darn dogs. That's what got me arrested."

"No," Bernie said. "You got yourself arrested. And now you're driving too fast. I've seen pickups come through these intersections, and they don't stop to look for traffic. You have to pay enough attention for you and the other guy."

"Anything else, Ms. Backseat Driver?"

"Yeah, as a matter of fact. That officer—"

Darleen's phone rang, and Bernie interrupted herself. "Don't answer it, it's not safe—"

Darleen picked up the phone, glanced at the screen, then reached back to hand it to Bernie. "You get it."

Bernie touched to answer. "Hello."

She heard Chee's familiar voice. "Well. Finally. How's everything?"

"OK," she said. "Sister is driving me back to our house so I can get to work. She was telling Mama and me what happened."

"Our house? I thought you were with Mama for a few days. What did happen in Farmington? I got the overview, but not the details. Is she looking at a fine, community service?"

"I'm not sure yet." A lot about Darleen's abbreviated story didn't quite make sense.

"I can see it now. Darleen at the wheel, talking away. Mama in the front seat. You in the backseat, surrounded by assorted junk."

"You've got the picture."

"And your sister's driving is making you crazy."

"Wish you were here?"

"Yeah. Sitting next to you, trying my best to distract you from worrying about your sister or your mother."

Bernie laughed. "I miss you. What's happening out there?"

Chee filled her in on Paul and Bahe's request that he start the Monument Valley assignment early. He told her about finding Melissa, the trespassing teens, and the grave. He sounded good over the phone. Happy. Happier, she thought, to be working as a cop than he was as a cop on vacation.

"It's great to hear your voice," she said. "It seems like we've been apart forever. When will you be home?"

"Oh, a few more days. I figured you'd need to stay

at Mama's at least that long to get Darleen straightened out."

"Actually, I'm going back to work. Remember that traffic stop, and the guy who tried to bribe me?" She told him about the problem with the camera. "The DEA is taking a look at the car today, and I want to be there for that. I'm curious about what was in there that was so important."

"I was hoping you'd cruise on up here again once you got Mama situated." She heard the disappointment in his voice.

"But you're working, and you're helping Paul, too."

There was silence on the phone, and then he said, "I still wish you were here."

After he hung up, she tried not to feel sorry for herself because she'd come in second to his cousin and a movie about zombies. Darleen and Mama were talking about school, but as soon as they finished, Bernie planned to redirect the conversation back to the arrest.

"They say that Diné College has good teachers," Mama was saying. "And you know that girl from your class who went to San Juan College. Then some people like that UNM in Gallup."

"After what just happened, I want to go somewhere away from here, Mama. Someplace where I wouldn't run into people I know who like to party. Remember, the IA?"

Bernie chimed in. "Institute of American Indian Arts." A good, tough school in Santa Fe, but too far from home for her little sister.

Darleen asked, "How come you know about it?"

"Our cousin's wife's nephew went there. Peewee."

Darleen laughed. "That guy!"

"Some famous artists taught there—Fritz Scholder, Charles Loloma, Allan Houser."

Darleen turned on the signal to pass. "I'll find out what I need to do to get in."

Right, Bernie thought. "I bet you have to have your GED first."

Darleen pulled up in front of Bernie's Shiprock trailer and parked. She left the motor running.

"You two want to come in?"

"No. I need to get over to the library to use the Internet for the IA. OK with you, Mama?"

Mama nodded. "You and Sister talk about that Eye school some more."

Bernie walked to Darleen's open window. "Call me tonight. Be careful driving home, and no drinking."

"Anything else?"

"Watch out for those dogs."

"Hey, thanks for buying gas."

"Your tires were low, and I put in some air. Keep an eye on that."

Bernie spoke to Mama. "Remember to drink plenty of water on these hot days."

"That's right," Darleen said. "You drink more, and I'll drink less."

Bernie stood in the drive watching as Darleen's car disappeared. Then she walked past the loom and climbed the steps into the trailer. The house, stuffy and lonely, added to her out-of-sorts feeling. A phone message from Louisa contributed to her funk.

"Can you call me when you get a minute? Or stop by anytime, you two. It always brightens Joe's day to have you guys over." Joe, of course, was the man she called the Lieutenant, the legendary Leaphorn, her mentor and Chee's former boss. Recovery from the damage a crazed woman had done with a bullet to his brain was coming slowly.

She hadn't been to see Leaphorn or Louisa, his housemate and more, in over a week. Life moved too fast. She'd be in touch after she learned what schedule Largo had planned for her. The only certain thing about police work, Bernie thought, was that you never knew what might come next. Largo mentioned that the techies had removed the questionable camera from her unit, and the DEA, or whoever, would check to see if perhaps someone could salvage the recording and the incriminating conversation it should contain.

She showered, put on her uniform, and headed to the office, hoping to take another look at the boxes of dirt before the DEA folk arrived. Coming in the station's back door as she always did, she hadn't even sat down when Sandra, the receptionist, buzzed her.

"There's a gentleman here who needs to file an accident report."

"I'll be right out."

She didn't see many men wearing ties in Shiprock. A good bolo, maybe, but seldom an official necktie, even if the guy was due in court or running for Tribal Council. The light-skinned gentleman in the business suit, his hair cut close to the scalp, was the sort Bernie only encountered when she'd been arm-twisted into representing the department at a meeting someplace fancy.

"I'm Officer Manuelito," she said. "What can I do for you?"

"I need to report some damage on my car. I was at that little restaurant down the highway from here, and somebody backed into me and then drove off. Not a lot of damage, but any little thing costs a fortune to fix." His straight white teeth gleamed when he smiled at her. "So I need to file an accident report for my insurance."

"I can help you with that." She knew the café. It sat right off the main road north to Cortez and south to Gallup. It was Shiprock's most popular place for travelers, both Navajos and *bilagaana*, and for locals too. The tight parking spots and steady traffic contributed to frequent accidents.

She called up the necessary file on her computer and typed in the date, learning that he drove a black Porsche Cayenne. He showed her a photo of the damage.

"I've never seen this kind of SUV. It looks like somebody crunched into your front bumper with a trailer hitch."

"That's what I thought. Whoever did it was long gone when I came out, and I didn't hear a thing. Made an interesting dent. The car's a hybrid, runs on battery power as well as gasoline. Helps save the planet, at least until we can buy solar cars."

Bernie nodded, glad that the accident didn't involve injuries or other complications. She'd finish this quickly and examine the dirt. "Your name, sir?"

"David Oster."

"Address?"

He gave her an address in San Francisco.

"San Francisco? You're a long way from home."

"That's right. I'm missing the fog but enjoying the sun."

"Welcome to Navajoland. I'm sorry about your car. What brings you out this way?"

"The sun, actually. I'm with Primal Solar."

"Primal Solar?" The name stirred a memory in the back of Bernie's brain. "I've heard of that."

"We're the company responsible for some of those photovoltaic panels that got ripped in half by the wind or crushed by the snow. I'm here to make good on those mistakes and to find a site for our next solar farm."

"Solar farm?" As far as she knew, every farm used the sun to make things grow.

"That's engineer talk for an array of panels installed together to create a lot of energy, enough for the reservation and to ship to California. Solar power is the way of the future. Clean, renewable, nonpolluting. I can't imagine a better project to spend time on."

Some twenty thousand families lived on the reservation without power, as though they were in a third-world country. It was ironic, Bernie thought, since the Navajo Nation was home to some of America's biggest reserves of coal and uranium, as well as abundant sun and wind for alternative energy. Bernie knew people who had tried solar power. At first they had been happy with their electricity for lights and refrigerators, then sad when the panels stopped working.

Oster continued explaining. "We'll do some training and leave a pool of support personnel homeowners can call if they have problems down the line. We're hiring." He handed her a business card. "If you hear of people who could use a job, ask them to call or go to the website."

"Do you have an office in Shiprock?"

"I'm working from my motel in Farmington for now, but I need an office here while we're doing the assessments and making the repairs or replacements on the old system. Do you know of any space available?"

"Check the shopping center near Smith's," she said. "They had some empty storefronts last time I looked."

"Smith's?"

"That's the big grocery." She told him where to find it.

Bernie printed two copies of the form she'd put together and gave them to him. He pulled a slim silver pen from the inside pocket of his jacket, tapping it against the paper.

"I noticed that you spell Shiprock here as one word. I thought it was two."

"The rock itself, the big blackish formation, that's two words. The town is one word. The US Post Office wanted it that way."

He smiled. "One more thing to confuse us newcomers. Here's another question for you. Is there a Starbucks around here? Or someplace where I can get a latte and use Wi-Fi?"

"We're still waiting for the first Shiprock Starbucks." The wait would be indefinite, she thought.

No one she knew would pay those prices for a cup of coffee. Well, maybe Darleen and her friends. "The library has Internet and computers. It's across the highway from the medical center, near the Boys and Girls Club. As for coffee, I think the best is Giant."

He looked puzzled.

"The Giant service station."

He nodded. "Giant. That's a new one on me. When I hear Giant, I think of the baseball team."

Now she was puzzled.

"You know. The San Francisco Giants? The team that has solar panels at the ballpark?"

"I'm not really up on baseball. Basketball is king around here. The station is up there past the bridge."

"I must have missed it."

"Hold on." She opened the filing cabinet and found a file labeled "Maps." Amazingly, the one she wanted was in the front. It showed the intricacies of the Shiprock metropolis, population 8,000. She circled the shopping center, the Giant station, the library, and the police station, and handed him the map. "Good luck with your project. Where will the new panels be?"

"We're looking at several sites. It's on the way. The world is changing, and Primal Solar is making it happen."

What a zealot, she thought as Oster left. But at least he was working for a good cause. She'd be curious to see a solar-powered car.

Bernie went to the front to sign out the key to the evidence storage room. Sandra turned on the camera that monitored the area.

"Be sure that thing is working," said Bernie. "I had a bad experience with my dash cam."

"Yeah, I heard."

The dirt looked like regular dirt, nothing mixed with it except the material nature provided—tiny fragments of snakeskin, little cacti, black seeds that might have come from saltbush—and a bit of man-made litter. The boxes and their contents seemed innocent, but why did Miller have this stuff in his trunk, and why wouldn't he talk about it?

There must have been something else in his car, something she'd missed in the dark. Something worth more than the money he'd offered her. She knew guilt when she saw it.

When she left the evidence room, she noticed another man in a suit, the second one that day. His back was to her as he talked with Captain Largo.

"Manuelito, I think you'll remember Agent Jerry Cordova." Largo nodded at Cordova. "Use my office."

Chee got to the station at 6:45 that morning to find a stout woman in a Navajo Police uniform waiting for him. There were streaks of gray in her smooth dark hair.

"*Yá'át'ééh*." He introduced himself.

Rosella Tsinnie did the same, Navajo style, with parental clans. "I've heard about you from Lieutenant Leaphorn. Heard about you for years." From her tone, what she had heard wasn't necessarily complimentary. "How is the one who retired doing?"

"The Lieutenant is recovering from that bullet."

She moved toward the door. "Let's go to this burial you found."

"Don't we need to wait for Captain Bahe?"

"No. I'll drive."

"You know where the site is?"

"I read your report. You can talk to me about what you didn't put in there on the way out."

Although he had never met Tsinnie, Chee realized he knew her by reputation. She was one of the first women criminal investigators in the department, smart and irascible. She'd paid her dues with her time at Window Rock and later at Kayenta, and she could have retired, but Chee had heard she was supporting a young granddaughter and a husband who had developed cancer after a career as a uranium miner. Like Leaphorn, she was a legend.

Tsinnie climbed into her unit, moved an insulated lunch bag from the passenger seat, started the engine, and pulled out as Chee fastened his seat belt. She drove fast and well, a person who knew the Monument Valley road and its idiosyncrasies as well as her own driveway. With their early departure they avoided the buses crammed with sightseers, encountering only a few local pickups raising clouds of dust. Chee looked out the window at the buttes, noticing how different they seemed in the morning's soft light.

"OK, Chee, review what happened last night for me. Start at the beginning. Don't leave anything out, even if you think it's not important."

The question reminded him of the Lieutenant. He summarized his conversation with Bahe, his search of viewpoints outside the park, his discovery of the RV and his decision to ignore it, the cruise along the Monument Valley Park loop road, the encounter with the woman who had noticed the red car. How he heard the music, found the car, and removed the keys from the ignition.

"I followed the footprints in the sand up a rise, down, and then up again to the ridge. I saw Melissa standing there. She gathered up her equipment, and

I led the way back, a shorter route. That's when we came across the site." He described Melissa's fall, his discovery of the rocks around what looked to be a grave, and his search of the gravesite, noticing the tightness in his throat and tingling on his skin as he spoke. "That's about it."

Tsinnie kept her gaze on the road. "What did you talk to the woman about?"

"Photography, mostly, at first. The movie business."

"What else?"

"I told her that her friends were worried about her. She told me she wasn't lost."

Tsinnie passed a pickup towing a horse trailer. The driver acknowledged her by raising his index finger from the steering wheel.

"So what do you think? What does your gut tell you about that place? Is it really a grave?"

"It has something to do with the movie people. Bahe thinks it may be part of a set. The call about the missing woman might have been a way to draw attention to it—but what would be the point of that? Of getting the police involved?"

"Keep talking."

Chee took a breath in. Exhaled. "My instincts say the woman I found didn't know about it." He stopped, surprised at the conviction in his own voice.

Tsinnie slowed down as they passed a cluster of cows and calves walking on the other side of the road. "Did you see the grave first? Or did the lost woman point it out to you?"

Chee paused. "I heard her grunt when she fell. I

turned to help her; that's when I noticed it. If she hadn't tripped, I could have walked right by it." Melissa could have faked it, Chee realized. The entire call could have been a setup. "She said she didn't know it was there—she had never seen it before. She seemed to be as surprised as I was at the discovery."

"Anything else?"

"The boss guy, a man named Robinson, laughed it off when I mentioned the grave to him. But some others I met out there, Navajo guys, they knew about it. They didn't want to talk, but I could tell from their reaction."

"What else?"

"Nothing at the moment."

Chee looked out the window at a row of distinctive red sandstone spires. American explorers had named the formation Three Sisters because it reminded them of a short procession of nuns. He had heard that these were Holy People who had stopped at this spot to argue and turned to rock.

Even though it was relatively early and Tsinnie had the air-con on, Chee felt uncomfortably warm. By the time the visitors at the new hotel finished their breakfast and checked their e-mail, it would be in the nineties. In the valley, most of the rare shade came from the angle of the sun on the monuments. The few trees grew only along the washes.

The enormity of this landscape made him feel humble, a small cog in the huge wheel of the universe. Made the puzzle of the grave seem unimportant. Unless, of course, a murder was involved.

"I think it's a publicity stunt," Tsinnie said, "creating a fake grave for us to investigate as a way to get the media out here. Since you're not from around here, you were an easy target."

Chee said nothing.

"Of all the places in Tsé Bii' Ndzisgaii that she could have gone for pictures, why was she there? Why Rabbit Ridge? You didn't ask her, did you?"

He wasn't Lieutenant Leaphorn, but he'd seen plenty of ploys, dishonesty, smooth talkers, and skillful liars. He resented the implication that he'd been used.

"Rabbit Ridge? So that's what it's called."

Tsinnie's earrings, some sort of red-and-orange stone surrounded by a narrow border of silver, moved when she turned toward him. "Right. We're getting close to the site. Tell me where to stop."

She parked, and they hiked away from the road, following the prints he and Melissa had left in the sand the night before. Tsinnie looked at the tracks. "So these big ones are yours, and these others are hers?"

He nodded. Tsinnie seemed to be memorizing the patterns of the shoe tread.

The monuments glowed, the sun bronzing the stone soaring up from the sandy valley floor. They looked just as they had been presented in the stories from Chee's childhood. Landscapes like this put humanity in perspective, he thought. They ensure that we humans know our small place in this vast universe.

He trudged toward the ridge ahead of Tsinnie, his boots sliding on the sand. She was wearing sneakers—not uniform, but smart. She kept up with him.

He noticed a delicate chevron pattern, the path of
a snake. Chee was careful to avoid it. He still remembered his grandmother telling him not to walk in a
snake's trail or the creature would follow him home.
Elsewhere he spotted the thin lines made by lizards'
tails and the tiny impressions left by their delicate
clawed feet. He saw bird footprints, too, and the
place where a raptor had swooped up dinner, shap-
ing the sand with its wings. Chee liked this kind of
art better than old paintings at a museum. It was
free, and frequently changing, too.

"Up ahead," Tsinnie said. "Is that it?"

"Yeah."

"You know, Chee, I was hoping you'd made this
up. Been hallucinating or something."

It looked less sinister in the daylight—a mound of
reddish dirt surrounded by a ring of stones of vari-
ous sizes, invisible from the road. The perpetrators
had created it in a depression where, Chee guessed,
it would be fairly easy to dig.

Tsinnie gave the orders. "Look for tire tracks,
signs of somebody hauling grave-digging machin-
ery down there close to the road." She chuckled.
"Let me know if you stumble across something interesting."

Chee reminded himself that his assignment
here was only temporary, Tsinnie a passing irritation, like indigestion. She only knew him through
Leaphorn's comments, and the Legendary Lieutenant had always given him more grief than praise.

He sauntered along slowly enough to take in whatever disturbance might be on the roadside, noticing
tough desert grasses and the hoof prints of cattle.

He had decided to give it another five minutes and then turn back when some different indentations caught his eye. A vehicle, probably a backhoe, had moved from the hard-packed dirt onto the sand.

He took a picture of the tracks with his phone, then followed the scar with his eyes until it disappeared over a rise. He walked up the hill, knowing that the grave lay on the other side.

Tsinnie's voice broke his concentration.

"Chee, come over here. I found some footprints that you and not-really-lost girl managed not to step on."

"OK. I've got some backhoe tracks down here." He jogged back to the gravesite. She pointed to two sets of prints. Both looked to Chee as if they'd been made by hiking boots. "Get some pictures of these in case this is a big deal." The tone of her voice suggested that she sincerely hoped it would be a little deal. She opened the bag she'd brought along and handed him a camera. "Know how to use this?"

Chee examined it. "Any trick to it?"

Tsinnie raised an eyebrow ever so slightly. "Point and shoot. Take some exposures of these before the wind does more damage. You see anything interesting?"

"I found some wide tire tracks and the place where the machine left the road and then went back to it. Looks like a backhoe did the work on this."

"I'm going to search for more boot prints. Find me when you're done."

The camera was simple, an older digital model with a zoom. After he took pictures of the boot prints and the route of the backhoe, Chee hiked to the road, where Tsinnie was standing by the unit, drinking from a water bottle.

She glanced up at him. "We're going out to the movie camp now to talk to the man in charge," Tsinnie said. "We can tell him they'll have to pay a fine and clean it up. No one who lives out here would have used a backhoe to make a grave."

It seemed to Chee that more evidence was called for, but he didn't argue. Maybe the force of her personality would make Robinson confess.

The camp was quiet. A few people clustered in little groups outside in the shade created by the food tent. He overheard snatches of conversation, zombie actors talking about kids and the baseball season as he led the way. The detective following. What an odd world. He didn't understand the fascination with zombies. To his way of thinking, there was enough unexplained evil in real life.

He knocked on the production office door and, when there was no answer, went to the one with the Administration sign. The woman behind the desk told them that Robinson wasn't at work yet. Could she help?

"Is he the top man here?" Tsinnie asked.

"Yes, ma'am."

"Where can we find him?"

The woman hesitated. "He worked late last night, so he's probably still asleep in the green trailer with the Land Rover parked in front. That way." She pointed. "Like I said, they all had a late night filming. He's probably not—"

Tsinnie charged off while the woman was still talking.

"Thanks," Chee said.

He caught up to Tsinnie as she approached the front door. She looked at him. "He knows you. You knock."

Robinson—hair mussed, bare-chested, in pajama pants—opened the door more quickly than Chee expected. "Officer Chee. What's the problem? What time is it, anyway?"

"Time to tell us about the grave." Tsinnie took charge, introducing herself tersely.

Robinson looked at Chee. "What the— We went over all this last night."

The trailer was equipped with blackout shades, Chee noticed. A computer screen glowed blue in the darkness beyond the doorway. "Detective Tsinnie thought of some questions I didn't ask you."

"We were at the gravesite," she said. "This is important, or I wouldn't waste my time here."

Robinson exhaled. "OK. Let me get dressed. I'll meet you in the crew tent in five minutes."

"No, we'll talk now in your trailer."

Chee knew the technique. Catch a contact off guard, off balance. Surprise him into telling the truth.

Robinson started to say something, then turned and walked into the room, leaving the door open. He sat at the desk. Tsinnie stood next to his chair, looking down at him, and Chee stood by the door.

Even in the semidarkness Chee could see that, unlike the neat office, Robinson's personal trailer was a mess. The laundry, papers, and unwashed dishes reminded Chee of the low points of his bachelor days, the debris of a life moving too fast.

Tsinnie got to the point. "Tell me why that grave is out there."

"No idea. I don't know anything about it. I told Chee that last night."

"You guys want some extra publicity, so you decided to use the Navajo Police to get it. That was a bad, bad decision."

Robinson stood. "Listen. Why would I want to waste time talking to the police? We're on a tight shooting schedule. Whatever distracts from the filming costs us money. That certainly includes this nonsense. The planet is full of bones and graveyards. Why is this a big deal, anyway?" Robinson rubbed his hands through his hair, amplifying the bed-head effect. "This is crazy."

Chee watched Tsinnie bristle, stand a little taller. "I live out here. I know everyone. I would have heard about that grave. I didn't. It's new with you people. It wasn't here before you came."

Robinson walked to the corner of his trailer that served as a kitchen. Chee watched him run water into a coffee mug and put the cup in the microwave.

Tsinnie raised her voice over the whir of the oven. "When the grave is exhumed and we come up with nothing, that could look like a way to get attention for a zombie movie. But it will be bad news for you, or whoever came up with this idea. And expensive."

And, Chee thought, embarrassing for the Navajo Police.

"Like I told you, detective, and like I told Chee, I don't know anything about this."

"Who would?"

"Well—" The bell on the microwave cut him off.

Chee watched him remove the cup and add the instant coffee powder.

"How do you guys come up with sites anyway?" Chee asked. "Does somebody look around for places to film the scenes?" Tsinnie glanced in his direction, her expression neutral.

Robinson took a sip of the coffee. "That would be the location supervisor and the scouting team. They went all over the place."

"Call the supervisor," said Tsinnie. "I want to get this settled."

"Once we start filming, she moves on to the next gig. She's not here."

Tsinnie said, "Then get her on the phone."

Robinson put his cup down. "BJ has all that contact information."

"Are you making this hard on purpose?"

"BJ, the administrative assistant, office manager, etcetera. Next door in the office. She can—"

Tsinnie turned her back to them, leaving the door open. Chee felt the trailer stir as she clomped down the metal steps.

"Tough gal," Robinson said.

"She's only doing her job."

"Nah. She enjoys being a big shot. We've got some of those around here, too."

"Are any of those folks who helped with the scouting still here?"

"Mike Turner stayed on. He works with us in case we need some fine-tuning. The best time to find him would be tonight at the meal tent before the filming starts."

"Thanks."

"By the way, what did you think of Samuel last night? I mean, the way he dealt with the trespassers?"

Chee considered the question. "They were high school girls. He frightened the younger one. She was too scared to talk about it, but I wonder if he hurt her arm."

Robinson put his cup down. "He told me he found a gun on them."

"They dropped it before they got to that actress's trailer. They're kids."

"You think he was too heavy-handed?" Robinson didn't wait for the answer. "I'm going to get rid of him. I'd decided that even before last night, but Melissa talked me out of it. He enjoys being a tough guy too much."

Chee met up with Tsinnie outside the central office. BJ had found the location scout's number, and Tsinnie had left a message on a voice-mail system. Chee filled her in about Turner, hinting that he might be a better source.

"I don't like dealing with these people. I'm telling Bahe to have you do it. I'll handle the Navajo end, if there is one. You can come back and talk to Turner. Let's get out of here."

Chee had been around enough strong-willed women to know better than to argue.

"Hey there, Jim Chee." Melissa trotted up to them. "What happened with those trespassers last night?"

"They were teenagers. I gave them a lecture and turned them over to their dad. Robinson called me in because Samuel said they had a gun, and one of them mouthed off to him. No big deal."

"Samuel? Trouble follows that man like a shadow."

"I thought you liked him. Robinson said you saved his job."

Melissa shrugged. "One of the worst mistakes I ever made."

Tsinnie asked, "You the woman who was lost?"

"That's what they say. Did Chee tell you about the grave we found in the middle of nowhere? Spooky, huh?"

Tsinnie stiffened. "We're looking into it."

"A grave turns up on the site of a movie about zombies. How much weirdness is that?" She turned to Chee. "So now I've got new earrings as good luck."

Chee looked at them. Beautiful silverwork framed the turquoise stones of robin's-egg blue. They reminded him of some his grandmother had worn, the stone given to the Diné as a sign of protection. "They are beautiful."

"I got them at the gift shop at the visitor center. I couldn't afford them, but I decided to splurge. After all—"

Tsinnie interrupted. "Chee may need to talk to you again as part of the investigation."

"Of course. Did he tell you how that arm reached up from the depths and grabbed my ankle? He beat it off with my tripod and saved me from certain death. Or, I guess, undeath."

Tsinnie didn't crack a smile.

Chee enjoyed the way the detective negotiated the road hazards, handling the ruts and washouts, loose animals, herds of sightseeing buses, and tourists driving like idiots because of the enchantment of the scenery. Nothing she encountered behind the wheel upset her. She kept her equilibrium, drove like a pro.

As they approached the John Ford Point turnout, she said, "Tell me about that blond girl."

"She didn't have anything to do with the grave. She was genuinely surprised when we found it."

"You've said that already. What's her job?"

"She's a bookkeeper."

"I'm like your Lieutenant Leaphorn. I don't believe in coincidences. Why was she there by the grave? Why there instead of someplace else? That woman is in on this. That grave is nothing but a big headache for us. Too bad you had to find it."

They drove past a black horse and a rider in a red shirt and white hat posed against Ford Point's backdrop of mesas, buttes, and spires.

"What are you doing out here anyway, Chee?" Tsinnie slowed to avoid a cloud of dust from an open-air sightseeing van.

"It's a long story."

"I've got time."

"Well, my wife and I were due some vacation. I'd spent summers here when I was younger, but I hadn't been out for a while. I thought it would be great to show her this place. And my clan brother who lives out here asked me if I could help him with a project."

"I know Paul. They say he's going into the tour business."

"We'll see what happens."

"My uncle does tours, too. He started a couple of

years ago. He works hard at it. He and his wife have three kids."

And that, Chee thought, explained a lot.

Bahe met with them at the station and listened to Tsinnie's report and request. He leaned back in his chair and looked at Chee. "No one has complained about you yet, so I'd like you to see this through before you get deported to Shiprock. Since you already have connections out there in Lala Land, follow up with the movie people."

Chee nodded.

"Tell them if the Navajo Nation has to dig up that grave, the bill goes to them. That's on top of a citation that comes with a fine for not having a permit to work in that part of the park."

"Sure thing."

"You don't think there's a body under there, do you?"

"No, sir."

"Me neither. I hope we don't have to prove it."

Since Tsinnie knew the families in the valley, Bahe assigned her to those interviews.

"It's a big waste of time." Tsinnie studied the desktop. "These movie people did it. They cause a lot of problems. Making noise all night, scaring livestock, a bad influence on our kids."

Bahe took a breath. "The president and the Tribal Council want to bring more movies here. We need the jobs, the fees, the tax money they pay. When a company has a good experience, the word spreads." He leaned in toward her. "Ask around out there, even though you'd rather not."

Tsinnie stood. "You need me for anything else?"

"Go." He turned to Chee. "The movie company scouted the sites and must have taken pictures to help them figure out where to film. If they built the grave, they must have planned it. They ought to have a picture of the place without it—or with it there, if they didn't create it. Talk to this Turner guy and ask him to show the pictures that prove they are innocent.

"Talk to the publicity director, too. If this is a scam, she's probably the one behind it. They hire these people to find ways to keep the movie in the media. And in case something happens that might generate news, like somebody being made an honorary Navajo or stumbling over a grave."

"You know a lot about this," Chee said.

"They don't call Monument Valley the Hollywood of the Rez for nothing."

"Does anybody call it that?"

Bahe grinned. "When you find the publicity person, impress on her—they tend to be women— that the Navajo Nation has laws against illegal burials and that her company will be charged for the exhumation and fined, too. Tell her a crew of folks digging up the grave would bring the production to a stop and add to their expense. Money gets their attention."

"If I get lucky, maybe I can clear this up with a couple of phone calls."

"Don't some horror stories mention a zombie having to sleep on the dirt of his own grave? Something like that?"

"I'm not into that stuff."

"Maybe that's what Bernie found. Boxes of zombie dirt."

"So you heard about her traffic stop?"

"Some news travels fast." Bahe opened his desk drawer and removed some cards. "Here's another little job for you. Check in with the heads of security at Goulding's and Monument Valley Inn and Spa." He handed the cards to Chee. "We just call it the Inn. Ask what's new, anything cookin' we should know about. Maybe they'll remember somebody asking if there were any graveyards nearby." He chuckled at his own joke. "It's good to stay in touch with those guys, and I haven't been able to do it."

"Will do."

Chee handled the interview with the Inn's security chief with one phone call. The director, Brenda Erdman, had time to chat.

"I heard you found a grave out there," she said. "Weird."

"It's true. Where did you learn about it?"

"One of the tour guides mentioned it this morning. A new operator, Paul something, with Hozhoni Photo Tours."

The chief of security at Goulding's Lodge was Norman Haskie. "Bahe asked you to check in with me?" he asked.

"That's right."

"Did you know somebody found a grave out in the valley?"

"Yes. Actually, I'm the one."

"Well, then, you might be interested in something that happened here. I'd rather not mention it on the phone. Can you stop by?"

Haskie was waiting when Chee got to his cubbyhole of an office. Chee learned that Haskie had been in the marines before he went to work at Goulding's and that he loved his job. He had worked with Leone Goulding, better known as Mike, and told Chee the story of how Mike and her husband, Harry Goulding, had traveled from their ranch in Monument Valley to California. Harry threatened to camp out in John Ford's office in his efforts to lure movies to the valley. Impressed with photographs Harry carried with him, the renowned director came with film crews. Over the decades, Goulding's Lodge had grown from a base for movie companies into a destination for tourists from all over the world.

Chee liked the story, even though he'd heard it before. Haskie's affection for the lodge, Monument Valley, and his job was palpable.

"Guess we better get down to business." Haskie turned on his computer and clicked at a file, opening it to reveal photos of a hotel room.

"See that?"

"Blood?"

"That's what the maid thought. That's why she called me. But don't get too excited. We didn't find a body." Haskie put his elbows on the desktop. "Somebody phoned down to the office about eleven p.m. and said the folks next door were raising so much ruckus he couldn't sleep. The night clerk called the noisy room. No answer, so he called security. I was working that night and went on over. I stood outside the door and listened. Didn't hear anything. I figured the honeymooners had worn themselves out. Next morning, the manager on duty called me at home. He said one of the maids saw some bloody towels and a fresh red stain on the carpet through the doorway. She refused to enter the room in case there was a dead person."

Chee wondered what would come next.

"So I went to check it out. I saw the carpet and some soiled towels piled in a corner by the door, all neat like. No one in the room. No knife, no gun, nothing that looked like a weapon. Just the stain and the towels. This was the same room I got the call on the night before."

"Interesting."

"People do strange things in hotel rooms, you know? Things they would never do at home. It looked bad, but it could have been some loony trying to give himself a body piercing. That would make me holler. I gave housekeeping the go-ahead to clean up. And then I got another call. The maid came across something else."

Haskie walked to an old-fashioned filing cabinet, the kind Chee remembered Lieutenant Leaphorn using. Selecting a key from his key ring, he opened the top drawer. He thumbed through the folders, stopped, pulled out a Ziploc bag, and handed it to Chee. "She found this between the bed and the frame when she was changing the sheets."

Inside the bag was a silver chain with a pendant and an index card. Chee recognized the necklace as a handmade Navajo piece, high-quality old silver with greenish-blue turquoise. Chee put the bag on the desk. "What's the procedure when something valuable like this turns up?"

"The front office calls the guest. We say we found a piece of jewelry, a watch, a wallet, whatever. Have them ID it and then mail it off. That's what we tried to do here, but the registration information turned out to be bogus or missing."

"What do you mean?"

"We didn't have a phone number. The letter we sent to the customers at the PO box they used for an address came back stamped 'Unknown.'"

"When did this happen?"

"Early spring. I meant to talk to Bahe about it sooner, but when nothing came of it, I figured it was just people acting weird. Then I heard about what you found out there; I thought it wouldn't hurt to mention it."

Chee looked at the necklace again. "What's on the card?"

"That's the registration he filled out."

"Could you give me a photo of this?"

"Give me a minute. Let's do this right." Haskie opened the bag and put the necklace on his desktop, adjusting it so the pendant, the clasp, and part of the chain were in the frame.

"Wait a second." Chee reached into his pocket. "I think I've got a quarter or something we can use to show how big the stone is." He pulled out the poker chip he'd found near the gravesite and put it by the pendant.

Haskie clicked off some shots. "I'll send them to Bahe, too."

Chee was impressed with how well the man had covered all the details. "So, why do you think this might be tied to the grave?"

"Whoever stayed at that room that night had something to hide. Otherwise, why not register with a real name? And there's the blood."

Haskie handed Chee a slip of paper. "Here's the name of the maid, in case you want to talk to her. She's off now, but will be back in the morning."

"Thanks for the information."

Haskie rose to see him out. "You know, I probably shouldn't have wasted your time with this. I bet whatever happened here has nothing to do with what you found."

That was likely to be true, Chee thought.

He went back to the station, typed up his report, and was ready to head back to the movie camp to interview Turner when his phone buzzed.

"Hey there." Paul's voice rang with exuberance. "Good news, bro. I booked more customers for the tour. You're bringing me luck."

The tour. He needed to get back to fix the People Mover. "That's great. Is it still at sunset today?"

"No. Sunrise tomorrow. That's better. Not so hot."

"Are your clients more Norwegians?"

"No, these people sound like they're from Texas. Do you think I could give them bologna sandwiches in the morning? They're traditional, right? You and I grew up on them. Breakfast of champions."

"Let me think on that." Chee hung up and finished his notes, rehashing the session with Haskie. He considered the phony registration, the commotion, the bloody towels, and the unclaimed necklace.

Suspicious? Yes. Criminal? No evidence of that. Would someone commit murder in a hotel room and then take the time to bury the body? Highly unlikely, especially considering that a backhoe was involved. And if this happened in the spring, say three months ago, would the backhoe tracks have survived?

He thought again about Melissa and the way they had discovered the grave. Tsinnie was right. It was too coincidental. Chee stood and stretched. He needed to get this silly thing settled and get back to Bernie. He had hardly spoken to her, between the spotty phone service in the valley and his focus on his work. Missing her, he called her cell phone. It rang until her message came on.

Finally he called the movie office, asked for Turner and learned that he was unavailable.

"Would you give me his cell number?"

The receptionist hesitated. "He usually doesn't answer his cell. Mr. Turner is due here for a meeting in an hour. I'll have him call you if I see him."

Chee doubted that Turner took orders from his secretary.

9

Cordova opened the door for Bernie and sat behind Largo's desk. Bernie settled into her usual spot, the folding chair.

Cordova smiled. "Nice to see you again, Officer. You're looking well."

"Thanks. I'm surprised that you're here. I thought we'd be dealing with the DEA on this."

"It was a multi-agency operation." He didn't elaborate, but Bernie knew the FBI had been working on human trafficking and credit card fraud. "I want to go over your traffic stop to make sure we don't miss anything."

"Great. It's been on my mind ever since it happened." Cordova had interviewed her before, and she remembered how thorough he was. "I assumed the whole encounter was on tape. The record light came on, but Largo told me the equipment wasn't working."

"Stuff happens. Maybe it was the universe's way of putting me back in touch with a beautiful woman."

He took a slim recorder from his pocket and spoke into it, setting the place, date, and time and specifying that he was interviewing Officer Bernadette Manuelito of the Navajo Police. Then he placed the machine on the table between them.

He started by asking Bernie to recount what happened, noting that he would interrupt her for more details from time to time. He stopped her when she mentioned that Miller stepped out of the car to go with her to get the gun. "Tell me more about his demeanor."

Bernie thought about it. "His coordination was good and his speech clear, no slurring. His eyes looked OK, not watery or bloodshot, and the pupils normal. Before he got out of the car, I noticed perspiration beading up on his forehead and that he was fidgeting. He grew more nervous later."

Cordova got to the handgun. "Where was it in the glove box?"

"Right on top."

"Did you see anything else suspicious in there?"

She thought about it. "No."

"Elsewhere in the car?"

"I looked on the seat and the floor. Nothing unusual, nothing worth sweating over."

"Did he say what he was doing out there?"

"He said he was driving from Albuquerque to Gallup, with a detour to see Ship Rock."

"That's a long detour. Did he give a reason?"

"He told me he could never be in the Four Corners area without seeing it."

"Really? Did you follow up on that? Ask him why he liked Ship Rock so much?"

The moon was bright, Bernie remembered, and Ship Rock had resonated with beautiful mystery that night.

"No."

The look Cordova gave her said he thought she'd made a mistake. "Go back to the conversation. Tell me everything you remember, even if it seems irrelevant or inconsequential."

"He mentioned Northern Arizona University." Bernie tapped a finger for each point. "He told me about his dog. He talked about staying at the Comfort Suites in Gallup."

Cordova interrupted. "Did he mention any other specific places he had been?"

Bernie thought about it. "No. Oh, wait. He said he'd been in a meeting in Albuquerque. Mostly he talked about Flagstaff. Told me he worked in construction, mentioned that the town had a good brew pub, said he liked to walk with his dog around there. Nothing that seemed noteworthy."

Cordova's questions became less routine, more interesting. "At what point did he offer you a bribe?"

"Before he opened the trunk."

"He offered you five hundred?"

"First a hundred. Then five hundred."

"That's right." Cordova smiled at her. "Why?"

"Two reasons, I guess. I didn't respond when he made the first offer. Maybe he would have offered more, but he said that was all the cash he had. After I saw the rifle in the trunk, he told me I could have that, too."

"Anything else stand out from the encounter?"

"Before he offered me the bribe, he asked how I found out."

Cordova looked up from his notes. "Found out about what?"

"That's what I wondered. Why are you guys interested in Miller?"

Cordova clicked off the little recorder and placed it gently in his pocket.

"I can't tell you. But we're glad you stopped him. It looks like you did everything by the book."

"Tell that to Largo. Everyone at the station is giving me grief about confiscating two boxes of dirt."

"Gives them something to talk about. Our man is examining the recorder. If nothing else, he can get it working for next time. I'll be in touch. Let me know if something else occurs to you."

"So has the crew looked at Miller's car yet?"

"They went over it yesterday."

"What did they find?"

"It was clean."

"Clean?"

"Well, besides the dirt you found, there was a bunch of dog hair." Cordova grinned at her. "I can't say much except Miller is on our radar, and your instincts about him being up to something are probably correct."

"Did your guys look at that dirt? It could have been contaminated. Miller told me he was in construction. Maybe someone hired him to cover up some illegal spills, chemical dumping, uranium tailings, stuff like that. Did you have it tested?"

Cordova sighed. "You don't give up, do you? I'm

not sure exactly what tests they did on the dirt, Manuelito, but don't worry about it."

"They might have missed something. You could—"

He shook his head before she'd finished the request. "They did whatever was required. End of story." Cordova stood, letting her know the interview was over. "Tell Largo he can get rid of that dirt. Unless you want some as a souvenir."

After Cordova had gone, Bernie wondered what to do next. Maybe one more look at the evidence would inspire her.

Sandra gave her the key again, then picked up her water bottle and took a sip. The dispatcher was on a new water diet. The idea was that if you drank enough, your stomach would be full and you wouldn't be hungry. As far as Bernie could tell, it also worked by requiring you to use energy in more frequent trips to the restroom. "I guess that guy was a rock collector or a dirt collector or something."

"Are you going to give me a hard time about this, too?"

"Not really. I think you'll catch enough grief without me."

The boxes sat on a table next to the cabinet, lined up side by side. Bernie leaned over to examine the first one. It was maybe four inches deep, with "Foodclub" printed on the outside, the kind of container canned goods came in for stocking in grocery stores. Someone, probably Miller, had shoveled in dirt to fill it halfway. Now that she had better light, Bernie spotted grayish sticks, a shiny beetle carapace, partially disintegrated paper, a few tiny cacti, eroded lava rocks the size of the jawbreakers she liked as a kid, and black specks that looked like seeds. She put her face close to the dirt and inhaled deeply. No chemical odor she could detect.

She looked at the second box, spending another ten minutes with it, finding similar contents and nothing that smelled odd. The mystery remained unsolved. She relocked the room, turned in the key, and came up with an idea.

Largo looked up from his computer when she rapped on the doorframe.

"How did it go with Cordova?"

"Well, I learned that Miller is some kind of untouchable the feds or DEA or somebody has on their radar. Bribing a tribal officer is small potatoes. Even if I'd had it on tape, I think Cordova would have dismissed it."

"Don't let it bother you."

"Cordova says they're done with the dirt, but I have an idea, sir."

"Somehow that does not surprise me."

"I'd like to have the soil tested for contamination. You know—oil spills, uranium debris, chemical leaks. Stuff like that."

"And you know what the budget is like. And the feds already cleared it."

"Cordova gave me the impression they just looked for drugs."

Largo hesitated. "You can't let it go, can you?"

"It bugs me."

"If you can talk someone into doing the tests for free, go ahead. I wanna keep you happy, Manuelito."

"Would you mind if I took some of those little cacti home? Maybe I can get them to grow."

After making a few calls, she found a contact at the San Juan County extension office who knew someone who could do the soil testing as part of another batch of samples he was working on. He'd come by for the dirt that afternoon. If the boxes didn't contain anything special, she would stop obsessing about them. If she came up with something and outsmarted Cordova—well, a little humility might be good for the man.

When she went into the break room to get cups to put the plants in, Bigman was alone at the table with a sandwich in front of him. "I hear that was some haul you came up with the other night. If it had been me, I would have made that scumbag tell me where that dirt came from and drive out there and put it back. Did you ask him to empty out his shoes and take off his socks? Maybe there was some sand lurking between his toes."

"You bet I did. You can't be too careful."

"Speaking of lurking, when is your husband coming back from zombie duty?"

"I don't know. Not soon enough. I miss him."

"Seems like a cool assignment. Hanging out with the stars." Bigman looked at the sandwich, offered Bernie half. She declined.

"How famous do you have to be to get a job as a zombie?"

"I heard that Rhonda's in the movie." Bigman took a bite of his lunch.

"Rhonda who?"

He chewed, swallowed. "Rhonda Delay. Even you

must have heard of her, Manuelito. She's everywhere. TV, ads, on the Internet. She has a new record out."

"I'll ask Sister. She keeps up with that stuff."

"How's that girl doing?"

Bernie wondered if Bigman had heard of Darleen's latest predicament. "Now she wants to go to art school. She's looking into that one in Santa Fe."

"The IAIA?"

"That's it."

Bigman rewrapped what was left of his sandwich. "And your mother?"

"She's OK."

"Glad to hear it."

Bernie grabbed a pair of Styrofoam cups for the cactus plants and got the evidence room key one final time. She scooped up some of the gravelly dirt and gently moved several of the little cacti to a new temporary home. She left them on the table; then she told Sandra about the man coming to pick up the boxes.

The late June heat must have made criminals lazy. Her afternoon's assignments ranged from tedious to downright boring. As she drove toward Shiprock High School to check a vandalism report, she heard an electronic chime. It seemed to be coming from the backseat of her unit. The noise continued for several cycles and then stopped. When it started up again, she pulled to the shoulder, killed the engine, got out, and opened the back door. She saw nothing, so she raised the lid of the trunk to investigate. Nothing unusual there, either, but she knew she hadn't imagined the sound. She checked the rear seats again, more closely, then squatted down to peek beneath the front seats.

This time, she found a slim black cell phone.

One of the technicians checking for drugs must have dropped it, she thought as she picked it up.

Then she looked at it, and radioed Captain Largo.

"Remember that guy I arrested? The one Cordova talked to me about?"

"Miller. Go on."

"I found his phone on the floor of my unit."

"How do you know it's his?"

"When I touched it, the screen lit up with a picture of him."

"I'll mention it to the feds. Remember to drop it off when you get in."

"Yes, sir."

"And Bernie, we saved those cups with the dirt for you when the guy came in to get the boxes. They're on your desk."

She looked at Miller's phone again. The home screen displayed several missed calls. None were familiar, but two of the numbers that came up more than once showed a 505 area code. That meant her part of New Mexico—Sheep Springs, Shiprock, Newcomb, Sanostee and also beyond the reservation, as far out as Albuquerque and Santa Fe. She made a note of those numbers, and several other frequent connections.

Then she touched the camera icon. The pictures were mostly shots of the landscape. She saw several views of Ship Rock, some sunsets, pictures of the Grand Canyon, blooming flowers. No photos of people, but about a dozen shots of a large, hairy black dog.

She would have checked the phone into the evidence room before she left for the day, but Sandra had gone home, and Largo was out. Instead, she locked it in her desk drawer for the evening, finished her paperwork, and drove to her trailer along the San Juan River.

Bernie wasn't used to being home by herself. Since their marriage, she and Chee spent their time off together except when she needed to sleep at Mama's. The place felt empty without him. She straightened up the house and then went to the deck and moved the cacti from the white cups into small flowerpots, using the same gravelly dirt. Since the plants were only three inches across, she'd assumed they were babies, but now she noticed tiny dried flowers. They must be full grown, some sort of miniature barrel cactus. She'd look them up in her cactus guide when she got a chance. Something else to keep her mind off her missing husband.

She checked the refrigerator and remembered that she and Chee had done a good job of eating everything before they left for vacation. Oh, well. She didn't have much of an appetite anyway. She turned on the TV and turned it off again. Picked up her book, but found herself staring out the window instead of reading. When the phone rang, she wished it would be Chee, but it was Darleen.

"Drive out and eat with us. Mama says the *atoo'* is even better now. And I want to talk to you about that school idea."

"I don't know. It's hot. I'm tired."

"It's as hot there as it is here. Hold on."

"Wait. Don't put Mama—"

Mama's voice came on the phone. "Come over now, daughter. I need to give you some of this food.

It's too much for your sister and for me. And she wants to say something to you."

"I'm not very hungry."

"And bring the Popsicles."

Then Darleen was back. "We'll wait to eat dinner until you get here. Just because Cheeseburger isn't there doesn't mean you can feel sorry for yourself."

"Thanks a lot."

"Don't be grumpy. And hurry up."

Her appetite had returned by the time she got to Mama's, and the stew smelled wonderful. It was always better the second day. After they ate, Mama put some in two containers. "One for the Cheeseburger. One for the one who got shot." Bernie put them in the freezer, along with what was left of the Popsicles.

Darleen had been quiet during dinner. Now she was watching the news on TV. Bernie joined her on the couch. "Hey," Darleen said. "There was just something on about a movie at Monument Valley. Something with zombies. Rhonda is the star. Rhonda! Whoa. I wonder if Cheeseburger is working near there. Maybe he'll get to meet her."

"Bigman was talking about Rhonda at work. I've never heard of her."

Darleen made a clucking sound. "Seriously? You must have seen her in one of those movies, and then she did the way-cool videos, and then she was on that TV thing, you know, with those cute guys? Has your husband seen her yet?"

"I don't know."

"Maybe he could take a picture of her for me. That would be awesome."

"I'll ask him."

Darleen said, "You sure were grouchy on the phone."

"I had a bad day at work."

"What happened?"

The question surprised Bernie—Darleen's world focused on Darleen. But she filled her in on the details.

"Dirt Guy sounds like a weirdo to me. I'm glad he didn't shoot you or something."

"Me too."

"Why won't the FBI tell you about him?"

"I don't know." Bernie wondered how she could get more information out of Cordova.

Darleen changed the subject. "I found some forms for signing up for the IAIA at the library, and I printed them. Can you, like, help me if I have questions and stuff? I want to get the forms to Santa Fe as soon as I can."

Bernie glanced at the TV. A commercial with cats. "I think we should wait until we know for sure that you won't have any more repercussions from getting arrested. The IAIA might not be the right place, and this might not be the right time."

"Don't be negative. On the website, they said students could submit a portfolio to be considered. What's that?"

"They mean a collection of your art—drawings, paintings, photographs, sculpture, poetry, whatever."

Darleen looked puzzled. "Seriously? How does that work?"

Bernie felt sorry for her. "Make a list of questions,

like the ones you're asking me. Call somebody there and ask them. I really don't know everything. I leave that to Mama."

The walker squeaked in the hall. "What do you leave to me?"

"Bernie was telling me what to do." Darleen got up off the couch. "I'm gonna work on some drawings."

Mama said, "Draw some horses, OK?"

"I'll do one for you."

Bernie heard the door to Darleen's bedroom close.

Mama sat carefully on the couch. "We will need a plan for Darleen to go away from here. I can take my old rug to the Toadlena Trading Post. The one with the double-diamond design. See if that man will buy it."

Bernie remembered the rug from her childhood. She'd sat next to Mama as the rug grew, day by day, inch by inch. Out of necessity, Mama had sold every other rug she made, but she'd held on to this one, and Bernie couldn't imagine Mama's house without it.

Bernie had financed her education with scholarships and a part-time job. "Sister might be able to get some grants to pay for school, maybe even a loan. If she went to school around here, she could live with you. That would be less expensive. I will check on that."

Mama listened without responding. At least, Bernie thought, she didn't argue. Maybe the notion of selling the rug was just a way to spur Bernie into action.

Bernie helped Mama get ready for bed, turned off the TV, and loaded the stew in her cooler. She knocked on Darleen's door. "I'm going home."

"Drive safe. Watch out for those dogs."

"Why don't you do your drawings in the kitchen sometime? Keep Mama company."

"I can't focus with the television blaring. Why don't you—" Darleen cut the comment short, but Bernie heard the criticism. "See you later."

On the way to Shiprock, Bernie stopped at the convenience store for a Coke. The clerk, who Bernie usually thought of as cranky, was smiling. "Looks like you're having a good night," she said.

"Just when you think you've heard everything. A tourist guy came in here. You know what he wanted?"

"Directions?"

"Well, yeah. He was looking for a house out by Ship Rock. But he wanted something else, too."

"What?"

"Organic dog snacks."

"What is that?"

"That's what I asked. He looked at me like I was as dumb as a board. Then he said we need to make sure dogs eat the same high-quality food as people and, oh man, he went on and on."

Bernie waited for the punch line.

"I handed him a package of jerky, that new, expensive stuff that says organic on the front and is made from buffalos. I told him that was what we used around here. He looked at it and bought four, no questions asked. For his dog!"

"Crazy, is it?"

"Amazing."

As she headed for home, Bernie sipped her drink and thought some more about Cordova. She was eager to get the results of the tests on the dirt. Would the lab be able to find ancient pollen? Maybe the dark specks were scraps of charcoal from an archaeology site. Maybe Miller was a would-be grave robber. She was glad Largo had authorized the soil analysis, but if he hadn't, she would have done it anyway on her own, just to scratch the itch.

She thought about Chee, pictured him happily working with the fancy movie people, too busy to call her. Then she remembered that she hadn't called Louisa back. She'd stop by there tomorrow and talk to the Lieutenant about all this. Without Chee around, the days seemed longer. The distraction of a visit to Louisa and her mentor would do her good.

She made the call when she got home and Louisa picked up right away. "I told Joe you were coming, and he nodded. I know he'd like to see you, too," Louisa said.

"I've neglected you guys."

"I thought you were going on vacation. Monument Valley, wasn't it?"

"That's right." Bernie explained about Mama needing extra help, without going into detail. And about Chee's temporary assignment.

"Can you stay for lunch tomorrow? Company would be nice."

Bernie heard the loneliness in Louisa's voice and realized that she was lonely, too.

"If you need to do errands or something, I'm

happy to sit with the Lieutenant. I want to get his opinion on a situation at work."

She heard Louisa fumble for words. "You know, I haven't been out of the house except to take Joe to therapy or to make a quick trip to the grocery while he waits in the car. I might take you up on that offer. We'll see. Drive safely."

When Bernie hung up, she put Mama's stew in the refrigerator and wrote herself a note to take it with her in the morning. Then she found one of Chee's T-shirts to use as a nightgown and went to bed, listening to the rush of the San Juan River in the darkness until she fell asleep.

Louisa hugged Bernie at the door, invited her to sit on the couch next to the Lieutenant, and brought three cups of herbal tea. Bernie would have preferred coffee, especially in the morning. She took a sip out of politeness and noticed that the Lieutenant's remained untouched.

"Thanks for the stew and that little cactus," Louisa said. "What kind is it?"

"Some sort of barrel. I couldn't find it in my cactus book."

As they chatted, the Lieutenant seemed briefly curious about the conversation, then turned his attention to the view outside. This was the first time Bernie had seen the scar on his scalp, the place where the bullet had entered. He looked better than when she'd last visited, but his stillness surprised her. She had never seen him not reading, making notes in his little book, typing at his ancient computer, or talking on the phone and pacing as he puzzled out a crime. Now he looked out the window at a hummingbird feeder that hung in the shade of the back porch. Just watching. Just sitting.

"Since the Lieutenant can't speak yet, how does he tell you what he wants?"

Louisa laughed. "I guess at it. He taps once for yes, twice for no. Sometimes he nods. He can write, but it's difficult for him, frustrating. I'm getting pretty good at reading his mind." Louisa put her hand on top of Leaphorn's. "We spend a lot of time here with those beautiful little birds. They remind me of jewels with wings."

"*Dahetihhe.*" Leaphorn turned toward Bernie when she said the word. "That's what we call them in Navajo."

After Bernie assured her that she was happy to keep Leaphorn company, Louisa drove off to get a haircut. In fact, Bernie welcomed the opportunity to have the Lieutenant all to herself.

Without Louisa there, Bernie could speak in Navajo, Diné Bizaad, and the Lieutenant seemed more attentive.

"You remember how you always helped Chee on his tough cases? Well, something happened at work that puzzles me. I am hoping you and I can come up with some new ideas. Or maybe you will just tell me I'm crazy to be obsessing about this."

He tapped his index finger once against the top of the table next to his recliner.

"Does that mean yes, I am crazy?"

He tapped twice.

Bernie smiled. "Well, you might be wrong about that. Especially when you hear what happened."

She told him about the traffic stop and the dirt. "The man offers me five hundred bucks and the rifle to give him a speeding ticket. Weird, huh?"

She looked toward Leaphorn. He was watching her.

"I arrested him because I knew he was guilty of something. But his car was clean: no drugs, no explosives, no hot credit cards. Not even any bootleg liquor. I don't understand it."

A cat—the cat she and Chee had fostered while Leaphorn was in the hospital—quietly jumped onto the Lieutenant's lap. Bernie took a sip of tea, wishing she had more sugar for it. The cat had curled into a ball, and the Lieutenant was stroking it.

She told him about the soil testing she'd ordered and about finding Miller's phone and her plan to follow up with the phone numbers. "Ever since I stopped that man, I've been wondering why he tried to bribe me if he had nothing to hide. I can't get it off my mind. I know he got away with something. But what? Does this make sense to you?"

He tapped three times.

"Three? What is that? Maybe?"

He tapped once.

"I'll have to tell Louisa that."

He tapped once. How frustrating it must be for him to be unable to speak.

She watched one little bird drive another away from the feeder. "Maybe he planned to use that dirt for claim salting or something. Do you think that dirt is important? It's tickling my brain, you know, like an itch that won't go away."

Leaphorn put his fingers together and made a circular sign with his right hand. She knew he wanted to write something. She pulled her notebook and a pen out of her pack. She found a blank page and handed him the pen. Slowly he printed, painstakingly forming each letter. He handed her the paper: one of several Navajo words that meant "Be careful."

"Will you help me figure this out?"

This time the nod was strong, unmistakable.

When Louisa came back, she looked more relaxed. And she had an idea.

"I'm going to show Joe how to use my laptop computer. Since he can tap, I bet he could type." She turned to him. "Do you like the idea?"

He nodded and tapped once.

"What about his old computer? He was used to that."

Louisa laughed. "That dinosaur? It's ready for a computer museum. No wonder he found computers frustrating." Leaphorn's old desktop machine had been hauled down to the office in Window Rock during the investigation into his shooting. Afterward the technician had returned it to Leaphorn's office, but he didn't get down on the floor to hook up all the wires again.

Louisa placed a plate of cookies on the table, crisp pink wafers with a sweet white filling of pure sugar, and went to get the laptop. Chee loved these cookies, and Louisa must have assumed Bernie did too. She ate one just to be polite. Leaphorn had eaten two and was munching on a third when Louisa came back with the computer.

"Could you set up Joe's e-mail before you go?"

"Do you have an Internet connection?"

"Yes, I got it for my work, to stay in touch with the university. I'm glad we have it."

Bernie quickly created the e-mail account, adding her e-mail, Chee's, and Captain Largo's in Leaphorn's address book.

10

Chee called Turner's cell phone before he left the station, and a man answered.

Yes, he was Turner. Yes, he'd worked on location scouting. Sure, they could meet, but not tonight. He'd see Chee at the movie site in the morning.

By the time Chee returned to Paul's compound, his cousin had assembled an assortment of tools, including some actually designed for working on cars, and spread them out on a towel. A couple of friends had arrived, ostensibly to help. One of them had brought a welding torch. Someone had jacked up the People Mover on one side and spread out a blue tarp against the sand beneath the vehicle, covering the places where the oil had dripped out. The assembled group waited, drinking sodas from the can.

Chee changed clothes, then handed Paul his phone before maneuvering beneath the old vehicle.

"If Bernie calls, let me know, OK?"

"Sure. If it's the bill collector, I'll tell him to talk to Bernie instead."

"Just say the check's in the mail."

"No worries, man. You want some music while you work?" Paul didn't wait for a response. In a few seconds, Chee heard a Navajo rock band. Nice!

Removing the old part took longer than it should have. After half an hour of lying on his back beneath the vehicle, struggling with bolts that hadn't been loosened since they'd been installed decades ago, he was glad when Paul squatted down to talk to him.

"You need a break, bro? Wanna soda?"

"I'm almost done." Chee removed the final bolt, eased the oil pan onto the sand, and scooted out from under the vehicle. Paul's buddies carried the pan to the welding area. Chee stood, stretched, rubbed sand on his hands to strip off the worst of the grime, and then walked to the ramada, where the man with the torch and solder went to work on the hole. Because of the desert's dryness, the metal looked good otherwise. No rust.

Replacing the oil pan was harder, and Chee's neck and shoulders ached when he finally finished.

"I appreciate it, man," Paul said. "I could never have done what you did." He patted his ample belly. "Even climbing down under there would have been tough for me."

They added oil, and Paul started the engine, with Chee in the passenger seat. The friends left, and the two of them drove the half mile to the park road with no problems.

At the junction, Paul stopped. "How far is it from here to the place where you found the lost woman?"

Chee told him.

"Let's go. I'd like to see that view she was so crazy about."

Chee offered directions. They parked on the road, climbed the ridge—studiously avoiding the grave or any mention of it—and sat in the warm sand, watching as the moon began to rise over the monuments. The still air smelled of dust. They heard coyotes singing in the distance.

"Young ones," Paul said. "I like their music better now that we aren't running sheep. I'm glad we came here, man. I was restless, you know, nervous about the tour tomorrow. I feel better now."

Chee looked at the hint of stars appearing in the growing darkness and shifted to rest his back against a rock, adjusting until he found a smooth place, enjoying the evening. The raucous young coyotes reminded him of the two teenagers he'd met last night. Why were girls that age so infatuated with celebrities? He heard Paul begin to snore and nudged him with his foot. "Let's head back. I want to get everything set for the breakfast so we can move quickly tomorrow."

"I got the bologna and the bread."

"I stopped at the store and bought what I need for burritos."

"Fried bologna is good for breakfast," Paul said.

As they hiked back toward the vehicle, Chee thought about the grave. Even though he didn't like the idea, since he was this close, he should take another look. Wouldn't it be wonderful if his call to Turner had had an effect, and the company had done the right thing and removed the grave?

"I need to look at something for work."

"I figured. I'll meet you at the People Mover."

Unfortunately, the ring of rocks and the mound of dirt inside were still there. Chee lectured himself about it. There was no good reason a fake grave should spook him. He took a breath, and thought about how beautiful the evening was, how fortunate he was to be in this special place.

Then he saw what looked like a bone protruding from the red earth. Pushing back the impulse to walk away, he squatted down, pulled out his phone, turned on the flash, and took some pictures. He was careful not to touch it. Even so, an uneasy feeling spread from the top of his head to the soles of his feet.

Chee rose early to make breakfast for the group, cooking the onions, scrambling eggs with them, adding bologna and then cheese to the mix, and rolling it in warm flour tortillas for the expected customers. After the Norwegians' problems with spice, he was tempted to leave out the chile to make the assembly quicker. But he'd worked with some Texans and remembered that they liked things hot.

Paul set up the coffee in his big black campfire pot and assembled cups, napkins, and some oranges. He loaded an eight-gallon thermos of water onto the People Mover.

The sky had lightened when Chee started his truck to follow Paul. He drove with the windows open, enjoying the cool air. From somewhere amid the monuments, he heard the raspy cry of a raven.

Paul made it to the Inn to pick up his customers

without trouble, and Chee headed in to the police station. Today he'd talk to Turner and wrap up the grave problem. Maybe the bone he'd seen came from a chicken or something, another movie prop. Nothing to fret over. Bahe would rejoice at his competence and let him go home to Bernie a few days early.

He strolled into the office with a spring in his step.

Bahe had left a faxed copy of the contract between the movie company and the Navajo Nation. The contract clearly specified places that could be used for filming, and the area where the grave had been discovered was nowhere on the list. The company had agreed to restore each site where they worked to its original condition or better.

Along with the contract was a note Bahe had scrawled in red pen. "Prove they did it. Settle this today. Tsinnie's contacts all say the grave came with the zombies."

Guilty until proven innocent, Chee thought. He typed a note about the bone fragment and sent Bahe the photos. He wrote his report about yesterday's contacts with the hotel security people, including the towels and necklace at Goulding's. Then he picked up the copy of the contract and the citation Bahe had drafted and headed out to find Turner.

The film base camp buzzed with activity. Chee wondered why they bothered with the tent for the dining area. Sanitation rules or something? He would have rather seen the view. And it was hot inside, even early, despite the fans and the portable air conditioners the movie company had hauled in, all of it running by generator. However, the tent made an excellent container for the wonderful aromas of grilled bacon and plump sausages, pancakes with warm, sweet syrup, and the sweet fragrances of the bakery section. The plates of food the staff members enjoyed looked delicious. These people always seemed to be eating.

There were as many staff here now as when he had stopped by last night. A few people in zombie makeup and costumes chatted with normal-looking folks in shorts and sleeveless shirts over plates of omelets, bagels with cream cheese, whatever. The crowd was mostly young and white, with some Navajos and Hispanic-looking people among the crowd. Samuel was sitting by himself.

Chee unsuccessfully surveyed the room for a fellow searching for him. He thought it odd that most of the cast ignored his presence, a rare experience for a cop in a room of civilians. Even a Navajo cop, an extra-rare species, couldn't compete with zombies.

Seeing a couple of men about his age in boots and jeans eating eagerly, he walked toward them. The cinnamon rolls they had looked good.

Chee introduced himself. "I need to find a Mr. Turner. Is he in here?"

"Never heard of him, but that guy might know," said one of the men, gesturing to the left toward a man with a clipboard. "He's one of the big shots."

The man scooted his chair back from the table and rose as Chee approached. "I'm looking for Mr. Turner."

"Michelangelo Turner at your service. Call me

Mike. You must be Officer Chee? What can I do for you, Officer?" Turner looked to be in his late fifties. He was well-built, an inch taller than Chee.

"I'm investigating a grave we discovered out by Rabbit Ridge. I need to see scouting pictures to determine if it was there when the movie company arrived. Mr. Robinson said you would have them." After he took a look, Chee thought, he would present the citation and be on his way.

"I never heard of Rabbit Ridge," Turner said. "I have no photos to give you. I could have told you that on the phone. I'm sorry you wasted a trip."

"You're sure?"

"Of course I'm sure. Hard to miss a grave here in the naked desert, don't you think?" Turner turned, ready to walk away.

Chee had seen this attitude before. "Sit down." He didn't like dealing with jerks. Turner frowned and sat, and Chee took the chair across from him. The man's height was all in his legs. Sitting gave Chee an edge.

"I agree. It would be hard to miss a grave, and the people who live out here never noticed it until the zombie crews arrived. I'd like to learn that what some people think is a grave is actually just a misunderstanding. That's where you come in."

Turner scowled. "I don't know anything about this. What do you want from me, man? We're behind schedule, over budget. I don't have time for this stuff."

"Someone takes pictures as part of the site scouting. If you have a photo that shows the grave was there when you guys first came, no problem.

Easier for us is better for you. Otherwise, things get complicated, people start talking homicide investigation."

Turner made a sound, a sort of a snort. "My assistant and I took photos all over the place. I didn't see a grave. We stayed in the Jeep, didn't do much walking around. It was March, freezing cold. And now it's hotter than Hades."

Chee heard the frustration but said nothing.

"Look, if there's any problem with permits or stuff like that, Delahart is the man to talk to. He's where the buck stops. Not with me or even Robinson." Turner stood.

Chee stood, too. He remembered what he'd learned about dealing calmly with difficult people. "My boss wants me to get this settled. If you don't have the photos, then I guess you and I need to drive out there together so you can see what I'm talking about. That might refresh your memory. The drive, and hiking to the gravesite, driving back, that's at least an hour." Chee looked down, then raised his gaze. "Longer, probably, because you'll have a hard time getting traction in those shoes, and the heat will slow you down."

Chee knew that Turner wanted to argue, so he kept talking. "That is, unless you don't want to cooperate with this friendly investigation. In that case, you'll probably need to go to Phoenix, or maybe it's Salt Lake, to explain to the federal court why the Navajo Nation is wrong to view what we've found as an illegal burial and fine your company for desecrating sovereign land."

Now he had Turner's attention.

"But if you could remember where the scouting photos are, and I can take a look at them and see that the grave was there and had nothing to do with your operation, that would save us both a long, hot afternoon hike or a lot of complicated paperwork. And you won't have to change your shoes."

"Give me fifteen, twenty minutes. Wait here, and I'll have a girl bring them over."

"A girl?"

"My assistant. Claudia. An intern."

Chee nodded.

"Fifteen minutes."

He watched the crowd. Why the eternal fascination with zombies, werewolves, vampires, ghosts, mummies, aliens from other planets, giant mutant creatures of all sorts? He'd take a good action movie any day, especially with a car chase that involved aerials and explosions.

Melissa interrupted his daydreaming. "Hey there. Are you now the official zombie officer?"

"Looks that way." Chee explained his errand.

"Want to join me for something to eat while you wait? I'm starved."

"Coffee would be good."

He followed Melissa through the food line. The aromas made him hungry, but he hoped to leave as soon as he got the pictures. He selected Guatemalan Atitlán from the fancy push-button coffee machine because Melissa recommended it. Next time, he'd try a double *café noisette*—whatever that might be— because the name made him smile.

Melissa set her tray with a boiled egg and a single piece of toast on a table close to the buffet line, and

Chee settled in across from her. "I'm glad I ran into you. What can you tell me about Turner and Mr. Delahart?"

"Delahart? Don't tell me—he's in trouble?"

"Not that I know of. I keep hearing his name."

"Delahart's the big boss, the producer, the man who authorizes the checks. He doesn't associate with us underlings except to give us grief about spending too much money."

"I thought Robinson ran things."

"Well, Delahart is the big boss, but Greg—uh, Mr. Robinson—does the work. He's an associate producer, and does a good job of running interference for us with Delahart. Turner works under Robinson."

She was almost pretty when she smiled, Chee thought. The turquoise in her earrings was close to the color of her eyes. "I might need to talk to Delahart about the grave. Is he here?"

She shook her head. "He's too important to be with us peons."

"Seems like he'd want to see what's going on, if he's paying the bills."

"Actually, I pay the bills. He signs off on them, but I don't think he even read the reports or looked at the statements until recently. He'd rather dabble in PR, mostly posting stuff about Rhonda's new hairstyle or what she had for breakfast. Social media trivia for the trivially minded." She made a dismissive cluck and shook her head. "Delahart won't tell you anything about the grave. He probably couldn't even tell you what state we're in. He likes that air-conditioned room at the Inn better than the glory of Monument Valley. That makes him weird, in my book."

Chee took another sip of the Guatemalan coffee, savoring it. It was delicious, possibly even better than the coffee Bernie made.

"I don't see how you can drink coffee on such a hot day." She jiggled the ice cubes in her cup.

Chee asked the question Tsinnie had prompted. "How did you find that spot on Rabbit Ridge? It was perfect for the moon between those monuments."

"It wasn't really me being smart. Or even good luck. Mike suggested it."

"Mike?"

"Turner. I thought you'd met him."

"Oh, yeah. I talked to him. Did he tell you how to find it?"

"Drew me a map. I tried to get him to go with me. He's worried about the production schedule, and all that wind last week really slowed us down. Expenses have climbed, and some sponsorships I thought we'd land haven't come in yet."

A young woman in black jeans walked to their table. "Are you Officer Chee? Mr. Turner told me to give this to you." She handed him a flash drive and a business card. "He said to tell you if you have any more questions, please contact Mr. Delahart. That's his card."

"Did he really say please?"

The young woman looked surprised. "No, sir. That sounded better than what he said."

"Thanks. I appreciate it."

He'd expected printed photographs he could thumb through quickly, not another session back in the office at a computer. He put the device in his pocket, said good-bye to Melissa, and walked out into the heat.

It would be hours before the June warmth reached its peak, and much longer before the day cooled off. The sun made the handle on his unit's door so hot he could barely open it. He slid gingerly across the too-warm seat, turned on the ignition and the air-con. Gerald waved as he drove away.

Back at the station, Chee plugged the portable drive into a computer and waited as a long thread of images appeared on the screen, reminding him that sometimes computers and their kin, an inescapable part of modern law enforcement, actually made his job easier. He enlarged them and sorted out a subset that showed the landscape near the gravesite, finding scouting shots similar to the view Melissa had photographed from the ridge but nothing that looked remotely like a grave. Great, he thought. The grave had not existed when the movie company came to scout, and now it did. Case almost closed.

He called Delahart's cell number again, with another diversion to voice mail. Then he called the Inn and asked for Delahart's room. The person who answered spoke with what sounded to Chee like an East Coast accent. "Delahart here."

Chee introduced himself. "I need to talk to you about an investigation that concerns the movie production."

"Talk to Robinson, the honcho out there. I'll give you the number."

"I've already spoken to him, and to Mr. Turner. They told me you were the only one who could provide the information I need. This involves publicity."

Chee heard a round of coughing on the other end of the phone. Then Delahart spoke. "I'm in a meeting now, and even if I could squeeze you in, I make it a point never to talk to cops. But you made me curious. What's the problem?"

"An illegal gravesite on Navajo Nation land."

Delahart coughed again. "No kidding? Whoa. Call in the Mounties."

Chee didn't let his irritation show. "I'm finishing up something here, then I'm on my way to the Inn. I'll see you around two."

"You think I know something about a grave? What grave? You're nuts, man."

"We can talk there at the hotel, or you can meet me here at the police station. Your choice."

"OK, fine. We'll talk here. Whatever. Your time to waste." He gave Chee the room number.

Chee did a quick background search on Delahart, finding business addresses for him in Hollywood and Las Vegas, lists of movies the man had been involved in producing, the story of two messy divorces completed with the help of high-profile celebrity lawyers, records of political contributions in California races, and a couple of lawsuits, settled out of court, in which stars claimed Delahart had spread lies about them.

Chee still had half an hour before the meeting, so he went to Goulding's. The maid, Mary Toledo, the woman who had found the towels and the necklace, ought to be at work now. As he drove, a feeling of relief and something else, something like happiness, settled over Jim Chee. He wasn't exactly sure what he'd expected from the photos, but whatever he'd expected, it wasn't this—a chance to wrap up the grave case and, if Bahe was willing, head home to Bernie earlier than anticipated.

Mary Toledo seemed only slightly surprised to see a policeman. After introductions, Chee asked her to sit down, explaining that he was on loan to the Monument Valley department from the Shiprock substation. He told her she wasn't in trouble, but he had a few questions for her.

"I know your clan brother who lives out here. They say he's starting up a business," Mary said.

"That's right."

"He's a good man." She looked at the floor. "I believe you came to talk to me about what I saw in that room, but I don't like remembering it. Something bad happened there."

"Mr. Haskie told me the story of what you found. I was wondering if you noticed anything else that might be important, anything besides the towels and the problem with the carpet and the chain with the turquoise pendant. Anything odd."

She examined her fingernails. Chee understood her reticence. "They say you do your job here well," he said. "Did you have an opportunity to straighten things up, throw anything away, before you called Mr. Haskie? You know, try to clean up a bit so he wouldn't see such a mess?"

"I didn't clean it until later, after he looked around. I didn't feel right in there."

"I found out that the man who rented that room used a fake name."

Mary rested her back against the wall. "From the way the bedcovers were, two people slept there. I found long hair in the drain in the tub when I cleaned it, and lipstick on the plastic glass in the bathroom wastebasket. I think they were elderlies."

He thought about the best way to ask the next question. "Did you find anything else in that room? Maybe something little that didn't amount to much. After the shock of seeing those towels, it would be easy to forget about that. But when time passes, sometimes other memories come back."

He waited.

Mary squeezed her lips into a thin line and stared at the ceiling for a moment. "I found two empty soda cans in the garbage. I hadn't seen that kind before. Special Dr Pepper. Caffeine-free. I took those because otherwise they get thrown away. I save them until there's enough to sell at recycling.

"And those people gave me a tip, a five-dollar bill."

If whatever happened in that room was evil, Chee thought, how odd that the criminal would leave money for the maid.

When she got to the station, Bernie found two messages.

The first was in Captain Largo's precise handwriting: "Rotary of Farmington wants a speaker tomorrow from the Navajo Police about what we do. I booked it but now have a meeting all day in WR. Pls. handle this." The note included the name of the person to contact and a phone number.

WR meant Window Rock, and Bernie knew that saying no was not an option here. Public speaking turned her stomach inside out. Even the idea of it made her grumpy. At least he'd said please.

The second, a note from Sandra, read "Call Cordova." She handled that first.

After some pleasantries, the FBI man got to the point. "I understand you found Miller's phone in the back of your unit."

"A phone, anyway, that wasn't in the car before he

got there. And when I picked it up, his picture came up. So I'm betting it's his."

"Do you have it handy?'

"It's locked in my desk drawer. Want me to get it?"

"Right. You know how when a phone comes to life sometimes, a message screen shows missed calls, voice mails, new texts, stuff like that?"

"I know."

"Does anything like that flash up on Miller's phone?"

"Before I check, tell me why you're interested in him."

Cordova hesitated. "Because he's a person we're interested in. Your turn."

Bernie took out the phone and pushed a button to turn it on. "Will Miller be brought in for more questions about the bribe he offered me?"

"The Phoenix office is working on that."

She took that as either a *none of your business* or more probably a *no*. "Did someone tell him I found his phone?"

"It's hard to reach him when his phone is in your unit. Guess we'll have to write him a letter." He paused a moment. "You know, if I found the phone of some guy I'd arrested in my car, and I was curious about what he'd been up to, I might look at the screen and see recent calls, texts sent and received, frequent contacts, what he has photos of."

"If I had done that, I would have noticed a bunch of calls to what looks like Farmington, but might be Gallup. No texts."

"OK. Send that info to me."

A pause, and then she said, "Nothing labeled

Drug Supplier or Human Trafficking or Evil Companions. I could help you better if you'd give me a clue as to what you're looking for."

"Are you taking care of yourself, Manuelito? You sound out of sorts. Is the heat getting to you?"

"I'm fine. I don't like being kept in the dark. I am really annoyed that some jerk who tried to bribe me could get off without even a slap on the hand." And the Rotary assignment hadn't improved her mood.

"Hey, chill. Miller has been a bad boy in more ways than you think, and he's on the radar. You did good to stop him. Keep at it, and you'll be my hero. Lighten up."

After Cordova disconnected, she explored the phone in more detail, scrolling a few screens deep to find Miller's contact list. A private residence in Gallup was listed under Frequent Contacts, with the name "Roberta." A girlfriend? She found numbers in Las Vegas and Utah in the frequent category, along with another New Mexico listing, an upscale motel in Farmington.

She looked at Miller's photos again, wondering if she'd missed a drilling rig or a tailings pile in the background, something that would support her asking for the dirt to be analyzed. She didn't find anything helpful, but enjoyed his shots of Ship Rock, the beautiful Tsé Bit' a' í—the Rock with Wings. Cordova found it odd that Miller said he liked the place, she remembered, but it made perfect sense to her.

When she was done, she filled out the paperwork and put the phone in the evidence room.

She called about the soil sample and learned it wasn't ready yet. Then, with no other distractions available, she contacted the Rotary club. The woman there confirmed that the meeting Largo had assigned Bernie was tomorrow, told her how long they wanted her to speak, and where to show up. "I'm so glad he's sending a female officer," she said.

Bernie got up, stretched, and went to the break room for water. Sandra buzzed her just as she was getting ready to make some notes for the talk.

"Head out on US 64 toward the state line. Some tourist stopped at Teec Nos Pos and said he saw something that looked like a body along the side of the road, a few miles before he crossed into Arizona."

"A human body?"

"The caller thought so. Near the junction of BIA 5713."

"I'll take a look."

Bernie could tell even before she got close that the "body" wasn't a person but a bag of garbage that must have fallen from a truck on the way to the dump. Animals had explored this treasure trove, ripping through the plastic to get to the edibles and uncovering worn-out jeans and an old plaid shirt. Maybe at seventy miles per hour a person with a good imagination could picture a dead body there.

She pulled onto the shoulder and turned on the light bar. She put on gloves and moved the worst of the mess, obstacles that caused vehicles to swerve, off the highway. She looked for identifying information, an envelope with a name and address that might lead to the offender, but came up empty. She took care of the safety issue and radioed Sandra to tell the road crew that they had a cleanup job.

Driving on to the trading post for a cold Coke and to see what was new on this part of the rez besides littering, Bernie recognized the person at the gas pump. She'd encountered Mrs. Benally and her son, Jackson, when Mrs. Benally's car had been stolen from a grocery store parking lot and then returned. The woman was driving something different now, a burgundy Ford van circa 2000.

Bernie greeted her. "New wheels?"

"That's right." Mrs. Benally squeezed off the last drops of gasoline and replaced the nozzle. She patted the side of the van. "It runs all the time. I can get in lots of groceries, even my neighbors'. We could even haul some hay. Take a look."

Mrs. Benally slid open the side door, and Bernie peered inside. Spacious, indeed.

"This looks like a good vehicle." Bernie remembered Mrs. Benally's old sedan, a better car than the one Darleen was driving. "Someone might be interested in your other car. The green one."

"Oh, I gave my son that one. He will be moving in August to be closer to school."

"Wow. Jackson gets his own car. You must have had some lucky aces at Fire Rock or some good numbers in the lottery."

Mrs. Benally rummaged in her purse. Instead of a lottery ticket, she extracted a white card. She handed it to Bernie. "That's the man who gave me the money for the van."

"Why did he do that?"

"We made up a contract. I told him it was OK to put some of those mirrors that make electricity on my land. I call him Mr. Sunshine."

Bernie looked at the name. David Oster. Living up to his word. A bright spot in her day.

She was happily anticipating the end of her shift when Sandra called on the radio.

"Largo wants to talk to you. Said to tell you to reach him at home." Sandra gave Bernie the number, even though she knew it by heart.

"Do you know what he wants?"

"Nope. Things are quiet here."

Largo got to the point right away. "I'm wondering if we ought to invite the Lieutenant to join us for one of those breakfast sessions again. You were out there for a visit. What do you think?"

The question surprised Bernie. "Well, he can't speak yet, but he looks stronger. Seeing his old crew might help him get better. I'm sure Louisa wouldn't mind bringing him."

"I want you to come with him."

The warmth in her unit suddenly felt stifling. She hadn't been to the breakfast meetings, or the restaurant that hosted them, since the day the Lieutenant nearly died in her arms.

"You there, Manuelito?"

"Yes, sir. When do you want to do this?"

"It depends on how the Lieutenant is feeling, but I'm thinking of next Monday. That work for you?"

"Chee should go with him. He hasn't been to one of those meetings in a while."

Largo grew silent for a moment. She could practically hear him thinking.

"Have you heard from your husband lately?" he asked.

"Well, we talked yesterday." Bernie's brain raced. She seldom worried about what might happen to her, but the knowledge of what could happen to Chee followed her whenever he left on assignment. If something were wrong, Largo would have told her upfront, not wasted time with talk about meetings. But she had to ask. "Is he OK?"

"He's fine, but if I know Chee, he's probably grumbling. There's a new development in that grave he stumbled on. Bahe wanted him to stay out there until he's settled it and given out a citation." Largo chuckled. "Knowing Chee, that could be a while."

Bernie wondered why she had to hear this from her boss instead of her husband.

"Guess that's it," Largo said. "Say hey to the Lieutenant for me when you go out there again. If it seems right, invite him to join us next Monday."

"I will."

"Oh, one more thing. Your pal Miller came by and picked up his phone."

"How did he know we had it?"

"He told Sandra he remembered where he was when he saw it last."

After Largo signed off, Bernie sat in her unit, thinking about Chee, relieved that he was OK, sad that he wasn't coming home, annoyed that Largo had been his messenger. Why hadn't Chee given her the bad news himself? Too busy? Bad phone service? Logical answers, but they didn't ease her disappointment.

She called him, first his cell, where she left a message, and then at the Monument Valley substation. To her surprise, he answered.

"Hi there, beautiful. Nice to finally hear your voice."

"Yours, too. Largo told me there's a new development in the case and that you have to stay out there longer. What's happened?"

"I was going to call you when I got done here, but you beat me to it. I found a body."

"Are you talking about the grave you stumbled on?"

"No, this is different." And he told her what had happened, starting at the beginning.

12

Chee walked to the Inn looking forward to the conversation with Delahart, even though, based on first impressions, he expected the man to be a jerk. He anticipated a confrontation, lies, and denial in spite of the evidence. He'd ask the required questions, get the expected non-answers. Chee could explain the statutes the grave violated and the penalties the Navajo Nation would impose, and suggest, as Bahe had instructed, that if Delahart would make the grave disappear quickly, at least some of the legal complications might disappear, too.

So soon, maybe even by the end of the day tomorrow, the fake grave could be gone. Another page in the saga of bizarre and questionable adventures in the amazing real-life world of law enforcement.

He walked into the lobby, a simple, high-ceilinged room made elegant by the stunning views of the monuments and the way the design incorporated nature's panorama as part of the decor. He'd seen the buttes and mesas every day that week, but this angle gave him further appreciation for their massive beauty.

Then a mountain of suitcases and backpacks caught his attention. Was all this luggage on its way to the guest rooms, or on its way out with departing travelers? The group had recently arrived, he decided. A noisy flock of predominately gray-haired women accompanied by a few senior men loitered around the suitcases. Most of the elderlies had name tags on cords around their necks and wore shorts or khaki pants and hats.

He paused for a moment, observing the confusion at the front desk. The registration clerk stood alone behind the counter, dealing with a man in a plaid shirt and a straw hat. From their posture, Chee decided neither person was enjoying the encounter.

A broad, carpeted staircase with a wooden railing circled up from the lobby through the atrium to the upper-story guest rooms. Good, he thought, he could avoid the elevator. When he and Bernie were in Hawaii on their honeymoon, she'd teased him about climbing the stairs at that fancy hotel on the beach—twenty-seven flights—so they could see the view from the top floor. The only elevator he knew of in Shiprock was at the hospital, and the only way he would ride in that tight little box would be as a patient on a gurney. He'd take the stairs any day.

At the top, he continued down the carpeted hallway, looking for the room number Delahart had given him. He rapped on the door, announced himself, and waited. Thinking he heard something on the other side of the door, he knocked again and called, "Mr. Delahart, it's Officer Chee. Here for our appointment." There was no reply.

Chee went back to the lobby, found a house phone, and called the room number. No response. A silver-haired woman with big red earrings approached him. "Excuse me, sir. Are you a real policeman?"

"Yes, ma'am. I'm with Navajo Nation law enforcement."

"Oh. I heard they were making a thriller out here. I thought maybe you were an actor, you know, somebody famous."

"No, ma'am."

"You look handsome enough to be in the movies. Could I get a picture of us together?"

"OK, I guess." Handsome enough to be in a movie about zombies. He'd have to tell Bernie about this.

"Millie," she called across the room to a lady in loose jeans and a white blouse. "Come take a picture of me with a Navajo policeman."

Millie's camera was buried at the bottom of a purse that could have held Chee's entire wardrobe. After she extracted it, she took a few minutes to get it turned on, and a few more to take some shots with the flash and some without.

When that was done, Chee made his way to the hotel security office.

From their phone conversation, he'd expected security director Brenda Erdman to be older. She was in her late thirties, professional-looking in a red shirt with the hotel logo and "Security" embroidered beneath it. She sat behind a desk and motioned Chee to a single straight-backed chair in her office, but he stood, hoping to keep his visit short. He noticed her America's Favorite Desserts desk calendar as he explained the Delahart situation.

"I need you to let me into his room." Chee gave her the number. "We had an appointment. I talked to him half an hour ago, and he confirmed it."

"Where's Bahe? He usually handles calls at the hotel." She looked at Chee. "You need to give me a good reason to open a locked door for you."

"How about a safety check? The guy up there was expecting me but didn't answer the door. Something might have happened to him."

"Maybe he decided he didn't want to talk to the police. Is he a parole violator or something? Do you have an arrest warrant?"

"No."

"People have a right to privacy."

Chee thought about it. "I'm investigating a possible crime, and this guy is important to the case. I'm here on Bahe's orders."

"No. I can't do it. It's against hotel policy. Our guests have a right to let the phone ring and ignore a knock on the door. What if he's, uh, romantically involved, or dying his hair in the bathroom, or sleeping with earplugs? He will raise holy hell, and I'll be looking for a new job. I'm sure you know this without me explaining it. It has to be a matter of life and death."

Chee appreciated the hint. "I'm not kidding when I said something may have happened to him. He was coughing like crazy when I talked to him on the phone. He could barely speak."

She pursed her candy-apple-red lips.

"A dry cough is one of the signs of heart failure. Delahart couldn't even catch his breath."

"I'll call up there. What's the room number?"

Chee gave it to her.

She put the phone on speaker. Chee counted ten rings before she disconnected.

"That's a suite," she said. "Expensive. You gave me another reason not to create an angry customer."

"Or another reason to worry. What if he was your father up there, having a heart attack? Come on. I'm convinced this man is not safe, and you're the person in charge of security. Rich guys, corporate types, have families who care about them, too."

When she looked at him now, Chee sensed a change.

"You're working with me to do your job, Ms. Erdman, acting on important information. You're making sure nothing bad has happened up there."

"OK." She opened the bottom drawer of her desk and picked up a first aid kit, then led the way to a service elevator.

"Wouldn't the stairs be quicker?"

"No. I can give us an express ride."

She put a plastic key card in a slot and pushed a button. Chee heard the elevator groan and felt it begin to rise. He took a big breath, watched the numbers on the display change, told himself to relax.

"Last time Bahe talked me into this, he told me about how he'd saved a woman who'd tried to kill herself with pills at that new Navajo casino hotel near Flagstaff. Your heart attack story and mentioning my dad was better. Tell him that."

Chee caught a glimpse of the green gum she was chewing. The air around her smelled like peppermint.

"Did Bahe say what happened to the woman?"

"He did chest compressions until the EMTs arrived. He saved her life." She looked at Chee. "I grew up in Gallup. I have enough Diné friends so I know how hard it must have been for him to do that."

The elevator door opened, and Erdman headed down the broad hallway with quick, sure steps. Chee hurried out behind her, noticing the security camera.

"What's a suite like?" he asked. "More than one room?"

"A living room with a balcony and a separate bedroom. There's a guest powder room in the front and a bigger bathroom with a Jacuzzi tub off the bedroom. They're nice. Larger than my house."

"Sounds bigger than mine, too."

As they approached the suite, Chee noticed that now the door stood slightly ajar. He took a few quick steps and knocked on the doorframe.

"Navajo Police. Mr. Delahart, are you OK?"

When he received no response, he pushed the door open and announced himself again.

The first thing Chee noticed was a service cart carrying an ice bucket with an inverted wine bottle and dirty white plates stacked to one side. A split second later he felt hot air flowing toward him and realized that the sliding glass door was open to the balcony. Beyond the wrought-iron railing Merrick Butte stood against the brilliant summer sky.

"Mr. Delahart. It's Sergeant Jim Chee. Everything all right here?" He took a step into the room and noticed a brown shoe protruding from behind the couch, and then the leg attached to it. A few more steps, and he saw the body, facedown and motionless on the beige carpet with a crimson stain on the back of his shirt.

This was the part of police work he dreaded most.

He heard Erdman gasp. She moved to the body, squatted down, and put her hand on the man's thick neck. "No pulse. He's not breathing, but his skin is warm."

Chee heard a noise to the left and reached for his gun. A door began to move.

"Police!" He yelled the word. "Open the door slowly. Push your weapon out."

The door moved a few inches.

"I don't have a weapon." The man's voice sounded like it was coming from the floor. "For the love of God, why do you think I'm hiding in here? Some maniac—"

"Are you alone in there?"

"Yes." And then a cough.

"Mr. Delahart, come out slowly. Put your hands out where we can see them."

A bearded man staggered into the room. He was wearing shorts and a gray muscle shirt with King Kong on the front. He had blood on his hands. He stared at Chee and at the security guard. Then his gaze went to the floor behind them.

"Oh my God. He's dead, isn't he?"

"Did you shoot him?" Chee asked.

Delahart shook his head, and then sank down to the carpet. "I can't believe this."

Chee turned to Erdman. "Do you have your weapon?"

"Right here."

"Take him out into the hallway."

She nodded. "Come with me, sir."

"I didn't do anything."

Erdman reached for him, but Delahart squirmed away. "I gotta get, ah, my watch from the bedroom."

She grabbed his right forearm, and Chee gripped from the other side. He felt Delahart tense.

"Hey, who do you think you are?"

"A Navajo policeman in charge of a murder scene talking to a bloody guy I found with a dead man."

They steered Delahart out to the hall, where Chee released his grip. "Sit with your back against the wall."

Erdman reached for her walkie-talkie. "I'm putting the place on lockdown." Then she spoke into the radio.

Delahart stood next to the wall for a moment, and then attempted to lurch back toward the room. Erdman blocked him.

Chee frowned at the man. "Don't mess with her. She knows exactly what to do in situations like this."

He doubted that Erdman had ever been in a situation like this, but she squared her shoulders and spoke with a confidence he hadn't heard before. "Sit. Your watch can wait. I'll tell you what time it is— time to behave yourself."

Weapon in hand, Chee pushed the bathroom door open with the toe of his boot. He saw blood on the sink and more blood on the bright white floor tiles. No gun in any obvious place.

He walked through the living room, past the body, into the bedroom. No weapons, no sign of a struggle, nothing unusual. The bed was made, and built into the floor—no way to hide beneath it. The door to a second, larger bathroom stood open. He saw a fancy watch with a gold band and, next to it, a vial of white powder on the vanity. He left them there.

He quickly rescanned the living room and then walked onto the balcony. The outdoor furniture, two chairs and a round table, seemed undisturbed. He looked down at the sandy red earth two stories beneath him and noticed depressions, what could have been footprints. It wouldn't take a lot of athleticism for a person to jump from here, land unharmed, and run.

He called Bahe at the station and explained the situation.

"I'll be right over," Bahe said. "I'll contact the feds." Homicides on reservation land belonged to the FBI. "Get hotel security to keep people from going back there where the tracks are."

"Sure thing. Erdman's already put the place on lockdown."

"You know something, Chee?"

"What?"

"Life has grown more interesting in this quiet corner of Navajoland since you got here."

Chee came in off the balcony and took a final, slow look at the living room, forcing himself to study the area around the body. He left the murder scene and took a couple of deep breaths. Erdman and Delahart had moved from the hallway floor onto the big stuffed chairs near the elevator. The man had his head back, staring at the ceiling, a tissue pressed against his nose.

"There are tracks in the sand out there, down from this balcony. Can you make sure nobody disturbs them?"

"Sure," Erdman said. "What else?"

"Do the surveillance cameras up here work?"

She nodded. "We have them in the lobby and the restaurant, and at all entrances and exits too."

Delahart interrupted. "How long do I have to stay here?"

"Until the police are done with you," Chee said.

"I want a lawyer."

Chee gave him a cold look, then turned to Erdman. "Can you go downstairs and make sure the front desk staff and the room service guy who brought the cart are available for questions?"

"Of course. Anything else? Whatever I can do." There was energy in her voice, and her eyes were shining.

"Those tracks in the sand off the balcony. Make sure nobody goes behind the building."

"Will do. You told me that already. I'll have the tape for you in my office."

After she left, Chee moved the chair she'd been sitting in to give himself a clear view of both the hallway and Delahart. "Why did you shoot that man?"

"I didn't. You knew him. He told me he'd met you when I said you were coming to interview me."

"Who was he?"

"He was that big guy, Samuel, the rent-a-cop from the movie camp."

"What made you kill him?"

"That's crazy talk. I'm lucky I'm not dead myself and you treat me like a criminal."

"Then set me straight."

Delahart coughed. "Samuel got here right when my nosebleed started. I was in the little bathroom dealing with it when I heard him talking to somebody. I thought he was on the phone. But then I heard the gunshot."

He's had time to work on his story, Chee thought. "So you heard the shot and went out to see what happened?"

"Hell, no. I thought whoever shot the guard might be looking for me. I hunkered down in there until you two showed up."

In that time, Chee thought, Samuel had bled to death. If he'd done his job and come straight to the room instead of posing with those tourists, Samuel might be alive.

"So, if you didn't shoot him, who did?"

"I told you I couldn't see through the closed door. Do you think I'm Superman or something?"

"Were you expecting any visitors?"

"No. Yeah, you." Delahart removed the tissue from his nose.

"Did you recognize the other voice?"

Delahart shook his head. "Hard to hear well through the door."

"So let me replay this. A mysterious stranger comes to your hotel room and shoots your security guard while you're in the bathroom. Is that your story?" Delahart's nose was bleeding again.

"That's what happened."

"Do you usually have a bodyguard?"

"Samuel wasn't my bodyguard." Delahart wiped his nose, reapplied pressure with the tissue. "He was doing some special assignments. He wanted to talk about that."

"You might as well tell me."

"One of the women in this movie is a hot ticket, so she gets extra security as part of her contract. Samuel would let me know if she was planning to go to Las Vegas for the weekend, had an argument with her boyfriend, changed the color of her toenail polish. I'd send out some tweets: the Zombie Queen sleeps late. Stuff like that."

Chee shifted in the chair. "Was she OK with someone spying on her?"

Delahart coughed and moved the tissue back to his face. "Guess I forgot to ask her. The price of fame."

"Did Samuel want more money?"

"He was whining about an ex-wife breathing down his neck for more child support. I told him he could quit working for me if he wasn't happy with the arrangement. His ex wasn't my problem; I've got two of my own to contend with."

"Did he punch you? Is that how you got the nosebleed? Maybe you shot him in self-defense."

"How many times do I have to say I didn't shoot that obnoxious son of a gun? The nose problem is the dry air in the desert."

Dry air and nose candy, Chee thought. He wondered if too much cocaine would cause a cough, too.

"Who is the star Samuel was spying on?"

"Rhonda Delay. Hey, maybe she offed him. Zombie Queen claims a new victim."

Chee frowned. "You're lucky she didn't shoot you, too." Delahart seemed more like a petty criminal than a murderer. He might have hired someone to do the deed, but he didn't seem reckless enough to do it himself.

"Rhonda knows the way the game's played. If you're looking for a person who wanted Samuel dead, I'd start with his ex. From what I hear, he had a thing for young girls." Delahart looked at the blood on his hands. "Can I go to the room and wash up?"

"No."

"How long do I have to sit here?" A cough.

"Until my boss stops by to take you to the police station for safekeeping."

"You're joking, right? I've got a million things to do, man. I can't afford to sit around." Delahart made a move to rise. "I have to go get my phone, make some calls."

Chee put a hand firmly on Delahart's arm. "You better get used to waiting. If I had to guess what happens next, I'd say you'll be waiting in jail."

Everything about Delahart irritated Chee—the grating, high-pitched sound of his voice, his arrogantly unkempt look, the know-it-all attitude. But most of all, the lying.

"I came by hoping to talk to you about something that looks like a grave, remember?"

"Do you take me for a mortician? We're busy making a movie, man. We don't have time for a stunt like that. Like I told you before, I don't know anything about a grave."

Chee frowned. "So if you won't tell the truth about something as easy as that, I figure you must be lying about everything, including murder."

"You wanna know about the grave? What do I get in exchange?"

"Maybe I won't volunteer the information about what I saw in the vial next to your watch."

Delahart exhaled, made a sound as he cleared his throat. "The grave is a prop. Turner and I came up with the idea when he was scouting. I thought it would create a little buzz. Sorry it got your panties in a knot."

"Clever to add bones to make it more realistic. Animal remains or something?"

Delahart laughed. "That's a good one. I wish I'd thought of that. We ought to hire you to help with this promotion stuff."

And this time, Chee realized, Delahart was telling the truth.

When she got off the phone with Chee, Bernie returned Darleen's call. Her sister answered on the third ring.

"Howdy, sis. How's it goin'?'"

Darleen had been drinking. Bernie's heart sank.

"I got a buncha drawings done for that portfolio. When can you come over so I can show you? I'm celebrating now."

"You aren't driving tonight, are you?"

"Duh. That's why I called, so you can come over here. Mama and I are watching an old movie on TV. I forget the name, but it's funny. Here, she wants to talk to you."

Bernie could hear the phone being transferred.

"Eldest Daughter, how are you?"

"I'm fine, Mama. Did you and Darleen have dinner?"

"Yes. Pancakes. Everything is fine here."

"Except that Darleen has been drinking."

"We have an agreement now. She only drinks at home, and I have her car keys."

"I don't think that school in Santa Fe is a good idea." Bernie spoke without her usual caution.

"It is a good idea for her to have something to look forward to."

"Tell Sister I'm tired tonight. I will look at her drawings tomorrow when I come to see you."

Bernie was getting ready for bed when the phone rang. She checked the ID, and was relieved to learn that it wasn't work, or Darleen calling back to argue.

"Hi, Louisa."

"Hey there. I wanted to tell you that Joe is enjoying the laptop. We installed the Navajo language font."

"Great."

"He's doing research on hummingbirds. And he's looking up that cactus you gave me to see what kind it is."

Bernie thought of the necklace Chee had mentioned, and explained the situation to Louisa. "I'm going to e-mail the Lieutenant a photo. Maybe he can find out something about it. He has Chee's listing in his address book, so he can respond directly to him."

"Good idea. Joe is really taking to this computer. You know, his spirit has been up and down. The physical therapist says that he's frustrated, and it's all part of the brain injury. But he's got some of his old sparkle back."

Bernie couldn't imagine the Lieutenant having mood swings. She'd seen him satisfied, if not actually happy, when a case came to conclusion, and noticed brief, rare flashes of irritation, usually directed at Chee or the feds, but that was it. *Sparkle* was not a word she ever would have used to describe the Lieutenant. But she didn't know him the way Louisa did.

Bernie woke early, went for a run, took a shower, and ate a tortilla with some peanut butter. She put on her uniform for work and headed to Mama's.

Mama was sweeping the porch when Bernie drove up, using the broom for a bit of support.

"You're working hard this morning. Did you have your breakfast?"

"I made the coffee." Mama indicated the chair against the front of the house, next to her walker. "You sit here while I finish."

It was nearly nine. Bernie asked, "May I fix you something to eat?"

Mama shook her head. "Youngest Daughter set up oatmeal in that envelope. She leaves me a bowl, even the water in a cup." Mama swept the last of the dirt off the porch and moved carefully toward the walker. "She likes that beeping machine and those little packages."

The microwave oatmeal Darleen had purchased was full of sugar, not as healthy for Mama, and more expensive than the regular kind. "I'll tell her how to make the oatmeal you like."

"I already showed her." Mama laughed. "You explain how to make it in the *bee na'niildóhó*. That's the way she does it."

Bernie smiled at the Navajo word for microwave oven. It translated to "you warm things up with it."

Mama looked good this morning. Relieved, no

doubt, that what seemed to be a major problem for Darleen turned out to be less than that. Bernie would talk to her sister about the ramifications of her arrest, and learn what came next, if anything.

"How are you, my daughter? There's some trouble in your voice."

"Oh, a little problem at work."

"And with the one you married?"

"I miss him."

"He works hard, that one. He won't forget you. Can you stay here with us today?"

"No, I have to patrol this afternoon. I just came by for a quick visit and to take a look at Sister's new drawings."

"That's good. She's in the kitchen."

Darleen had opened a Mountain Dew, and sat at the table with two piles of papers in front of her. She wore silver hoop earrings that reached her chin and a knit shirt with a butterfly on it that, Bernie thought, would have fit better a size larger.

Bernie sat next to her. "Where are your drawings? I'm glad you did some."

Darleen sighed. "I looked at them this morning. They still need work." She put her elbows on the table. "And I don't know about all this. I never was good at school."

"You're smart, you just weren't motivated." Bernie glanced at the paperwork Darleen had assembled—an admission application, student housing requests, and forms for financial aid. "Did you call the school and find out about the deadlines and the GED?"

"I left a message. No one called me back." Darleen shoved a booklet toward her. "Look at this. They want to know all kinds of stuff. I don't get it."

Bernie opened the cover and thumbed through it. It was the application for financial aid, a universal form that many colleges used. Darleen had answered the questions requiring basic information but left most of it blank.

She could take over, Bernie thought, but she wasn't going to. She poured herself half a cup of coffee. "Want some?"

"No, thanks. I made it too strong this morning."

Bernie picked up the financial aid application again. "How much is tuition anyway?"

"I don't remember. It's here somewhere." Darleen started shuffling through the piles.

"When the person from the school calls you back, ask about that too."

"Are you going to help me?"

"When there's something I can do. For now, you can handle all this."

And if you can't, Bernie thought, you shouldn't be going away to school.

Darleen sighed. "You know, I just want to be an artist. This is really complicated."

"Life's complicated."

"Like you and that guy with the dirt?"

"Yeah," Bernie said. "Like you getting arrested. What's next with that?"

Darleen shrugged. "I got a ticket. Twenty-five dollars. Stoop Man is all mad at me and his sister for being drunk. He'll get over it."

Bernie said, "I don't like you getting drunk either. Neither does Mama."

"I'm OK. I just do it to celebrate or when I don't have anything better to do. Don't nag me anymore."

Bernie took Mama some coffee. The rug Mama loved, the rug she planned to sell, was on the couch, folded into a rectangle. Mama ran her hand over it as she focused on the TV. "When I feel this one, I think of those sheep we had then. We had a time with some of those *dibé yázh*, the little lambs."

"I remember that spring when it was so cold, and the lambs came early." Even though she had been small herself, Bernie had bottle-fed one of the newcomers. She could hear the rhythmic sound the lamb made as it sucked and see the way its tail wagged as it gulped the milk. It grew to have wool the color of chocolate and became one of her favorites. The brown in the rug's double diamonds came from its fleece.

As she drove into Shiprock, Bernie noticed the building clouds, potential thunderheads that held the flirtatious promise of rain. Had it rained somewhere on the sprawling Navajo Nation? She hoped so.

She arrived at the police station a little earlier than she had to for her shift, and ran into Bigman finishing his reports.

Bernie greeted him. "A couple of days ago, you said you wanted to ask me a favor?"

"Oh, that's right. It's for my wife. She's interested in weaving. She asked me to see if I could find somebody who might be willing to teach her. She'd like to start soon, while she's still off from school."

A couple of years ago Bigman had married a *bilagaana* who taught at Shiprock's elementary school.

Bernie didn't know her very well, but she liked the woman.

"Learning to weave takes a while. She won't be able to pick up a whole lot before she has to go back to work."

"She wants to keep at it, evenings and on the weekends, depending on how much she has to do for her classes."

"Does she know anything about weaving?"

"She knows how to get to the auction at Crownpoint."

Bernie laughed. The auction, held each month at the Crownpoint Elementary School, drew weavers from across the reservation and plenty of buyers, too. "I'll see who I can come up with." She wondered if Mama, probably the teacher Bigman and his wife had in mind, would be willing.

Her afternoon's most interesting assignment involved two males with fake IDs, apparently underage, turned away from Falling Water Casino. They remained loitering in the parking lot, drawing the attention of a security guard who thought they might be working up the gumption to break into vehicles. The boys disappeared before Bernie could find them, vanishing at the first glimpse of her police car. The guard knew one of them because his teenage grandson had played basketball with the boy, and he agreed to have a word with that boy's mother. The whole thing took longer than Bernie expected.

Next she talked with a man accused by a neighbor of siphoning gasoline. The gas thief explained that he was merely borrowing the gas. He had gone over to ask his neighbor if he could have some, but the neighbor didn't come to the door, so he helped himself. He meant to explain the situation, but he got busy. Bernie took him to the complainant's house, where he apologized and promised to buy more gas than he stole as soon as he got his check. Apology accepted, case closed.

The day dragged on. She checked with the soil analysis lab and got good news; results should be available by the end of the day. She'd talk to Cordova when she found out what was in the dirt, tell him about the frequent calls to Las Vegas and Utah she'd seen on Miller's phone. Maybe she could parlay the new information into an explanation of why Miller warranted federal attention.

The promising clouds vanished, pushed away by a hot, dry wind that unrelentingly blasted the landscape, stirring tiny bits of sand into dust devils. Bernie remembered walking on the dirt road near her house as a girl, the airborne dirt stinging her arms and legs. In high school, waiting for her events in track, she dreaded feeling the wind-blown sand buffet her skin, and she would shut her eyes and turn her back to the gusts.

She watched the swirling spirals move from the earth into the sky, as much a part of summer as rodeos and roadside flea markets. Diné tradition taught that, like everything in nature, the wind had its purpose—scouring the earth clean. Nonetheless, it made her feel edgy.

She heard the radio call for her.

"Largo wants you to head over to check out a burned car." Sandra gave her the route number and directions to a house closest to the car. "Somebody who was driving out there called it in."

"OK." Bernie knew the area—a good place for mischief, complete with old stories of evil ones.

She soon saw and smelled the smoldering car, or what was left of it. She drove her unit off the road and parked. The cases of burned vehicles she knew about on the reservation had all been tied to revenge, and a few had involved grisly murders. She hadn't been the responding officer on those calls. Once, as a rookie, she had been on duty at a house fire. The family survived, but she never forgot the stench and sight of the dog that had burned in the blaze chained to the back wall.

As she walked closer, she realized the vehicle looked like the car she'd pulled over, the one with the boxes of dirt in the trunk. Even in its blackened condition, she was almost certain that she recognized it. She remembered Miller at the wheel, sweaty and uneasy, and hoped she would not encounter what was left of him now. Bernie's aversion to associating with the dead had begun in childhood, learned from the example of her relatives and from the stories she'd heard as a little girl. The spirits of the dead, *chindis*, roamed restless and out-of-sorts. She tried not to imagine what she might find inside the car, but she had paid too much attention during training to return to naïveté. The thought of the body and the stink of the smoldering car made her queasy.

Reminding herself that she was a Navajo police officer, she stood straighter as she walked to the driver's door. She forced herself to look through the broken window at the blackened remains of the seats. Empty seats. No burned body. She exhaled and stepped away. She took a few deep breaths, then walked back to the vehicle and found the VIN near the windshield, above the melted dashboard. She went to her unit to radio in the ID number, along with the good news that no one remained inside, then realized this place was a communication dead zone. No radio meant no cell phone service either.

Bernie surveyed the scene around the car: empty beer cans, broken glass, shredded plastic, and the usual accumulation of windblown trash. No obvious clues. When she'd seen enough, she drove to the closest house, a tiny home with a porch added on, covered to provide some shade. Whoever lived here might have seen the car burn.

An elderly man in a cream-colored cowboy hat sat on a wooden bench outside the house. A small flock of sheep watched from the corral as Bernie got out of her car, taking a couple of bottles of water with her.

On a calm day, the view of Ship Rock from this spot would be spectacular; today, the Rock with Wings rose against an ugly brown haze. The man was sheltered from the wind, but Bernie struggled to keep her hair out of her eyes as she walked toward him. She introduced herself, and the man, Mr. Tso, reciprocated, inviting her to sit down in a chair next to him. She offered him one of the bottles of water. He accepted and placed it on the porch beneath the bench.

Mr. Tso looked out toward the horizon. "You are the daughter of the one who weaves in Toadlena."

"That's right, sir."

"My sister, she knows your mother. Your mother helped her string the loom for one of the big rugs." Mr. Tso described his sister's weaving in detail.

They sat, watching a raven plane down, struggling against the wind to examine something on the side of the road, then soar again. After a while Bernie said, "Someone called about that burned car. That's why I am here."

"That's what I thought. My daughter made the call. I have coffee from breakfast, it could still be warm. Would you like some?"

It would be rude to refuse, even though the heat of the day made coffee less appealing.

"Do you want sugar in it? I like mine sweet."

"No, sir. Just the coffee would be fine. No sugar for me."

He hobbled in, leaving her to enjoy the view of Ship Rock. Even in the harsh afternoon light, Tsé Bit' a' í held majesty. Bernie knew the story of the winged monsters who once lived on Ship Rock and how the Hero Twins killed them but spared their children, transforming them into eagle and owl.

When Mr. Tso came back with the coffee, Bernie noticed that he used a rope to hold up his pants. He handed her a blue enamel cup that reminded her of the ones she'd seen at Paul's house. She tried a sip. It tasted worse than she'd imagined; stale, sharply acidic, and about the same temperature as the day. To make it worse, he had added so much sugar that it could have been coffee syrup.

She listened to Mr. Tso's stories about serving in the marines in Korea. He made her laugh, but she knew he must have darker memories of that time, things left unspoken. He finished his coffee and the story at the same time. "My grandson was going to sign up for the marines, too, after high school, but then he never did. He says he's looking for a job, but he's not looking in the right places."

"Speaking of jobs, I need to ask you questions about the car that burned. It could happen that whoever did this will do it again. People will suffer."

Mr. Tso frowned. "It's dangerous to talk about these things. I am an old man, but you, you need to stay safe to help your mother."

"My job is to help keep other people stay safe, too. People like you, my mother, and your daughter and your grandson." She paused to give him time to consider what she'd said. "Did you see the fire?"

He leaned back, resting his thin shoulders against the wall. With some difficulty, he twisted the lid to open the bottle of water that Bernie brought. "Yesterday afternoon, I had a pain in my hip, so I was resting in bed when I smelled something." He took a sip. Screwed the cap back on. "I opened my eyes and still smelled something strange. Then I came out here to the porch and that's when I saw the flames over that way."

He moved his chin toward the site of the burned car. "After a long time, the flames got so low I didn't see them, just the glow and the smoke. My daughter saw that car when she came for me so we could go to Gallup to the clinic. When we got to town, we went out to eat at a big restaurant, you know, one of those places where you get your own food? They have Jell-O with those little marshmallows. Red Jell-O is the best."

Mr. Tso stopped talking.

Bernie turned the conversation back to the car. "Did you see any people out there? Anyone driving by or driving away?"

"Not people. Only the thing we don't talk about."

The area had a reputation for skinwalkers, shape-shifters who could outrun a car, who changed from human to animal and back again. Evil creatures. She shared the Lieutenant's view on this, more skeptical than Chee when it came to supernatural malevolence. But she did not doubt that evil existed and that some of it defied ordinary explanation. Traditionals like Mr. Tso believed that to talk about shape-shifters invited their attention, gave them power to trouble you.

Bernie sat with Mr. Tso for a while, watching the light change on the Rock with Wings. The gray volcanic core looked massive, sharp-edged, beautiful.

"Tell the police that car should stay there," Mr. Tso said. "It can remind people to keep away from that place."

In the background, Bernie heard the sheep bleating in their pen. She remembered spending summers traveling with her mother's flock to the greener pastures in the mountains, enjoying the outdoors, the freedom, and even the work.

"Your mother might like that restaurant my daughter knows about. The Big Corral, or some name like that. You should take her there next time you go to Gallup." He finished the bottle of water and put it down beside him. "I would like you to come back to see me. But we will not talk about that fire."

She walked to her unit, feeling the push of the hot wind against her pants and shirt, narrowing her eyes to slits to keep the dust out. She felt worn out from the tips of her toes to the top of her head, and Mr. Tso's old coffee sat in her stomach like an acid bath. She had hoped for a clue from the old gentleman, not skinwalker rumors.

She drove back to the burned vehicle to look again for tracks, for an empty gas can, for some sign of how the fire started other than a theory of supernatural evil. She was more thorough this time, examining debris the wind had anchored to the shrubs and rocks and hiking up a hill above the vehicle, hoping the overview might give her a better perspective on the crime. Pausing when she reached the ridgeline and turning out of the wind, she glanced down toward the blackened car. It looked like a carapace, the discarded outgrown body of a giant insect, even darker than the lava that formed Ship Rock and its dikes.

Bernie knew that geologists described Ship Rock as the core of an ancient volcano. The dikes, or stone walls, that radiated from it had once been lines of liquid glowing lava that spewed up through the earth rather than pouring from the volcano's mouth. One Diné story, also violent, told of Ship Rock as the home of vicious birds that swooped up the People and fed them to their fledglings. Geologists disagreed about the age and force of the volcanic field that created Ship Rock and the dikes, just as her people's stories of the rock's origin and purpose varied depending on the storyteller. As Bernie saw it, the diversity of stories reinforced the idea that there are many valid ways to see the world and live in harmony, in *hozho*, with nature and your fellow humans.

She looked around the ridgetop again, seeing some indentations, possibly what the scouring wind had left of footprints in the soil. She followed them for a few minutes until she came to a place where the earth had obviously been disturbed. A piece of wood, thin and painted, had been shoved into the soil. At first she thought it might be a prayer stick of some sort, but it wasn't. It reminded her of the little stakes used at construction sites. Something had been removed from this spot, and if she had to guess, she'd say it was dirt. The same kind of dirt she'd seen in the trunk of the car that so closely resembled the burned vehicle at the bottom of the ridge. She took some photos of the stake with her phone. She took out the plastic Ziploc bag she always had with her in case she found some interesting seeds, or something else worth collecting, and used her hands to scoop in some dirt. Hiking down, she walked around the burned car again, taking more photos.

On the drive back to the Shiprock station Bernie thought about Miller. Why had he come to the reservation instead of going home to Flagstaff? And where was he now, the man who loved the desert? Why had his car burned? Who would destroy something so useful? She'd have plenty of questions for the Lieutenant to ponder.

As soon as she had service again, she radioed in the charred vehicle's VIN. The check could take a while, and the business day was nearly done. But by the time she arrived at the office, Sandra had a message: "Arizona Motor Vehicles confirmed Michael Miller as the burned car's registered owner.".

Bernie checked her e-mail and found a message from the soil sample lab, with a report attached. She opened it eagerly. "No organic or chemical contamination discovered. Soil resembles that found near Ship Rock, more gravelly than loamy, with traces of pulverulent clay."

Disappointed, she read on to discover highly detailed information about soil structure. Unfortunately, none of the details offered obvious clues to Miller's motivation. At least now she knew that the dirt was just dirt, and where it came from. It wasn't the answer she'd hoped for, but it led to a new series of questions.

"Do you have a phone number for the daughter of Mr. Tso, the woman who reported the burned car?" she asked Sandra.

"Here it is. Roberta Tso." Sandra gave her a slip of paper. Before she called, she checked it against the number for the Roberta she'd noticed on Miller's phone. Bingo. But why?

Roberta Tso remembered the burned car very well.

"By the time I got there to pick up Dad—he was spending the night with me because his appointment at the clinic was early—the fire was nearly out. I'd never seen a car burned like that. It was amazing. Scary. I had to wait until we got back toward Gallup to call it in." The voice on the phone stopped. Bernie heard Roberta sigh. "I worried about my father living out there by himself even before this happened. I'd like it if he'd move in with me in Gallup, but he's a strong-willed man. It will take even more than a fire-starting maniac to make him change his mind."

"When I spoke with him, he didn't have much to say about the fire."

Bernie heard Roberta chuckle. "He's not a big talker unless it's war stories. He knows all those details, but the rest of his memory seems to be fading. Sometimes he can't tell the difference between what happened to him and what he dreamed or imagined. My father mentioned that he saw something strange a few weeks ago. He didn't want to talk about it, but I could tell it made him nervous. Now he thinks whatever he saw was tied to the fire. I don't like the idea of Dad out there alone, with something like that going on."

Bernie noticed the anxiety in the woman's voice. "Do you have an idea of what frightened him?"

"No. He just changes the subject when I ask, so I stopped asking. He might have just imagined something."

"Does your father have any other relatives or neighbors who check on him? Anyone you know of who might have seen something suspicious?"

"My boy, his grandson, goes by now and then. Aaron. Aaron Torino."

"Would you give me his number? I'd like to touch base with him."

There was silence for a moment. "I'll give you his phone number if you want, but I don't know how helpful he'll be."

"Why is that?"

"Oh, he's our problem child."

Bernie changed the subject. "How do you know Michael Miller?"

"He's been talking to me and Aaron about some solar panels he would like to install out by Dad's house. I think he's a nice guy, but Dad doesn't like him, and he says the panels are ugly."

"Do you know how Miller's car ended up out there?"

"Oh, no. That was his car, the one that burned?"

"Yes."

"Maybe he was looking for an alternative site, since Dad was so adamant about not wanting the solar stuff. Was he hurt?"

"I don't know."

Bernie told Roberta she might have some follow-up questions, and hung up.

She called Aaron Torino. Her efforts to build rapport by telling him how much she had enjoyed talking to his grandfather fell flat. Torino asserted that he hadn't seen anything and didn't know anything. From the noise in the background, she suspected there were others in the room with him. The nervousness in his voice was palpable.

"My granddad says the skinwalkers hang out there. He has some crazy scary stories about that stuff. Ask the old dude."

She spoke before she could stop herself. "*Shicheii*. That's what we call our mother's father, our grandfather. We speak of them with respect."

After he hung up, she decided she needed to talk to Aaron Torino face-to-face. Preferably at Mr. Tso's house.

14

The hotel elevator doors opened and Bahe stepped
out, looking more serious than Chee had ever seen
him. A tall, thin man, obviously FBI from the tai-
lored cut of his clothes and his demeanor, stood next
to Bahe. He introduced himself as Agent Burke, not
volunteering his first name.

"I'm surprised to see you here, Chee. I thought
you were based in Shiprock. I heard about you from
Agent Cordova."

"I'm on loan to Bahe while some of his folks are
in training. I had an appointment with Delahart
here, and—"

Burke cut him off. "Bahe filled me in. Are you
sure no one else has been in the suite? No cleaning
people or food service? I see you here and the crime
scene down the hall."

"No one has been in there since I left." Chee kept
his voice level.

"I saw that security gal out there instructing

some kid in a T-shirt to keep everyone away from the back of the building. I hope it's not too late."

"She did her job well. She gave me a lot of help."

The agent stared at the blood on Delahart's face and hands and turned to Chee again. "What'd you do to him?"

Delahart spoke first. "Let's get this over with. He didn't do anything, and I didn't shoot anybody. I hid in the john, and I couldn't see what happened. I've got a life. I can't sit here growing old."

Burke ignored him. "I'll take a look, see what you missed, get some photos. The body's still there?"

"Yes."

"The man had a name. Samuel. He worked for me." Delahart's voice had an edge. "When you go down there, bring me my phone. I need to make some calls, get some work done."

"Of course you do, and I'm here to wait on you." Burke's smile was totally devoid of good nature. They watched him stride down the hall. His walk reminded Chee of students strutting onstage at graduation.

"Are all FBI guys like that?" Delahart asked.

"No." Chee turned to Bahe. "Shall I take Delahart to the station?"

"I'll do that." Bahe walked over to Delahart and stared down at him a moment. "Agent Burke is in charge of the murder investigation, but you have some business to settle with the Navajo Nation for digging a grave outside your permit area. Chee here looked at the photos your people took. No grave before you arrived."

Delahart shrugged. "We talked about that. Take

it up with Robinson. Give him the citation and tell him I said to pay it."

"What about the body at the gravesite?"

"There is no body. We dug a hole, lined up some rocks. It was a joke, a prop."

Bahe said, "Well, there's something there now. Detective Tsinnie sent what we found for analysis, but it sure looks like bone fragments."

Delahart's jaw dropped. "Samuel drove the backhoe we used to dig the hole. I was gonna say you could talk to him about it, but I guess you can't. He might have found some animal bones or something to make the grave realistic."

Chee was remembering the chip he'd found near the grave. "Was Samuel a gambler?"

Delahart shook his head. "That guy had a bunch of issues, but gambling wasn't one of them. When Robinson and I took him to Vegas with us on the plane, I never saw him even put a quarter in a slot machine."

"What did he do for you?"

"Whatever I asked. He was a mean son of a gun."

Chee left Delahart with Bahe and found Erdman in her office. She rose when he entered. "Hey. I owe you a big apology. You were right about that room. If I'd listened to you, we might have arrived in time to save that guy, or maybe see who shot him."

"You were doing your job. You did well up there. Very professional."

She handed him the surveillance tape.

"Did you look at it?"

"I saw the big guy who got killed getting out of the elevator. Room service bringing up the cart we saw. Miscellaneous men, women, teenagers, a guy with a hat. Old folks struggling with big suitcases, a couple sneaking in their dog."

"What aren't you telling me?"

"Because of the way the building curves, you can't see the door to the room where we found the dead guy. It's a flaw in the way the camera was installed. I'm not sure how much this will help you."

"Agent Burke will be in touch if he needs something else."

She gave him a hotel business card with her name and extension. "Give him that, too. You know, I'd never seen a dead person before."

"They say you get used to it. I never have."

"Do you really think I did OK?"

"You held your own just fine. If you ever get tired of doing this, you ought to consider becoming a real cop."

Chee typed up his report, relieved that this was not his case or his business. He included as many details as he could recall, even the most minor things, in part to demonstrate that he wasn't some hick cop but mostly to get it out of his brain and to minimize contact with Burke in the future.

He also typed out the notes from his interview with Mary Toledo about the bloody towels and the necklace. When he was done, he found Bahe at his desk on the phone. He motioned Chee to sit, and ended his call.

"What's your take on Delahart? Did he kill Samuel?"

"Maybe. He strikes me as a guy who thinks the rules don't apply to him. Maybe not. The sight of the body shocked him." Chee took the poker chip out of his pocket. "Did I show you this?" He placed it on Bahe's desktop. "I found it on the road where I saw that missing woman's car, before we discovered the grave."

Bahe looked at the chip, turning it over in his hand. "They don't use these at any casinos around here that I know of. Kind of pretty."

"I wonder if Delahart dropped it when he was out there supervising Samuel. Maybe he kept it as a good luck token or something."

"It didn't work very well." Bahe gave the chip back. "Maybe whoever shot Samuel was really after Delahart, but that's a federal case. Our concern is still that grave. The bone fragments make it more complicated. Without that, we could have just ordered the movie folks to remove it. Now comes the wait for lab results to see if what we found was human."

Chee appreciated the "we," even though he knew his discovery had caused the complications. "Will that take long?"

"Normally, yes. But the medical examiner has some eager interns looking for stuff to do. We ought to know pretty soon." Bahe stood. "Go back to your cousin's place and get some rest if he'll let you. You look beat."

"I'm OK."

Bahe nodded. "We work with a *hataalii* here, a good man. Maybe you've heard of him." He gave Chee the name. "I'm going to ask him to help us with that back there." He nodded in the direction of the hotel. "If those bones are human, by some bizarre chance, we can deal with that, too."

Chee knew of the healer by reputation but had never attended one of his ceremonies. He appreciated Bahe's concern. "Let me know, and I will come back for that with Bernie. It would be a good thing."

Chee called Bernie before he ventured into his cousin's land of no phone service. To his joy, she answered. She was at work, and she talked about the burned car and Mr. Tso's grandson and the old man's skinwalker theory.

"How's your day going?" she asked.

He told her.

"I think that big shot from the movie company killed Samuel," she said, "but it was an accident. He and Samuel were in the drug business together, and Samuel wanted more money."

"Interesting guess."

"Anything new in the case of the bloody towels?"

"No."

"What if the necklace belonged to a tourist woman who found it in a pawnshop or an antique store or something? She has plenty of jewelry. She hasn't even missed it. Mystery solved."

"So why were she and whoever making so much noise in there? Why the blood?"

"And how is it tied to the man with the cocaine and the dead person?" Her laugh made him miss her all the more. "You know what the Lieutenant would tell you?" She continued before he could think of a good answer. "He always said to trust our instincts. What does your gut say?"

"The necklace belonged to a person, a woman, who slept in the room and is connected to the bloody towels. Something bad happened to her, or she did something that she's ashamed of there. She never would have abandoned that necklace if she could have claimed it. And whatever happened wasn't a crime of passion."

"Why not?"

"Beside the laundry, the person left the maid a tip." It felt good to brainstorm with Bernie.

"I was going to e-mail the Lieutenant the photograph of the necklace you sent me. I forgot." She gave Leaphorn's address to Chee. "You can ask him to help. I think he'd like to be involved with police work again."

"Speaking of passionately missing something, I can't wait to see you again."

"I thought you were enjoying your work up there."

"I am. Bahe's great, and it's nice to spend some time with Paul in the evenings, help him get his business going. This movie stuff is interesting, too. It's giving me—"

"I've got to go." Chee heard a siren in the background and the squawk of Bernie's radio. She hung up without saying "I love you," or giving him time to say it either.

Before he switched off, Chee found his photo of the necklace. He sent it to Leaphorn with a cc to Bernie and a note: "Can you help ID this? Might be linked to a crime."

As he logged off, he heard someone approaching behind him, the sound of footsteps on the hard floor. Instead of heading to the break room, Officer Tsinnie was walking to his desk.

"*Yá'át'ééh*," said Chee. "Are you enjoying your day?"

"It's OK. I heard Paul had a bad time this morning. His funny Jeep broke down out there. My uncle's company had to come and get his customers."

Poor Paul, Chee thought. He should have done a better job on the repair. "My cousin was lucky your uncle could help. Do things like that happen very much out here?"

"Not with the good operators." She waited a beat and then said, "There's a young woman out there who asked to see you. Her eyes are red from crying."

"Me?"

"She says she met you at the movie site."

"That slender blond woman, Melissa?"

"No—a teenager with one of those little metal rings here." Tsinnie pinched her right eyebrow.

"Is there another girl with her?"

"One groupie isn't enough for you?"

"It's not that—" But Tsinnie had already left.

Chee found Courtney pacing in the lobby.

"What's up?"

"Can I talk to you? It's complicated."

"Take your time." He motioned her to some folding chairs by the wall and sat next to her. Her bravado from last night had faded, leaving a scared young woman in its place.

"It's about my dad and Alisha. She ran away or something, and now he's gone too. I'm worried." She got up, shoved her hands deep into her pants pockets. Sat back down again.

"Go on. What happened?"

"You remember how Alisha was acting the other night? All quiet and weirded out?"

"Yeah."

"This morning, Dad noticed some big bruises on her arm. Dad asked her if you had hurt her. She shook her head, and then she said it had nothing to do with you, that you were nice to us. And then she started to sob, and Daddy hugged her. When she stopped crying, she said she didn't want to talk about it."

Chee remembered Alisha rubbing her arm. He listened intently now.

"Dad kept saying that nobody had the right to hurt his daughter, saying she needed to tell him whatever happened so he could take care of it. Finally, she told about the pictures. Then Dad got really mad, and she ran outside and she didn't come back."

"Are you talking about something that happened at the movie site?"

"You remember that guard guy?"

"Samuel?"

"He caught Alisha because she had the flashlight and didn't turn it off. I was running ahead of her, and I hid behind the trailer. I couldn't see them, but I heard him yelling at her and her crying and him yelling more, and then it got quiet. I didn't know that guy was a creep. I should have helped her instead of hiding, but—" Courtney pressed her lips together and then relaxed them.

"You're helping her now by talking to me. Go on. What pictures?" He remembered Samuel claiming the girls wanted a picture of Rhonda and her trailer.

Courtney compressed her lips more tightly. Took a breath. "Alisha said Samuel made her lift up her shirt like they do in those *Wild Girl* movies. He said he would put the pictures on the Internet if she told anybody. She's my little sister, and I shouldn't have let him do that."

"He might have hurt you, too, and you couldn't have stopped him. Don't blame yourself. You said that Alisha ran away. Is she still missing?"

Courtney nodded. "After she told Dad, Alisha started crying again and went outside into the parking lot. I started to go after her there, but Dad said to let her be because she needed to calm down and have some alone time. When she didn't come back, we walked around the hotel looking for her. Then he got in the car and told me to stay there to let him know if she returned. That was a long time ago."

"What time did all this happen?"

Alisha had gone missing a few hours before Chee found Samuel's body, according to Courtney.

"You did a smart thing by coming here now. Maybe he found her and they are both back and worried about you. Come on. I'll drive you to Goulding's."

But Alisha wasn't in the hotel room, and neither was her father.

Courtney asked, "Will you look for her?"

"Sure. But you need to stay here as our information center so you can let me know when you hear from your dad or your sister. Give me your phone number, and I'll call or text as soon as I hear anything."

"But maybe I should—"

He interrupted her with a shake of his head. "You don't want Alisha to come back and find this place empty. She may need to talk to you about what happened. Are you clear on that?"

"Yep. OK."

"Why don't you call your dad now?"

Courtney dialed the number, and it went to voice mail.

He read her disappointment. "He's probably somewhere phones don't work. And don't worry about Samuel. He won't hurt you or your sister anymore."

"How do you know?"

"Trust me. I know that for sure."

Back at the station, he told Bahe about the missing girl and Samuel's connection with the situation.

"You met this guy Isenberg," Bahe said. "Do you think he could have shot Samuel?"

"Well, his daughter said he was furious. He had a gun in his car. He knew Samuel worked for the movie crew. He could have called out there, asking for the man's boss, and been referred to Delahart."

"I'll mention this to Burke," Bahe said, "and he'll want us to look for Isenberg in the park, at the movie set. You know how these guys are."

Chee could tell from the captain's tone that he wasn't finished.

"Now for the bad news. The preliminary results are back from the bone fragments. I'm afraid they were human."

Chee felt as though he'd been punched in the gut. Shocked and then angry. What made Delahart think he could desecrate a human body for a movie promotion? And to blatantly lie about it? What kind of scum was this?

Bahe's voice scattered Chee's thoughts. "The medical examiner told me something else interesting. The intern said the little bits of bone had been burned. Cremated. Like a mortuary does. The whole idea of it makes me sick." He handed Chee a sheet of paper. "I drew up a new citation to include illegal disposal of human remains as well as the earlier charges."

Chee looked at the citation, remembering that the original was in his unit. "We ought to make Delahart remove every one of those little bits of bone on his hands and knees."

"I agree."

Chee put the paper aside. "I don't like the idea of that girl out there somewhere."

"You can look for her on your way to serve the citation. I'll call hotel security and ask Haskie and Erdman to look around for the girl. Maybe she's at the restaurant, having a soda."

After so many trips over the rough road, Chee had learned to avoid most of the holes and ruts and other obstacles in the dirt loop. He knew where the wide spots came that made passing the tour buses easier. He kept the windows up to reduce the dust, appreciating the air-conditioning.

His concern about Alisha Isenberg was tempered by his experience as a policeman. Unless parental abuse factored into their motivation, runaway children usually returned home or showed up at a friend or relative's house. He assumed Alisha hadn't gone far, and would head back to the hotel room once she came to terms with her embarrassment. But if she'd walked to the park, a several-mile hike in the hot sun, the story changed. Dehydration, sunstroke, and vast empty spaces to get lost in—that was more complicated. She'd already been traumatized, and he didn't want her to suffer anymore. He'd had good luck finding Missy; he hoped Alisha turned up safely too.

Spotting a blue car in the Wildcat Trail parking area, he pulled off the road. He couldn't see what kind of sedan it was, but it resembled Isenberg's vehicle. When he got out of his unit, he realized the day had gone from hot to sizzling, and that the car was not Isenberg's Audi. He stretched, felt heat seep through his skin into his bones.

A couple in shorts and floppy hats using metal walking sticks approached. The man spoke first. "Hi there, Officer. Everything OK out here?"

"I'm looking for a missing girl." Chee described Alisha.

"This is a big place to be lost in," the woman said. "We haven't seen her."

The man said, "If I were lost, I'd try to get to the road and follow it back. You can see the dust rise."

That gave Chee an idea.

He stopped to chat with the next tour bus driver, and the next and the next. Bus number four had pulled over to let the customers get photos of Elephant Butte from the overlook. Chee drove close, lowered his window, explained that he was looking for Alisha.

The driver, a portly woman wearing a straw hat, had news.

"I saw that girl walking on the road. She looked bad, sunburned, beat down by the heat. I stopped and asked her if she needed some help. She started crying and asked me if I could take her back to the hotel. I told her to get in and I'd get her there but it would be a while yet because the bus had to make vista stops. I gave her some water."

The woman paused, gave Chee a knowing look. "We're not supposed to pick up people along the road, but I was worried she could have a heat stroke or something. Ford Point, that was the next stop. She sat here in the cab with me. The customers got out for photos and to look at the jewelry and stuff and to get a can of soda or something. She just sat.

"Then this car pulled into the parking area, and as soon as she seen it, she jumped right out and started waving and yelling. The car slammed on the brakes. And then she's running over to it and the driver's door opened and this man got out and he swooped her up like you see in the movies.

"I went over there to make sure everything was OK. I've got a daughter myself, you know." The gold cap on her front tooth sparkled when she smiled. "Turned out the guy was her papa. I think they'd had an argument or something."

Chee couldn't call in the good news because of lack of service, so he texted Courtney and Bahe. As soon as his phone picked up bars, they'd get the message. One problem solved, two left: the citation to deliver and the People Mover to fix. Well, two and a half: Who killed Samuel? For the girls' sake, he hoped it wasn't Isenberg, but he figured that was Burke's baby.

He continued through the valley with a lighter heart. As always, the beauty of Dinetah spoke to him, the vertical red stone against the blue dome of the sky lifting his spirits. Why was it, he wondered, that those polls that measured well-being focused on income and home ownership and never asked about the view?

He pulled into the movie parking area and realized that Gerald wasn't on the job. Vehicles had parked haphazardly, some clustered under the juniper trees, some in uneven rows, looking as though their owners had stopped without a plan in mind.

Perhaps because it was daylight, the movie camp seemed quieter than usual. He went to the administration trailer and asked for Robinson.

"Sorry, he's not here today," BJ said. "Want me to have him call you?"

"No. Do you know when he'll be back?"

"We have a big group meeting tomorrow." She gave Chee the time. "I know he'll be here for that. You could catch him afterward."

Or before, Chee thought. He would serve the citation directly ahead of the meeting and not have to listen too long to Robinson's protests of innocence. "I'll stop by then. Is Gerald off today? The parking lot looks like a disaster area."

"He got terminated. You know, fired."

Chee put on his I'm-interested look and waited for her to say more.

"Oh, he's a good guy. It wasn't anything he did. One of those budget shortfall deals."

"Too bad. He lives around here. There aren't a lot of jobs."

"If somebody had to get fired, it should have been Samuel. That guy was nothing but trouble."

With her use of "was," Chee assumed she knew Samuel was dead. "Why do you say that?"

She glanced down at the desktop, then back toward Chee. "He was Delahart's stooge. Eavesdropping on our conversations and feeding him information for that dumb blog and all the other ways he gets publicity. But Delahart pays the bills, and Samuel was Delahart's golden boy, so we all put up with it."

"The FBI investigator, Agent Burke, will probably want to talk to someone here about that."

"If he wants to ask me about why Samuel got shot, he better be quick. I'm leaving next week."

"Is that when the filming will be done?"

"No. But most of the administrative functions, like this job, shift back to California to save money."

"Well, good luck to you."

She smiled. "You look like you could use a cold drink. You know how to find the food tent. Help yourself."

That sounded like a good idea. Maybe a bottle of cold, cold water would get him in the right frame of mind for working on the People Mover on a very warm afternoon.

In the tent some local crew members nodded to him and motioned him over. Randy said, "I heard your cousin ran into some trouble with that big vehicle he uses for tourists."

"I heard that, too."

"Tell him my boy used to drive one of those at Canyon de Chelly, taking folks to the Canyon del Muerto and the ruins. He knows what makes them tick." The man gave Chee his son's name and number. "Paul knows me, but we haven't seen each other for a while."

Chee was leaving with his water and an oatmeal cookie when he saw Missy. She was chatting with another woman, but Chee knew it would be rude to ignore her. She introduced him to Trish, a tall brunette wearing a T-shirt with an eagle design.

Trish smiled. "So you're the one who found my friend here?"

"That's me."

Melissa said, "I wasn't lost. I keep saying that, but no one listens. Hey, I heard about Samuel. How awful. Do you know what happened?"

"Not exactly."

"Someone told me Delahart shot him," Trish said.

News traveled almost as fast in the movie company as it did on the reservation, Chee thought. "That's interesting. Did he say why?"

"That guy was a slimebag."

"Which guy?"

"Take your pick. Sorry to speak ill of the dead, but it's true. Samuel would make up lies based on little things he heard or saw. Then Delahart would put stupid gossip in the movie blogs, fan pages, whatever. He didn't bother to check to see if it was true, or fair."

Melissa said, "Delahart never seemed like a guy who would shoot anybody. Spreading rumors about them, innuendo, that's more his style."

"So that leaves about a hundred other suspects. You, me, BJ, even Rhonda," Trish said.

"Rhonda, she's another story. She's got an ego

and a temper, and Samuel's lies didn't do her any favors."

Trish laughed. "Seriously. I think you're confusing the real Rhonda with the Zombie Queen."

When Melissa shook her head, Chee noticed that she wasn't wearing her turquoise earrings. He asked about it.

"I loved those earrings, but I took them back to the shop. I decided they were beyond my budget. Delahart had Robinson announce his budget cutbacks, and I figured I shouldn't have been so extravagant."

"BJ told me that parking-lot Gerald lost his job."

Melissa sighed. "We were expecting more underwriting, but it didn't come through. I feel bad about Gerald, and there's more layoffs to come."

Chee left the air-conditioned tent for the late-afternoon heat. He'd never minded summer, even at its peak. What was the point of calling anything in nature "bad"? Weather was weather, hot was hot, cold was cold. He didn't see the need to attach judgment.

While he still had phone service, he called his cousin on the off chance that Paul was somewhere within range of a cell tower and had his phone with him.

Paul answered. He had just finished filling his water tanks and was heading for home.

"I'm about done, too, ready to get back to your place," Chee said. "I thought I'd see if you had any idea what was wrong with the People Mover."

"You heard about that?" Paul sounded remarkably upbeat for a man who had looked business disaster in the face earlier that day. "Yeah, I guess I'm famous all over the valley now."

Chee waited for Paul to bring up his botched repair job, or to ask him to work on the People Mover. He did neither.

"I've been thinking some more about this food deal. You know, what to feed the customers. Something easy but good. I'm doing the research, man. You can be my test subject. You know, like a crash test dummy?" Paul chuckled.

Chee didn't appreciate the comparison. "What about the vehicle?"

"Don't worry, bro. It's under control."

On his way through the valley, Chee cruised past the former campsite of the German tourists. They had done a fine job of cleaning up. Except for tire tracks, the place looked as though no one had been there. He wondered if the movie people would do as good a job when they left with the burned bones with which they had desecrated Navajoland.

15

The next day the memory of the burned sedan, the stench of rubber and plastic, still bothered Bernie. She pictured the scene again. She wondered if it had to do with gangs, some sort of initiation. Another thing to mention to the Lieutenant. Talking to him always helped.

She steered her mind to happier thoughts. The Lieutenant using the computer. Wonderful news. Another step in his recovery.

As she drove into Window Rock, her cell phone vibrated. She was surprised to see that the caller was Officer Wheeler, a colleague stationed there. She put him on speaker.

"Hey, Manuelito. So the Captain has you tracking down a burned car?"

"That's right."

"I've been investigating incidents like that out here. I can give you some info, share my files. I heard you were coming out this way to see the Lieutenant.

Meet me at the Navajo Inn, and I'll pass all this off to you. I want to talk to you for a minute about that guy Miller, too. I'm almost at the parking lot now."

"OK, thanks, but—" And before she could suggest an alternative place to meet, he hung up.

She would have suggested that they get together at the chain restaurant down the street or the Chinese place in the little mall. She had always enjoyed the Navajo Inn, but now the thought of going there felt like a cold wind on her neck.

She forced herself to park in the open spot by the door, the same place where the Lieutenant had parked his truck the day he was shot. Even looking at the building made her edgy. She climbed out of her Toyota, straightened up, took a breath. She knew she had to do this sometime, and now was as good a time as any. She walked through the big doors and into the dining room.

Wheeler sat at a booth by the back windows, looking at the oasis of shade and water the restaurant and adjoining hotel had created. Bernie slipped in across from him.

Bernie's favorite waitress, Nellie Roanhorse, handled their section. Nellie came by for their orders and smiled at Bernie. "Good to see you again. I've missed you here. How's your friend, the one who got shot?"

Surprisingly, it was a relief to talk about him. "He's getting stronger, doing better. He's able to use the computer now, working a little."

"You want some fries today?"

"No, just a Coke."

Nellie brought the Coke, and an iced tea for

Wheeler. Bernie sipped, focusing on each sweet, cold swallow, forcing herself to drink slowly when she wanted to gulp it down and order six refills. Cokes weren't the best thing for her, she knew. She usually limited herself to one a day. Nellie understood her weakness, however, and took her glass for a refill while she and Wheeler talked.

Bernie opened the discussion. "You mentioned that you'd learned something about Miller. I'm curious about that man. Do you know why the feds are so interested?"

Wheeler put down his glass. "When I heard the story about you and the dirt, I remembered him from a DWI road block this spring. He was suspicious then, too."

Bernie wondered why, of the hundreds of motorists Wheeler had dealt with, Miller stood out. She waited for the story to unfold.

"I talked to him like you do to everybody, to see if I smelled beer or something. The man wasn't drinking, and he was driving OK, but he sure was nervous. He's telling me about how he moved from Las Vegas. I asked him about the casinos in Vegas, which ones have the best odds, and he clammed up, like I'd said something dirty to him. I checked his license, registration. All good, same as you found. When I told him he could be on his way, he asked me if I'd ever heard of something called the Red Rock Highway and how to get there. I told him yes and explained where it was."

Bernie knew the Red Rock Highway—BIA Route 13, the scenic route over the Chuskas, which wound through forests and red cliffs. Off this route, someone had burned Miller's car. "Did you ask him why he wanted to know?"

"He said he had some business out that way. Funny, huh? There's not much there."

"He told me he was a contractor. Is that what he said to you?"

Wheeler rubbed a thumb against his jaw. "I remember he mentioned that he did some landscaping. That might be what he planned for the dirt you found, a mini project on someone's patio."

"Do you know why the feds are interested in him?"

"Maybe they're bored or something."

She picked up the car fire folder. "I appreciate this. I'll show it to the Lieutenant. Maybe he'll have some insights."

"Tell him hey for me. Let me know if any of these cases are related to yours, maybe gangster activity spreading out that way. You've made me curious."

When Nellie came closer, Bernie asked for the bill.

"My treat today. You come back and bring the one who got shot."

Louisa opened the door before Bernie could knock, and told her the Lieutenant was taking a nap. "He usually sleeps about half an hour, so he ought to be awake soon."

In the kitchen, Louisa asked about Mama and Darleen. Bernie answered briefly, not going into detail. The cat came in, lapped some water from its bowl on the kitchen floor, and pranced away again.

"What's happening with your work?" Bernie asked. They had talked before about Louisa's research for a book comparing the origin stories of southwestern tribes, a project she'd been involved with for years. Louisa also worked as a consultant in American studies with her colleagues at Northern Arizona University.

"I haven't been doing any consulting lately. I miss interviewing for the book, but it will be there when the time comes."

"Captain Largo asked me to invite you and the Lieutenant to join him and some of the top brass for breakfast at the Navajo Inn. It's an open invitation. Whenever he's up for it. I thought it might be better to ask you about the idea first."

Louisa ran her hand through her cropped gray hair. "I'll talk to Joe about that. Give him time to consider it. Would you be there, too?"

"Largo wants me to, yes. I stopped at the restaurant today to meet with another officer. I wasn't looking forward to it, but I did OK."

"You've got a lot on your shoulders, between your mother and sister and the job and that handsome guy you're married to. So, how is your mother's health these days? How's Darleen doing? And how are you holding up with Chee at Monument Valley?"

Bernie had noticed that white people often asked more than one question at the same time. She liked it; it meant she could answer whatever question she wanted.

"I'm fine. Missing my husband. How are you feeling?" She knew Louisa had some health issues, things she rarely talked about.

"I'm all right."

Bernie heard a shuffle in the hallway and turned.

Leaphorn walked slowly, using his cane, coming to join them. She remembered seeing him in the hospital, pale and near death, and how Louisa had stayed with him in that tiny room, cheered him up, brought him home. "The Lieutenant looks better every time I see him. Now he's getting around without using the walker. Wonderful!"

"It is wonderful. You know, only ten percent of people who are shot in the head survive." Louisa's voice quavered. "I thank my lucky stars that Joe beat the odds. And that he's recovering. I celebrate his being alive every day."

"Remember that congresswoman from Arizona, the woman who was shot? She went skydiving to celebrate the third anniversary of her survival."

Louisa laughed. "Can you imagine Joe jumping out of a plane?"

Bernie turned toward Leaphorn as he entered the kitchen. "*Yá'át'ééh*."

He nodded to her. He looked sleepy, she thought.

Louisa pulled out a chair so Leaphorn could lower himself more easily, but didn't offer to help him beyond that. "We're going to Gallup for Joe's physical therapy tomorrow. It was good that you could come today." She rose. "Can I bring you something to drink?"

"No, thanks. I just had a Coke." Bernie looked at the Lieutenant. "Do you like that therapy?"

He made a sound and then tapped twice, the signal for no. Then again once, for yes.

Bernie laughed. "I guess that means you're not sure."

"They make him work, and that's exhausting. But

he's getting better because of it. The staff helps him with balance, standing, walking."

Bernie thought about how hard it would be to have to relearn all of that. "Do they help you with talking?"

The Lieutenant made another sound, but Bernie couldn't understand it. Louisa said, "That's the speech therapist's job."

"What a lot of appointments. No wonder you haven't had any time for your research."

"This is my work now. My work and my joy. Whatever I can do to help Joe."

Louisa looked exhausted, Bernie realized. What if Chee had been the shooter's victim? Would Bernie be as open-hearted? What if she'd been shot? How would she feel about Chee putting his job on hold to help her regain some of what the bullet took away? She thought of people she knew who had come back from Iraq or Afghanistan with injuries, and how they and their families struggled. People did what they had to do, and she admired those like Louisa who kept their balance in a whirlwind of change.

Leaphorn tapped on the table, using all his fingers and both thumbs.

"Joe, the computer is in your office." Louisa turned to Bernie. "I know you've got police business to discuss with him. You'll be more comfortable in there, and you can talk Navajo without having to translate for me."

The Lieutenant pushed himself to standing, using the table for leverage. He reached for his cane and, step by slow step, began to move toward his office. Bernie followed. With some effort—and a look that yelled leave-me-alone when she tried to help—the Lieutenant settled into his favorite reading chair. The cat tagged along, too. Leaphorn motioned for Bernie to put the computer on his lap.

"Do you remember I mentioned to you that I'd stopped that man with the dirt in his trunk?" Bernie asked in Diné Bizaad, the language where her best thinking lived.

Leaphorn tapped once: yes.

Bernie told him about Miller's car being burned near Ship Rock.

Leaphorn typed in Navajo: *Who?*

"That's what I want to know. Who did it? Wheeler has been investigating stuff like this here in Window Rock. Those cars were burned as revenge or gang initiations. He gave me a folder about all that. Oh, and he said to tell you hello." Bernie sat down in the desk chair and rolled it next to the Lieutenant. She opened the folder and showed him the photos, but he didn't seem interested in them or in the printouts Wheeler had included.

"So, who could have burned the car? *Hosteen* Tso, the old one who lives out there and saw the fire, thinks it was a skinwalker. Wheeler told me the gang activity he's tracking might be spreading. Mr. Tso has a grandson who sounded kind of rough on the phone. Maybe he did it. That might take us back to the gang angle."

Leaphorn moved his right hand over the keyboard, picking out each letter: *why?* Bernie wondered if the injury had affected his hand-eye coordination or his ability to remember where the letters were. Maybe he had always been a hunt-and-peck typist.

"Why? Good question."

She felt her cell phone vibrate and looked at it. Captain Largo was on the line.

"Excuse me," she said. "It's the boss."

"Manuelito," Largo said, "I just got a call from Agent Cordova I thought you'd be interested in."

"Yes, sir?"

"He told me Miller reported that his car was stolen from outside a bar in Farmington the night before it burned."

"Interesting."

"The report is on your desk. You'll probably want to talk to the deputy who interviewed him about it."

"Thanks. What do you think?"

The line was silent for a moment. Then Largo chuckled. "It could have happened. It has the same probability as the Navajo Rangers capturing Bigfoot. Are you with Lieutenant Leaphorn now?"

"Yes, sir. He's sitting right across from me."

"Let me talk to him."

"You know he—"

"I know."

She handed the phone to the Lieutenant. He put it to his ear and, after a moment, turned away from her. When he turned back, his eyes were glistening. He handed her the phone; Largo had disconnected.

She told Leaphorn about the stolen car report and Largo's skepticism. "That adds a new wrinkle. If it was some random guys who decided to take it, why bother to steal something and not sell it? Or keep it?"

Leaphorn kept his hands still.

"What if whoever took it had been tracking

Miller from Flagstaff or Albuquerque because he wanted whatever contraband the guy had? Maybe Miller had reneged on a deal, and this guy thought he was smarter than the feds, or he didn't realize the feds had already searched the car. When he couldn't get what he wanted, he got angry and torched the car."

Leaphorn tapped twice and typed: *Not there.*

"You mean I'm not there yet with the answer? Or the drugs weren't out there in the car?"

Why burned there?

Bernie thought for a while. "What about this? Imagine some lowlifes have Miller on their watch list because of the drugs. They carjack him and force him to drive out there to get him to tell them where the drugs are, or the weapons or explosives or whatever he's involved in. They threaten to hurt him if he doesn't talk. He tells them where to look, and then they burn the car to scare him. He escapes and makes up the stolen car story because he's embarrassed to tell the truth. And so his insurance company will pay."

Leaphorn typed a Navajo word that meant something like "complicated."

Bernie smiled. "You always did encourage us to go for the obvious solution first. Now all I have to do is think it up. But, if not, at least I have the complex one."

Leaphorn looked better than when she'd arrived. He was sitting straighter now as he typed again.

Why feds involved?

"That's my question too, but no one will tell me. I don't know enough about Miller to figure it out but I could tell by the way he reacted when I stopped him that he's not squeaky clean. I'm guessing it's white-collar crime—not sex trafficking or terrorism. Maybe he's involved in a mortgage scam or Internet fraud."

Leaphorn didn't respond. Was he getting tired, or processing the information? The cat stretched out on his lap.

Another idea came to her. "Largo doubts the stolen car story. Maybe Miller drove it out there himself and burned it to destroy whatever evidence the feds and I missed, and then claimed it was stolen. Since the original traffic stop was part of a drug interdiction, I expected the DEA to be involved, but instead I talked to an agent named Jerry Cordova. He asked some questions, but wouldn't tell me why."

Leaphorn started typing: *What ?s.*

"What Miller had been doing at that meeting in Albuquerque, where he said he'd been, whether I'd seen anything else suspicious in the car besides the dirt. I told him I didn't know, and no. Later, after I found Miller's phone, he asked me where he'd been calling. If the guy really worked in Flagstaff, I thought it was interesting that he didn't have many Flagstaff numbers in his phone. I mean, it's summer. The time for building out there in the mountains before the ground freezes again."

dirt?

"Cordova didn't ask me about the dirt. But I keep coming back to it."

Who is M?

The cat leaped to the floor by Leaphorn's feet and then onto the windowsill, where it sat, watching an assembly of hummingbirds at the feeder. They looked like airborne jewels, iridescent green-blue, their wings moving so fast Bernie could only see a blur. The cat's tail twitched.

"I don't know, and I can't seem to find out, either. I feel like my logic is going in circles, using lots of energy to stay in one place, like those little birds." She looked to Leaphorn for a response and discovered that he had closed his eyes.

"I'm tiring you out with so much talking."

He looked up at her and typed: *thinking*.

"Me, too. It's making my brain hurt."

Leaphorn typed something else.

"Chee? Oh, right, I haven't given you the update."

She filled him in on the discovery of Samuel's body, the man hiding in the bathroom, and Paul's adventures setting up the tour company. She remembered what Chee had wanted her to ask. "Hold on a second. I left my backpack in the living room, and I need to show you something."

She located the backpack on the coffee table, then remembered her phone was in her pocket. She called up the photo Chee had sent her of the necklace.

"Chee said he e-mailed this to you, but he wasn't sure it came through. He asked me to get your opinion. Does it look familiar?"

Leaphorn studied the photo, then tapped three times, his code for maybe.

Why.

"You know Chee. He doesn't like loose ends." She told Leaphorn the story of the bloody towels. "He's been wondering why someone would abandon something so beautiful. It doesn't sit right with him. Like me and those darn boxes of dirt."

She watched the hummingbirds for a few minutes more while Leaphorn typed. Not a message this time; he was calling up his e-mail. Chee had managed to send the Lieutenant the same photo.

Leaphorn switched out of e-mail and typed. *Will get back to Chee.*

"Have some tea first," Louisa said when Bernie went to say goodbye. "It's herbal. Good for you. Better than all that coffee you and Joe drink. I won't keep you long, but you have to try this."

Louisa poured a cup for Bernie, one for the Lieutenant, and one for herself. "You know, when Chee gets back from Monument Valley, you both should come over. That would be fun. Joe and I will rent some of those old John Ford movies that were filmed out that way."

Bernie took a sip, then added some of the honey Louisa offered. It didn't seem to help. If she drank half a cup, that would be polite enough, Bernie decided. Then she could be on her way.

She glanced at Leaphorn, sitting in his familiar place. His eyes were closed, his tea untouched.

On the drive to the office, Bernie puzzled over Miller without coming up with any ideas, then turned her thoughts to the Rotary speech. She'd finished a mental list of the major talking points when her phone rang. She put it on speaker.

"Mr. Tso's daughter called," Largo said. "She says her dad asked her to call you. Says he remembered something else and wants to talk to you."

"About the car?"

"I asked her that. She said he wouldn't tell her. He said he could only talk to the police about it. He said it was important."

"OK. I'm near that turnoff, so I'll stop and see him now."

"The daughter said to tell you that his grandson will be there, too."

Bernie hoped surprise would work in her favor with Aaron Torino.

When she got there, the young man's posture told her he hadn't expected his grandfather to have company. She started over, introducing herself with her clans. Some young people reciprocated. Some looked puzzled. Some saw this link to tradition as old fashioned. She watched Aaron's attitude shift from surprise to impatience. He gave her a hard look but didn't speak. The man could use a refresher course in manners, she thought.

Mr. Tso said, "Officer Manuelito is curious about the car out there. I told her you might know something."

Aaron was older than Bernie expected, probably mid-twenties, but he acted like a teenager. She wondered if he'd been arrested. He had the sort of arrogance she'd observed in ex-cons.

"My grandson was bringing us some beans," Mr. Tso said. "You have some, too."

"Only a small serving." She didn't want to hurt his feelings by refusing. And they couldn't be as bad as Louisa's tea or Mr. Tso's ultra-sweet coffee, could they?

Aaron disappeared into the house. She heard some noise, and then he came back to the doorway. "Gramps, you got any salt?"

"It's here on the porch."

Mr. Tso motioned Bernie to the wooden chair again. There was room on the bench next to him for Aaron, but the young man squatted on the porch step, balancing the plate on his lap. Bernie studied the pinto beans he'd given her on a plate with a chip in the rim. Then she tasted them, lukewarm and old. "I'm the officer who talked to you on the phone. I'm investigating the car fire, trying to find out if anyone out here saw anything. Your mother and your grandfather both suggested that I talk to you."

He tossed his head toward Mr. Tso. "Talk to him. He has nothing to do but pay attention to what happens out here."

"Your grandfather tells me he wasn't feeling good that day. That he was in bed resting, and then he smelled something, and when he got up he saw the fire. Is that right, sir?"

Mr. Tso gave a quick nod.

Aaron took a bite of beans. Chewed. Swallowed. "You know a dude, a cop named Wheeler?"

"Officer Wheeler. Yes."

"He's been riding one of my friends pretty hard. If he lets up, I might remember something."

"I don't have any control over what Officer Wheeler does. He told me there have been a bunch of car fires lately in Window Rock, too."

Aaron laughed. "That guy stays up with the news."

"He's wondering if this one might be tied to those. He mentioned the idea of gang involvement."

Aaron took another bite of beans, added salt.

Bernie heard Mr. Tso's bench creak as he shifted his weight. Then he spoke. "I have been thinking about the questions you asked me about that fire." He pressed his palms together. "Some young people might go out to where that car is. They drink, play loud music. My grandson, I tell him not to go there. I tell him to make those boys go somewhere else."

"That party was nothing," Aaron said. "You make it sound like a big deal."

"Come up here and sit with me. Don't make the lady talk to you down there on that step."

To her surprise, Aaron rose and joined Mr. Tso on the bench. "Grandfather, you didn't tell me you'd been sick."

"It was because of what I saw up there on the ridge." Mr. Tso continued. "It was in the late afternoon, after you brought food for the sheep. Sometimes it looked like a man. Then it was low, like a coyote. Then a man. I saw it before the car caught on fire, my grandson. That's what I needed to tell the officer, too." Mr. Tso turned his attention to the west, where a few high clouds caught the beginnings of the sunset color show. The day had started to cool a bit. "No more talk of that."

Aaron looked at his grandfather's empty plate. "Would you like more food?"

"No." He handed the plate to Aaron. "Bring me some water."

Aaron headed inside, and Bernie followed. He turned to her. "You're bothering an old man. I left before the fire, OK? I don't know anything about it."

"Your grandfather invited me here, and he was glad for my company. I think he gets lonely."

"Lonely, so then he makes up stories. Do you think he is crazy?"

"I think *Hosteen* Tso is a fine old gentleman. A warrior. What do you think?"

Aaron looked at his empty plate. "I think he imagines things, maybe because he's mostly here by himself. Sometimes he can't sort out what happened last week from what happened a long time ago."

"Has he talked about a creature prowling on the ridge before?"

"Yeah, he mentioned it the first time a few months ago. He said he'd seen something out there walking. He was shook up about it, too. He called it human and then said it could have been a big dog or a wolf. Or something else. He told me to be careful, and to be sure to leave before dark. He worries about me the same as he did when I was a kid."

The same way Bernie's mother worried about her and her little sister, she thought. It didn't matter how old she got, how good a cop she was, Mama would always envision her as a child whom she needed to protect. She pulled her attention back to Aaron's story.

"A few days ago I brought him some groceries, wire to fix the fence, gasoline for his chain saw, other things he asked for. I hung here longer than usual to help because his hip and back hurt. He said he thought the pain came because of what he'd seen on the ridge." Aaron didn't use the word for the evil creatures either in English or, more descriptively, in Navajo, Bernie noticed.

He walked to the stove and turned off the propane burner beneath the pot of beans. "It was the same story that he told out there on the porch. He tells those stories over and over, and I can't tell if the same thing happened again. He comes up with stories he heard as a boy to make sense of things."

"The old stories are part of what makes us Navajo. They give us a framework. They've helped me when I have to do a job I'd rather not face." Bernie put her plate on the counter next to the other two. "You asked me about his story, if I believe it. I've seen some things at night when I've been working alone that I don't talk about. A lot of what happens leaves me puzzled, makes me wonder."

"Wonder what?" Aaron was giving her his full attention now.

"Wonder what was going on, and if I'd seen something or just imagined it."

"I thought he was trying to scare me into staying out here with him when he told me what he saw before the car burned. I told him I couldn't. I've got to get a job, and this place doesn't even have a telephone."

"So we're back to the car. What do you know about it?"

"Nothing. I told you already. But let Wheeler know it's not connected to the vehicles that burned near Window Rock, and to give those dudes a break. And tell him that my friend, the one he's hassling, he's not hanging with them anymore."

"What is your friend's name?"

"Vernon Vigil."

"I'll mention it."

Aaron took a mug to the big red thermos that sat on the kitchen counter and pushed in the button to start the flow of water. "You're a cop. You stay up with stuff. I need to ask you something. Do you know anything about a new solar project out here?"

"It sounds great to me. A way to provide power for people like your grandfather, and the extra power would help other people. They've been experimenting with it a long time and the new technology seems dependable and safe."

"They want to put some of those collector things by this house. Someone has been talking to me and Mom about it, and we think it sounds like a good deal. Grandfather could get electricity as well as some money, but he won't do it. He says the panels would spoil the view, and he wants to see Ship Rock as it was meant to be seen. He would rather live in the dark out here alone than change his mind." Aaron sipped the water. "What do you think?"

"I think solar power is great, but people have a right to say no."

"You sound like him. Mom and I are trying to persuade him to come and live with her in Gallup. That way he wouldn't have to see the panels. Or he could stay here with lights and a refrigerator. Have shows on TV instead of just looking at the scenery and watching the dust settle."

Aaron poured a second cup of water. "Want some?"

"No, I have to go." She stood a little straighter. "Are you sure you don't want to tell me anything about that car?"

"Nothing to say."

She went back to the porch and said good night to Mr. Tso.

"Come back," the old man said. "I have stories for you."

Aaron walked to the car with Bernie. "If you're really a cop, how come you aren't driving a police car instead of that thing?"

Bernie gave her Toyota a pat on the hood. "No patrol unit because I'm off duty, on my way home. Any shortcuts back to Shiprock?"

He looked at her vehicle again. "You've got enough clearance to make it." He gave her directions that sounded simple. Straight, a right at the big fork, then a hard left before the old windmill. Watch for ruts.

She found the big fork—at least, she assumed it was the right junction—easily enough, thinking about Aaron and how he stood to benefit if the burned car scared his grandfather into moving. She considered the connection between Roberta Tso and Miller. Decided that the stolen car report on her desk would have Miller's contact information, and that he needed to answer some questions.

It was getting dark, the last rays of the long-lasting June sunset bathing the landscape in dusty pink. She drove on, savoring the fading light and the cooling air. She avoided most of the teeth-shaking holes in the road as she searched for the windmill without luck. She prided herself on her sense of direction. How could she miss a windmill? Maybe Aaron had given her wrong directions. She switched on the headlights and decided to turn around if she didn't find the windmill at the top of the next rise.

Then, instead of the windmill, she saw an animal standing in the road, its eyes reflecting greenish gold in the fading light. In her years of cruising back roads on the reservation, beginning long before she was a legal driver, she'd encountered scores of coyotes. This one was huge, unlike any coyote she'd ever seen. She slowed down to let it move aside, but it held its ground. Goose bumps rose on her skin.

Her logical mind tried to make sense of it. Maybe it was a hybrid, an animal born of a large coyote and an even larger dog. Maybe a wolf hybrid had escaped from that refuge near Ramah and trotted out this way.

She slowed some more. The animal watched, challenging her to proceed. When she honked, it began to lope toward the car.

Without hesitation, Bernie made a U-turn back to Mr. Tso's place, glad that the dirt was hard-packed here and, for once, happy that there had been no rain to soften the soil. She glanced in her rearview mirror, wondering if it would chase her, but the animal had disappeared.

She drove faster now that she knew the road, her brain repeating the soothing words of the old prayers. When she passed the house, Aaron's truck was gone, the porch empty, the place dark.

At the burned car, Bernie slowed down to study the ridge above. Its rocky profile cut into the blue-black of the early evening sky.

16

The People Mover sat in Paul's yard like a prehistoric monster. Chee parked beside it. Next time someone wanted to make a horror movie, he thought, they should consider using all the dead cars and pickups in Navajoland. Have them come back to life and stalk their former owners, punishing them for neglect and abuse.

His cousin rested under the ramada with a book: *John Wayne's Kitchen: Favorite Recipes of Monument Valley*. A covered pot simmered over the wood fire.

"Hey, is there a recipe for True Grits in there?" Chee said.

"Haven't gotten to that yet. I'm looking for something easy I can fix when I start having guests in the hogan. And when you abandon me, bro."

Chee sat next to him. At that level, he could smell something interesting coming from the pot. "An officer I work with told me you had some trouble with the People Mover."

"No worries. It came out all right. Ron Good-springs took the customers, and I rode along as sort of his assistant. He said you're working with his niece. Was she the one who told you?"

Chee nodded. "I thought I had fixed the problem for you. I'll take another look and see if I can figure out what went wrong."

Paul gave him his classic grin. "You don't have to play mechanic. The one who helped me with the customers figured out what the problem was. All fixed." He went back to the book. "You remember pigs in blankets?"

"I sure do. Hot dogs with a biscuit on the outside. Your mother made them all the time, and we loved them. Is that what you're cooking?"

"Nope."

"So are you going to explain what went wrong with the beast?"

"I was hoping not to, but here goes." Paul put the book down so he could use his hands to tell the story. "The man who helped me had an idea that maybe the thing wouldn't run because it was out of gas. He loaned me a gas can and took me to the station after the tour. I bought gas. Then he gave me a ride back to the People Mover. I poured it in and—*gr, grr, grrrr, grrrrrr, vroom!* Off we went. That sucker uses a lot of gas, and the gauge doesn't work."

Chee smiled. Another lesson in the futility of guilt and worry. "So what's for dinner?"

Paul handed Chee a rag. "Take a look."

Chee tripled the thickness of cloth against his skin and lifted the handle on the heavy pot. Inside was a concoction he couldn't recall seeing before. "I give up."

"I call it Monument Valley Surprise. It's an experiment. If we like it, I might serve it as dinner to the folks who come to stay here overnight. The recipe says to cook it another half hour."

As it turned out, half an hour wasn't enough. But Paul declared it fit for visitors and had three helpings. In addition to a bit more cooking, Chee suggested fewer onions and chiles and more potatoes and meat.

Chee slept poorly, troubled by images of Samuel's body and upset at the idea that the man had hurt and embarrassed little Alisha, and probably other girls too. He missed Bernie and wondered if she missed him. When he finally did fall asleep, he dreamed that Darleen was in jail for stealing Melissa's earrings.

He awoke feeling unsettled, said his prayers with corn pollen, started a fire from last night's embers, and cooked enough eggs for breakfast for two. Paul joined him, and they watched as morning brought the color back to the monuments.

Chee took the smoother route back to the office. When he reached the pavement, he noticed the undelivered citations on the seat next to him, the original and the new citation, which included the addition of human remains to the illegal gravesite. He'd check in at the office and start the paperwork with Bahe that meant he could go home. He could deliver the citation on his way back to Paul's. Or maybe Tsinnie could be the gofer. As he pushed the button to lower the window, he realized that he'd miss driving this unit—it worked better than the one he used at

Shiprock. And he'd miss Bahe. He would recommend that the station look into luring Erdman away from the hotel, putting her to work for the Navajo police. She wasn't Navajo, but you didn't have to be to join the department. She was smart, she knew the area, and she had good instincts. Perhaps a woman would get along better with Tsinnie.

Bahe was on the phone when Chee got to the office, so he read the digital edition of the *Navajo Times* and then checked his e-mail. Something from "leaphornj."

He opened it. The Lieutenant's reply to his request for help dispensed with pleasantries and got right to business:

necklace 1930s. museum-quality heirloom Persian turquoise? Robert Etcitty

Etcitty was a jeweler Chee had heard of, a man too young to have been born in the 1930s.

Leaphorn had typed a line of inverted triangles to separate the next section:

vvvvv

poker chip = Stagecoach

Chee pulled out the chip and looked at it to make sure. No, it didn't have a stagecoach on it. The impression was of an eagle. The photograph he sent must have been blurry or something.

Chee walked outside, gathering his ideas, considering what to send as a reply. The June heat radiated off the walls and terraces of the visitor center. He noticed it more outside the station than in the valley itself, probably because of the added warmth generated by the air-conditioning units and the pavement and concrete. He climbed the steps to the vista point and spent a moment taking in the procession of vehicles stirring up dust on the vista road and the view of the Mittens and Merrick Butte against the cloudless turquoise sky. Merrick Butte took its American name from a soldier turned silver miner who died at the spot. But unlike the grave Chee had inadvertently discovered, Merrick's place of death had an impressive natural marker, a massive tower of red sandstone rising over the desert. Chee took the poker chip out of his pocket and studied it again.

Back in the office, he first thanked the Lieutenant for the information.

I must have not given you a good photo of the chip. The design is an eagle with three arrows in its talons. I just sent it to offer you an idea of the size of the necklace. Are you sure about the silversmith? I know a man by that name, and I believe he would be too young to have made it.

He inquired about Leaphorn's health and Louisa and clicked send. He felt a twinge of sadness. In all the years they had worked together, he had never questioned the Lieutenant's mental fitness, but evidently the brain injury changed things. He hoped the change was temporary.

Chee saw the neat pile of papers he expected, the forms he had to complete to mark the termination of his assignment at Monument Valley, on Bahe's desk. But the captain didn't give them to him immediately.

"Remember that message you sent me for Burke, the one about the photos Samuel supposedly took of the girl?" Bahe wasn't as jovial as usual.

"Sure. What do you need?"

"Burke found the pictures, still on that phone, along with quite a few more. Similar poses of other women, and maybe some minors, too. Since that teenager was the only one we had a name for, Burke tried to reach Isenberg to talk to him and his daughter. No luck."

"The only phone number I have is the sister's cell phone. I'll give him that. The family is at Goulding's."

"They left yesterday. Burke thinks that's suspicious. Burke doesn't have any suspects in the murder at this point except Delahart, and maybe this girl's father."

"Did he find the gun?"

"No. It wasn't in the room." Bahe paused. "He asked if we could give him a hand. Burke wants us to review the security recordings from the hotel."

"Us? Why? It's a federal case."

"I owe the guy a favor. So look at the tape and see if you spot Isenberg or anyone you recognize from being out on the movie set."

Chee thought about it. "You know, the camera only captured people leaving the elevator and walking down the hall. Other movie people might have rooms on that same floor."

"So check that out too." Bahe tapped the flat end of his pencil on the tape. "Monica can set up the player. She's good at that stuff."

Bahe pushed the pile of papers, the exit forms, toward Chee. "I know you're ready to get home. It's been exciting having you here, to say the least. Just leave these on my desk before you head on back to Shiprock."

Monica dealt with the technology smoothly,

showing Chee the necessary buttons on the remote to run the TV monitor and the DVD player. Why was every one of these things just different enough to make life complicated?

"Any questions? And no, I won't bring you popcorn." She walked to the door and then came back. "I forgot to tell you to check your voice mail. You know that upset girl who came in yesterday? She called while you were talking to Bahe. I put her through to leave a message. And your wife called. She sounds nice over the phone."

"She's nice in person, too. I'll introduce you when I'm back here for the sing." She would know he meant the healing ceremony with the *hataalii*.

"Good. I'm looking forward to that." Monica smiled at him. "If you have any trouble with the machine, give it a slap on the top with the palm of your hand."

Chee pushed play and saw the elevator door and an empty hallway. Then came Samuel, walking toward Delahart's room. More empty shots, and then he watched a man in a hotel uniform roll the room-service cart down the hall. Erdman's assessment had been correct. People struggling with suitcases, a couple of older women holding little dogs, dry kids in swimsuits getting into the elevator, wet kids in swimsuits getting out of the elevator. The hallway was busier than he'd expected. After some serious boredom, Chee realized he could listen to his phone messages and watch the procession of people at the same time.

Courtney's voicemail thanked him for yesterday. Then she changed the subject. *"Hey, I've been on the movie's fan page, and they had a story that said a police-man found a grave out where they've been filming, and now everyone is investigating. Do you know about that? Way bad!"*

Delahart's back at work, Chee thought. Would he use Samuel's murder as a promotional tool too? He was surprised that Courtney's message didn't mention human bones.

He slowed the tape a few times and made note of a person or two whose body language seemed suspicious, and then fast-forwarded through a section with no people as he listened to Bernie's message: *"I miss you. Hope you're OK and not working too hard. Call me."*

He was ready to punch in her number when something on the TV monitor caught his eye. He put the phone down and hit rewind. Someone who looked like Greg Robinson left the elevator and walked down the hallway toward Delahart's door. Chee hit rewind and watched again. As Delahart's assistant producer, Robinson probably had a million things to talk to him about. Chee decided he shouldn't have been surprised to see him on the tape.

All in all, not much to go on. Of course, whoever shot Samuel could have entered and left by the open back door, but he hadn't noticed any sand on the balcony's floor or on the carpet. And there didn't seem to be enough footprints in the sand for both coming and going. Chee focused on the images, waiting for Isenberg to appear and for Robinson to walk back to the elevator. He watched until he came to the footage of himself and Brenda heading for the room. No more Robinson. And no Isenberg.

The emergency exit staircase was at the end of the hall, he remembered, out of view of the hallway camera. Robinson could have left that way. And perhaps Isenberg, if he had been there at all, had come and gone on the back stairs, too. Erdman had mentioned other surveillance cameras that showed all the exits. Chee called her and left a message, asking her to have someone bring that tape over as soon as possible and deliver it to Bahe.

Bahe had left before Chee finished, so he wrote a note about Robinson and his request for the second tape, along with the paperwork to get a paycheck. Since he had to drive out to the movie set to serve the citation, he decided to do Burke a favor and ask Robinson face-to-face what he was doing at the hotel, clear up that loose end. It wasn't his case, but he was curious.

Without Gerald's oversight, the movie production parking situation had disintegrated into total chaos. He'd mention this to Robinson, too. The operation needed the parking attendant, budget crisis or not.

When Chee opened the door to the office trailer, the air-conditioned breeze bordered on too chilly. BJ looked up from her desk. "Hi. You're back."

"Yes, looking for Robinson again."

"Good timing. His meeting broke up ten minutes ago."

Bad timing, Chee thought. He'd hoped to arrive before the meeting started.

"Did you hear any more buzz about the murder?"

"No. I didn't hear any more news about that. But—" She hesitated. "What the heck, you'll hear this anyway. A lot more people are having their hours cut. Everyone's upset."

"Too bad."

"It's sad for the people who thought they'd have work for the next month or so."

"And for the locals, too." Chee heard something that sounded like a gunshot. "What was that?"

"Must be the special effects guys. You hear all kinds of things out here in zombie land. Don't let it spook you, Officer. Robinson ought to be in the tent still—a lot of people had questions for him. If he's not there, check his trailer. You know where it is."

In the tent, Chee saw rows of chairs that had been set up for the meeting and clusters of people standing and talking, but no Robinson. His goal was to deliver the citation, ask the man what he was doing in the hotel, finish the paperwork, and get back to Shiprock and Bernie.

But Melissa had noticed him and walked his way. She looked disheartened.

"Hi there," he said.

"Did you hear about the cutbacks?"

"BJ told me."

"It's my fault."

Chee remembered that she was the bookkeeper. "BJ said the word came down from Delahart himself. How could it be your fault?"

"I never should have let Samuel—" He heard the anger in her voice. "Can you give me some advice on something? I mean, could we talk privately somewhere?"

Chee wanted to say no, but what difference would

a few minutes make? "We could sit in my unit. It's parked over there."

He opened the passenger door for her and climbed in behind the steering wheel, lowering the windows to catch the breeze and create an illusion of coolness.

"You know, this is the first time I've ever been in a police car."

"That's probably a good thing."

She sat, staring out the windshield for a while. "I made a big mistake in the bookkeeping. It's complicated, but in a nutshell I gave the company credit for a big sponsorship that hasn't come in yet. Robinson trusted me and authorized the expenditures without asking enough questions. Delahart is the producer, so the buck stops with him, but I don't think he even looked at any of the reports. We weren't in the red yet, but it was just a matter of time.

"When I realized what I'd done, I went to Robinson with my resignation letter. He talked me into staying. He said that he and Delahart weren't working together very well, and if I left, Delahart would blame Robinson's management style and fire him. I didn't want him to lose his job over me. He asked me for a commitment to stick with it, and I gave him my word.

"He said that because I'd created the situation, I should figure out how to fix it. We knew the sponsorship money was coming, it was just a matter of treading water, doing more with less, until then."

"What does this have to do with Samuel?"

"I'm getting there." She looked out the window at the sunlight reflecting off the other vehicles.

"We trimmed expenses—Delahart was always harping on that anyway, so it didn't look suspicious. But Robinson felt bad about what would have been the next step, cutting some people's hours or letting them go. I had another idea. I'm good at blackjack, and I said with some luck, I could make up the deficit."

Chee felt his jaw tighten. Gambling to pay debts was one of the top ten terrible ideas of all time.

Melissa didn't notice his reaction. "Because I'm on the management team, I get to claim one of the empty seats on Delahart's corporate plane. He goes to Vegas every weekend to meet with investors. Sometimes he'd invite Rhonda, our zombie queen, and tell Robinson to go along. I finagled an invitation, went to a casino with my own paycheck, and came back with about double. I showed Robinson how I put the winnings into the line items that were short. I did it three times, traveling with Delahart, Samuel, and some other folks who wanted to get away. I played at a different casino each time, and had more good luck. With a few more successful trips, I could have fixed the deficit without anyone knowing it had even been there."

Melissa stopped talking. Chee thought about Delahart's investors, about the cocaine, and Samuel's spying. He doubted if the money problems were all due to Melissa's error. "If you had almost fixed the budget problem, and Delahart didn't know about it anyway, why did he decide to cut people's hours now?"

"He's a jerk. He wants more money for himself and his Las Vegas investors."

"I still don't see how this ties to Samuel's murder."

Melissa swallowed. "Samuel always went to Vegas because he was Delahart's man. He decided I had a gambling problem, and he threatened to tell Delahart I was embezzling to cover my gambling debts if I didn't pay to keep him quiet."

"Were you using company money to gamble?"

"No. Only my own. Robinson and I kept a second set of books, so when the sponsorship came in, I'd get back the money of my own that I'd loaned the company."

A second set of books was another very bad idea, Chee thought. "So you let Samuel blackmail you?"

"I knew I shouldn't have paid him. He started tightening the screws. Every time I got on the plane, the price of his silence escalated. That was why I had to return those beautiful earrings. I needed all the money I could find to keep Samuel quiet."

Chee remembered something. "Robinson said he planned to fire Samuel before the incident with the girls, and that you talked him out of it. Is that right?"

"Another mistake. Samuel knew he was about to get canned because of the same sort of bad behavior you saw—getting too rough with trespassers, especially girls. He came to me and said that if Robinson fired him, he would go to his boss, Delahart, and say Robinson canned him because he knew I was embezzling, and Robinson was covering it up. Somehow Samuel knew about the second set of books. So even though I hated Samuel, I went to Robinson and begged him to give the jerk another chance."

Chee let the silence sit between them until he

figured out how to phrase what he wanted to say. Parts of her story didn't make sense. "So Samuel was blackmailing and intimidating you and spying for Delahart on the rest of the company. Maybe he was blackmailing other people, too. It sounds like you weren't the only person out here who would have been happy to see him dead."

"I could give you a list of names as long as my arm. But they're actors and technicians and extras and gofers. Not killers—unless it's make-believe."

"What about Robinson or you?"

"Sure, I wished him dead, hit by a truck, a heart attack, something that would remove him and the trouble he made. But I figured what goes around comes around, you know? A karma sort of thing. I hoped the havoc and pain Samuel caused would catch up with him in the end. I guess it did. I can't say I'm sorry."

Chee had been around people enough to figure she was telling the truth, at least mostly.

"What about Robinson? He asked me how Samuel treated the girls, and when I told him, he said he was going to fire him. Did he?"

"You'll have to ask him about that. He didn't mention it to me. I guess he didn't want to hear me whining to save that weasel's job again."

She looked tired, he thought. Older than when he'd first met her on the sandy rise in the moonlight. She sighed and sat up a little straighter. "I'm thinking about how I'm going to explain this all to Delahart. I made a commitment to Robinson to finish the job, and I will if he doesn't fire me."

"Anyone can make a mistake. It sounds like you've taken some pretty creative steps to fix things. Maybe Delahart will hire someone to come in and help you straighten things out."

"Yeah." She made a sound that was somewhere between a laugh and a sigh. "Without Samuel on the payroll, he'll have some extra money for contract labor. But he'll probably use it for nose candy."

Chee opened the car door. "I'm going to talk to Robinson. You want to come?"

She shook her head. "Do you mind if I sit here a minute? I'm still figuring out what to do about this mess."

Chee had the keys, his weapon, and his handcuffs with him. It was against regulations, but he didn't see a problem. "That's fine. Just be sure to lock the doors when you leave."

It was, Chee knew, none of his business how the movie company handled its finances. Not his concern that Delahart stayed at an expensive hotel and ordered room service while a local guy who probably had a bunch of relatives he was helping out lost his job as a parking attendant because of budget cutbacks. His job, he reminded himself, was to serve the citation for the grave and to ask Robinson a few questions about his visit to the floor of the hotel where Delahart's room was, and how he left without using the elevator.

As he walked toward the trailer, he replayed his conversation with Robinson about Samuel. Robinson hadn't exactly said he was going to fire the man—he said he planned to "get rid of him." Chee

had interpreted that as the same thing. But maybe
not.

He knocked on Robinson's trailer door and noticed a young woman coming toward the place. Not
exactly pretty, but handsome in an athletic-looking
way. She looked familiar. Maybe he'd seen her in the
food tent.

She stopped at the base of the steps. "Is Greg still
here?"

"Robinson? I hope so. I'm waiting for him to
answer the door."

"He was upset after the meeting, dealing with so
many angry people. They're clueless. They don't
realize Delahart makes the money decisions. That
dude is a coked-up rat bastard, but Robinson takes
the blame." She looked at Chee again. "He might be
on the phone or something. We were going to fly
out to Durango for a break from the heat. He was
supposed to meet me at the car so we could head to
the airstrip. Probably got a call."

Chee knocked harder this time. "Mr. Robinson,
it's Officer Chee. I need to talk to you."

"You're a real cop?"

Only on a movie set would he be asked that question. Chee introduced himself.

"Sorry, I thought you were with the production.
I'm Rhonda."

"I hear you're famous."

"That's me. Queen of the Zombies." She flashed
him a beautiful smile. "Are you here about Samuel?"

"Not exactly." He didn't want to elaborate.

She walked up the steps, knocked, and yelled.
"Greg, open the door. It's hot out here, honey. You

need to talk to the policeman, and then we need to go."

Nothing.

Rhonda pulled a key from her pocket, put it in the lock, and looked up at Chee. "You do it. I'm getting bad vibes here."

17

Morning light nudged Bernie to wakefulness. It was already almost dawn. She ran, showered, had a bite of breakfast, put on her uniform for work later, and headed to Mama's house. She wanted to talk to Mama about helping Bigman's wife. If Mama had the energy, it might be a good solution to several problems.

As she drove, she thought about weaving. Making beautiful rugs took supple hands and multilevel thinking. Traditional Navajo weavers like her mother held several ideas in their mind simultaneously, moving one to the forefront and then another, focusing on details while simultaneously remembering the big picture and making the process seamless. She remembered how Mama could get lost in her weaving, sitting until it finally grew too dark to work and then stirring as if from a dream to consider what they'd have for supper or to ask about schoolwork. That was before arthritis took its terrible toll.

Darleen had the same ability to concentrate. When she was working on her drawings, it was as though she was in a trance. Weaving seemed to Bernie to be a more practical art, but at least her sister had something in her life that gave her pleasure and might be useful.

Bernie considered herself a practical, down-to-earth person. She liked facts, nailing down loose ends, corralling rowdy details one at a time and closing the case. She wanted to make the world a better place, not with art but in a concrete way. Her contribution as a police officer was to help make sure people like her mother and Darleen could live in peace.

If she hadn't become a cop, she thought, she never would have met Chee, the man who made her life more beautiful. She'd come to a realization last night. Her husband would always love his work. She could be jealous of that passion, or accept it as something she'd known about him from the first day they met. It was who he was. And, she thought, loving his job didn't mean that he didn't love her, too.

She pulled up to Mama's house and heard the blare of the TV through the open windows of her Toyota. Mrs. Darkwater's big black-and-brown dog barked and charged at her car. It quieted down when she stopped. Bernie climbed out of the car and stiffened as the animal rushed to her. She thought it meant no harm, but she didn't like dogs so close, sniffing at her. She hurried to the house and closed the door behind her.

The two elders sat side by side, watching a game show, one of those where the contestant gets the prize behind the door. They were giving the woman on the screen advice.

"No." Mama leaned closer to the TV. "Pick number two."

"You're all right with number three," Mrs. Darkwater said.

Bernie stood behind them. "Hello there, ladies."

Mama patted the couch next to her, motioning Bernie to sit down. "Welcome, my daughter. You will like this show."

Mrs. Darkwater moved over so Bernie could squeeze in next to Mama.

The woman on TV didn't listen to Mama. She stayed with number three. The prize was a year's supply of frozen pizzas. The shiny new RV was behind door number one.

The scene switched to commercials. Mrs. Darkwater said, "I heard that someone's car got burned over there by Ship Rock."

"It's a bad place," Mama said. "When people go out that way, things happen."

"Did you hear why it happened?" Bernie asked.

Mrs. Darkwater spoke first "They don't need a reason." Bernie didn't need to ask who "they" were. She could tell from Mrs. Darkwater's tone that the reference was to skinwalkers.

Bernie wondered if her little sister was still asleep. Then she remembered that Darleen's car was gone. "Where's Sister?"

"Oh, she had to go to Farmington. She got a letter from the court."

"Really? What did it say?"

"I don't know. She said she didn't understand it, so she drove over there."

"Why didn't she call them?"

"You ask too many questions." Mama got up, using her walker to provide some leverage as she rose from the couch and to steady her steps to the bathroom.

"I think that one isn't feeling good." Mrs. Darkwater fluffed up the pillow Mama had positioned behind her back as she spoke. "She told me she has a pain in her side. Right here." Mrs. Darkwater put her hand on her own ribs. "I had an uncle with that pain. He went to the hospital in Farmington. They took out the gall bladder. Then he had a stroke. He's better now." Mrs. Darkwater gave the pillow a final pat and put it back on the couch.

Bernie knew how lucky she was that Mama had such a concerned neighbor. "If Sister goes to school somewhere, it wouldn't be good for Mama to stay alone here in the house. Something could happen."

"You worry too much." Mrs. Darkwater frowned. "When you think about problems, you get more problems and they get bigger. That's what happens." She patted Bernie's hand. "If something happens, you'll do what you need to do then."

It wasn't the response Bernie was looking for, but she agreed with the logic. First things first. Still, she wanted to have a plan in place.

She fixed an early lunch for them all, and then Mrs. Darkwater headed home for an afternoon nap. To Bernie's relief, the dog, which had been napping on the porch, followed after her. Mama looked tired.

"Before you take a nap, I need to talk to you about something."

"I know," Mama said. "Your sister and that school. I want to take a look at that place. How far is it?"

"About a four-hour drive."

"Darleen will come with us. You both can drive."

"I don't think we need to do that yet." Darleen should be in on this conversation, Bernie thought. The letter from Farmington must have to do with her sister's arrest. "We should talk about this later, when Sister is ready."

Mama had a question in her eyes. "When we go to Santa Fe, to see the school, will we drive by the car that burned?"

"No, you can't see it from the highway."

Mama nodded. "Good. What happened to the one who was driving?"

It never failed to amaze Bernie how quickly news spread on the reservation. "I don't know, but at least he was not burned in the car."

"I'm glad about that."

Bernie mentioned Bigman's wife and her desire to learn to weave. "Perhaps you know someone who could help her. She's a good woman. She works at the school as a teacher."

Mama didn't respond except with a quick nod. Message received.

Bernie helped Mama lie down for a little rest, asked her about the pain Mrs. Darkwater had mentioned, and learned Mama didn't want to talk about that.

Before driving back to the station, she walked over to Mrs. Darkwater's house. The dog wagged its tail from the shade of the porch but, to Bernie's relief, didn't rise. Mrs. Darkwater sat working on a crossword puzzle. She tapped the point of her pencil gently against the page. "You're a smart one. What's a word that means 'threatened'?"

"Scared? Or bullied?"

"Longer. Ten letters."

Bernie thought. "Try frightened."

Mrs. Darkwater looked at the page. "No. Third letter is a D."

"Hmm."

She glanced up at Bernie. "Drive back safely."

"I will. I wanted to ask you something. How did you hear about the burned car?"

"Arthur told me. You met him. He's my husband's relative who drives the trucks with the packages. One of the other drivers saw it on fire out there."

Back in the car, Bernie turned up the radio so she could hear it over the wind noise. KNDN's broadcasts included a community calendar she always found interesting. That and the music kept her from thinking too hard about the talk she had to give to the Rotary, or about the mysterious Mr. Miller and how his stolen car had ended up burned and abandoned. Clearly, Miller hung with the wrong crowd.

She drove and listened, warm and windblown, and had almost reached the pavement of 491 when she heard her phone chime—a new text. She glanced at it when she stopped at the stop sign where the dirt and pavement met. A note from Darleen: *call u 2nite*. Bernie called her, and her voice mail picked up on the third ring.

She cruised past a new billboard touting Primal

Solar and a herd of lean horses standing in the shade of the sign. Pulling off the highway to check on a pickup truck parked on the shoulder with its emergency flashers blinking, she realized it was empty. A car obviously speeding passed her, and she flashed her lights. She thought again of Miller's car. Was it stolen for a joy ride? Of all the cars in Farmington, why his? Of 27,400 square miles of reservation, why there? And why would a guy in such a big hurry to get back to Flagstaff be in Farmington? She remembered the calls on his phone to the Farmington motel. Interesting.

When she got to the office, a domestic violence call was waiting, the kind of case she dreaded. Usually it meant a husband or boyfriend hurting a woman, sometimes with the kids as witnesses. Those incidents made her angry, broke her heart, and left her feeling totally ineffectual. Largo knew she'd rather deal with drunks or druggies, gang fights, even suicides. Anything but DV and men who let anger and fear, usually fueled by alcohol, transform them into pathetic monsters. It wasn't the danger—that was an integral part of police work. She hated the devastation of beaten women and terrified little ones.

She ran into Bigman in the coffee room and told him the truth, at least part of it. "Largo wants me to settle this burned-car deal. I've got to track down a potential witness and see if I can reach Miller—you know, the guy who owned it. Can you take the DV?"

"I was going to volunteer for it," Bigman said. "I've dealt with these two before. And I owe you for that Rotary talk tomorrow. I'd rather face a wife beater than those men in suits any day."

"What about the new guy?"

"I'm taking him with me. It might get dicey out there."

"I meant for the speech. I told Largo I'd do this one, but there will be more requests."

"You want to scare him into resigning already?"

Bernie called the deputy in Farmington who had handled the report on Miller's stolen car and left a message. She made more calls, attempting to get in touch with the delivery driver who might have seen the burning car. Then, while she waited for callbacks, she got busy with the task she wanted to postpone indefinitely—creating the Rotary talk from the outline she'd made in her head. She didn't mind writing the speech, but the talking part bothered her.

She envisioned the Farmington event. She'd be an outsider in a group where everybody knew everybody, a woman among mostly men, a Navajo in a group that was white with a few Hispanics, a young woman in a crowd contemplating retirement. But no matter what the audience, public speaking didn't come easy to her. She was slightly more comfortable with it than Chee, or maybe even Captain Largo, but that only meant that she'd faced a roomful of strangers eighty-five percent terrified.

The Rotarians had requested an overview of the work the Navajo police did, so that was what she focused on: the history of the force, the size of their jurisdiction, how they worked with other agencies like the New Mexico State Police and the San Juan County sheriff's office. Then she'd touch on the issues that continued to face the department and the people they served: lack of community activities as alternatives to crime, the growing influence of gangs and drug trafficking, too few officers, too few resources, too much territory to cover.

Bernie had made a decent start when Sandra buzzed her. She had a call from a truck driver.

"Yes, ma'am, I saw that blaze. It was somethin'. I couldn't figure what it was at first. I thought it might be a house. I wanted to turn down that dirt road and have a look, but I was already off schedule."

"Do you drive that route all the time?"

"A couple times a week I might have packages out that way."

"Did you notice anything else?"

She heard silence on the phone, and then he said, "You mean, like somethin' I didn't usually see out there?"

"That's right."

"Well, now that you remind me, I saw a hitch-hiker trying to thumb a ride out to 491. I notice them every once in a while. Not too often, because there's barely any traffic out that way. I can't pick nobody up. Company's strict about that. One time my pal Mario, well, he stopped for this kid—" The driver's tale grew elaborate, wandering away from the investigation Bernie was pursuing.

When he paused, she steered him back to the hitchhiker. "You mentioned that in addition to seeing the fire, you saw a person trying to catch a ride. Why did you think that was odd?"

"Well, he was wearing hiking shorts and had a dog with him. He was tan, but not an Indian, no offense. I wondered if he'd been climbin' Ship Rock or something. I know that's against the rules, but people try to do it anyway."

"Do you remember how tall he was, anything else about him?"

"He looked like an average guy in a ball cap. Maybe thirty or early forties. He had on a long-sleeved shirt with those shorts." The sketchy description of the hitchhiker matched her memory of Miller right down to the baseball cap.

After Bernie hung up, she talked to Largo about her interview with the driver.

"It's summer, Manuelito. Shorts really aren't suspicious unless you see me wearing them."

Navajos of Largo's generation dressed conservatively, with a tip of their Stetsons toward the cowboy tradition. The generation above them, elders like her mother and Mrs. Darkwater, had been raised to be even more modest. Bernie remembered Mama always in a skirt until Darleen had persuaded her to wear sweatpants for a big, messy job around the house. Their mother had become an instant convert, but still always wore a long skirt, a velvet blouse, and her best jewelry to visit friends and relatives.

Largo leaned back in his chair. "What I wonder is who burned that car and why, and whether we'll be seeing more of this out here. Follow up on that gang stuff Wheeler copied for you. I would like to get this off the books. Any luck reaching Miller?"

"No, sir. I called the number the deputy gave me. No answer, no way to leave a message. I called his old cell phone. Same results."

"OK. Back off. Cordova handles that, understand?"

"Yes, sir." She stood to leave. "How did that domestic violence call work out?"

"The man was gone when Bigman and the new guy got there. The wife had a bloody lip but didn't want to press charges. She and the kids were shook up. The new guy did OK." Largo moved forward, resting his elbows on the desk. "You know, Manuelito, sometimes women feel safer with another woman. You could do some good on those cases. You ought to think about that."

"Yes, sir."

"I know you don't want to be pigeonholed. But because of what they've been through, a lot of these ladies don't trust men much, even a nice guy like Officer Bigman."

"Yes, sir. I'll call Cordova and tell him about the hitchhiker."

"You're changing the subject. We could use a specialist in domestic violence. I could get some training for you."

"Yes, sir. Anything else?"

"You're stubborn, too. Good luck with the Rotary tomorrow."

"Thank you, sir."

She left a message for Cordova that she had news of Miller, but nothing more. Maybe she could use the hitchhiker sighting to finally coax some information from his sealed lips. As she prepared to get back to work on the talk, she saw that the Lieutenant had sent her an e-mail:

Cactus = Sclerocactus mesae-verde, endangered, grows in Shiprock area. See below.

Listed as threatened by the US and on the NM and CO rare plants list.

He had included information copied from his research site:

Found on tops of hills or benches and slopes of hills, from gravelly to loamy and pulverulent clay soil, the plant is very small, with a maximum size of only 2 to 2.5 inches in height, 3 to 3.5 inches in diameter, and with up to 14 spiral-like ribs. The flowers are white to cream-yellow, 3 cm long, 2 cm in diameter and do not open completely. The fruits are green, spherical, with a diameter of 1.25 cm. The fruits brown with age, and split horizontally. The seeds are black. Wild-collected specimens usually die in cultivation.

The part about the little plants not surviving in captivity caught her attention. Interesting and sad. But it said "usually," not always. A glimmer of hope remained for her little transplants. Certainly they would have died if they had been dumped in the garbage along with the dirt in the boxes. Had Miller known what the cacti were when he dug them up, or was it accidental that they were in the boxes? If he knew they were endangered, protected by the Navajo Nation, the state of New Mexico, possibly federal regulations, that would explain his reluctance to open the trunk, and his attempt at bribery. *Endangered*, she realized, was the word Mrs. Darkwater had needed for her crossword puzzle.

Even though a person could acquire beautiful, healthy cacti with a money-back guarantee from nurseries, poaching had become a growing problem in the Southwest. Bernie had read about thieves in Arizona digging up heavy, centuries-old saguaros to sell for top dollar. Other poachers went after rarer varieties, sometimes on special assignment from plant collectors. The National Park Service tried to save cacti popular with poachers by inserting microchips in the plants to identify them if they arrived in the resale market, but plant thieves usually got away with it.

Since Bernie enjoyed botany, she understood that successful poaching involved more than simply heading into the desert with a shovel. Many cacti looked similar. Some needed time for exposed roots to harden before they could be replanted. Most, like *Sclerocactus mesae-verde*, didn't transplant well. To make top money, the seller also needed a buyer who appreciated the rarity of the species as well as its beauty.

Miller had told her he made a living as a contractor. Wheeler had said the man also did landscaping, so the idea of his moonlighting as a cactus thief had some legs. Bernie found her list of numbers from his phone and printed it for Sandra to check. Perhaps some of the contacts were cactus customers. She remembered Miller saying that he loved the desert.

Then she argued against her theory. Miller struck her as a wheeler-dealer and a man in a hurry. Would those little plants have sold for more than $500? It seemed unlikely. She went back to "just a coincidence," but that didn't sit right either.

She sent Leaphorn a thank-you and asked if he could find out anything about the market value of the cacti. Then she had another thought. Maybe Aaron had been in on the deal, digging up the plants for Miller to sell. But it wasn't Aaron's number in Miller's phone. It was his mother's. She remembered Largo's admonition: leave Miller to the feds. But Largo had instructed her to follow up on the burned car, and that brought her back to Miller.

She put the issue out of her mind and focused on polishing the Rotary talk until she couldn't bear it, then went outside for some air.

Bigman had nabbed the spot in the shade where Largo usually parked, and was heading into the building. He greeted her, asking, "Did you ever come up with an idea of someone who could work with my wife on weaving?"

"I mentioned it to Mama. But don't get your hopes up."

"Did she say no?"

"She didn't say anything. But she isn't weaving anymore because of her arthritis and she gave away her loom." Bernie watched the native grass at the edge of the parking lot move in the breeze, wishing she'd shared this news with Bigman earlier instead of leaving him disappointed. "But Mama still knows the weavers around here. She may come up with a name for you."

"Could you tell your mother she wouldn't have to weave much? Only enough so my wife could get the idea. I bet that loom they used to have out back at the Toadlena Trading Post is still there. Maybe they would let your mother use that. I could pick

her up, drive them both over there, and then take
her home."

Bernie knew the *bilagaana* couple who ran the
post, wonderful people who sometimes hosted tour
groups in the century-old building and invited local
weavers to offer demonstrations. Perhaps Mama
could work with Mrs. Bigman there. But they'd run
the risk of having an audience, not the best environ-
ment for a beginning weaver.

"I'll talk to her about that."

"Maybe it would be better if we stopped by to
visit. Once she meets my wife, she might change her
mind."

"Mama likes company. But just remember that
she hasn't agreed to anything yet."

Bigman cleared his throat. "I've been meaning to
ask, what's happening with your little sister and that
incident in Farmington?"

"I don't know." That reminded her that Darleen
had promised to call, and hadn't. She sighed, and
went back inside to finish the draft of her talk and
print it before going home.

"Hey, Manuelito, you okay?" Sandra looked up
from her desk as Bernie walked in. "You don't look
so good."

"Really?"

"You seem kinda pale, girl. You know all the
sugar and caffeine in Coke isn't good for you. Rots
your teeth, too."

A Coke would be great, Bernie realized, but some
cold water would suit her fine.

Sandra reached into her desk drawer. "Try this."

"Thanks." For a happy second Bernie thought it

was candy, then realized Sandra had given her some kind of health snack, an energy bar. She'd tried them before, and they reminded her of sweetened cardboard.

"I have a message for you, too."

"Cordova?"

"Oh, yeah, him, too. He's on your voice mail. But this is the one I meant." Sandra handed her a note from the Rotary organizer with home and cell phone numbers. Bernie smiled. Maybe the talk had been cancelled.

She called Cordova first. He sounded preoccupied. "Just checking to see if you've learned anything new about Miller that might be helpful."

"You're working late," she said. "I've got some new info."

"Go ahead."

"You need to tell me why you're interested."

"No, I don't, but nice try."

"Why are you such a tough guy?"

"I was born this way. Just tell me what you've got, Manuelito."

She told him about the truck driver who'd seen a man resembling Miller hitchhiking, and about the questionable cacti. He listened without interrupting, and then he said, "Thanks."

"That's all I get?"

"I'll buy you a Coke next time I see you. Happier now?"

"No, of course not. If you guys were more cooperative—"

"Gotta go." And he disconnected.

Bernie called the Rotary woman next.

"We've had a great response to your coming to talk. Lots of reservations. We've never had a representative from the Navajo Police. I'm so glad they are sending a woman. I know people will have a lot of interesting questions for you about your job and how you became a police officer." She recommended that Bernie come a little early so she could meet the club's officers and get a good parking spot.

So instead of leaving for home, Bernie looked over her speech again, made some changes, and printed out a new copy. The energy bar wasn't half bad.

18

Chee turned the key in the door of Robinson's trailer and heard the lock click. He saw Robinson lying on his back and instinctively stepped in front of Rhonda, blocking her entrance and her view with his body. Then he spoke calmly. "He's hurt. Run to the office and ask BJ to call an ambulance. If there are any EMTs around, we could use them."

"What? Why?"

"Do it. Then come back and keep everyone else out of here." Chee had stepped into the room as he spoke, moving toward Robinson. From her gasp, he realized Rhonda had seen the blood.

"Oh, my God." And then he heard her clatter down the steps and run.

Chee squatted down. Robinson's chest rose and fell slightly with each breath. Chee scanned for something to use to stop the bleeding. There was a dish towel on the counter. He grabbed for it, knocking a sheet of paper to the floor, and pressed the towel against the chest wound.

Robinson looked at him, and Chee moved his mouth close to the man's ear. "Hang on. I'm here to help you, and more help is on the way."

He held the pressure, feeling the warm blood on his hands. Glancing around the room, he didn't see any disturbance or signs of conflict. The door had been locked from the inside, but whoever did this could have locked it on the way out.

The towel was red and saturated now, and the bleeding seemed to have slowed. Robinson's lips had a bluish tinge. Chee kept talking, encouraging him, but his eyelids fluttered and then closed.

The trailer swayed, and Chee heard footsteps on the entrance stairs. He listened to the door opening behind him, and felt someone approach. He kept his gaze on Robinson's face, willing him to keep breathing.

A man with a first-aid box knelt beside them. He spoke loudly. "Mr. Robinson, it's Kevin Green, the EMT."

Robinson opened his eyes again.

Green had already slipped on gloves. "Gunshot?"

"Looks like it," Chee said.

"Anyone else hurt?"

Chee realized he hadn't looked. "I don't think so. As soon as you take over, I'll check. I haven't heard any noise."

"An ambulance is on the way from Kayenta. Can you find another towel?" The tone of Green's voice said he had taken charge of the medical emergency.

Another EMT had entered with a blanket to wrap

around Robinson's lower body. Maybe they could keep him from going into shock, keep him alive.

Chee stood and found three towels on the counter, clean and folded. When he bent down to hand them to Green, he spotted the piece of paper he'd knocked to the floor earlier. He picked it up and, after he checked the empty bedroom and the bathroom, read what was on the page. Then he folded it and put it in his own pocket before making his way past the medics to the trailer's door.

Rhonda was waiting at the bottom of the stairs. A few others had gathered there, too. She put her hand on his arm when he reached her. "What happened?"

"A chest wound. The medics are working with him."

He saw the color drain from her face. She took an awkward step backward. Chee grabbed for her arm, catching her just before she collapsed and supporting her. "Sit down a minute. Put your head between your knees."

"I'm OK. What happened to him?"

"I'm not sure. I need to call the police station."

Bahe was out, so Chee spoke to Tsinnie, explaining the situation and saying that he would stay on the scene until the ambulance arrived.

"Hey, I have news for you." Tsinnie seemed almost friendly.

"Go ahead." He hoped it wasn't more bad news about Paul.

"That guy with the nosebleed? The FBI wanted him on money-laundering, racketeering, and other heavy stuff."

"No kidding. Did they say if Delahart admitted to putting the bones out there?"

"Nope. Not to me and Bahe, anyway. Bahe said he knew that man must be guilty of something, just from the way he acted. I don't think they've charged him with murder yet, but I bet he did it."

Chee wasn't a gambling man, but he would have bet against Tsinnie.

Outside Robinson's trailer a group of about a dozen people had gathered, standing in clusters and talking among themselves. They watched Chee approach.

"The EMTs are helping Mr. Robinson, and an ambulance is on the way," he said. "I don't know what happened yet, except that he has a chest wound. There's nothing to see here."

Rhonda stood, less shaky now. "We've got work to do, so let's get to it. That's what Robinson would want. Mike Turner will be the guy in charge."

Melissa stayed behind. "Did someone attack him?" she asked Chee.

"I don't know what happened for sure."

"Who would want to hurt him? He's the nicest—" She noticed Rhonda and turned toward her, raising her voice. "You. You witch. Your publicity caused all the problems with Delahart. You never get enough attention, do you? I couldn't blame you for shooting Samuel, but why—"

Chee grabbed Melissa's arm as she swung toward Rhonda. She was stronger than he expected. Rhonda stepped away and looked at Melissa, the sort of stare Chee remembered teachers giving him before he got the *final* warning. But her voice was surprisingly gentle.

"Calm down, Missy. I was mad enough to kill Samuel, but I only do that in the movies. I'm crazy about Greg, and I respect the job you've done, too. We've got enough drama here. We have to focus on wrapping this up, finishing the movie as soon as we can. We owe Robinson that, no matter what."

They heard the wail of an approaching siren.

Things moved quickly after the ambulance came. The EMTs brought out the stretcher, ordering bystanders to clear the way. Robinson's eyes seemed to be looking for something. They found Rhonda, and he gave her the ghost of a smile, then focused on Chee.

Chee walked up to the stretcher, had a word with one of the EMTs, put his head close to Robinson's to hear what the man strained to say, and nodded once, twice. He slipped the piece of paper he'd picked up in the trailer into Robinson's shirt pocket.

After the ambulance drove off and the crowd had dispersed, Chee spotted Melissa standing in the shade on the side of the trailer.

"Do me a favor and make sure nobody goes in there, OK? Wait for me. Robinson gave me a message for you."

She nodded.

Chee got what he needed from his police car, then climbed Robinson's steps. He took a few crime scene pictures, although he doubted that anyone would need them, found the gun that had done the damage, and sealed it in an evidence bag. Picking something up from Robinson's desk, he locked the door behind him with Rhonda's key.

Melissa stood where he'd left her.

"I need to give you a message from your boss, but before I do, are you ready to tell me the truth now?"

She sighed. "I don't know where to start."

"Start with the stuff you left out about the money."

"I never thought it would come to this."

Chee waited.

She sighed. "Remember I told you that I was trying to fix the shortfall we had because of the sponsorships I'd anticipated that were late?"

"I got that."

"Well, other money was missing, too. It took me a while to click to it, but when I looked at the bank statements, I realized someone was using a debit card and withdrawing a bunch of cash. Robinson has a card on the account. Not much use for it out here, but it's different in Vegas, of course, and he flew there every week.

"I could see that he was taken with Rhonda. I figured he was buying her gifts, maybe getting them a fancy room at a hotel there, using cash to avoid a stink. It wasn't really wrong, since stars get pretty much whatever they want. But I need to be able to categorize where the money went. ATM withdrawals look suspicious, and I need to keep things on the up-and-up for the sponsors.

"But when I mentioned the ATM withdrawals to Robinson, he acted like he didn't know what I was talking about. That hurt, and it made me mad."

"Is he the only one with a debit card?"

"I don't have one on that account. Not Samuel. Not even the Zombie Queen herself."

"What about Delahart?"

"Uh . . . I don't know."

"You ought to find out. You might have made a faulty assumption."

She studied her shoes for a minute.

"Whenever I talked to Delahart about money, he told me not to worry about it. He laughed at those ATM charges and said his investors would take care of everything." She looked at Chee. "Do you think one of them shot Samuel? Or did Rhonda do it? She had as much reason as I did, and a shorter fuse."

"None of the above."

Melissa raised an eyebrow.

"The feds are investigating it. They'll look at Isenberg, the father of one of those girls I talked to, the ones Samuel manhandled and embarrassed. Isenberg is furious about that, but he didn't do it. Samuel's death was an accident."

"I saw you put a piece of paper in Greg's pocket. Was it a confession? A suicide note?"

Chee considered his answer. "Ask Robinson about it when he recovers."

"You don't have to be cagey. I'm the gambler here, remember? I'm good at reading people and at keeping secrets. I'll tell you what happened."

Chee waited.

"Robinson went to talk to Delahart, man to man, to tell him Samuel was blackmailing me and that he'd taken those nasty pictures and that he planned to fire him before the production got sued, and probably turn him over to the police. He planned to tell Delahart he'd quit if Samuel stayed on.

"But Samuel answered the door, laughed in his face. Robinson got angry and said he'd call the police. Samuel pulled his gun. They struggled. Bingo."

Melissa was crying now, but she kept talking. "He didn't mean to kill him and then he panicked afterward. It was the last straw. Money troubles and the layoffs, that stupid stunt with the grave, the production behind schedule, all of that. Robinson would have died if Rhonda hadn't had the key to his trailer and if you hadn't been here. And it was all because of me. If I'd only let him fire Samuel when he wanted, none of this would have happened."

"He asked me to make sure you got this." Chee handed her a bag he'd seen in the trailer with her name on it.

She took out a box and a small envelope, opened the envelope, read the note inside, and handed it to Chee. "Missy, none of this is your fault," Robinson had written. "Enjoy your life and think of this beautiful place as often as you wear these."

Inside the box were the earrings with the robin's-egg turquoise, the ones she had started wearing after the day she and Chee stumbled over the grave.

In the tent, Rhonda and Turner were engrossed in conversation with BJ and half a dozen others. He'd wait. He pushed the button of the fancy coffee machine. This time he selected something called Ethiopian Yirgacheffe. It was great, almost as good as the coffee he remembered drinking as a boy when he helped his aunt and uncle at sheep camp each summer.

When he took Turner's two citations out of his pocket, he found the poker chip. The chip made him think of Leaphorn's e-mail about the necklace and the silversmith. Maybe the excellent coffee had clicked his brain into gear. He had misread the Lieutenant's message and underestimated his mentor.

Melissa had come in and joined the meeting wearing the turquoise. Good. He finished the last of his delicious coffee and walked over to deliver the citation.

It was warm in the SUV, but Chee didn't mind. He powered down the windows to let in the desert air and searched in his wallet for the card that the trespassing camper, Gisela, had given him. Before he left the movie parking lot—and the end of cell phone coverage—he dialed her number.

She and Heinrich were in Kayenta, staying at a motel, planning to leave in the morning.

"I've got something important and interesting to show you," Chee said. "Can you meet me at Goulding's in an hour?"

"What is this about?"

"I'll see you up on the terrace outside the trading post."

"Are we in trouble again?"

"No, ma'am. It will be worth your time, I promise."

Then he made another call, this time to Bernie, to give her an update. She didn't answer. He couldn't wait to see her again.

He called Bahe and then Captain Largo to give him an update and arrange to get back on the schedule at Shiprock. After that, he called Haskie at Goulding's and explained the situation.

By the time he'd done all that and driven to Goulding's, Haskie was waiting in the hotel lobby. They walked together to the terrace, where the elderly tourists were sitting on the bench beneath a ramada. Gisela wore a sleeveless shirt that showed off her sunburn. She gave him a faint smile.

Heinrich got right to the point. "Why did you ask us to come here? Are we to be arrested?"

"No, sir. Mr. Haskie here has something that I think belongs to your wife."

"That can't be," he said. "We have never come to this hotel before."

Haskie took the bag with the necklace out of his pocket. He removed it from the plastic and put it on the table in front of Gisela. "Sergeant Chee thought you'd like to see this."

Gisela picked it up. "Oh, it's beautiful, but why—" She studied it for a moment, and her expression softened. She began to sob. Heinrich looked puzzled, then put his arm around her. She reached into her purse for a handkerchief and wiped her eyes. "I thought I would never touch this again."

"There's one thing you have to do before you can have it," said Chee. "You have to tell us about the necklace."

"I will tell you what I know. But where should I start the story?"

"When I met you at your campsite, you told me that your grandfather had been out here. Begin with him."

The woman had regained her composure. "As a young man, Karl, my *Grospapa*, wanted to be an actor. His family found his dream quite shocking. Karl's father served as a doctor in a little town in Missouri. He had immigrated from Germany, created a life from hard work, saving every penny he could. The idea of his son onstage, wearing a costume or a fake mustache out in California? Unsettling, unprecedented. But this was America, a new world. He let Karl sow his wild oats."

Heinrich interrupted. "Karl became a farmer?"

"No, dear. That means he had a chance to rebel a little." She leaned forward on the bench. "My grandfather went all the way to Los Angeles on the train. He wanted a role in a movie, and eventually he met someone who knew someone who knew John Ford. One thing led to another, and Karl had an opportunity to work on *Stagecoach*. He only had a small part as a cowboy, but it meant the world to him."

Heinrich took up the story. "Meeting John Wayne and John Ford, that was the most exciting time in his life. He loved to speak of it, and he retold the story many, many times."

"Did your grandfather make a lot of movies?" Haskie said. "Maybe he ran into some of my relatives out here. They got to be Indians."

Gisela looked puzzled, then laughed. "No, he only worked on *Stagecoach*. He missed his family, so Karl returned to Missouri, became a doctor like his father. He married, had two sons. The younger was my father, Charles. He served in the army as a doctor. When I was a teenager, he was stationed in Germany. That's where I had the good fortune of meeting Heinrich."

"Get on with the story," Heinrich said. "These men have important things to do."

Gisela patted his hand. "My father often told me about the trip he made with Karl out here when he was a boy. How he loved the blue of the sky and the red of the earth. They camped, just the two of them, and Papa liked this place as much as *Grospapa*. Maybe even more. He showed me the pictures of the two of them standing at Ford Point."

"Tell about the necklace," Heinrich said.

"Well, when *Grospapa* Karl was in the movie, he met an Indian named Robert, and they got to be friends. He loaned Robert some money—not that he had much—and Robert gave him a necklace as collateral. *Grospapa* kept it, and when he and *Grosmama* married, he gave it to her. The necklace passed on to my father, and he gave it to my mother for their tenth wedding anniversary. She loved it, and she always said she wanted to see where it came from.

"Meanwhile, I graduated from high school and college, went back to Germany, and married Heinrich. After Papa retired, he and Mother came to Germany to visit us, and we talked about *Grospapa* Karl's movie stories and Monument Valley. We'd pull out our copy of *Stagecoach* and watch it together, waiting for the barroom scene where Karl was an extra."

Heinrich said, "You're giving out too many details. Get to the point."

"It's fine," Chee said. "It's an interesting story." Haskie nodded in agreement.

"Then, last year, Mother said it was time to see this place for herself. She was sick, but she tried to squeeze in every last minute of life. Papa hadn't been out here since that camping trip. I hoped to return to the States to accompany them, but Heinrich was involved in a big project at work, so we couldn't make it. Mother told me she planned to wear *Gros-*

mama's necklace for the whole trip. So they rented a car—"

"Not just a car. A big Lincoln," Heinrich said. "Charles told me he loved driving it."

Gisela smiled. "They'd been frugal their whole lives. Never went on vacation. I can just see them in that Lincoln. And we always camped, but this time Papa splurged on a hotel. Anyway, by the time they reached Monument Valley, Mom was really weak. They drove out, took pictures, and called me, so happy and excited. Papa told me they could see the monuments from the hotel room. Mother died a few weeks later."

Heinrich said, "If Gisela's mother left the necklace here, why didn't the hotel return it to her or her husband?"

Haskie explained. "For some reason, they registered with a fake name. They left the line for vehicle information blank except for 'California' and 'Lincoln.' We couldn't follow up."

Gisela said, "He wouldn't have recalled the plate number. But why a fake name?"

"A lot of hotels won't let you rent a room without a credit card," Chee said. "How did they get around that?"

Haskie shrugged. The couple looked at each other, and then the woman laughed. "They had a card they somehow managed to acquire in the name of their dog. They got it years ago, kept it for emergencies, but they never had emergencies. Dad always paid cash. He told me that way he never spent more money than he had."

"The address on the card was a post office box."

"That's right. The post office was on the way to his office."

"The maid found a stain on the carpet," Haskie said. "I've been wondering—"

Gisela interrupted. "I know. Papa told me how embarrassed my mother was to have made such a mess."

"What happened?" Chee asked.

Heinrich sighed. "We don't know all the details. A hemorrhage. If Charles hadn't been a doctor, his dear wife would have passed to death there in his arms. He managed to stop the bleeding. He told us she insisted that he clean up the room as much as he could and that he leave a tip for the maid before they left for the hospital in Kayenta."

"A few weeks after her funeral," Gisela said, "I asked about the necklace. Papa thought it must be in one of their suitcases, but he never found it. He was depressed, sad, adrift after she died. A missing necklace was the least of his concerns. When we lost him a month ago, we intermixed his ashes with my mother's." She smiled at Haskie. "I'm sorry my parents caused you so much trouble."

"I'm glad I can give this to you."

Gisela took the necklace out of the bag and put it around her neck. Heinrich helped fasten the clasp. Then she pulled out the paper.

Haskie said, "That's their registration card. You can take that, too."

She studied the card her father had filled out for the room. "You wondered about the names they used to register. Here they are: Mr. and Mrs. Postkutsche." Gisela chuckled. "That was their dog's name. It means 'stagecoach' in German."

Chee reached in his pocket and put the white chip with the eagle design on the table. "And you might want this. Or did you mean to leave it with the ashes?"

"You know about the ashes?"

Chee nodded. "Did you know what you did was illegal?"

"I told her we should bring them home with us," Heinrich said, "not leave them here in the wilderness, but this woman has a mind of her own."

Gisela sighed. "When I picked up the urn with their ashes from the mortuary, I thought I would send a bit of my parents off with the wind in a place that meant so much to them. As Heinrich looked for a campsite, we noticed that old grave. Since it was already there, it seemed like a gift, and so—" Her voice started to shake. She stopped talking and wiped her eyes with the back of her hand.

"Leaving the ashes and the bone fragments there showed great disrespect to our land and our culture," said Chee. "The same goes for scattering ashes to the wind over Navajo land. But it's done now."

"I apologize." Gisela picked up the chip. "I left this on the road by the grave. A talisman for my parents' lucky travels in the great beyond. Was this how you found us?"

"Sort of. I have a very smart friend who helped me. Robert, the jeweler you mentioned, was Robert Etcitty. His work is well known. You can see his picture as a young man in the museum, along with some actor cowboys. Maybe one of them is Karl."

"So now, do you arrest us for the ashes?" said Heinrich. "Do we pay a fine? Go to jail?"

"None of the above. I'm heading home. You two behave yourselves. Let the dead rest in peace."

Gisela moved her thumb over the silver and turquoise pendant. "When I wear this, I will remember your kindness."

Chee left Haskie and the couple and headed to the parking lot. He thought about Gisela's parents and their farewell trip. Would he and Bernie be blessed with so many years together? Would they cherish each other more in a few decades than they did now? He couldn't imagine loving her more than he already did, but he'd learned that many wonderful and surprising things were possible.

By the time he got back to the substation, Bahe had left, so Chee typed him a note explaining the source of the bone fragments. He told the captain he had delivered the original citation, the one that charged the company for the fake grave but did not mention the remains, since *The Undead Return* couldn't be held responsible for that. He found a message: "Call Melissa."

"Hey, I thought you might want to know that Robinson is going to be OK."

"Glad to hear it. I told the feds about the gun I found in his trailer. It was Samuel's."

"Are you coming out here again?"

"No, not even for another cup of that good coffee. I'm going home."

"We're gone in a few days, too. Rhonda will put up the money to finish the movie. She's the new producer. BJ's staying, and Gerald is coming back. We're going to use him as an extra."

"Great. I've gotta run."

"Just one more thing. You remember those girls that Samuel caught trespassing? Rhonda wants to send them a photo."

Chee found Courtney's phone number. "Can she send one to me, too?"

"A souvenir of your time in zombie land?"

"Not for me. I've got a sister-in-law who would love it."

19

When Bernie returned from her morning run, she found a message from Chee: *"Wonderful hearing your voice, even on the answering system. I'll call back and you call me, too."*

She called, and he answered on the second ring.

"Hi. Everything OK out there?" she asked.

She could hear the smile in his voice. "As good as can be expected without you here. At least I didn't have to give a presentation to the Rotary. How did it go?"

"It's later today. Don't remind me."

"Which Rotary group are you talking to?"

"There's more than one?" Obviously, she thought—otherwise he wouldn't have asked the question. "It's the San Juan County chapter."

"Are you nervous?"

"Who, me?" She told Chee what she planned to talk about. "After that, I'm going to the Farmington sheriff's department and see what they know about Miller's car being stolen."

"If you can swing it, go there before lunch. They've got good coffee there, and usually cookies, too." Chee gave her the name of an officer who specialized in car thefts.

"What's happening with you?" she asked.

He told her about the Germans and the necklace and Delahart's arrest by the FBI.

"I knew there was something off about that guy," he said. "I couldn't figure it out. It all came down to money laundering in Las Vegas, using the movie as a cover. Above my pay grade."

"I feel the same about Miller. When will you be able to come home?"

"Not soon enough."

They hung up, and she showered, put on her uniform, looked at herself in the mirror, and had an idea. She ran her *be ezo*, a traditional brush made with dried muhly grass, through her hair until it shone and gently gathered it into a thick ponytail. She took some yarn and tied it up, folding the ponytail over three times until it reached the back of her head, forming a loop. She wrapped the yarn tightly around the center and then fanned out the ends, creating the traditional *tsiiyeel*, the Navajo bun. She decided the hairstyle made her look more business-like and perhaps a touch more mature. The elders said that pulling the hair in close to the scalp kept the thoughts contained—just what she needed for her venture into public speaking.

She checked in at the station before heading to Farmington. Captain Largo motioned her into his office.

"I haven't had a chance to read your report, so

give me the short version. Anything new on the burned car?"

"I told Cordova the hitchhiker story, and he was unimpressed, to say the least. I haven't spoken to the grandson again yet. Aaron thinks his grandfather has some dementia, but he seemed sharp to me." She told Largo Mr. Tso's skinwalker theory.

He shook his head. "I could tell you some scary stories. Anything else?"

"Remember those plants Miller had in his car?"

"No."

"The cacti?"

"I don't think of those as plants. They're a nuisance."

"Well, turns out the ones in the box were an endangered species. Miller is a plant poacher."

"Whoa. A dirt thief and a plant poacher?" Largo's phone rang. He looked at it. "Any other big news? That's hard to match."

"I'll let you know if I think of something."

She turned to leave, and he called to her. "Your hair looks great today. Good luck with your talk."

At the Farmington sheriff's office, she met the deputy Chee recommended. He found Miller's stolen car report.

"I took the information over the phone. He said he'd left the Malibu parked outside a bar, and when he came out, no car. He had the license number and all the make and model info, but he also knew the VIN. Besides his being so organized, two things struck me as off about it. First, if it was gone when he left the bar, why didn't he report the car stolen until the morning?"

The waiting-until-morning thing would be explained if Miller were drunk, Bernie thought. But the deputy wasn't done.

"Second, the bar was closed that evening because some gal drove into the back wall the previous night and did a bunch of damage. I wouldn't have realized it, except we always get at least one call for fighting or rowdy drunks or something from there. That place is notorious. Since they'd had to close, it was peaceful. So I wondered why Miller would have parked there."

"Did you ask him?"

"I didn't realize it was closed until I double-checked when the FBI guy asked about it."

"When was that?"

"After you found Miller's car torched. I wonder why the feds have his number?"

"Me too."

He asked about Chee, and then whether Darleen Manuelito was related to Bernie. "You know," he said, "she might be eligible to get into that new diversion program. It works pretty well. Of course, she'd have to stay with it."

"What program?"

"You must have heard about it. The one for first-time offenders that the county got that grant for. Alcohol and drug rehab, counseling, that sort of thing. It's a trial, designed to keep down DWIs and reduce repeat offenders."

"I have to talk to her about it. Thanks for the Miller stuff."

"Here, take this with you." He opened a desk drawer and pulled out a full-color brochure: *San Juan County Fights DWI*.

She put the brochure on the passenger seat of her unit. Someday, she'd like to feel proud of her sibling, happy for her accomplishments instead of ashamed. Would that day ever come?

Bernie noticed a thrift store as she headed toward the restaurant for the meeting. An empty parking slot beckoned, so she stopped. Sometimes she could find zip-up sweaters or ones with big buttons that were easy for Mama to handle. She didn't see a sweater she liked, but when she passed a rack of belts, she thought of Mr. Tso holding up his pants with a rope. She invested a dollar in a canvas belt with a D-ring for a buckle so he could adjust it to fit.

She drove toward the restaurant, thinking about the fake stolen car report instead of her talk. It was inconvenient to set your own car on fire in the middle of nowhere and then have to hitchhike. She remembered the ridge, the places where the earth had been disturbed, and the yellow pieces of wood. Miller must have used the stakes to mark the cacti when they bloomed, the easiest time to spot them. She smiled. The pieces were coming together, but many were missing, including Miller himself.

As for Mr. Tso's apparitions, perhaps he couldn't see very well. Maybe, as Aaron suspected, his grandfather's brain had slipped into decline, wobbling between reality and imagination.

She parked in the restaurant lot, noticing that it was nearly full, and picked up her backpack, double-checking to make sure her notes were there. She put on a bit of lipstick, squared her shoulders, and walked into the room where the meeting would be. She felt almost as unsettled as when she'd met Chee's relatives for the first time.

The sixty-something woman at the door in the gray business suit introduced herself as the program director and the person Bernie had talked to on the phone. "We're so glad you could join us. You're younger than I expected. Have you met our president?"

"No, ma'am." Younger than expected? That didn't sound like a good thing.

The woman ushered Bernie to a round table, where a man in a business suit and well-polished cowboy boots was talking to a small group of people. The man in the boots extended his hand. "Clayton Sanchez, president of this bunch of rowdies, at least for a few more months. We're pleased you could come today." He introduced the other men at the table: a Farmington banker, a gentleman who owned a drilling company, and an insurance broker. Only the banker wore a suit, and he had a bolo with a piece of coral in place of a necktie.

Bernie nodded, wishing she had Chee's gift for remembering names. Clayton reminded her of clay, and she pictured his boots encased in claylike mud. Maybe she could use sandy clay, whatever that might be, for the Sanchez part. She felt the men watching her while Sanchez spoke.

"Captain Largo and I got to know each other pretty well when I was with the Farmington Police Department. He's a good cop." Sanchez talked about a meth case he and Largo had worked together. The man knew his way around a story.

The room had nearly filled. A flock of waiters and waitresses in black pants and white shirts began delivering plates of salad to the tables.

Sanchez interrupted himself. "We better sit so the young lady can eat before she has to talk."

The salad looked good. So far, being in this room with the Rotary group wasn't the heart-stopping experience Bernie'd imagined, but the hard job was still to come.

A tall man wearing a white shirt open at the neck and a sport coat approached. Bernie thought he looked familiar, and struggled to place him. He introduced himself to the group just as Bernie's brain had churned up his name: David Oster.

"I'm the guy working on that big solar project. You all may have heard our radio ads: 'Harnessing the power of the sun to provide electricity to our families and the rest of America.' "

"The rest of America? That sounds great. Ambitious." Sanchez winked at him. "Join us here? We've got an empty seat." Sanchez turned toward Bernie. "This is Officer Bernadette Manuelito. She's our guest speaker today."

Oster smiled. "We've met. Officer Manuelito was the one who had to give me the sad news that the town of Shiprock didn't have a Starbucks."

Sanchez chuckled. "We've got three here in Farmington. Did she tell you that?"

"No, she didn't. Your secret is safe with Officer Manuelito." He sat across the table from her. "It's nice to see you here."

"So you're a Rotary member?"

"I'm with Rotary in San Francisco, and as part of

our membership, we have a standing invitation to visit other clubs when we're in the area."

"How's your project coming?"

"Fine. Except for the wind, the weather has cooperated. Once we smooth out a few bumps in the road, we'll have the perfect site for a large installation."

"We've got plenty of sun out here, that's for sure. What kind of bumps?"

"Oh, nothing too serious. There seem to be some people who still don't understand the value of solar power. My contractor and I are working to change some minds, open the naysayers to the possibilities of nonpolluting, renewable energy. Where would we be without the sun?"

"Good question. And good luck with your project."

"I don't need luck. It's a natural, you know—the wave of the future, the way the world is moving."

Bernie looked at her salad, carefully pushing the strawberries to one side and the pecans to the other. She tried a bite of the lettuce and a little red tomato and found them acceptable. Chee would have appreciated this fancy dish, she thought, but give her iceberg lettuce and ranch dressing any time.

Bernie heard Sanchez pushing his chair back, and she took a breath. Show time on the horizon. She felt her chest tighten.

Sanchez went to the microphone, and everyone stood for an invocation and then faced the flag for the Pledge of Allegiance. When he invited them all to sit and began to read extensive announcements, Bernie moved her plate to the side and took out her notes. One more quick review.

He introduced her, and she walked to the podium, suddenly regretting the salad she'd eaten. She adjusted the microphone, lowering it to pick up her voice. She felt her knees wobble.

"Ladies and gentlemen, *yá'át'ééh*. Good afternoon. Thank you for inviting me here today. And for the free lunch."

A few of the attendees chuckled.

"This is the first time I've been asked to speak on behalf of our department." She looked up from her notes. "I thought I would start by explaining that if you want to be on patrol with the Navajo Nation police, you have to enjoy driving. Each officer who works on our force is responsible for about seventy square miles of reservation land. That's about twice the area of Grand Rapids, Michigan. Or think of it this way: the whole country of Liechtenstein is only sixty-two square miles."

People in the audience smiled. She relaxed a little, looked at her notes for the next point she wanted to make, and kept talking. "In the rest of rural America, there are about three officers for a thousand civilians. Out here, when our department is fully staffed, there might be two of us for that same population. But I'm not complaining. I love my job, and I like to stay busy."

Most of her nervousness had evaporated, amazingly. She moved on to the next point and the next. It was over before she knew it.

By the time she sat down again, the rest of her table had finished eating. The waiter brought her a large white plate filled with noodles shaped like ridged tubes covered with a mysterious sauce. She recognized mushrooms, green peas, and circles of sausage. If Chee were there, he'd probably figure out how to make it and experiment on her.

She finished the salad, eating the strawberries and pecans separately, and followed it with her bread and butter. The noodles scared her.

Then the waiter brought something delightful to the table. Chocolate cake beneath white frosting dotted with pastel sugar sprinkles sitting next to a big serving of whipped cream. He came back with hot coffee, filling cups carefully, and offering decaf to those who declined. Being a speaker wasn't as bad as she'd imagined, especially when it included cake. She'd have to thank Largo for the assignment.

At the podium, Sanchez asked for any final business, reminded the group of the speaker for the next meeting, and then, with a bang of the gavel, adjourned the meeting until next month.

Oster stood to tell her goodbye.

"I ran into Mrs. Benally at Teec Nos Pos," Bernie said. "She told me the two of you had done some business."

"Lovely woman," Oster said. "I wish everyone out here were as easy to deal with."

Bernie went back to the office to get her assignments for the rest of the day and to tell Largo about the talk. Sandra got her attention.

"Hey, your sister has been trying to reach you. She wants you to call her."

She wondered if Darleen had an emergency, the rationale for calling her at work instead of at home or on her cell. Bernie called Mama's phone. Busy. She called Darleen's cell and left a message.

Then she logged into the database to do a quick search on Aaron Torino and, while she was at it, tossed in the name of the mysterious Michael Miller. The system chugged, and then her monitor locked up. She tried every trick she knew with no luck, finally finding Sandra, the closest thing they had to tech services.

She'd go outside to call Darleen again while the computers were down, she decided. She took a deep breath, looked at her phone for a moment, and then pushed in Mama's number. Sometimes she wished she'd had a big brother instead of a little sister.

Darleen sounded happy. "I wanted to talk to you about going to Santa Fe tomorrow. Remember? Mama wanted to check out the school? I called you at work because I thought you might need to get the day off or something. Hope I didn't freak you out."

"I was just in Farmington, and a sheriff's deputy told me you're being considered for the alcohol and drug diversion program."

"That's cool."

Bernie had expected Darleen to be embarrassed, or at least surprised. "Cool? So you got arrested for drunken driving? Not just drinking a beer and mouthing off, like you told Mama and me?"

"Well, not really. It's a long—"

"You lied to us."

"I didn't exactly lie. I just—"

"Grow up. I can't deal with this."

"You don't have to deal with anything." Darleen sounded angry now. "You never listen. You always know what I should do. I didn't tell you every little thing that happened because I didn't want another lecture. I felt bad enough without you nagging on me. I made a mistake. Who hasn't?"

She stopped talking, and Bernie let the silence sit.

When Darleen spoke again, she'd stopped shouting. "Come over to Mama's tonight so we can talk. It's not as bad as you think. Seriously."

Bigman appeared at the station door, waving to Bernie to come in.

"I've got to go."

"When do you think you'll be here?"

"I don't know. Before dark. I have to take something to the old man who lives near that burned car."

"This isn't as bad as you think," Darleen said again.

"Yeah, right." Bernie hung up, furious. She walked inside the building to find Largo looking for her.

"Manuelito, what have you done to the computers?" He sounded more annoyed than usual.

"I was doing a search, seeing what I could find out about Tso's grandson."

"Sandra's having trouble getting things back to working again. We may have to talk to Window Rock."

Largo seemed to be waiting for her to say something.

"Sir, lunch went well. People seemed to like the talk."

"Good. I owe you for that."

It seemed like a good time to ask for the next day off, explaining that she had an unexpected situation to deal with concerning her mother. Largo gave it to her without asking questions, and she spent an uneventful afternoon placing unreturned calls to Aaron and catching up on paperwork. The highlight was a residential burglary report. The thieves had absconded with the victim's jewelry, cash, and meat from the freezer. The woman held her brother's drinking buddies responsible.

After work, Bernie went home to change clothes, then stopped at City Market to buy Mr. Tso a can of coffee and some plums, which she rinsed at the store. When someone hauled water, every drop was precious. She put everything in her backpack, then added Mr. Tso's thrift-store belt. His house wasn't that out of the way to the turnoff for Mama's place. Maybe his view of Ship Rock would offer some inspiration.

She stopped on the way and parked her well-used Toyota close to the burned shell of the Malibu. She wanted another look at the ridge to see if there were any more of those little cacti or any strange tracks she'd missed. She remembered the animal she'd seen in the road the evening she got lost. The thought made her uneasy, but she convinced herself it was a dog, or maybe one of those big wolf hybrids.

An assembly of clouds hung in the late afternoon's huge, brilliant sky, a hint at the undelivered promise of rain. She stood on the sandy earth and took in the sight of Ship Rock, more rugged than it looked from the angle at which she saw it most often. She had met people who found this landscape unsettling, people from elsewhere who felt uncomfortable without a green canopy of trees overhead. She liked trees well enough, as long as she could still look out and see the sky. She considered the piñons and junipers that lived in co-existence on much of the Navajo Nation's land to be nature's best tree creations. It took the piñons a hundred years to grow twelve feet, and they provided tasty nuts. Juniper was used in ceremonies and as medicine. She'd grown up drinking juniper tea when her stomach felt uneasy, and as a girl she had used the little brown seeds inside its blue berries to make bracelets and necklaces. Good trees, and they didn't usually block the view.

Her eye caught a flash of motion near the ridgetop. She focused. Saw it a second time. In addition to coyotes and dogs, there were horses out here, although an animal that large seemed unlikely on the rocky slope. She kept her gaze on the ridge, but she didn't see it again.

The vibration of her phone in the backpack surprised her. She fished it out of the front pocket. Chee!

"Hey there." His voice sounded as strong as if he'd been standing beside her. "I talked to Bahe, and I can head back to Shiprock."

"It seems like you've been gone forever."

"Sounds like you're standing in a tunnel, sweetheart. Where are you?"

"I'm getting ready to visit *Hosteen* Tso. You know, the man who lives near Ship Rock. When I leave, I'm spending the night at Mama's. Darleen and Mama and I have a lot to talk about." She'd save the bad news for when she saw him, after she'd interrogated Darleen. "I can't wait to see you."

"I can barely hear you, honey. Call me when you get to Mama's, OK?"

"Sure thing."

She ended the call, wondering not for the first time if the aggravation caused by all the times cell phones didn't work was offset by their convenience when they did. She still voted in favor, but the margin was slim.

She climbed the ridge, wishing the day were cooler and that she'd worn her hiking boots. She saw a lizard nicely camouflaged against the gray rocks, but no cactus plants, or yellow markers for them. No more tracks, either.

The old man was sitting on the same wooden bench where she'd seen him last. He stood when she stopped her car and hobbled out to her, greeting her in Navajo and adding the word for "friend." He motioned her to the side of the house. "Put your car there, where you saw my grandson's truck. Get some shade from that tree by the corral." She parked, grabbed her backpack, and walked to the porch.

"I like your hair fixed like that, the old way. It keeps the wind from stealing your thoughts. I used to wear my hair like that, too, back when I was young." She wasn't surprised; the hairstyle was part of the Navajo tradition.

She showed him the bag with the plums and the coffee. "These are for you, Mr. Tso. I thought you might enjoy them."

"*Ahéhee*. Thank you."

Then Bernie gave him the belt. He ran his hands over the fabric. "A nice one. Soft." He started to hand it back to her, but she shook her head.

"It's for you. You can wear this when your daughter takes you to that big food corral."

He looked puzzled. "I don't know about a place like that."

"It's in Gallup. You mentioned that you liked the Jell-O there."

Mr. Tso shook his head. "Maybe the heat is bothering you. Come and sit with me."

Bernie didn't press the point. She took her place in the chair next to Mr. Tso's bench and shared the view. They watched a pair of ravens soar against the deep blue sky.

"My grandson came earlier today to tell me he has a new job. The people who want to put up those mirrors hired him." She sensed a grandfather's pride, but something else in his voice as well. Concern?

"The solar company? That's wonderful for him. Maybe you will see more of him now."

But Mr. Tso shook his head. "They are the ones who gave me those lights down there." He moved his head toward the side of the house where she had parked. "Go take a look. Then I will tell you more."

She stepped off the porch and next to a chain saw and the red plastic gas can, she found a row of little lanterns mounted on long metal stakes with pointed ends. Each of the six had a flat dark rectangle on the top of a little box that was glass on all sides. They looked new.

She returned to Mr. Tso. "Those are interesting. Do they work?"

The old man frowned. "The one who wants to put those mirrors out there, he gave them to me. He and my grandson pushed them into the ground. When the sun went down, when the first stars could be seen, they turned themselves on." He shifted on the bench. "No good. They make light when it should be dark."

Bernie pictured the scene. She thought solar lights were an excellent idea, especially for a house without electricity.

"When I was a boy, we respected the darkness. We went to sleep when it got dark, got up when the sun rose. In the winter, the long nights gave us stories."

A coyote yipped in the distance, joined by another. Then came barking dogs. Mr. Tso began talking about a pack of dogs that had killed his goat when he was a boy, a story he had told her the first time she visited. An old shotgun was propped by the bend on the porch. It reminded her of the gun her uncle had kept for creatures who threatened the sheep.

It was not uncommon on the Navajo reservation for feral dogs, perhaps interbred with coyotes, to attack livestock and even children. Perhaps, Bernie thought, even an old man. She understood why Mr. Tso's daughter and grandson worried about him. "Those lights might help you see if a coyote or a dog pack is bothering your sheep. Maybe you should ask Aaron to put them by the corral."

"Those are my daughter's sheep. With the lights, the sheep couldn't sleep." Mr. Tso chuckled. "They would have to start counting people. Not enough people out here to make them sleepy."

Bernie said, "Your daughter worries about you because of that burned car. I think that you know more about the burned car than you have told me. If you helped, maybe the police could find the one who burned the car, and your daughter wouldn't worry so much."

Mr. Tso stared out at Ship Rock. Finally he said, "Some evil things the police cannot help us with."

They sat watching the shadows grow deeper on Ship Rock, and then Mr. Tso spoke. "A man came in that car that burned. I saw him out there on the ridge when I was checking on the fences. It was in T'ą́ą́chil, so the snakes were waking up. It was near dusk." T'ą́ą́chil was the Navajo calendar's equivalent of late March and early April, Bernie knew. The sun set early.

"I saw him walking on the ridge. I wondered what he was doing up there, and I thought that I should tell him to beware of the snakes. But when I looked again, the man was gone. An animal, dark and bigger than a dog, was on the ridge in his place. I remembered it for many months. Then when the weather grew warmer, I saw the car again, parked over that way again."

He stopped talking for so long she thought he might be finished. When he resumed, she heard the fear in his voice.

"I looked toward the ridge. I saw something up there, something alive, big and black. Not a man. Its eyes glowed like fire. Then, the day the car burned, it happened again."

Mr. Tso turned his face toward the sky. The last of the sun's rays gave his skin a pinkish glow. He closed his eyes, and then opened them again.

"It came to me that the creature who rode in that car was not afraid of the snakes because they could not hurt him."

Bernie heard the muffled sound of a distant vehicle. "Is Aaron coming to see you tonight?"

"No. My daughter said they both will come again on Saturday. Tell me about your mother. Is she still weaving?"

"No. My mother's hands don't work very well anymore."

"She misses it, then. My wife would make rugs until she couldn't see so well. She sold them to those traders in Fruitland, the Hatch Brothers. She would sit where you are now, and we would talk. She had some sadness that we never had more children, but her sister's children were ours, too."

As Mr. Tso talked on about the extended family he and his wife raised and other adventures that happened before Bernie was born, she watched the vehicle make the turn from the highway onto Mr. Tso's dirt road, a rooster tail of dust rising behind it to hang over the route. At that distance, she couldn't tell if it was a car or a truck.

The monologue over, Bernie rose. "I enjoy your company, but I need to get going now."

Mr. Tso stood too, and made his way to the side of the porch. "Look down there. You take those things. Give them to your mother. She's getting old now. She could use them."

When Bernie stood next to him, she could see that the little glass boxes on the posts had started to glow. Pretty. They reminded her of light in a jar.

"Maybe your daughter would like them," she said. "They're new and useful."

"You take them. See if they can fit in your car."

"I can't take them now because I really need to get to Mama's house. I'll get them later."

"That makes me happy. I have another visit with you to look forward to."

Mr. Tso sat on the bench again. "That one coming might be a friend of my daughter or my grandson. Sometimes those young men come here looking for him. Sometimes my daughter asks her people to check on me. They want to make sure that I'm still keeping an eye on Tsé Bit'a'í."

Bernie could see now that the vehicle was a white minivan, exactly the kind of vehicle she'd expect one of Roberta Tso's middle-aged lady friends to own. If she had left a few minutes sooner, she could have driven off with a wave to whoever was in the car. Now, though, it would be rude not to stay to greet Mr. Tso's visitor before heading out. A few minutes wouldn't matter that much. She dreaded the conversation that awaited her with Darleen.

The road stopped at Mr. Tso's house, except for the rutted track where she'd gotten lost and that Aaron said ultimately led to the highway. There were no occupied homes on the way here. Mr. Tso's place was not a spot a person came to by accident.

"Could you bring me some water?" Mr. Tso asked.

"Of course."

"Maybe, if you aren't tired, you could make us some coffee."

"I will. Would you like one of those plums, too?"

He smiled. "A soft one. Maybe our visitor will have one also."

She went into the house, happy that she still had enough daylight to work with without the bother of using his kerosene lamp. Mr. Tso lived in one room, and he was a good housekeeper. His bed was made, the couch clear, and the kitchen area free from clutter. The only thing that seemed out of place was a pile of white papers on the table, a manila envelope next to it.

Bernie added water and some of the coffee she'd brought to the old coffeepot and found a match to light the propane to fire up the burner. She noticed Mr. Tso's can opener, the old-fashioned kind that involved stabbing into the can with a sharp point and then peeling up the metal along the edge of the circle. The pungent fragrance tempted her to change her mind and make a cup for herself. But no, she wanted to talk to Mama and Darleen before it got too late. She'd say hello to the visitor, let the guest serve the coffee, and be on her way.

She heard the car door open and then a man's voice speaking English. "Hello, sir."

She thought the voice sounded vaguely familiar. As she searched for a spoon to measure the coffee, she worked to remember who it was, wondering whom she and Mr. Tso would know in common. Mr. Tso's bench creaked, and she assumed he was rising to meet the visitor.

"I would have called, but you don't have a phone. I have to talk to you about something very important, and we don't have much time. That's why—"

"*Doo yá'áshǫǫ da!*" Mr. Tso spit out the words.

Why, she wondered, did he think this man was evil, intending to harm him? Was it his dementia?

"I don't know any Indian." The stranger's voice sounded tenser now. "But I'll take that as welcome. That's my buddy, Buddy, sniffing around. Hey, hold on there."

She heard the crack of the shotgun, a high-pitched animal cry, and then, "What the heck? You crazy old coot. Wait a minute now, don't shoot me."

Bernie rushed to the porch and pulled the weapon away from Mr. Tso. The elderly man was shaking. "Stop. No more shooting."

"*Yeenaaldlooshii*."

Bernie spoke in Navajo. "No. He's not a skin-walker." She looked at the visitor, recognized him. "See, he's not even Diné." There might be non-Navajo skinwalkers, but she had never heard of one on the reservation.

Bernie leaned the shotgun against the wall and helped Mr. Tso sit down.

She switched to English. "Mr. Miller, are you OK?"

Miller looked confused and shaken. "He shot at my dog."

Mr. Tso stared at the porch floor, clearly avoiding the possibility that Miller might look him in the eye. "I saw the *yeenaaldlooshii*. I shot it."

Miller stayed where he was. "What's he talking about?"

"He thinks you and your dog are cursed."

"Cursed? I guess he's not far from right. I found Buddy at the shelter. He's like me, you know? Lived a hard life." Miller had a bottle and something that looked like a Frisbee in his hand. He pushed the pseudo Frisbee open into a bowl and poured in some water. "This is for Buddy when he comes back. When he gets over being scared. I hope he's not hurt." He put the bowl on the ground next to the porch.

Miller turned to Bernie. "You're the cop who stopped me, right?"

She stood next to Mr. Tso, relieved that he had stopped trembling. "And you're the one who offered me five hundred dollars and a rifle. And lied about it. Why are you here?"

Miller glanced at his watch. "Long, sad story. Basically, to apologize for scaring Mr. Tso the other night and to discuss the forms I left."

"What are you talking about?"

"Mirrors that make energy." Mr. Tso's voice was weak. "This one brought the lights. He wants me to sign to put the mirrors here so I won't see the view so good. I told him no. He doesn't listen."

Miller turned to Bernie. "I offered him every deal I could think of for the lease. He says the panels will spoil his vista of rocks and dirt. The man I work for told me to be more persuasive."

Mr. Tso leaned away from Miller. "Go away now."

Bernie said, "You said you wanted to apologize?"

"Well, yeah. That's right."

"What did you do?"

Miller pursed his lips and released them. "I thought if I couldn't encourage Mr. Tso to sign the papers, I could scare him into leaving, or get his family to think he was crazy. I got the idea when I came in April. That's when a kind of little cactus blooms. The yellow flowers make them stand out; otherwise, they blend into the gravel real well."

"We'll come back to that, but tell me about frightening this man."

"OK. With my binoculars, I could see Mr. Tso on his porch, and I knew he was the main obstacle to getting the lease done. I'd learned some things about Navajo skinwalkers from a program at NAU, you know, that college in Flagstaff? I got Buddy to give a good howl so the old gentleman would look up here. It was cold, so I had packed the poncho with me. I took it out of my backpack when I got out the string to mark the plants so I could come back for them later. I put it on over the pack and moved up and down among the rocks, like those skinwalkers are supposed to do. I knew his daughter was worried about him being a little off, so I figured even if it didn't scare him into moving away, if he told her the story, she might think he'd flipped. She and the grandson would move him out of here, sign the papers, and we'd be in business."

Miller stopped talking and looked out toward Ship Rock. "Buddy. Buddy. Here, boy."

Binoculars, Bernie thought, catching the sun. That explained the glowing eyes Mr. Tso had mentioned.

"Was that it?"

"Well, no. I did the same thing, walking on the ridge like that, when I came back to dig up the plants. That time, we snuck up to his house, too. I had Buddy scratch at the door and jump up and paw at the window in his bedroom. I read that skinwalkers act like that."

Mr. Tso was staring at the deck, ignoring Miller as though he wasn't there. Bernie felt her anger rising. "You should be ashamed. Is that why you set your car on fire—one last effort to terrify Mr. Tso? Or was it for the insurance money?"

Miller's eyes widened. "Me? Not me. I needed that car. I don't know what happened, and that's the honest truth. I went up there the third time to see if there were any cacti I'd missed and to give Mr. Tso another jolt, get him to think moving was a good idea. I heard something strange, so I looked down and saw the flames. No other cars out there; no people around. It scared the you-know-what outta me. Buddy and me scrammed as quick as we could."

Bernie watched Miller wipe the sweat off his forehead. He was nervous, just like he'd been the night she first encountered him. She looked over at Mr. Tso. Hard to know what he thought.

"But now you're back, and you're nervous," Bernie said. "Tell me how that makes sense?"

Miller hesitated. "When the car burned, I had to hitch a ride out of here. It took a long time before someone stopped, and as I was waiting for a ride for me and Buddy, I decided I'd had enough of this whole thing. I figured I'd try a new plan, telling the truth. So, besides saying sorry for what happened on the ridge, I came to warn the old gent that he really should sign those papers before something happens."

"Go away now." Mr. Tso moved toward the shotgun, but Bernie put a hand on his arm.

"Hold on, sir. I need to find out something before he goes." She focused on Miller. "Since you're now into honesty, tell me more about the cacti. How do you sell them?"

"Through the Internet. Phoenix, Tucson, Palm Desert. I ship them out as quick as I can."

"Is that why the feds are interested in you?"

"The feds? You think I'm, like, the orchid thief of the desert?" Miller chuckled. "The cacti are just a few hundred bucks a pop. But why not sell them? I have to dig them up anyway, so they won't cause trouble with the greenies and slow down construction where the road for the panels would go." Miller looked at his watch. He called, "Buddy. Here, boy. Buddyyyy."

"You didn't answer the question. Why do the feds have you on their radar? That's the reason you got away with trying to bribe me."

Miller walked to the edge of the porch, studied Bernie's backpack perched on the step, walked back. Probably creating a lie to satisfy her, she thought.

"The feds want to know about some of my old Las Vegas contacts. I got tired of their questions, came out here, got a job. When you stopped me, I was on a con with some guys in Albuquerque who know how to use credit card numbers creatively. I figured somebody ratted me out. Sure enough, the feds are on my tail again." She could see the moisture glistening on his forehead as he turned to her.

"I wasn't supposed to have that rifle. I wasn't supposed to be driving out here. The cacti? I figured I could make a few bucks on the side, after the boss told me to get them."

Miller called for his dog again and stared into the distance. Then he turned back to Mr. Tso. "I'm sorry about all this. I told the boss I would deliver the papers, or report back that you'd had a fatal accident, but Buddy and I are headed to Phoenix."

Bernie said, "Who is your boss?"

"A West Coast guy. He's got me by the short hairs. I'm telling you, Manuelito, because I'm done with lies, with cons, with the low life. I'm not the straightest guy around, but no way could I kill this old man."

"Oster?"

"I just call him boss."

If she hadn't heard so many creative fabrications and cons, she would have bought Miller's entire story. A credit card scam would have caught the feds' attention. Scaring Mr. Tso to get him to sign the lease sounded plausible, but she couldn't imagine a businessman like Oster would condone it.

Miller turned toward the road and whistled energetically. Mr. Tso frowned. Even though it wasn't quite dusk, loud whistling such as Miller's attracted the attention of evil spirits. And whistling after dark violated a traditional taboo; the sound summoned up *chindis*.

Bernie saw the old man cringe as Miller whistled again. "Stop that noise," Mr. Tso yelled at Miller. "Go away now."

A set of headlights had left the highway and turned onto the entrance road that led to Mr. Tso's house. Bernie saw Mr. Tso watching them, too. His voice had steel in it.

"If that is your boss man, I will talk to him about you. I think there is no boss man. Who would kill an old man over a machine with mirrors?" Then he said something in Navajo, an insult. Bernie didn't translate.

Miller looked at Bernie. "Is there another way out of here?"

"Sort of." She told him about the back way. "What about your dog?"

"The dog ran off the same way that road goes," Mr. Tso said. "Maybe it will hear you calling for it way out there if it's not dead. I shot it good."

Miller rushed to the van and started it. They watched his vehicle disappear in the dusk, bouncing down the rutted road in the shadow of Ship Rock. His shrill whistle was enough to summon a corpse.

It was, Bernie realized, one of the most beautiful times of day, dark enough now for headlights with automatic sensors to turn on, dark enough that Ship Rock seemed to glow and the air had begun to cool. Dusk but not totally black. Time to get to Mama's house, but first a moment to savor the evening and the silence after all that talking. But even though Miller's story might have no substance, she hesitated to leave Mr. Tso alone.

Mr. Tso seemed to read her thoughts. "Your mother will be waiting for you. But we forgot to have a plum."

She went inside and took Mr. Tso a plum and found one for herself. Soft and sweet, it reminded her that it had been a long time since lunch, and that cake and salad didn't make a stick-to-the-ribs meal. When Mr. Tso took a bite, she saw that most of his teeth were gone. He wiped the juice from his mouth with his shirtsleeve.

"In this car coming, it must be a friend of my daughter. You go now. I will explain if anyone asks why you drove away. She can bring the coffee."

Bernie thought Mr. Tso looked tired. "Whoever this is, please tell her you need to go to bed soon. And now, you can sleep well. You don't have to worry about the evil ones. It was only that lying man, Miller, and his dog trying to scare you."

Mr. Tso said, "You need to leave. If the man comes back, or his dog comes, I have the gun. I can take care of myself."

20

Bernie went inside and turned off the fire under the coffeepot. Like all good desert dwellers, Mr. Tso kept his windows tightly closed until the day cooled, then opened them to welcome the evening breeze. The heat from the stove had added to the accumulated warmth. "I can open the windows for you. Shall I light the lamp, too?"

"I know the dark as well as a mole. Just open the window in the back by my bed. I'll do the rest when it gets cooler. Go see your mother."

She made her way around the piles of yellowed copies of the *Navajo Times*, neatly bound with twine, and what looked like junk mail in paper bags on the floor and pushed the window up to let in the evening air. She gathered her backpack from the porch and waved goodbye, walking to her car past the warm glow of the solar lights Mr. Tso objected to.

Miller had left Buddy's water bowl on the porch. Above Mr. Tso's dark little house, the stars shone clear and beautiful, keeping company with a moon that looked as though someone had shaved a sliver from its right side. She thought about Miller as she started the Toyota. If he was on the feds' radar for credit card fraud, that would explain the pressure on Largo to drop her bribery complaint.

She decided to drive up the road a bit, then park to make sure the visitor was a friend. Maybe, as Darleen complained, she didn't have to act like a cop all the time. But Miller's story was believable enough that she'd invest a few more minutes here before she headed to Mama's house. And she wasn't eager to confront her sister; better to sit and gather her thoughts.

The breeze through the car's open windows felt good on her skin. Her bun kept her hair from blowing in her face. She'd have to wear this hairstyle more often, she thought. Next time she'd get Mama to help her with it.

As she looked for a place to pull over, she considered Miller the mystery man again. She and Cordova had built some rapport during a previous case they'd worked on together. She even thought he'd been flirting with her. Now he treated her like a spy or worse, like a schoolgirl. The man annoyed her. When she had phone service, she'd call him and mention that she'd seen Miller again and had news for him. See if Cordova would confirm the credit card story.

She swerved to avoid a rock in the road and remembered the numbers she'd seen on Miller's phone. The calls to Las Vegas might be connected to the credit card scam. What about the California number? Probably tied to the cacti.

She slowed down to spare her little car the worst of the ruts, found a place to pull over, and turned off her headlights. Her shoulders felt heavy, her neck stiff. A long day. None of this was her concern anymore, of course, but she didn't like loose ends. What about the calls to the Farmington motel? A partner in the cactus business? A girlfriend? Another con man?

Mr. Tso's visitor's vehicle came closer. Maybe a pickup? Its lights bounced up and down with the ruts on the dirt road. It was that awkward time of night when headlights didn't help much, but at least they made it easier for other drivers to notice your vehicle on the road.

She considered happier thoughts. She'd been right to suspect something illegal in the boxes of dirt. Thanks to the Lieutenant, she'd learned about the cacti. She could tell him how he'd helped her solve the mystery. She and Chee had researched several cases for their old commander. Now the seasons had shifted, and he could assist them. In the future, perhaps the Lieutenant's insights would provide even more help. Nice to be a team again, she thought, even though the dynamics had changed.

Chee would be home soon. Life was good, except for Darleen, and she'd deal with her in the morning. A shower, whatever Darleen had saved for her for dinner, and then into her little nest of a bed on Mama's couch. She'd use the old blanket Mama planned to sell at the trading post to keep off the evening chill, and maybe dream about the lamb.

The oncoming vehicle passed her, a big black SUV with a strange depression in the front bumper.

It looked like a truck with a tow ball on the back had plowed into it. She'd seen it before, but where?

She started the engine. When she got to Mama's, she'd set up the coffee for the morning so after she came back from her run it would be ready. Coffee. Starbucks. California. A motel in Farmington. Oster.

Her fatigue vanished. She swung the Toyota back around toward Mr. Tso's. She didn't know why, exactly, but Oster held the key.

The Porsche Cayenne had parked close to the porch. Mr. Tso was sitting where he always sat, and Oster was in the wooden chair, still in the business clothes he'd worn at the Rotary meeting.

"Officer Manuelito, what are you doing here? It must be my lucky day to see you twice."

"Mr. Oster, I could ask you the same question."

"I'm here to talk to Mr. Tso. We have a little unfinished business."

"Is Miller working with you?"

"Miller?" It was too dark to see Oster's face at this distance. "Oh, yes. That's what he calls himself now. You know him?"

"I stopped him because I thought he was suspicious."

"Well, you were right about that. I'm afraid he's done considerable damage to my business and threatened Mr. Tso."

Mr. Tso stood. "That man who works for you is evil."

"I was trying to give a hand up to an old acquaintance. I thought I could help him, and the next thing I know, he's selling endangered plants. And trying to scare Mr. Tso with that skinwalker business. I apologize for the late visit and for Miller's brutish behavior. His audacity in trying to scare this gentleman embarrasses me profoundly. I didn't want to put off making amends for another day." Oster rose and offered Bernie his chair. "Please join us."

She shook her head. "Mr. Tso has had a long day, and I need to get to my mother's house."

"I understand. It will only take a moment."

Bernie's innate politeness trumped her fatigue. She put her backpack on the porch next to her chair, in reach just in case some of what Miller had said was true and she needed the gun that was in it. "If Miller is so despicable, why did you hire him?"

"What can I say? An error in judgment. I was invited to give a talk at Northern Arizona University about solar energy. He was in the audience, and I remembered him from a trade show in Las Vegas. But when I used his name, he grew flustered and offered to buy me a beer. As it turned out, he was in Flagstaff because of the Witness Security Program."

"What? You mean the US Marshals were keeping an eye on him? Why?"

"My question exactly. The man is a notorious liar, but I believe that he was actually in the program because of his reaction to meeting me, someone who'd known him in his earlier life before his identity had been changed. He said he had agreed to testify in a money-laundering scam that involved real estate, the entertainment industry, and his Las Vegas colleagues. He was working as a building contractor and landscaper in Flagstaff with his new Michael Miller identity, but not making much money. He seemed to have some skills that would help me with the solar project, so I offered him a job."

"A bad man," Mr. Tso said. She heard the weariness in the old man's voice. Time to wrap this up so she could get to Mama's.

"Yes," Oster said. "He told me he scared you into signing the papers. There's no need to be scared now. I came to tell you that you did the right thing. You'll be a hero out here when the electricity comes. And Aaron and Roberta won't worry about you so much."

"I signed nothing."

"He also said that, if you didn't sign, he would arrange an accident. Obviously, he lied about that."

"I want to go to bed," Mr. Tso said.

Bernie expected Oster to leave then. Instead, he stepped closer to Mr. Tso. "I don't think you realize the value of solar energy and how it can make a real difference to your family, friends, the Indian people out here, even the world itself. You will be a big man around here once those panels go up. And—"

Bernie interrupted. "Wait a minute, sir. Mr. Tso is tired. He's already said no, and he's asked you to leave. I know you're passionate about this, but Mr. Tso has the right to refuse your offer."

"I don't understand why you are involved in this, Manuelito, but no, he doesn't. It's selfish, putting his desire for a view of that ugly hunk of rock ahead of the well-being of his people. You know how important solar energy is to the Navajo Nation. To America, to the world. This is a perfect spot for the panels. It doesn't make sense for one old man's lack of vision to imperil the project."

Oster turned to Mr. Tso. "Your daughter wants you to move in with her. If you do that, you won't have to look at the panels. You won't have to worry about skinwalkers, or goblins, or anything else like that." He put his hand on Mr. Tso's shoulder. "Let's go inside and get the job done."

Mr. Tso pushed Oster's hand away. "You leave now. When I die, my daughter and my grandson, they can do what they want."

Bernie turned to Oster. "It sounds like you will get what you want if you have patience. You're badgering Mr. Tso. It's time for both of us to leave. I'll follow you out so he can get some rest."

Oster ignored her and pressed a finger against Mr. Tso's chest. "I don't have patience. I have loans, a contract for the power, and I don't have time to wait. The planet can't wait, either. We are about out of time, thanks to Miller's bungling. The other pieces are in place, but this property is central, and you're acting like a selfish old goat."

Mr. Tso rose from the bench. He spoke in a hoarse angry shout. "Go away now. I have nothing else to say to you."

Bernie stood, too, hoping to defuse the situation.

"We've all had a long day. You've got a big drive back to Farmington."

"OK, then, as you wish. Talking is done. I have one more thing to show you before I go."

In one quick move, Oster pushed Mr. Tso down on the bench and pulled a gun from beneath his jacket.

Bernie thought of the gun in her backpack. "What are you doing?" she said, keeping her voice

light. "You're smarter than that, to threaten someone with a gun. Especially in front of a cop."

"Shut up."

When she saw Mr. Tso reach for his shotgun,
Bernie leaned down for her backpack.

With surprising quickness, Oster grabbed her,
kicked her feet out from under her, and pushed her
hard into Mr. Tso. The old man grunted as she fell
against him. He grabbed for her, throwing her farther off balance. She heard the shotgun slide along
the porch and into the dirt below with a dull thud.
Mr. Tso's lean body hit the porch hard, the kind of
impact that could break fragile ribs.

Oster grabbed Bernie's arms and twisted them
behind her back. She automatically moved to free
herself, but he acted quickly. From the level of pain,
it felt as if he'd dislocated her shoulder.

His voice stayed calm. "I'm not much for violence, Mr. Tso, but we need to get things moving.
Enough talk."

He grabbed Bernie again, yanked her to standing, and pressed the gun to her back. She forced
herself to stay calm.

"Stand him up, and we'll go inside and get the
papers."

She heard Mr. Tso's ragged breathing as she
reached to support him. He moaned. She spoke
to him in Navajo. "Grandfather. Think strong
thoughts. You are a brave man."

Oster's gun prodded her kidney. "What are you
saying?"

Bernie switched to English. "Do what the man
says."

"That's right. Listen to this smart woman."

Because of the pain in her shoulder, Bernie used her left arm to help Mr. Tso to his feet. He was shaking, and he did not put any weight on his right leg as they moved to the door.

"We're going in so you can sign the papers. That's the only way you both stay alive. Clear?"

Tso grunted.

"Lean on me," Bernie said. Tso was several inches taller than she was, but about the same weight. He quivered as he gripped her arm. Bernie willed herself to come up with a plan to save his life.

It was darker in the house than on the porch, but she could see the outline of the sofa. She walked toward it, Mr. Tso clinging to her and Oster urging them forward with the pressure of the gun.

"Let go of her now."

She felt Mr. Tso loosen his grip. Oster slapped her, hard enough to snap her head against her neck and force her backward. Her skull hit the wall as she sank into the couch, and she tasted blood from where her teeth had torn her cheek.

Oster pointed the gun at her. "Old man, take off that rope of a belt. Do it now."

Mr. Tso did as told, his stiff hands struggling to move it out of the pant loops. Oster grabbed it.

"Now sit next to her."

Mr. Tso slumped down on the sofa.

Bernie said, "My fellow officers know where I am. They are probably on their way here already." She hoped the darkness made it hard for Oster to read her face. "There's no way you can escape without being caught unless you take the back route. It's impossible for a stranger to find it in the dark, but I can explain it to you. But only after you toss your gun into that bucket of water by Mr. Tso's stove and agree to drive away. He and I will say nothing about this as long as you promise to leave us alone."

Oster looked at her as though she'd never spoken and handed her the rope, keeping the gun leveled at Mr. Tso's chest. "Wrap this around your ankles." He watched as she complied. "Tighter. OK, now make it tighter."

"Now wrap it around the leg of the couch." She leaned over to comply, looping the rope around the couch leg, fastening her ankles to it.

Mr. Tso coughed, and she heard fluid, a bad sign in a person with a possible broken rib. Oster spoke to him.

"Now, Mr. Tso, slip that twine off those newspapers over there and bring it here. Quick now."

She felt the gun in her side.

The old man did as told, leaving the newspapers scattered where they fell.

Oster pushed Bernie's ribs with the gun again. "Get up and put your hands behind you."

Oster stepped back, and Bernie stood awkwardly, off balance because of the narrowness of her stance. She swung her good left arm toward his face, aiming for his nose with the heel of her hand and all the power she could summon. She made contact just as she felt the weight of the gun come down hard on her injured shoulder. She crashed to the floor chin first. Before she could reach his feet to trip him, Oster grabbed both her arms. He twisted hard as she struggled, sending another shot of hot, raw pain through her right side. He kicked her and stepped on her back, putting his weight into it, as he bound her wrists so tightly it felt like wire cutting into her bones.

Bernie lay still, telling herself to ignore the pain and think.

"Let's finish here. Where are the papers?"

Mr. Tso remained silent.

The longer Tso delayed, the longer she had to think of an escape plan. Bernie felt Oster remove his weight, and in the next split second he kicked her again, harder this time, connecting with her hip. She moaned automatically. She knew the old one would not want to contribute to her suffering.

Mr. Tso said, "Look on the counter."

"I can't see them. What do you do for light?"

"The lantern on the shelf."

"What shelf? Oh, here. That's right. Miller told me you used kerosene."

Bernie quietly turned her head so she could see and breathe better. She watched as Oster took the lantern to the table and removed the glass dome. A match scraped as he lit the wick, and she saw the yellow light. "I don't see the forms. Oh, there they are. They weren't on the counter, they were right here on the table."

There was a scratching sound, as if something outside were trying to get in.

Mr. Tso said, "Skinwalker out there."

"Don't try to scare me with that mumbo-jumbo. I'm going to make this as easy as I can for you. I'm bringing the papers to you, and a pen."

Bernie twisted her wrists against the twine. It

hurt, but the sweat on her skin helped her gain some momentum. She pushed at the rope with her legs, keeping the movement subtle to avoid Oster's attention. The darkness on the floor worked in her favor.

She saw Oster's feet moving toward the couch. Bernie held still. "It's easy." His voice reminded her of a college professor. "All you have to do—"

Bernie heard Mr. Tso laugh, a wild, unearthly sound of derision and disgust. She turned her head, ignoring the pain in her neck, but could see nothing. She heard the sound of skin on skin, a hard slap, and heard a dull thunk, possibly the back of Mr. Tso's head hitting the wall.

"I'm sure you realize that you'll both be dead in the immediate future, but you can control what happens before that, old man. The sooner you sign, the less you'll have to listen to your friend here screaming."

Mr. Tso said a few words in Navajo, something about regretting her suffering, before she heard Oster hit him again. Then he coughed, a harsh sound that made Bernie wince. "No Navajo. Don't forget again."

"He said he needs to think about it," Bernie said.

"There's nothing to think about," Oster said. "He's lucky. He has a final opportunity to sign the papers, a hero in his daughter's eyes and to his grandson, on the side of good. Doing his part to save the planet. It's a fine way for a deceased father to be remembered."

She heard the scratching again, this time from the front door. She didn't know what was out there, but it couldn't be more evil than what was in the house. "I know you are a smart man. I can't believe you think you'll get away with this. The captain knows where I am. He's already dispatched a unit here. This is all a mistake. If you leave now, we could say that you had a mental breakdown or something."

The new tone in Oster's voice chilled the too-warm room. "I am the sanest person in the world."

"Then why go to such extremes?"

"Don't you understand the importance of returning to the sun for our energy, to save the planet? I told Miller that if the old man didn't cooperate, he should arrange a simple accident. It would have been a necessary evil for the greater good. A fall resulting in a blow to the head that would have spared Mr. Tso the further debilitations of old age, saved his daughter from additional concern about him, and helped our Mother Earth. Everyone wins. But Miller failed me and disappeared like a coward."

Bernie felt the floor shift as he moved closer to Mr. Tso.

"Inspired by your interference, I suppose, I've come up with a better plan. It will leave a bit of a mystery—the sad and untimely death of a rising star in the Navajo police force, who came to visit an arson suspect and died with him in a fire. Was it an accident, or did the deranged elderly gentleman start another blaze on purpose?"

"Mr. Tso is an arson suspect?"

"Who else would have burned that car?"

Mr. Tso coughed again and groaned. The broken rib from Oster's kick and the fall on the porch must have punctured a lung.

"Maybe Miller did it himself," Bernie said. "He denied it, but he's a proven liar."

The darkness was almost total now, except for the amber light of the kerosene lantern.

Oster walked to Mr. Tso with the contract. "Last chance?"

Mr. Tso said nothing.

Bernie's struggle against the twine had relaxed it a bit, but not enough. The subtle movements of her feet had done a better job. She had loosened the rope around her legs almost enough to pull free. She knew she had to keep him talking.

"What are you going to do with us?"

"So you want the details? Here are the bullet points. Fire, one of humanity's oldest discoveries in technology. Kerosene, propane, a closed house far away from any source of water. And I can put this unsigned contract to its next best use."

She heard him tearing the paper into pieces. "Old people get confused all the time and leave the stove on. What a tragic accident."

"You're risking a lot to make money."

"Money? It's not just about money. The survival of humanity has always depended on the sun. Everything, from those little cacti to giant redwoods, from the whales that eat the plankton that live on sun-fed algae to those of us at the top of the pyramid."

Oster's shoes made the wooden floor squeak as he strode toward the kitchen, and then there was a hiss as the propane rushed into the small room. She heard another sound from the back of the house, a loud, shrill rusty creak, like a sudden weight against old bedsprings. She felt the thud of something heavy landing somewhere behind her.

Oster yelled out. "What the—"

Bernie could see the black shape running toward him. She scooted to a seated position, squirming to free her legs while straining against the twine that bound her wrists.

Oster stayed upright when they collided, but she heard the sound of the impact. He kicked at the creature and dashed toward the front of the house. The creature followed, bumping against the table. She heard the glass of the lantern's chimney break as it crashed to the floor, along with the flurry of shredded paper. The flicker of the flame grew across the puddle of kerosene. She could not yet detect the odor of propane, but she knew it was inevitable.

The dark shape snarled and leaped at Oster again, and she heard his body ram against the wall. Oster grunted, struggled, and pushed the animal away. He managed to shove the door open, and Bernie heard it click closed behind him. She listened to his frantic footsteps, fleeing across the porch.

Then she noticed the whine, the panting, and her own body's rush of adrenaline. She forced herself to sit as still as death, hoping Mr. Tso would do the same, listening to the quick rhythm of claws on the floor as the creature ran to the bedroom, the groan of compressed springs as it leaped onto the bed, and the moan of release as it jumped through the open window.

The torn bits of the contract burned brightly now.

She called to Mr. Tso. "Can you stand up? We have to get out of here."

In the light of the fire, she watched him attempt

to push himself off of the sofa, then sink down. And then try again.

She heard the roar of the Porsche's engine.

Bernie put energy into her hands, finally wiggling them free. She used numb fingers and muscle power to release her legs.

The flames had consumed the kerosene-soaked contract paper and searched for more fuel, lapping toward the larger pool of kerosene and the flammable clutter of ancient newspapers.

She pushed herself to standing, waited until she was steady, and helped Mr. Tso. "I'll try not to hurt you." She put her arms around his torso. Half carrying him, she reached the front door, pulled it open, and dragged him onto the porch, smelling the rotten-egg stench of the escaping propane. He moaned as she shifted to support his lean frame with her back, his feet banging against her legs as she negotiated the steps. She ran from the house, carrying Mr. Tso, as far and as fast as she could, until her lungs burned and her muscles refused to respond. She tripped on a rock and collapsed, his body falling on top of hers.

She felt her heart pounding as she wrapped her arms around her head. She closed her eyes, and said a prayer of gratitude for her life, for her husband, for her mother and sister, for Mr. Tso. For the privilege of living in such a beautiful world.

21

The explosion shook Bernie's body as fire lit up the dark sky.

She stayed where she lay even after her breathing had slowed to something like normal. She felt the shallow movement of Mr. Tso's chest on top of her and gently pushed herself along the ground, out from beneath him. She couldn't hear the roar of the flames through the ringing in her ears.

She carefully rolled onto her back and glanced at Mr. Tso. From what she could see, he wasn't bleeding anywhere obvious. He looked frightened and tired, but he was alive.

She assessed her own physical damage, aware mostly of the pain from her injured shoulder. She sat up, watching for the creature that had attacked Oster. She thought about her backpack—with her gun as well as her car keys and phone—incinerated on what had been the porch of the house.

She remembered the sheep in their wooden pen

and looked toward the spot, but couldn't see it through the brilliant flames that were consuming the house. She wondered if the corral would catch fire. Poor creatures. She hoped they'd be safe. Then she smiled at herself. She must be a real Navajo to let the *dibé* into her thoughts before she considered what she would do next.

She saw another light, not from the fire but flickering in the distance. Vehicle headlights, she concluded, the motion caused by the bumpy dirt road. Had Oster grown disoriented in his search for the paved highway, driven out the wrong way, and come back? In the glow of the burning house, new terror showed on Mr. Tso's face. She kept her voice calm and spoke in Navajo. "We will lie down again and be still." He complied.

She supported her head with her palms, and watched until the vehicle grew closer. It was white, not black. Bernie stood as quickly as she could and limped to the road, waving her arms and shouting for help.

Miller stopped the van and yelled through the open window. "What happened? Why are you—"

"Mr. Tso is hurt. Help me lift him into the car. Hurry."

When Miller opened the door, the overhead light came on, and she saw Buddy sitting on the brown leather front seat. She stepped away, but Buddy didn't growl.

After they made Mr. Tso as comfortable as possible, she climbed into the backseat next to him. Miller drove away from the fire, toward the paved road and the hospital. He reached over to hand her a bottle of water.

"Why did you come back?" She unscrewed the lid and offered Mr. Tso a sip. "I thought you were on your way to Phoenix. Did you get lost out there?"

"No. I was nearly to the highway when I heard the explosion. I didn't know what happened, but it sounded bad. I thought maybe I could help. Remember, I said I told you I was turning over a new leaf. What about you? Weren't you going to your mother's place?"

"I left, but then I saw Oster's car and kind of put things together and came back."

She reassessed her own injuries. Besides her shoulder, her head ached, and her neck hurt. Her hip felt tender where Oster had kicked her, but amazingly, nothing seemed to be broken.

"Oster was there at the house?" Miller asked. "What happened to him?"

"The skinwalker got him," said Mr. Tso.

Bernie said, "I heard his car start and drive off."

The smoke from the fire drifted away from them. Miller rolled down the front windows, and Buddy stuck his head out. "What will you do about me and the plants?"

"The Navajo Nation will give you a fine. I'm not sure what the penalties are, under federal and state law. That is, if they can find you and figure out who you really are."

They drove in silence awhile. Finally Bernie asked, "After you take us to the hospital, are you really going to Phoenix?"

"I am. I need to check back in with the US Marshals, my keepers, who've been looking for me. I guess you figured out I'm in the program, and I don't mean AA. They need me to testify against a creep I knew from Las Vegas, a scammer who thinks he's a hotshot movie producer. Clever little twerp, and mean too. A guy named Delahart. I was trying to get out of it, work that card scam I told you about, but I'm tired of that."

He reached over and rubbed Buddy behind the ear. The dog ignored him. "In that program at NAU where I learned about skinwalkers, the guy talked about living in harmony with the rest of the world, walking in beauty. That sounds like my new plan."

"Much luck to you," Bernie said.

Mr. Tso coughed, and she felt his body shake. She put her hand on his forehead. It was too warm, she thought, and they had a long drive to the hospital.

"You know," Miller said, "I think it pays to be a good guy. I found Buddy on the road back there after I turned around. He'd been running, but he seems OK. I was worried. I thought Mr. Tso must have killed him."

Mr. Tso mumbled something.

"What was that? I couldn't catch it."

"He says, '*Ahéhee.*' Thank you."

"How's he doing back there?"

"He's a tough one. He's a fighter, but we need to get help for him as soon as we can."

Shortly after they reached the main highway, she saw the flashing lights of a Navajo Police vehicle and a black Porsche Cayenne pulled over on the shoulder.

"Slow down."

She spotted Officer Bigman standing over someone sitting on the ground. The person was wrapped in a blanket, even though the night was warm.

"Pull over and stop. Wait here. Don't disappear on me, Miller."

She walked past Bigman, noting the surprise on his face, and nudged Blanket Person with her foot. "Hey, there." Oster looked up when she spoke. "You'll have a lot of time to think about saving the planet while you're in prison." His expression matched the definition of a word she rarely used: *dumbfounded*.

Bigman said, "What happened to you? Where did you get that fancy van with the big dog? I thought you didn't like dogs."

"It's a long story. This guy you've got here tried to kill me and Mr. Tso. Mr. Tso is hurt and in the van. We're on our way to the hospital."

"Stay here. I called an ambulance for this one, and it should be coming shortly. Quicker than you can get to the hospital."

"So how did you know to arrest Oster?"

Bigman smiled. "I'm psychic? No, he crossed the yellow line and practically ran me off the road. I thought he was drunk, but when he pulled over I noticed the blood seeping through his shirt. It looks like he's got a broken arm and quite a few bite wounds. He's been raving about some animal attacking him and catching a house on fire."

"Actually, there is a house on fire." She pointed out the dim glow in the sky behind them.

"Guess I was too busy to notice," Bigman said.

Down the road now she saw the flash of colored lights: an ambulance heading toward them. "I'm amazed that you were out here."

Bigman chuckled. "I told you I was psychic. Actually, we have your little sister to thank. She called the station, worried. Sandra told her to chill, but she phoned back. Practically ordered her to get someone to come and find you. She mentioned the old man who lived near the burned car. I was driving out to look for you when that guy nearly hit me head-on. Glad you're OK."

"It's been exciting."

"I'll have to go to the hospital with Oster, since he's in custody, but Largo's sending somebody as backup. He can take you home."

"Probably the rookie," Bernie said.

The ambulance arrived. The attendants helped Mr. Tso out of the van, onto a gurney, and gave him immediate attention. Miller and Buddy drove away.

One of the EMTs came up to Bernie. "Can I do anything for you?"

She considered how she must look: dirty, disheveled, reeking of smoke, her mouth swollen from Oster's slap and her face-first fall. "I'm fine, except for my shoulder. Better, now that Mr. Tso is in good hands."

"Let me take a look." He did a quick examination. "It's not dislocated. Probably a sprain and some bruising. Ice will make it feel better. Still, you ought to have it x-rayed."

"Thanks."

Bigman said, "I asked dispatch to call Mr. Tso's daughter. She'll meet us at the hospital. Can you wait with my unit just until the backup guy comes?"

She wanted to say no, to go to Mama's, take a shower, eat something, and stretch out on the couch with an ice pack. But she was part of a team. And she realized she didn't have a car there. And she was missing her phone, her wallet, her keys, her gun, and all the other important things in her now-incinerated backpack.

"Sure. Can I use your phone before you go?"

Bigman looked at the ambulance. "Be quick."

Darleen answered on the first ring. "Sister? Are you OK? Oh my god, I thought you might be dead or—" And she stopped talking and started to cry.

"I'm fine. I'll be at Mama's later tonight."

The ambulance driver yelled, "Bigman, we're ready. They're waiting in ER for these two."

Bernie said, "I have to give Bigman the phone, but thanks for calling the station about me. I'm proud of you."

"I love you, that's all." And Darleen hung up.

Bernie watched the ambulance speed off, lights flashing, the piercing wail of the siren penetrating the summer night. She stood by the road, noticing that the glow from Mr. Tso's explosion was nearly gone. No one had arrived from the fire department, but it wouldn't have mattered. The old house was long lost.

Despite the ringing in her ears, she heard a coyote singing to the moon. She looked at the stars and the Rock with Wings, rising from the landscape. She thought about Miller and Buddy, wondering why Buddy got to ride in the front seat. Wondering about the animal that had attacked Oster. Wondering why she and Mr. Tso hadn't died in the explosion.

She'd talk to Mama again about teaching Mrs. Bigman how to weave, she decided. Not just ask, but try to convince her. They could use the loom Chee had built. No point in it sitting idle.

She climbed into Bigman's unit, watching the occasional vehicle drive past and flashing the light bar at speeders. After about half an hour, a Navajo Police car pulled to the side of the road behind her.

Chee opened the door almost before the vehicle came to a stop.

Despite her sore shoulder, his embrace had never felt so good.

22

Chee hadn't seen the Lieutenant since before his Monument Valley assignment. He was glad to have Bernie with him for the visit. She always managed to know what to say to ease the conversation forward, and when to stop talking.

Louisa greeted them at the door. She wrapped him in a quick hug. "Welcome, stranger!" Then she turned to Bernie. "What happened to you, sweetic? That bruise looks bad."

Bernie touched the tender place on her chin. "It's nothing. I did a face plant in the line of duty. How's the Lieutenant?"

"Joe is waiting in his office. I figured you all could talk there while I finish dinner."

"Can I make a salad, set the table, or something?"

Louisa nudged her away. "I'll call when it's ready. Go and chat."

The Lieutenant sat on an overstuffed chair with a view of the activity at the hummingbird feeders. He motioned them to the couch across from him. The Lieutenant had a computer on his lap. He looked better than he had at their last visit.

"It's good to see you." Bernie spoke in Navajo. "And before you ask what happened to my face— well, you should have seen the other guy."

Leaphorn turned to Chee.

Chee said, "She's OK. Nothing broken. No permanent damage. She's as feisty as ever."

The Lieutenant looked at Bernie again.

"I wanted to let you know your ideas helped solve that case in Monument Valley," Chee said. "What you wrote about the pendant and the poker chip? That led me to remember a tourist couple who had camped where they shouldn't have. It turned out they had carried the cremated remains of her parents out to the valley. That's where the bone fragments I saw came from."

Leaphorn typed something and handed the computer to Chee: *Etcitty too young.*

"What does that mean?" Bernie asked.

Chee said, "I was wrong about that. When the Lieutenant told me Robert Etcitty created the necklace, the only Etcitty I'd heard of is about my age. That's why I thought, well, that the Lieutenant might have been mistaken."

"Oh, right. Your friend who made my bracelet. So this man was his relative?"

"A great-uncle."

"Remember that old photo of the cowboys and Indians at Goulding's?" Bernie asked. "You mentioned that the man looked like Robert."

"I told the tourist lady about that photograph.

One of those cowboys might have been her grandfather."

They watched Leaphorn hunting for the letters
on his keyboard: *Chip?*

"You were right about that, too. I didn't realize it
was important when I found it. It was from *Stagecoach*, like you told me, in the poker scene. The tourist woman's grandfather saved it as a souvenir, and
she left it when she deposited the ashes. Without
it, without you putting it together, I wouldn't have
made the connection."

Leaphorn tapped three times.

"Three means maybe you would have," Bernie
said.

The Lieutenant typed: *Work w. Tsinnie OK?*

"Tsinnie? Who's that?" Bernie asked.

"Oh, a detective in Monument Valley. She knows
the Lieutenant."

Leaphorn typed: *Trained her.*

Chee hesitated. "We only spent part of a day together."

Leaphorn and Bernie waited. Finally she asked,
"And?"

"And, she's sharp. Asked tough questions. She reminded me of you, sir, in some ways. She made me
think."

Leaphorn nodded and tapped once, his signal for
yes, for agreement.

Bernie said, "Should I be jealous?"

Leaphorn looked at Chee, then tapped twice.

"OK, then. No jealousy."

He typed again: *Need to talk to Chee alone.*

Bernie said, "Sure. Maybe Louisa can use some

help now." But Chee noticed her frown. The Lieutenant had hurt her feelings.

At dinner, Chee tried to keep them entertained with stories of the gourmet coffee and characters he'd encountered during his movie duty. But the Lieutenant seemed distracted, glancing at Chee, then at Bernie, then turning away.

After the meal, Louisa said, "I made a special dessert tonight in honor of seeing you both again. And Joe has some good news too. So go out to the back porch while I get it ready, and we can sit and talk there."

The Lieutenant pushed his chair back and used the table to rise. He moved better than the last time she'd visited, Bernie realized. The therapy must be helping. She and Chee joined him at the glass patio table. Louisa had already put out the forks, white plates with an orange stripe around the rim, and matching orange cloth napkins. The Lieutenant's news must have called for a celebration with more than disposable dishes.

The back door opened, and Louisa emerged with a layer cake with chocolate frosting studded with piñon nuts. Who knew what deliciousness hid beneath it? Bernie felt herself salivate at the thought.

Louisa put the cake at the center of the table.

"Wow," Chee said. "That's beautiful. Did you make it?"

"I baked it this morning."

"So what's the special occasion? You're keeping Bernie and me in suspense."

Louisa smiled. "Joe and Captain Largo have been

e-mailing. Last night, the Captain asked Joe to come back to work for the department. Part-time, as much or as little as he feels up to, as a consultant."

Chee looked at Leaphorn. "And you said yes, sir?"

Leaphorn nodded.

"Wonderful," Chee said. "Now I won't be imposing on you when I ask for help on a case."

Leaphorn tapped three times.

"It probably depends on the case and how interesting it is," Bernie said. "I'm happy for you, sir. It will be great to have you back. I mean, even though it's on-line for now."

The Lieutenant nodded again.

Louisa served them each a piece of cake. Beneath the chocolate frosting were two layers of yellow cake and a red filling between them. Cherry? Raspberry? Whatever it was, Chee ate every bite and looked longingly at the uncut leftovers and the big, mostly uneaten slice on Bernie's plate. His wife had only eaten the frosting.

Louisa had moved on. "Who would like tea to go with this? It's herbal, good for you. Won't keep you up all night . . ."

"Gosh, not tonight," Bernie said.

Chee said, "Sure, that sounds good."

The Lieutenant shook his head. Vigorously.

Bernie changed the subject. "I saw your cactus over there." She glanced toward the little plant. "It looks OK."

"I think it's still alive," Louisa said. "I have more respect for the little guy after what Joe showed me about its being endangered. I guess we shouldn't really have it."

Leaphorn tapped twice.

Bernie smiled at him. "He's right. It's technically illegal, but it would never survive being transplanted again. Keep it. See if it blooms for you in June."

Louisa asked, "What happened to the old gentleman who lived near the cactus, the man whose house blew up?"

"He decided to move in with his daughter while he recovers from his injuries," Bernie said. "The grandson wants to rebuild the place, and the new house will have solar power. The company found an alternative site that preserves the remaining plants and the view of Ship Rock."

"Whatever happened to the cactus thief?" Chee asked.

"I don't know. Cordova is pretending he never existed. But somebody sent me a new backpack. And it has a wolf logo on it, the same as the logo that Miller had on his cap the night I stopped him. No note. No return address."

Chee somehow managed to drink half the cup of tea, and then they said their goodbyes.

Bernie didn't talk much on the trip home, but when Chee pulled into the driveway, she turned to him.

"OK. What did the Lieutenant need to tell you that he didn't want to say in front of me?"

Chee took a breath. Exhaled. "He scolded me for not taking good care of you. He doesn't like your bruise and your bum shoulder, and he didn't like the way you made a joke out of it."

"Every cop I know does that. Does he want me to be a crybaby or something?"

"I told him what happened, how you rescued the old one. I bragged on you."

"Any officer would have done that. The Lieutenant knows better than anybody that police work is dangerous. You weren't even there. If he has an issue with me, he should talk to me."

"He likes you, honey. That's why he's worried. He knows your injury had nothing to do with me. He was just venting." Chee put his arm around her.

"I'll have to talk to him about that," Bernie said.

"OK, but don't let on that you heard it from me."

Bernie opened the truck door and unfastened her seat belt. "What else aren't you telling me?"

"Nothing much. He passed along something Tsinnie told him. She thought I did a good job figuring out what those zombie people were up to." Chee chuckled. "I guess he mentioned it because I asked for his advice and actually followed it."

"I hope all the compliments don't go to your head. Next thing I know, you'll want that Monument Valley movie production assignment permanently."

"No way," he said. "The only star I'm interested in is you."

Acknowledgments and Disclaimers

It seems to take a village to write a book.

Detective Sergeant Michelle Williams of the Santa Fe Police Department graciously shared her experience, advice, and insights into the problems of traffic stops and other hazards; retired Navajo police officer Randy Johns generously offered great information on dealing with DWI arrests; and Farmington's Bill Stanley taught me a lot about alternative programs to address drunken driving. Thank you.

I appreciate the encouragement of engineer Sandra Begay-Campbell, and her knowledge of solar energy, the engineering profession, and the Navajo Nation. Thank you to botanist Daniela Roth for information on *Sclerocactus mesae-verde*, a real endangered cactus growing on Navajo Nation land, including the Shiprock area.

Ronnie Baird, general manager at Goulding's Lodge, planted the seed for part of this book with his colorful tales of working with Mike Goulding.

His generosity in speaking to the Road Scholar Tony Hillerman's Landscape tours helped me understand and appreciate the role of the movies in the lodge's history.

My appreciation to Alex Shapiro and the fine folks at the Institute of American Indian Arts for answering my questions, and for an extensive tour. Santa Fe's Aldea Book Club's astute insights into *Spider Woman's Daughter* helped me to craft this new Bernadette Manuelito story.

Thanks to my fellow writers, Rebecca Carrier, Jann Arrington Wolcott, Lucy Moore, and Talitha Arnold, who showed me how I could do better. My editor, Carolyn Marino, added her advice, support, and wisdom, as did my agent, Elizabeth Trupin-Pulli, and copyeditor Miranda Ottewell.

Thanks to my mother; to my business partner, Jean Schaumberg; to Don, my terrific husband; and to my son Brandon and his girlfriend, Lola Sandman, for their tolerance, advice, and encouragement. And to David and Gail Greenberg for their friendship.

And finally, a tip of the hat to all the fans of Tony Hillerman's work who took a chance on my first novel, *Spider Woman's Daughter*, and contacted me, asking for more. Without you all, this book would not exist.

Glossary of Navajo Words Used in ROCK WITH WINGS

adlaanii	"Lost one," an alcoholic
ahéhee	thank you
atoo'	mutton stew
bee 'adizí	Spindle Rock, known in English as Owl Rock
bee na'niildóhó	microwave oven; literally, "you warm things up with it"
be ezo	traditional hairbrush made with dried muhly grass

bilagaana	white person
chindi	restless spirit of a dead person
dahetihhe	hummingbird
dibé	sheep
Diné	Navajo people
Diné Bahane'	Navajo origin story
Diné Bizaad	Navajo language
Dinetah	traditional Navajo homeland; literally "among the people"
hataalii	Navajo singer, traditional healer
Hosteen	title of respect for an older man
hozho	a state of peace, balance, beauty, and harmony
hozhoni	happiness, oneness with the universe, arrival at a peaceful place
Késhmish	Christmas

T'ą́ą́chił	Early spring, the month of little leaves and when rabbits have their young and people prepare for the planting. Somewhat equivalent to late March/April.
t'ahi'go	angry
Tse Bii' Ndzisgaii	Monument Valley; literally, Vertical Rocks Undulating Line
Tsé Bit' a' í	Ship Rock; literally, Rock with Wings
tsiiyeel	classic Navajo bun hairstyle
Ya'iishjaatsoh	The annual time of gathering seeds, guarding fields, and asking the earth and Holy People to bless the plants in the traditional Navajo calendar. Roughly equivalent to July.
yá'át'ééh	hello
yeenaaldlooshii	shape-shifter